Summer Of Sunflowers

A Novel

CYNTHIA WOODTY

Published in the United States by Native Creative Works.
www.nativecreativeworks.com

Library of Congress Control Number: 2009911920

ISBN-13 978-0-615-29675-3
ISBN-10 0-615-29675-0

Printed in the United States of America by CreateSpace

Design by Cynthia Woodty
Edited by Jennifer Vogt

To men who helped raise me and are only here in spirit—

My brothers, Gene and Bruce,
and my father, Philip;

all men whom are missed dearly.

Author's Note

This is a work of fiction inspired by my life experiences and from what I observe as modern-day life on the reservation. None of the characters portrayed in this book should be considered as real persons. The events which take place in this book are not actual events and are spawned from my imagination.

I set out to write a novel, which portrays modern life on the reservation, as I lived it, remember it, or have heard from other peoples' stories. Having grown up on the Navajo reservation, I owe the land and people my respect, as well as my gratitude.

One of the driving forces for my choice of subjects to touch on in the book is my realization of the increased violence on the reservation. Although I do not live on the reservation any longer, I keep in touch with people from my childhood, and with family. It's through their accounts of violent, drug-related, and alcohol-related events, that I came to my realization. It's what has inspired me to write about these nagging issues, which Navajos, and many Native Americans face.

TABLE OF CONTENTS

Homeward Bound

Before me lies the body of a fragile, round-framed woman, on a bed draped with white, cotton sheets in a squeaky clean and colorless room. There is another woman in the room, who is sitting on a wooden and uncomfortable-looking chair beside the bed. Her body is slightly bent over, in a sort of hunch. Her head is hanging low and strands of her long, black and straggly hair are dangling in her face. Her hands are clasped together in her lap, fingers interlocked.

My feet are heavy. I feel as if I'm dragging a brick with each foot as I move slowly towards the bed. The woman on the chair does not raise her head. Instead, she sits quietly, as if in prayer. When I reach the bed and look closely at the woman lying on the bed, I realize it's my grandmother's frail body which lies before me. I do not want to wake her, but I want to hold her hand. So I proceed to search under the sheets for her hand. Her face slowly disappears. There are many layers of sheets. I frantically pull them back. They unravel and reveal nothing. The body which I saw in the bed seconds before is no longer there. It has disappeared into thin air.

The lady who is sitting on the other side of the bed speaks and startles me.

"She's not with us anymore," I hear her say in a familiar voice.

"Mom? Is that you?" I ask slowly with confusion in my voice.

No answer.

I grip the rails of the hospital bed and realize I don't really want an answer. I just want to see her face. I would be able to distinguish her features by looking at her face.

What seems to be an eternal moment of hushed silence passes and with it, a rumbling cart with squeaky wheels. The sound of metal surgical tools clanging against the metal cart fills the nearby hall and sends a shiver down my spine.

"What happened to her?" I quickly ask, still confused by the disappearance of my grandmother's frail body.

The woman in the chair slowly begins to lift her head and time stands still as excitement builds in my abdomen. By now, I am certain the woman is my mother.

What will I say?. I have so many questions for her and anticipate seeing her big, brown eyes light up when she sees me.

Bump. The car hits a bump. I wake from my dream and realize I am riding in my aunt, Jackie's, car. I remember that I'm on my way to my grandmother's house, along with one of my aunts, Jackie, and her husband, Jay. A song I recognize by Mary J. Blige is streaming from the satellite radio. As the painful, melodic voice of Mary flows from the radio, my aunt, who is in the front passenger seat, hums along to the tune of *'Not Gon' Cry'*.

I sit up straight. My butt is painfully sore. So in an effort to ease the soreness, I gently move it to another spot on the back seat. I stretch my legs as much as the back seat of my aunt's late-model Camry will allow, and remember how anxious I was to get to Grandma's house before I dozed off. I remember the dream of my grandmother and shrug it off.

We are rounding the last curb before the straight-away which will eventually climb the side of the plateau my grandmother's house sits on. I instantly notice familiar surroundings; the sagebrush plants covering the sides of the road, the tall and wispy grasses, the yucca plants, and then of course, the dirt, and more dirt.

The day is a pleasant one. The afternoon sun is beating down from a clear, blue sky with small puffy, cotton-white clouds.

I feel a cool, dry summer breeze coming from the southwest. The refreshing breeze is hitting my face as I sit in the back seat, with the window rolled down. Ahh, fresh air. There's nothing like it in the city. I let the fresh air fill my nostrils and my lungs. I am delighted to be home.

Although I will no longer be in the smog-filled city of Los Angeles we just came from, I will be on the rez, which is at the opposite end of the spectrum in terms of living conditions. The closest town, Winslow, is about seven miles back. So it's a little ride between Grandma's house and town, but not a bad one.

Grandma, however, thinks it's a perfect distance. She says, 'I'd rather be far away from all those crazy people in town than living with them'.

When I do have the privilege of staying out here with Grandma, I sometimes yearn for interaction with other people, for the hustle and bustle, and the convenience of living in a city or a town. However, I also recognize my inner desire to embrace the silence and peacefulness of this land. I usually let this desire take over and it allows me to reflect on my young life, to think, and to relax; all of which I am grateful for being able to do.

The breeze is gone and I feel warm air on my face. This doesn't bother me. I am content with the warm, dry air although I already miss the cool and moist ocean breezes in Los Angeles.

I look forward to the experience ahead and expect it will be a great one. There will be no television set to interrupt my thoughts, no noisy traffic to wake me from sleep, no loud and obnoxious neighbors banging on their own doors at two o'clock in the morning, and no unnecessarily loud sirens that you can hear ten miles away. Of course, I can't forget the blaring car alarms which are activated by the occasional bass-bumpin' passing car or something as trivial as the breeze. At last, I will enjoy the peace.

The past winter out here had been abundant with moisture; snow, rain, and sleet. According to the weekly reports over the phone from Grandma, it snowed heavily three times, and rained just about every week. Okay, the rain part could be a dramatization, but close enough.

Since Grandma doesn't own an automobile, she normally hitchhikes into Winslow, which I've only known as 'town' ever since I was old enough to understand words. Although she could spend countless hours in town for numerous reasons, she chooses only to go there for shopping, laundry, and her postal needs.

When she finishes her errands and has extra money for a call, she'll usually call us from a payphone at Wal-Mart. Of course, we didn't expect a call from her every time she made a trip into town. But one day, Grandma had called and said she barely made it into town, walking half of the way on foot, through snow up to her knees. Now that is absurd. But that's all fine with Grandma. She caught a cold that time and I was grateful it was nothing more.

Heavily moisturized winters like the past one usually bless the land with beautiful sunflowers in the spring and summer, which should now cover the valley at the foot of the plateau we're driving towards. Although I cannot see the flowers just yet, I imagine they are there, ahead of us, and I anticipate the sight of them.

I suppose you can say there is a balance effect—you pay dearly in the winter, and reap the rewards of nature's beauty in the spring and summer. Of course, not all of the land out here reaps the rewards. Some areas are still reddish-brown, other areas are somewhat beautiful; with light green shrubbery covering small sections of the land, partially hiding the reddish brown dirt underneath.

"We're almost at Mom's," I hear my aunt, Jackie, say from the passenger seat.

As active as my grandmother has been in my life, you would think I would call her 'Mom', too. You see, my mother left me with my grandparents by the time I was five. Her reasoning for this: "to go find herself." As upset as my grandparents were about the ordeal, they took me in and made the best of the unfortunate situation. And ever since then, my grandmother has been my foundation.

Now, I am sixteen and returning to Grandma once again. I just celebrated my Sweet Sixteen birthday and it was a special day because it marked my coming of age and indeed, I am feeling quite grown. I now feel like I am mature enough to carry a purse, which I am.

In recognition of my maturity, I decided to hang up my sweat suits, my collection of Nike basketball shoes, and my ponytail holders. I traded those in for more elaborate items, such as tight-fitting jeans and tops, sandals, and hair clips. And I can tell you the price of changing a wardrobe can be steep.

My hair is longer than it was when I left here and I know Grandma will be glad to see that. The last time I cut my hair short, she was UPSET. She said if I continue to cut my hair, 'I will be dumb and completely lose my identity…I will be lost…a lost Navajo girl, drowning in the sea of modern life.' Apparently, there's some kind of myth that says your intelligence and everything that defines you is in your hair. I disagree with the myth, of course, although I respect it. So I let Grandma go on believing that my long hair will keep my intelligence and identity intact.

As we get closer to Grandma's house, I anticipate the teachings, myths, and what I consider flawed predictions that she will share with me this time. In the past, she's shared traditional stories and myths with me over dinner or right before bedtime. These stories and myths are her way of teaching me about life, virtues and values.

Aside from the traditional lessons, she occasionally throws in unusual sayings, like the time she didn't hesitate to mention that I "need to act more lady-like, more like a young woman…because my breasts were showing more"! Oh no, not because I am getting older, but because my breasts are getting bigger, as if I want to hear that. I'd rather hear something like 'you're becoming more intelligent' or 'you are getting taller.'

This acknowledgement of my growing breasts started after I began my menstrual cycles, when my breasts weren't even showing yet. Still young and shy at the time, I laughed and giggled when I heard it, then Grandma sternly reminded me it's not funny.

'It's true,' she said. 'You just wait and see. Soon, you will be having sex and babies, too.'

So I did wait and I did see. My breasts did grow eventually, but everything else did not come true, or at least hasn't come true yet. I am still a virgin and that is a good thing. And I have not become pregnant or given birth to any babies, and that of course, is definitely good. A smile comes over my face, partly from satisfaction that I have not fulfilled Grandma's proclamation and partly from the anticipation of spending time with my personal heroine and listening to her sometimes absurd predictions.

I snap out of my musings and thoughts when the car hits another small bump in the road. As I straighten up from my slouched position, I can see that we are approaching the seasonal valley of sunflowers that I call Sunflower Valley, which means we have several more minutes before we will reach Grandma's house.

I take in the breathtaking sight as we pass—a barren patch of land now turned golden yellow. The deepest parts of the valley are covered with the most sunflowers, and I can see them all along the road, on both sides for miles; some are as tall as five feet, and others are much shorter. I want to reach out and touch them. But I don't follow my instinct. I just admire their beauty as we pass them; the beauty of their bountiful petals, and their delightful, round faces. I imagine they are welcoming me home as their faces lightly sway back and forth in the breeze; the tall ones with drooping faces and the shorter ones with erect and vibrant faces, looking right at me.

As we get closer to Grandma's, I am reminded by the hot beams from the sun that it is summer time once again.

Woo-hoo, summer time! No school! No studying. No catching the crowded city bus to school every day. Ugh! I am so relieved just thinking about being away from the city.

I absolutely dislike catching the city bus as you can tell. But since my aunt, Jackie, leaves home early on school days, I don't have a choice when it comes to transportation. So I catch the bus everyday to and from school with all those weird people; strangers with their peculiar ways; loud, attention-seeking people showing out, people picking their noses in public, girls wearing hoochie-mama clothes when they shouldn't be considered hoochie-mama material, waving their hands about and shouting all kinds of profane language.

Although I love the city in a lot of ways and for a lot of reasons, there are some things besides my city-bus-riding experiences I just can't get used to, or don't want to get used to, like the smog, and the craziness...crazy people doing crazy things, always having to watch my back...people getting robbed, women getting raped in their own homes...all craziness.

As much as I bout with my clash of preferences between the rez and the city, I'd rather be here on the rez and I would stay, but my aunt doesn't think the school system is good for me. She says, 'you will not be ready for college if you go to school around here.' I don't know where she would get such an idea: she *did* attend the nearby boarding school and she *did* go to college.

As common as boarding schools are on the reservation, none of our family members attend anymore. Somehow, by the time my generation came along, all of my cousins were living off the reservation, or rez for short, and I was the last in our family to receive an education from a boarding school. I attended the local one until my mother passed away four years ago. It was then that Grandma decided to send me to my aunt, Jackie, who lives in Los Angeles, and I have been adjusting to the city life since.

As Grandma's house comes into view, I feel my heart skip a beat. I sit up straighter and strain my eyes to see if I can see her silhouette outside from where we are. But I don't see anyone; just the outline of the yellow, cinder-block house, with its shadow in front of it.

"Can you clean up a little back there?" my aunt asks, as we approach the driveway to my grandmother's house.

Grandma has no fancy driveway leading up to her house. There are no streets to cross, no sidewalk to walk on, and no garage to park cars in. There is only a plain, old, dirt driveway which marks the front of her house.

I quickly gather up the empty McDonald's paper bags, stuff them with the food wrappers from our meal on the road, and ball up the trash. Thrilled about reaching our destination, I hastily slide the *Seventeen* magazines I brought along for reading, back into my oversized handbag. I leave the bags of groceries which my aunt purchased at a Safeway grocery store in Flagstaff, on the seat next to me. I check my face in the mirror of my compact. I would not want to show up at Grandma's doorstep with a bedhead look, so I gently comb through my slightly tangled hair with my fingers.

A Moment of Truth

My grandmother briskly walks towards the car, as we pull to a stop, with her arms open wide.

Before my aunt and uncle get out, I jump out to embrace my grandmother and squeeze her gently. I am delighted to see her. Up until now, I had missed her soft hugs, and the chubbiness of her body that makes her hugs so soft.

My grandmother is almost as tall as me, five foot three inches to be exact. I'm only a couple inches taller. Her figure is round and pudgy, yet shapely for a grandmother. The bun sitting atop her head has a mix of black and white hairs. The wrinkles around her eyes are soft and they somehow make her cuter. Her cheekbones are high, a characteristic very common in Navajo women, but her cheeks sag slightly. And her voice, her voice has what I call a rez accent: a deep, nasal tone with a touch of sweetness.

"You guys didn't have to buy food," Grandma says as she spies the bags of groceries in the back seat and gives Jackie a hug.

Jackie's shoulders are a bit of a reach for Grandma.

"Oh, it's nothing, Mom," Jackie replies, in her sweetest tone as she releases her mother's embrace.

"Hello, my daughter," Grandma says in Navajo.

"Hi, mom," Jackie responds.

"I went into town yesterday and brought some groceries home so I'm not starving or anything," Grandma says, as she embraces my uncle, Jay.

When she releases him, she adds, "And hello, my son."

"Yes, hello to you, too," Jay responds.

After she has hugged everyone, Grandma asks, "So when did school end, Shannon?" as she looks directly at me, with a bit of confusion on her face.

Although I told her the exact date over the phone a week ago, I decide to tell her again anyway. "Last Friday," I say, with an I-know-I-told-you look.

"I thought you guys were coming until next weekend," she says, switching her puzzled look from me to my aunt, who is standing a few feet from her mother, with her hands shading her eyes.

Originally, our trip out here was planned for next weekend, and I can tell she is fishing for more information from her daughter to explain the unexpected change in plans.

"Well, we are taking a trip to Miami next weekend, so we decided to drop her off this weekend," my aunt explains as she walks past her mother and takes a seat in one of the chairs on the shady, front porch which compliments the front of the house.

"Shannon couldn't wait to see you," my uncle, Jay cheerfully chimes in.

I know that isn't the whole story, but both my aunt and uncle looked content with their explanations. I had learned that Jay is leaving my aunt, and moving back to Miami, to be with another woman. And my aunt doesn't want me around to witness their break-up.

Although they tried to keep it under wraps, I overheard a few of their late-night arguments. There's only so much you can keep under wraps in a three-bedroom condo with modern and poorly-insulated walls. So I wasn't sure if my aunt suspected I had clued in, or if she knew I overheard quite a few arguments, but she did tell me Jay wouldn't be around anymore and that she needs some time to herself.

Not surprised by her daughter's intentionally vague response, Grandma takes a few steps up to her front porch, and after a deep sigh, asks, "Well, do you guys want some mutton stew and frybread?"

"No, we ate already," my aunt says, slightly shifting in her seat.

Knowing Grandma, I know she must have gone to great lengths to make mutton stew. She must've asked her sister for some fresh mutton or bought some off a neighbor. Fresh mutton isn't exactly a regularly-stocked item in the local stores and usually, only families with sheep as livestock are fortunate enough to enjoy the delicacy on a regular basis.

I see disappointment in Grandma's eyes, but she doesn't speak on it. Instead, she just stands on her porch, looking at her daughter with a distraught look.

I step up on the porch beside her, with bags in hand and say, "I'll have some," hoping to take her mind off her daughter's rejection.

And so we go inside the house and as she fixes my

bowl of stew, I set my bags down and take a seat on the couch. I think about how much I will miss Jackie and Jay. I decide now would be a good time to let Grandma in on what's really happening with Jay and Jackie.

So I walk over to her, near the stove, and whisper, "He's leaving her for another woman."

Grandma nods and simply says, "If it's meant to work out, it will and if not, then oh well, she can find another man." She makes no effort to speak quietly.

The relationship between my aunt and Jay had started several years before in Florida, while both of them worked for Royal Caribbean. Being the southern black gentleman he is, Jay asked for my aunt's hand in marriage after they dated for only a year.

And I can see why my aunt fell for the man. He is a well-built, tall, black man with bright eyes, and a nicely carved mouth; his lips are a mocha color, and plump, yet shaped to perfection. His smooth, flawless skin is a tender shade of chocolate.

"Do they know that you know?" Grandma asks me, as she hands me a piping-hot bowl of stew.

"I don't know," I whisper back. "I think Jackie knows I know."

"You know it's not good to talk about other peoples' business."

"Yes, Grandma," I reply, instantly ashamed of my gossiping.

I return to the porch and stand next to my aunt, who smiles up at me. I smile back and observe her for a few moments. I can see sadness in her eyes. I see my mother in her. It's no wonder everyone out here on the rez used to think they were twins. They shared the same flawless, almond-colored skin and the full lips with a deep wine color. They both had long, black hair and the same, slender, shapely form.

I imagine my mother's face and this image brings back a memory I have of her standing here on the porch one morning, brushing her hair. She brushed and brushed, all the while smiling and humming a soft tune. As I sat on the porch near her feet, I gazed up at her and remember feeling proud of my mother's beauty.

"Well, Mom, thanks for offering us some food," I hear Jay saying loudly, as I drift back to reality. Jay has always called my grandmother 'Mom,' and says it's because he feels it's respectful. Grandma, of course, loves this and has no qualms about it. Instead, she wonders why her other son-in-law, who is Navajo, I might add, still calls her by her first name.

"Okay, you're welcome," Grandma says, emerging from the kitchen.

"We will be heading back to L.A. tonight. I still have a lot of packing to do and I need to finish making arrangements for my trip," Jay continues.

"I-I thought you were both going to Miami?" Grandma asks, confused.

My aunt and uncle exchange quick glances.

"He's going ahead of me," my aunt haphazardly explains.

"You don't have to lie to me, Jackie," Grandma disappointedly says.

Before Jackie can answer again, Jay calmly and apologetically says, "Okay, Mom, we will not lie about this."

He looks again at Jackie and continues, "We are splitting up and I'm going back to Florida."

There is what seems like a long moment of silence.

"Oh dear. I am sorry to hear that,' Grandma says, obviously discouraged by the news.

"Sorry for not telling you sooner," Jackie says, as she nervously twists strands of her hair in a circular, winding motion.

Well, I'm going to miss you, son," Grandma finally says. And she proceeds to give Jay a long embrace.

"I'm gonna' miss you, too," Jay says, as he chokes back his tears.

My grandmother then gives her daughter another hug.

I continue to cool my stew by blowing on it. While I watch the exchange of hugs, I think again about how I will miss Jay, too. Without him as a father figure, who is what he has become for me, I wonder who I will turn to for advice on boys, for help completing my math and science homework, or for instruction on how to bake the best angel food cake. I am grateful for all he has taught me. I smile when I remember how foolish he looked wearing an apron and a hand-made chef's hat made out of a paper bag. Jackie had helped him make the hat and it looked like something a kindergartener would make. He wore the hat whenever he took on the duty of being a cooking instructor for me.

I will definitely miss seeing both of them together. I make a silent wish that my aunt will be okay, by herself again. She never seemed to have a problem with break-ups, though. Eligible men seemed to throw themselves at her, and I think she is a very lucky lady. Of course, she has some pretty high expectations, though; characteristics such as good looks, really good looks, and a fit body. She shared her list of must-haves with me in privacy, when we were lying on her bed, looking up at the ceiling, kicking our feet up, and letting our hair hang down from her bed. I laughed at her theories, more like giggled at them, and she went on to validate her theories, with details no young woman my age should hear about how a man's body is built.

Knowing my aunt and how confident and smart she is, I reassure myself she will be okay, and indulge in my bowl of mutton stew.

"I wish we can stay, but we really have to get going, and I would eat, but I'm not hungry," my aunt says to Grandma.

Truth is she doesn't like to eat Grandma's cooking; she always seems to be on a diet. She eats salads; all kinds of salads—Caesar chicken salad, potato salad, taco salad, and any salads that contain fruit. Her favorite meal by far is a California Cobb salad at TGI Fridays, with a glass of cranberry juice. All that food, but she can't eat fry bread or mutton stew. She claims 'they're unhealthy.' And I suppose she is right, but a helping every now and again wouldn't hurt.

Disappointment re-surfaces on Grandma's soft face and she says, "Young people, you're always rushing around."

While my grandmother, my aunt and Jay wrap up their small talk, I sip and then devour my stew. The mutton is savory, the potatoes are filling, and the soup is delicious; it's a bit creamy and seasoned to perfection.

When the bowl is empty, I return to the kitchen and in doing so, I realize how shabby the old kitchen looks; its walls are stained from many years of neglect. The cabinets which run along one wall are weathered and the paint is peeling. The white stove which is sitting crooked along another wall looks tired from years of cooking. The tiles on the floor are peeling; and the rickety, wooden table in the middle of the room is barely holding itself together.

I open the door to my mother's room, which sits right off the living room. The room still looks the same as it did when I left. A nice, framed, 8x10 portrait of my mother hangs on the wall to my right. It is her high school graduation picture and she looks pretty, with her short, shoulder-length hairdo nicely set in place with big curls. Her beautiful, brown eyes are gleaming. Her smile is generous, revealing her pearly whites.

"Hi again, Mom," I whisper, as I sit down on the bed and sigh.

It feels good to be here, in the presence of my grandmother and at the only true home I've ever known, the home my mother was raised in. I relish in the moment for a few minutes before returning to the porch again, where Grandma, Jackie, and Jay are saying their farewells.

Jackie excuses herself to go to the outhouse— Grandma's alternative to a real bathroom. Grandma once explained that a bathroom was not originally built into the house because running water was not something people planned for; it simply wasn't available.

Grandma speaks. "I sure hope you know what you're doing," she says, looking directly at her soon-to-be ex-son-in-law.

Knowing the conversation is none of my business, I turn back towards the entrance of the house to go inside.

Jay sighs and then turns around right where he's standing. "No, Shannon, don't leave. You need to hear a better explanation than what we've given you."

I take a seat on one of the chairs taking up space on the porch, and look up at my uncle-in-law, whose arms are now folded, and whose eyes are trained on the pebbly ground before him.

"Jackie and I have grown apart. She's going to stay in Los Angeles and I'm going to be in Miami. We have decided this would be best and we don't know if it will be permanent. But I want you to know that both of us care deeply about you," Jay explains.

When he raises his head, his eyes are full of sadness and the confidence he usually carries is no longer visible.

"I understand," I hear myself saying.

"I just want to make sure you don't blame yourself for any of this," Jay says, as he stands, shoulders shrugged, with his hands in his jean pockets.

"I will be alright. I am worried about you and Jackie," I say.

"Yes, I am worried about us, too," Jay confides.

"You take care of yourself, son and don't worry," Grandma says. She stands, wipes a tear from her eye, and gives him a hug.

After a few moments, my aunt emerges from the outhouse and smoothes out the wrinkles in her clothes as she walks back towards us.

When she returns to the porch, she sighs and says, "I guess we should be getting back on the road."

"Yes, yes, we should," Jay utters.

Jackie gets a good look at Grandma's tear-stained cheeks and softly says, "Oh, mom, don't cry," as she wraps her arms around her mother again.

For the next few moments, we all exchange hugs again.

When my aunt hugs me, she pauses for a moment, her arms still around my shoulders, and she smiles genuinely and looks right into my eyes, before she releases me.

"You take care of Mom, okay?" she says.

I nod my head.

"I'll be back for you at the end of the summer," she adds.

Jackie and Jay walk back to their car as Grandma and I follow them to say 'goodbye' one last time.

"Well, drive safe and have a safe trip," Grandma utters, in a flat tone, as my aunt and uncle-in-law get back into the car.

"Bye," my aunt says out the window, as she holds her hair up in a bunch behind her neck and fans her face.

Jay starts the engine, slips some lightly-shaded sunglasses over his eyes, and backs the car up. The sapphire blue car slowly rolls down the bumpy dirt road, leaving a small cloud of dust trailing behind them.

We wave as the car moves farther and farther away and the dust cloud disperses. There is a hidden silence, which now leaps out, as if it was locked in the ground and just broke free, and it surrounds us for a moment.

And just like that, we are alone. I look at Grandma and I could see the sadness on her face. I presume it's sadness from her daughter not staying long enough to visit with her.

I let out a sigh.

As we stand there, with our backs toward the evening sun, I think again of the summer ahead, I wonder what's in store. Neither of us speaks. We enjoy the silence and are still with time as we watch Jackie's car get smaller and smaller, farther and farther away.

Before I could say anything to finally break the silence, Grandma takes my hand in hers, and cheerfully says, "I have some soda in the ice box. We can drink some while we sit under the tree."

"Okay," I mumble, and manage a smile.

We both turn around and go inside the cozy, yellow, cinder block house with the white porch my grandfather built with "his own two hands", as Grandma proudly claims.

Being inside the house again brings on an uncomfortable feeling of sadness, not what I want to feel at the moment. So I tell Grandma I'll wait outside for her and I walk back out the front door and over to the large, shady elm tree which sits next to the house, the only elm tree for miles around, I should say. Two old, plastic, lawn chairs are propped up against the tree trunk. I unfold them and settle comfortably into one with a few missing plastic strands.

When Grandma joins me several moments later, with two tall, plastic tumblers of soda on ice, we talk mostly about school and how glad I am to be home.

I tell her all about my friends in L.A. and how much I enjoy their company. In an effort to portray their friendliness, I tell her about a time they jokingly hid my backpack for an entire day. Maybe not the best story to tell because she doesn't think they're friendly.

Instead, she says, "You should find new friends, ones that are serious about school."

Given my high level of respect for her, I do not disagree. Instead, I simply nod, and utter, "Yes, yes, I

21

probably should."

Of course, I do not intend to find new friends, but I'd rather avoid further scrutiny on the subject.

"You are very lucky to get a good education. When I was young, my parents took me out of boarding school when I was twelve, so I can work—I was a maid for a rich, white family in Tucson," she explains.

"I never knew you were a maid," I say, out of disbelief.

"Yes, yes, my older sister, Elsa, was a maid, too. But the family she worked for lived in Flagstaff, closer to home."

"So, were the people you worked for nice to you?" I ask.

"Yes, they took good care of me. But I used to get lonely for home," she says.

I sit quietly and enjoy the taste of ice cold Pepsi as Grandma recounts the two years she spent with the rich, white family.

She eventually gets back to her original point by saying, "Education is very important. If I finished school, I think I might've gone to college or found a good job."

"Grandma, I think you did a good job at being a mother," I say, hoping to put a positive spin on her outlook.

"Ah, yes, I think I did, too," she says, with a smile.

For the next few moments, we sip the last of our drinks and enjoy the cool breeze.

I calmly say, "I miss living here with you."

She looks to the ground as she nods and lets out a small groan. Then she says, "Yes, I miss the good old days, too—when it was me, you, your grandfather and your mother."

"Me, too," I say, almost in a whisper.

"Remember that time it snowed so hard that we all ended up stranded here for three days, trying to drive the truck out of the snow?" she cheerfully asks.

"Yes, I do. I remember shoveling the snow until my fingers were almost frozen."

"Your mother was such a princess, she wouldn't lift a shovel for anything. But she got out there with you in her high boots and fancy, furry coat," Grandma says.

"Yeah, and then she slipped and said she is never shoveling snow again."

We laugh at the memory.

"Yes indeed, your mother and Jackie were nothing like the other girls from around here. They used to act like Hollywood actresses or pre-madonnas," Grandma says, with a twinge of sadness in her voice.

The evening air is light and a light breeze blows from the west.

I absorb the peace and calmness of the land. I don't want to dwell on memories, so I cheerfully say, "Well, I'm glad to be back here, that's for sure."

"Me, too, I'm glad you're back."

Once again, we remain quiet. I appreciate the silence.

The sun begins to set. Grandma suggests we go back inside before the sun goes down. Out here, people go to sleep when the sun goes down because there is no electricity. And therefore, there is no reason to stay up late.

As I change into my pajamas, Grandma preps my sleeping area in my mother's old room. She changes the sheets on the bed and takes out a worn, checkered blanket for me. I recognize it as the same blanket my mother cherished

23

and favored. I sniff the blanket and the smell reminds me of my mother. It smells like strawberry and honey.

Either the smell of the blanket or the experience of being in her old room makes me think of her. I lie down with my hands clutching the blanket. The air is not cold or chilly, yet I hug the blanket tightly.

That night, I sleep and dream. I dream of my mother. She is in a field of sunflowers. It looks like Sunflower Valley. I see green and yellow everywhere. Green stems and yellow sunflowers. I don't see the brown dirt, or the flat land. I just see green and yellow. She is walking ahead of me and leading me towards the center of the flowery field. Every few seconds, she looks back at me with a smile. I squeeze her hand. I feel something wet on the ground, and it feels squishy but I don't look down.

We eventually get to an opening in the field, and there is a body, a slumped-over body that looks like it was just folded up right here on the ground. To my surprise, my mother turns the body over, as if she wants to show me the face of the body. And I see blood. Bright red blood.

I look at my mother and see a smile on her face. My stomach turns and the contents inside seem to whirl around. I am confused. So I run. I want to be near my mother, but I run from her and the body. I feel a burning sensation in my throat as vomit begins to erupt from within me.

"Shannon, wake up!" I hear Grandma saying, as she nudges me.

She is worked up into frenzy and I can see her face in the dark. She is sitting on the bed next to me, holding my shoulders with both of her hands.

The vomit continues to erupt and I nearly choke on it.

Grandma scurries off into the darkness with her flashlight and returns moments later with a wet cloth and a glass of water. She wipes off my clothes as I began to sob.

"Are you okay?" she asks, in her softest tone.

I tell her about the dream and she says, "Shhh…it's just a bad dream. You can sleep in my bed."

She hugs me close as she walks me back to her bed and tucks me in beside her. The comfort of her bed and knowing I am safe next to Grandma helps me relax.

I pull the covers up close around my neck while Grandma searches under her bed with her flashlight and retrieves something large, which looks to be a can. When the light from the flashlight shines on it, I recognize it as a Folgers canister. I watch her figure move about in the darkness. She sticks her fingers inside the canister and the next thing I feel is a gentle finger rubbing something powdery on my face.

I ask her what she is doing and her reply is, "When you dream about the dead, you're supposed to rub ashes on your face and pray for the dead. This will chase the spirits of the dead away. Don't you remember me doing this to you when you were a little girl?"

"Umm, no," I say, embarrassed of my poor memory.

While she whispers a prayer for me, I close my eyes and slip back into sleep.

We Mean No Harm

I wake to the smell of bacon, or maybe pork. Either way, I'm hungry and the smell is a comforting one. The clock on Grandma's dresser reads 1:40. I must've been tired from the trip. The sun has already begun to shine its beams upon the land. I rub the sleep from my eyes and look out Grandma's bedroom window to see a herd of sheep grazing close by. The sheep dogs that protect the sheep are barking and I can hear Grandma yelling at them.

She's hollering, "Go away!" in Navajo. They must've come to her begging for food like they usually do.

I sit up, on the edge of the bed. I remember the dream and coming to Grandma's room. I don't ponder long on the dream. Instead, I stand up and let my nose lead me into the kitchen, to the food. There are bacon strips, some scrambled eggs and a carton of orange juice on the table. A fresh breakfast in the middle of the day. I am extremely happy to be home. I can see by the dirty plate on the counter that Grandma has already eaten, so I help myself and eat to my fill.

When my stomach is full and I am satisfied, I wash up and brush my teeth in Grandma's bathroom, which is as dilapidated as the kitchen. Then I go outside and greet the beautiful and warm morning sun. It is going to be a scorcher. I can feel the heat on my skin already.

I walk to the side of the house where the shady, elm tree still stands its ground after so many years, and I see Grandma walking sluggishly back down from the slope behind her house. She has a set of binoculars around her neck and is wearing a floppy, straw hat.

As I unfold the same two old, lawn chairs we used while relaxing in the shade the evening before, I notice a moving vehicle in the distance.

I hear Grandma's footsteps behind me.

"Thanks for cooking a fresh breakfast for me," I say.

Grandma ignores my thank-you comment.

Instead, she says, "Your mother used to sit out here a lot and stare into outer space or something."

"I think she called it her moment of peace, and her beauty nap." I explain.

Before she could sit down, she mentions that she needs a pillow to sit comfortably on these chairs, so she heads back to the house.

"When I get back out, you must tell me more about Los Angeles and school!" she yells behind her, as she disappears back into the house.

It's not long before Grandma is back, and sits down comfortably on her cushion, when I notice the moving vehicle in the distance coming closer.

Unsure of whether or not Grandma sees the vehicle

approach from several miles away yet, I ask her, "Do you see that car coming up the road?"

She turns her head, and looks in an eastward direction towards what looks to be a van, and says, "Ohhh yes." Then in the same breath, she asks, "But who could it be?"

I can't even make out the type of vehicle yet. So I just squint to show that I am trying to figure out who it could possibly be.

"I don't know," I answer.

"Where did it come from?" she asks as she holds her hand up to shade her eyes.

"It came up from the east side of the plateau," I say.

After squinting, shading her eyes, and craning her neck this way and that, she worriedly says, "I wonder who that could be."

As I continue to observe the approaching vehicle, she slowly rises and cautiously folds her chair.

As the vehicle approaches, I make it out to be an orange Volkswagen van.

"Let's go inside!" she frantically says, as if someone is coming to kidnap us. She hurriedly scoops up her chair and begins walking towards the front porch, with her aging, plump body uneasily trying to keep up with her quick steps.

"Wait for me," I say, trying to fold up my chair fast enough to not get left behind.

"Oh dear, I hope it's not some winos," she says, as she quickly hobbles along.

She adds, "Your grandma, Elsa, said some drunks were out here a couple nights ago, fighting."

"What?" I ask in disbelief as I scurry after her, folded

chair in tow.

I figure Grandma is not in the mood for going into details, so I'm not surprised when I receive only a grunt in return.

"They probably already see us. I don't know that car. I don't know anybody with a van," she says as she hurries into the house.

Trying to remain calm, I offer a couple of possible scenarios. "Maybe it's just someone who's lost, or maybe it's the hippies from the border, on their way home. You know how they come through here sometimes." The border is the reservation border just to the south of us, where some real hippies live.

"No, look at the way they're driving, they're swerving all over the road," she says, exaggerating.

I, however, do not see the vehicle swerve at all. We get inside the house, and peek through the curtains of her bedroom window, and I could make out three silhouettes in the van. The vehicle is definitely an orange van, and it is a Volkswagen just as I thought.

"Who drives that kind of car?" Grandma asks, as if she's supposed to figure out who is driving from a quarter of a mile away. I'm sure she's normally used to figuring out whose vehicle is coming from such a distance, but her supernatural powers are not working today.

I don't answer her.

The van slowly pulls up to the dirt driveway, and stops about ten feet from the house. Grandma still hasn't figured out who these people are.

From the looks of the figures in the van, they look like white people, sober white people. So Grandma's expectations, I'm sure, are crushed. These people are not winos and they are definitely not hippies. I can tell by the way they are hesitant about coming to the door that they are strangers. If they were the hippies, they would be tightly packed into the van, all twenty of them, and they'd all be climbing out from every door and window as soon as the van stopped. And if they were winos, they'd be belligerent and falling out of the car.

Hoping they do not see us, but knowing for sure they already have, we slowly step away from the window and slowly close the curtains.

Grandma then whispers, "These people must be lost...let's wait to see if they knock on the door."

"Grandma, I'm sure they're going to knock, they can't just pull up and then drive away," I whisper back, only to make her worry more.

"I hope they get back in their van and drive away...just go away, people," she whispers again.

A few moments of silence pass, as we stand quietly near the window, but out of sight. I hear a door slam, and I hear footsteps, someone walking up the door, as the rocks beneath their feet make a crunching noise.

Knock, knock.

Before I can answer, Grandma says, "Shhh!" although I have not moved an inch or let out any sounds.

A few more seconds pass.

"They already saw us," I whisper, positively sure they already know someone is home, and saw us scurrying inside the house like mice. I laugh to myself at the thought of us hiding and these people already knowing we are here. I imagine they are laughing about us, and I feel embarrassed, but I let Grandma continue with her charades.

She makes her way to the door. "Who is it!?" she yells through the door, after a few more moments of silence.

For God's sake, Grandma, just open the door.

A voice from the other side of the door yells back, "My name is Adam Navarro! I'm looking for a man named Phillip ....."

Without opening the door, Grandma yells back, "Don't bother us!"

"So much for hiding and being quiet," I whisper under my breath.

The man yells again. "I'm the son of Daniel Navarro from California!"

To my surprise, Grandma doesn't yell back this time. Instead, she opens the door slightly and asks in her sternest tone, "Who are you looking for?!"

Before he could answer, she says, "We don't want trouble! Just go on and leave us alone!"

"Phillip Scott!" the man yells back.

I cannot see her face from where I'm standing, but I am sure she has a scowl on her face. That's just like the Grandma I remember. She is harsh and short when she doesn't know the people she's talking to, especially if they are a threat to her. She doesn't like strangers.

"Ma'am, sorry to bother you, but we are looking for a man by the name of Phillip Scott," the man says loudly in a polite and calm manner. He hurries his words out, as if to avoid another interruption.

This time, Grandma opens the door a little more, and asks for him to repeat the name again.

"Phillip Scott. My father was a friend of his. My

31

name is Adam Navarro, and my father's name was Daniel Navarro. I have a map right here," he explains.

Grandma opens the door a bit more and we watch as he fumbles to pull out a worn, folded piece of paper from his pocket. He holds it up to show Grandma, through the slightly opened door.

With this, Grandma opens the door wide enough to step outside with one foot.

I take my opportunity to have a closer look at the man. He is a tall and slender white man. He is wearing rimless glasses, khaki shorts and a white t-shirt. His eyes are what I call moon eyes, and are the color of the sea; blue green. He looks to be anywhere between 5'7" to 5'9". His shoulders are broad, and the sculpted muscles which make up his arms are modestly revealed.

I step a little closer to the door, but keep my distance.

"My husband's name was Phillip Scott," Grandma mumbles, as she cautiously takes the map from the man's hand and observes it.

The man calmly stands in his place, patiently waiting for a response from Grandma.

"Where did you say you are from?" Grandma finally asks, in a relaxed tone, after having a good look at the map.

The man's eyes lighten up and he quickly answers, "We are from San Francisco, and that is where my father met your husband. Before my father passed away, he told me if I ever wanted to visit Arizona, to make sure I visit Phillip..."

"I remember your father," Grandma says. "Phillip passed away a few years ago and it's just me now," she continues. "But I remember your father and San Francisco."

"Yes, I remember you, too," Mr. Navarro says with a

smile. He takes the map back and slides it into the right pocket of his khaki shorts.

"What are you doing here?" she asks as if it's a crime to visit friends of your family.

By now, I am more interested in the conversation so I inch closer to Grandma.

She opens the door wider now and holds her hand out to shake his, before saying, "It's good to see you again...the last time I saw you, you were about this high." She uses her other hand to show how tall he was then, or rather, how short he was because she holds her hand up near her hips.

"Yes, it's good to see you. I remember you, too, Mrs. Scott," Mr. Navarro says. He lets her shake go, and he looks back at the van.

"Who are you with?" she asks.

By now, I am in plain view, and I am sure the man is wondering who I am. When he returns his gaze towards us, I avoid eye contact with him, and look past him at the van with two more people in it; one in the passenger seat and one in the back. By their looks, I can see they are tired and as I am thinking this, the one on the passenger side opens the van door, but does not get out. I suppose he is stretching and turn my attention back to Grandma and Mr. Navarro.

"Those are my brothers," explains Mr. Navarro, as he points towards the two guys in the van, one of whom waves from the passenger side, and the other who nods from the seat behind the passenger.

"I remember your mom and dad, yeah, they lived down the hall from us in San Francisco," Grandma says, focusing her attention back on the conversation.

She steps out to the front porch, still talking to Mr.

Navarro, who motions to his brother, giving them the 'okay' to get out of the car.

"What are your brother's names?" Grandma asks.

"Jonah and Mikah," Mr. Navarro replies.

"Why don't you come on inside and sit down?" Grandma says.

I step out of the doorway and quickly snatch up my cosmetics bag and a clear tote bag full of my undergarments and socks from the living room couch and scurry into Grandma's room, where I toss them on her bed.

When I return to the living room, Grandma is holding the door open while the three men file into the house one by one. The two brothers whom waited patiently in the van moments before, take off their baseball caps, and nod at us as they walk through the white-framed doorway.

Grandma leads them into the kitchen, and pulls out chairs at the circular wooden table with wobbly legs, just big enough to seat four or five people.

"This is my granddaughter," Grandma says as she pulls me close. "She just came back from Los Angeles yesterday for her summer break."

The three visitors arrange themselves around the kitchen table, and all three tall men stand as they say 'hello.' They all have blonde hair and blue eyes.

Although I had not typically paid attention to white guys, and never found myself gawking at them, I instantly recognize the attractiveness of the three men sitting in front of me and find it difficult not to stare.

Adam introduces himself, then his brothers.

"I'm Adam," he says.

Now that he has removed his ball cap, his wavy and

dusty blonde hair is misshapen and he looks a bit rugged.

"This is Mikah, who is the second oldest," he says, as he points to the guy who sits next to him. Mikah is wearing his hair shorter than Adam, but looks very similar. His face is more square-ish and he has a nicely carved nose with a mustache and a goatee to top off his look. His deep-set eyes are a mysterious blue and when he blinks, I feel like I could be hypnotized by the beauty of them. Khaki pants, and a red, plain Polo t-shirt clothe his slender body. The muscles in his arms are just as well-defined as Adam's, and he has a pink, puffy scar running along the upper side of his forearm. His teeth are aligned for the most part, and his smile is a bit jagged.

"And my youngest brother is Jonah," Adam says, as he points to the guy who is sitting on the other side of the table.

Jonah is wearing knee-length khaki shorts; worn, leather sandals; and a simple, white t-shirt with the words 'Party? Anyone?' nicely lettered across the chest. He has a head full of healthy blonde, loose locks that move freely atop his head when he rises to shake hands. Talk about the Gerber baby look alike, he must be the boy in the picture on all the Gerber products, except he's all grown up with a patch of a beard on his chin.

"Hi," Jonah says, with a small wave of his hand.

"Hi there," Mikah adds, shyly.

I laugh to myself as I wonder how on Earth these attractive men ended up in Grandma's kitchen. They seem so out of place.

"Hi," I say as I nod at all of them.

Explanation, Please

Once everyone is settled and Adam, the oldest, has taken a drink of water from an Evian water bottle Jonah carried into the house, Grandma mentions she was not expecting anyone and their visit is a surprise.

"Sorry to intrude on you ladies," Adam apologizes.

I notice a couple of lightly-creased worry lines in his forehead, which give him an aged look.

"We would have called, but could not find a listing and I was not sure if you had a phone," he continues.

"That's okay. We don't have phones out here. Our visitors just hope we're home when they come to visit," Grandma says, with a short laugh that makes her entire body jiggle.

The men laugh uneasily.

"I'm glad you were home this time," Adam says with a smile, which forces his already-natural moon-shaped eyes to look more like crescent moons.

Grandma laughs again. "Yes, yes, you would'a come

all this way for nothing."

Adam continues to smile.

Mikah and Jonah sit calmly with their hands clasped in their laps. I figure they are still absorbing the sight of the kitchen.

"Well, we hadn't planned on making dinner, but now we have an excuse," Grandma says excitedly.

"Shannon, get the skillet out," she instructs me, with a wave of her hand.

I feel like a young servant, but am obliged to do whatever she asks.

"You guys can tell me more about your parents and San Francisco while I cook dinner for you," she says, as she gets up from the table, using both of her arms to steady her body as it rises.

"Can we help with anything?" asks the youngest, Jonah.

"Oh no, no, you sit," Grandma says.

I pick the shiniest skillet from the cabinet. I follow instructions from Grandma and make my way around the kitchen gathering the potatoes for mashed potatoes, and the flour for bread. I have always been shy, but I am especially shy around strangers, so I keep quiet and listen to the conversation between Grandma and the men. I put the skillet on the stove and pour some oil in it, just enough to cover the bottom half of the pan.

"So, tell me, where are your parents?" asks Grandma, while she takes out some chicken drumsticks from her ice chest.

Last year, her electricity was supposed to be hooked up and turned on, but the work's been delayed due to budget cuts from the Navajo tribe. Or at least, that's the story we were given. Nonetheless, she keeps her extra large ice chest well-stocked with all kinds of frozen meats and blocks of ice.

She always says 'you never know when you'll have visitors, and you have to make sure you can feed them.' Kinda' ironic.

Adam, the spokesperson for the men answers, "Well, our mother passed away from cancer three years ago, and our father died in a car accident the next year."

My grandmother and I both gasp, and she sympathetically says, "I'm so sorry to hear that."

Although I never met their parents, I can only imagine how devastating it is to lose both parents.

Adam simply nods, takes his glasses off and examines the lenses, before putting them back on. He moves about nervously in his chair and appears to be fighting back tears.

My heart suddenly aches for them, and I feel a shot of deep sympathy come over me as I look over at the small circle of men around the table.

I thaw the chicken in cold water, which becomes ice cold after only a few moments. As the chicken thaws, I take over the peeling of the potatoes. Being back in Grandma's kitchen is like learning how to ride a bike again. I had forgotten where all the pots and pans are kept, so it is a bit of a struggle for me as I navigate my way around again.

"Oh my, I am so sorry," Grandma says again, with a hand over her mouth and in a quivering voice. She begins to weep, so I rush over to hold her. I cannot bear to see her in pain.

There is silence for a few moments as Grandma

wipes her tears away.

"Since then, all three of us have lived together," Adam continues. "I graduated from college the same year my father passed away, and both of my brothers are still in college," he adds. He looks proudly at his two brothers, who just smile, hands still clasped in their laps.

"How old are you guys now?" Grandma asks, as she lifts a drumstick out of the ice cold water, rolls it in a mixture of flour and spices, and gently slides it into the waiting skillet of hot oil on the stove.

"Well, I'm 30 now," Adam says, putting one hand on his chest to further indicate he is speaking of himself. He looks at Mikah and says, "Mikah's 24," and then points to the youngest, and says, "And Jonah's 18."

Jonah and Mikah just nod.

I'm beginning to wonder if they know how to talk for themselves.

"Adam was just a little guy when we left San Francisco," Grandma says, looking directly at Adam. "You two weren't even born then," she adds, looking at Mikah and Jonah.

While Grandma cooks and I fiddle around with dishes, she asks them question after question and Adam does all the answering.

At some point, she asks Adam how well he remembers her husband. He says he remembers my grandfather through his father's stories mostly, and goes on to tell us about how his father worked at the same shipping dock as Grandpa. When he speaks about the two men, based on stories his father told him, I could see my grandmother's eyes light up.

39

He refers to my grandfather as a man he remembers as a true friend to his father. He speaks of memories he has of his family and Grandma's family getting together for Sunday dinners. At the time, Grandma had a son and a daughter, my oldest uncle, Anthony and my oldest aunt, Jeanette. Both were older than Adam at the time, but Adam remembers how they played together for hours on end.

As the discussion continues, I find myself stealing glances at Jonah. He and Mikah just sit and observe the kitchen. They are probably wondering how much longer it will hold up.

I am somewhat mesmerized by the looks of Jonah. His hands look quite rugged, as if he works with them a lot. But that face, it's so babyish and as close to perfection as I have ever seen. As cute as he looks, I remind myself again that I do not find white guys attractive, so I dismiss his looks and focus on helping Grandma prepare dinner.

Adam says, "I am excited about finally getting a chance to come see you and find out where you guys live." He pauses for a moment and looks at his brothers. I can tell he isn't finished talking, and everyone else seems to know this as well.

We all look at him and wait for him to finish. He fiddles with his glasses and then puts them back on.

Then he says, "After our parents passed away, I felt a strong need to see you guys again and I was really hoping to see Philip again."

Before sliding another floured piece of chicken into the popping grease, Grandma pauses, and looks at Adam with soft and saddened eyes.

Adam goes on to say, "I thought coming out here

would be a good idea for me...I really just decided I wanted to take a break from the city, so I invited my brothers since they are out of school...and voila, here we are."

Grandma goes back to turning browned pieces of chicken, and says, "We don't usually get visitors, especially all the way from San Francisco, and it's good to see you all again. It's been so long since we have lived there."

She takes a couple crispy pieces of chicken out of the skillet and puts more floured ones in. With all eyes trained on her and that scrumptious-looking chicken, she speaks again.

"I wasn't happy there and Phillip kept telling me to get used to it, but I couldn't and I was the one who talked him into coming back here." I can see Grandma's eyes take on a distressing look as she re-lives the memory for a moment.

Then with a sigh and a wave of her hand, she says, "Oh, it was just too crowded, so many people and it was always cold and rainy."

"Things haven't really changed since then, but there are still a lot of people and it still rains a lot," Jonah says, with a crooked smile, and a quick glance at his brothers, as if to ask them to agree with him.

"Yeah, nothing's changed...everything is just more expensive now," adds Mikah, sounding sarcastic.

Adam simply nods in agreement and sits at the table, with one leg casually crossed over the other.

"So how long do you plan on traveling for this trip of yours?" I ask, not really interested in an answer, but just wanting to join in the conversation. Heaven knows I know nothing about San Francisco and could add no value to their conversation.

Just as Grandma forks out a few more pieces of fried chicken pieces from the skillet, I put my hand in the bowl of water with the last pieces of drumsticks floating about. The temperature of the water has turned bone-chilling cold from the chicken, so I hand her the last pieces and dump the icy cold water.

"Well, we don't really have a set time, I just wanted to get out of San Francisco for a while, and take a road trip," explains Adam.

"What made you think to come here?" I ask, feeling stupid after realizing he already told us why they came here.

Nonetheless, he answers, "To be honest, I couldn't think of any place better to go than here."

Several seconds of silence follow, and I figure everyone is probably trying to think of things to say to keep the conversation flowing.

Finally, Grandma asks, "Where are you going to stay?" in a concerned voice as she covers the skillet.

"In hotels and our van," states Adam, letting his sea-blue eyes gaze around the room.

Before he could speak another word, we all hear a gasp from Grandma. "What!?" she exclaims, in disbelief, now standing with her hands on her hips.

Everyone at the table looks surprised or scared by the gasp from Grandma.

"Oh no!" she exclaims. Wiping her hands on her apron, and now with a very worried look on her face, she finishes with, "You can't do that...you can stay here until you're ready to leave."

Adam, Mikah and Jonah all look surprised but remain quiet.

"We don't mind having you here…right, Shannon?" she asks, looking at me, as if I am the decision-maker.

I look at the table with the three guys nicely huddled around, and see that their expressions have changed from surprise to confusion.

"Umm, yeah," I say, wondering if Grandma has lost her mind.

I'm certain Grandma reads the tension in the room, and goes on to say, "You guys can help me with a few fixes…I have been needing help fixing the bathroom up. I have most of the supplies, and my brother was supposed to fix it, but he's so busy and I hate to bother him."

This was her way of making everyone feel some kind of sorry for her. But instead of feeling sorry for her, I look at her with a puzzled look still lingering on my face.

"Well, what do you guys think?" Adam asks, looking at his brothers, with raised eyebrows.

"Umm, okay, I guess we wouldn't mind," Jonah simply says, glancing at Mikah.

"Are you sure you're okay with this?" Adam asks, looking directly at Grandma.

"Yes, yes, I'm sure," Grandma replies, with a bit of excitement in her voice.

Mikah matter-of-factly says, "We need to work on the van anyway."

"I suppose we can work on the van while we stay here, if you don't mind," Adam utters, with hesitation in his voice. He smiles at Grandma and his moon eyes become vividly curved to look more like crescent moons.

Why on Earth would white people want to stay here, on the rez of all place?' I don't speak my mind. I just stand

and listen to the arrangements unfold.

"Well, you can't stay in a hotel, oh no, we have room here…it's only the two of us and we're always scared, especially at night. It's spooky here sometimes, you know," Grandma explains, looking at me with her soft eyes, as if she wants me to add more.

I say nothing and laugh to myself, thinking she might just scare them away with an excuse like that.

"Are you sure?" Adam asks again, with a surprised, yet satisfied look on his face.

Mikah and Jonah smile at each other and shrug their shoulders.

We all wait for an answer from Grandma.

"Yes, you seem like some nice guys. As long as you don't cause any trouble, you can stay. I'm sure Phillip would have done the same," Grandma declares, as she casually begins to make her dough for tortillas. She slowly stirs the flour, baking soda and salt together, and adds small amounts of warm water until a ball of dough forms.

"Cool," Mikah says calmly.

"Thanks, thanks a lot…we will not be any trouble," Adam says, with a smile across his face that could've been big enough for all of them.

While Grandma kneads the dough and breaks off small round balls of dough, I turn over the chicken and the men watch Grandma's hands quickly roll the dough out onto her cutting board.

Mmm Mmmm yummy. I cannot wait to wrap a piece of fried chicken in my warm tortilla. My stomach lets out a little growl, and I try to remember the last time I ate tortillas. Seeing how my aunt doesn't cook very much, I'm positive it wasn't at her house. My mouth waters as I anticipate eating the warm, soft tortillas.

For the next few minutes, more arrangements are made and it is settled; the three young men will stay with us. It sounds like they will stay for a few weeks, and help out around the house as payment for room and board. As awkward as the situation seems, I manage to keep a straight face despite the surprise visit and unbelievable arrangements being made right in front of me. And eventually, I begin to take comfort in the thought of having three people I've not met before stay with us.

It is just like my grandmother to be so generous and sweet. I don't know many women who are so generous nowadays. Most of the local women I know are more concerned with what they will get in return for helping others. For instance, my grandmother's sister, Elsa, who doesn't live too far from Grandma's house, is known to be greedy, and will not do anything, unless you pay her cash, even for something as small as a ride into town. She could be considered a taxicab driver's wife out here. She collects and her husband drives. I can only imagine how much she would charge strangers to stay in her house...or even family members at that. She'd probably make her own family pay for using the toilet paper in her bathroom, if she could.

Just as I fork the last pieces of fried chicken from the skillet onto a serving plate, Grandma flips over her last tortilla in the skillet.

"Dinner is almost ready," Grandma says as she sets her plate of tortillas on the table.

Adam and Jonah rise from their chairs to wash their hands at our old, rusty kitchen sink.

"The sink doesn't work," Grandma informs Mikah and Adam.

Mikah turns the cold water faucet on, only to find no water coming out.

"Oh," I hear one of them say, with a hint of disappointment.

"You have to use a wash pan...fill it up with water...there's one in the bathroom sink," Grandma explains, with a tender, yet authoritative voice as she moves about, from the table to the stove and back.

"Shannon, show them what to do," Grandma directs me.

"Okay, there is a plastic wash pan in the bathroom sink," I say, as I point to the bathroom. "Can someone please grab that?"

Adam promptly walks into the bathroom and retrieves the plastic wash pan.

I take a kettle of steaming water from the stove and pour the water into the plastic wash pan which Adam has retrieved from the bathroom. Then I add cold water from a covered bucket of water which is sitting on a round, wooden table, next to the stove. I finally hand the wash pan back to Adam, whom carries the pan back into the bathroom. Mikah and Jonah follow like obedient students.

"You can unload your bags after dinner," Grandma says out loudly to the men.

"Grandma, it's called luggage," I say.

"Oh, whatever. Bags, luggage, all the same," Grandma retorts.

Grandma's plumbing has been a wreck for almost a year now. In the bathroom, the majority of the wall paper has peeled off, and the sink is about to fall off the wall.

The men don't make any complaints and quietly go about their business. Now that they will be staying for a while, I secretly hope one is a plumber, or at least knows how to get the water running again.

"I usually don't eat fried food," claims Mikah, as he joins us at the table again.

I see a blanket of disappointment cover Grandma's face in an instant.

I am sure he sees it and doesn't want to disappoint so he says "But I'll make an exception in this case," as he smiles at Grandma. He smiles at Grandma and reveals a distinct and somewhat mesmerizing jagged smile.

"Well, I can buy whatever food you eat the next time I go to the store," says Grandma, as she takes a plate and serves me. And she then adds, "As long as it's not too expensive."

"Can we go tomorrow?" I ask anxiously, quickly thinking of why I need to go. I hadn't bought any new CDs to get me through the summer, and look forward to a Wal-Mart shopping trip, so I can spend the money Jackie gave me and stock up on some new music.

Instead of answering me, Grandma replies, "Dig in…I'm sure you guys are hungry."

As Adam fills his plate, he looks at me with his blue-green eyes and says, "We can go into town tomorrow. I need to buy some parts for the van anyway." His dusty blonde, shaggy hair reminds me of a friend back in L.A., who wears the same shaggy do. I'm not sure if it's the blue-green eyes, the shaggy do, or something else about him that makes me feel comfortable in his presence.

At first, the mood around the table is somewhat somber. The evening sunlight shines its orange rays into the kitchen and onto all the dust particles which float about.

It doesn't take long for Grandma to make the mood more cheerful by sharing memories she has of my grandfather. She tells us he was "a stubborn old man," that he'd go out drinking with Daniel, the mens' father, even after she'd yell at him over and over. She mentions that she found him at a nearby bar once, sharing jokes with a group of other men; some white, some Asian, and some black. She complains about how she and the Navarros' mother would stay home and baby-sit all night, waiting for their husbands to return.

Adam confirms Grandma's stories about the men coming home late. He remembers staying up late with his mother most nights, waiting for his father to return. When his father did return home, he would stagger into Adam's room late at night and after his mother went to bed, tired of waiting. With the smell of liquor on his breath, his father would tell of the happenings at the local bar.

"He had this saying. He used to say, 'That Philip is the funniest Navajo I know and I only know one,'" Adam says as he reminisces. "He would laugh at his own joke, and I always asked him why he thought that was funny. Of course, he never explained," he adds.

Laughter fills the room.

When Adam asks about Anthony and Jeanette, Grandma goes into a schpiel about where all of her children are now.

And here's the jist of it. Her oldest son, Anthony, is in jail last she heard. She explains that he frequents the city jail quite a bit, mostly for minor misdemeanors like

Disorderly Conduct, or something along those lines. Jeanette is a social worker. She lives on the Sioux reservation, with her husband and two kids. Tom, who is next in line, is fighting fires for the Navajo tribe, somewhere on the East Coast. He lives on another part of the rez, about eighty miles away. Next in line is my aunt, Jackie. Grandma proudly speaks of Jackie's accomplishments; her graduation from ASU and her "big, important job" at Caribbean Cruise Lines. When she pronounces Caribbean, it sounds like Cariben. But everyone nods to show they understand. And then of course, there's my mother, Linda, who Grandma says was "her tail and baby."

"Linda passed away from a bad accident," Grandma says.

The men gasp when they hear this.

No further details of my mother's death are shared.

Before the men have a chance to ask questions, Grandma says, "My youngest son, Paul, was struck by a car on his way home from town."

Again, the men gasp.

When she is finished with the list, she sighs and says, "After all those births and all those years of raising children, I am left with only four children."

Adam sympathetically says, "I'm so sorry for your losses." The worry lines in his forehead deepen and his broad shoulders drop slightly.

Now that Grandma mentioned the deaths of her children, I remember how sad and dark both days were and I feel a twinge of sorrow seeping into my body.

A few days before my uncle died, I remember him leaving this house and walking out to the main road to hitchhike into town. As was typical, he had wanted to go to town and hang with his friends, which meant he wanted to go drink alcohol and wander around town aimlessly with his friends. And whenever this happened, he'd be gone for days at a time and return when he's gotten his fill of alcohol and mayhem.

But on the horrible day of his death, he was hitchhiking home, as usual, when he literally crossed paths with a blue Chevy truck, traveling at about 55 miles per hour. According to the police report, the man driving the truck claimed my uncle was walking in the middle of the road and he didn't see him until it was too late to swerve.

That happened four summers ago. But to this day, when Grandma speaks of it, her voice is cracked and sadness grows in her eyes. She drifts off into another world, as if she could see him walking down that road now. Tears slowly gather at the bottom of her eyes.

I close my eyes for a second as Grandma recounts the story to the Navarros.

After a few moments of silence, Grandma finally says, "And just when I thought I had gotten over Phillip's and Paul's deaths, my daughter dies."

Once again, no details of my mother's death are shared. Instead, Grandma stares into space for a few moments.

The cheerfulness which engulfed the table not very long ago is soon replaced with melancholy.

"We are so sorry for your losses," Adam warmly says.

"Thank you. It's been tough dealing with the deaths," Grandma says, with a deep sigh.

I close my eyes and listen to the conversation

continue.

While the men discuss their parents' tragic deaths, I sink into my own thoughts of the woman who gave birth to me.

My mother was an intelligent woman, but she never ventured too far from home like her sisters. Although she was intelligent and far prettier than the majority of women on the rez, she unfortunately had a weakness for alcohol, just like Paul and my grandfather.

I remember seeing her come home drunk once, and Grandma tried to tell me she had just gotten really, really sick. I knew from seeing my grandfather that same way that she was drunk.

As a child…I must've been about six years old, I had asked her once why she was a drunk, not knowing what the word really meant. I just knew that was what my grandmother called my grandfather when he came home the same way she did that night.

The next thing I remember feeling was a hot slap across my face.

'Don't you ever call me that again!' she yelled at me, with fire in her eyes. It was a look I'd see only once.

As I matured, I realized that from her perspective, she didn't consider herself an alcoholic because she drank "casually". And for her, it was okay to have a few drinks now and again. What she didn't understand was her father was an alcoholic, and Grandma had a few bouts with the poison as well, so it was in her blood; alcoholism was a part of her.

Unlike all of Grandma's other children, she seemed to have a close bond with her parents. After she had graduated from high school, she left home and when she returned a year later, she was noticeably pregnant. My grandparents let her stay home and rest until she was ready to release me into the world.

I snap out of my thoughts. The chicken bones on my plate are meatless, and the tortilla has been devoured.

I look at Grandma again and she still has a somber look on her otherwise-cheerful face.

"Oh, listen to me…I'm probably making everybody sad," she says.

"Oh, no, that's fine…you have to get that out…it's good to talk about it," Mikah says encouragingly.

"That is horrible," Adam says.

Jonah's shoulders sag as he nods his head back and forth.

"Well, enough talking about sad stuff, let's talk about something better," Grandma says, wiping a tear from the corner of her eye, with the sleeve of her shirt.

"Well, we can tell you about our trip here," Adam says, with a spark of cheerfulness, just enough to lift the gloominess from the table.

And so the men tell their story. They talk about their decision to take a cross-country road trip, and how that led Adam to remember their father's friend, my grandfather, and to convince his brothers to accompany him on a soul-searching trip.

"You really think that old van out there will get you all the way across the country?" I ask, out of curiosity.

"Well, it's been a good van all these years…it's never broken down. I suppose I could buy a new car or something, but I love that van…it belonged to our parents,"

Adam explains, with a shrug of his broad shoulders.

"So, you all just upped and left?" I ask, still confused as to how people can just up and go...across country.

"Yeah, we didn't have anything major planned for the summer. I needed a break from work...actually, I was laid off," Adam says in a tone that leads me to believe the change was not a positive one.

"I needed a break, too," Mikah explains.

"And I just came along for the experience," Jonah says.

Not knowing how to tell them the idea is a crazy one without hurting their feelings, I simply say, "Wow, that's pretty, pretty, umm, I've never heard of anything like that."

"Yeah, we thought about turning around a couple of times, and then of course, the van started acting up, in...what's the name of the town?" Adam says, looking at his brothers for support.

"Ummm, it was in between Williams and Flagstaff," Jonah says with assurance. He must've been the one in charge of the map.

"Yeah, just before Flagstaff," Mikah says.

Grandma interrupts before the men can figure out which town it was they began experiencing car trouble. "Well, I'm sure your father and mother would have enjoyed the trip...you know to come out here," she says.

"Yes, yes, I'm sure," Mikah says, confidently.

"When me and Phillip were leaving San Francisco, they asked us if they can come see us. That's probably when he made that map of yours for them," Grandma says.

I excuse myself from the table and proceed to take water out of the bucket sitting on the small, round, wooden table next to the stove. It is a table my grandfather made, and it's always been used as a water table, so the dark wood is slightly cracked and has inherited quite a few water stains. I carefully pour the water into a pot on the propane stove.

"Thanks for dinner, it was delicious," Jonah says as he rises from his chair.

"You are welcome," Grandma says cheerfully.

"What do you guys say we unload our stuff?" Adam asks his brothers.

"Sure, I think I ate enough for two and need to do some kind of activity," Mikah says.

"It is good to be full," Grandma adds.

And with that, everyone else leaves the kitchen; the three men to unload their belongings from their van, and Grandma to prepare my mother's bedroom for their stay.

I remain in the kitchen, putting my soft, nicely manicured hands to work. After I tidy up the old kitchen by washing the dishes with the hot water from the stove, wiping down the table, and sweeping the tile floor, I tend to myself. I wash my face using Grandma's Noxzema face wash, and I brush my teeth.

"You can sleep in my room," Grandma announces from her room, as I walk past her room, on my way outside to the old outhouse.

"Okay, Grandma, it's better than sleeping by myself," I say back to her.

On my short trek to the outhouse, I absorb the dry and cool night air while I think about our visitors. What a nice group of young men they are, and how on Earth did they end up here? It's not everyday that white people come to visit Navajos on the rez, and stay a while. You just don't see that stuff.

When I return to the house, I find Jonah outside, searching for something underneath the front seat of the Orange van.

"Great weather, eh?" I say loudly.

He is startled and jumps a little. I hear a faint thump and I am positive he has just bumped his head on the dashboard.

I giggle and say, "Sorry, didn't mean to make you jump."

"I'm okay, I didn't expect anyone else to be out here," he explains, with a smile, as he gets out of the van and stands, with his arms behind his back, leaning against the open door.

"So, did you think you'd end up in the middle of nowhere?" I ask.

"Nope, I mean yes, well, I actually didn't know where we were going, to be honest. I was just along for the ride and Adam knows how to pick the spots," he says.

He moves his arms up over his head and rests them behind his head.

"Ahh, I see. So do you guys do this often?" I ask.

He drops his arms back down by his side before answering, "Not really, we take a road trip every now and again."

"Cool."

"Am I making you nervous?"

"No, I just ummm....this is the first time we're actually staying on a road trip."

"I see. Well, I'm gonna' get ready for bed."

"I will be in shortly, just looking for something."

"Cool."

When I am back inside the house, I do the whole hand washing routine. I fill the wash pan from the bathroom with hot water from the stove, and then add the cold water from the bucket on the water table next to the stove. I do all that just so I can stick my hands in for a few seconds, rub my hands with a bar of soap and rinse the soap back off. And I can't forget the disposing of the water, where I pour the now-dirty water into another bucket which will be dumped outside once it's full. Yes, quite a few steps, all for the sake of sanitation.

After I change into my silk pajamas which I received as a gift for my sixteenth birthday, I say 'Good night' to our visitors and retreat to Grandma's room for the night.

I fluff the pillows in Grandma's room, and fix her bed up with some mismatched, but clean, Downy-smelling sheets and one of her homemade quilts—not a thick one, but a nice, colorful thin one. It has always been my favorite summer quilt, with patches of mismatched material from wherever Grandma could find scraps. Most of the scraps were my old clothes that I didn't fit into, so maybe that's why it is my favorite. Whatever the reason, I pull it up to my chin, close my tired eyes, and absorb the day's event, before I drift off into a world of sleep.

Appreciation of Beauty

When I wake the next morning, I hear people talking outside and when I listen harder, I can hear the familiar sound of Grandma's voice. I bounce out of bed with a newfound energy and do a few back and arm stretches I learned from my grandfather. Well, he didn't necessarily teach me, I just copied him. He'd get up every morning and stretch at the foot of his bed; his lanky body bending this way and that. Most of the time, I'd sneak into my grandparent's room in the middle of the night and I would still be half asleep when he woke, but I would watch him stretch, and after he'd leave the room, I'd get up and do just as he did.

I take a nice deep breath and examine the house a bit more. Although it looks smaller each year, I know it hasn't changed its size and it's just me, growing up. The house is of a decent size for a family on the rez; two bedrooms, a living room, a kitchen, and one bathroom—nothing fancy.

As I head toward the kitchen, I stop in the living room to take a good look around. I feel as if I've stepped backwards in time, and the house seems to have shrunk. The walls are still a dirty white, and the only thing different is a new cabinet near the entrance. This must be the one Grandma got as a gift from my other aunt, Jeanette, who lives in South Dakota. The same old, brown, 60's style couch is sitting in the same place, off to the left side of the room. The same small, round maple coffee table is sitting on top of the same old, olive green rug in the middle of the room.

"It's good to be home," I whisper.

In the kitchen, I pour water into a pot on the stove again, this time for washing up. Although I can do the cold water wash-up, I don't prefer it this morning and would rather feel the warm water splashing on my face.

While I wait for the water on the stove to heat, I help myself to a box of powdered donuts on the wobbly, kitchen table. My mouth is too dry to moisten up the donut so it moves painfully down my esophagus, bite after bite.

I hear Grandma's voice again. She is coming back into the house and chatter follows. Grandma is instructing Mikah and Jonah to carry boxes out of my mother's room and into her room. She doesn't let go of things very easily, so my mother's bedroom has basically been her storage room for the past couple years. You name it, it's in there—old stereos, old cassette tapes, old clothes, pots and pans, shoes, tools—all that. I call it junk. She calls them valuables.

With the heated water from the stove and a plastic tumbler filled with cold water, I prepare a sinkful of warm water in the broke-down bathroom sink. I can hear my mother's voice in my head, saying, 'Use warm water to wash your face...it opens your pores.' I smile and pour a little bit more cold water...just enough to make it lukewarm. I splash.

After washing up, I go to Grandma's room to help her straighten up and on the way, I say 'good morning' to the three men who are bustling about, following Grandma's directions. Her room has boxes stacked at least four feet high on one side of the room, and the closet is full of boxes, old clothes on colorful, plastic hangers, and more boxes of stuff.

I ask her why she holds onto so much stuff, and she simply says, "I don't know...these things are all still good...someone can wear these clothes again and use the things in these boxes."

Then she walks over to one of the shelves and opens a box, and pulls out some clothes. I don't know who's wearing dark green polyester suits these days, but apparently, she knows someone who is.

Before she can pull out more items, I build up enough courage to interrupt her and in a poor attempt to keep from discouraging her and hurting her feelings, I roll the words off my tongue, "Grandma, let's get the place ready for these guys, before you start pulling out stuff."

With disappointment, she tucks whatever piece of oh-so-fashionable garment she was taking out back into the box.

We move all of the clutter out of my mother's old room, and soon the place is transformed into a cozy guest room—gray and black Samsonite suitcases lying open on the bed, mens' sandals and tennis shoes nicely lined up on the floor of the closet, clothes nicely folded and sitting on the bed, and tightly-rolled, sleeping bags stacked nicely against one wall.

After all of our reorganization work is completed, the rest of the day is spent relaxing. I help Grandma sort through her boxes and boxes of junk for a couple of hours. When she decides she doesn't want to deal with it anymore, she plops down on a denim blue, round, oversized cushion next to more junk.

While I continue to sort through her prized belongings, she unveils her latest piece of work in the making—a five foot loom, half woven. It was covered with a huge sheet and I had mistaken it for more junk. But once she uncovers it, my eyes widen with delight.

Grandma proudly weaves still, not something most modern women on the rez find appealing anymore. It isn't as popular as it was say fifty years ago, that's for sure. Yet, Grandma clings onto the trade and claims it's something every young Navajo girl should learn.

"Wow, Grandma, can you teach me how to weave?" I ask. The thought of learning to weave is exciting and I follow my question, with a "Pleeeaase," desperately wanting her to say yes.

"I've been waiting for you to ask," she kindly says.

"Oh my gosh, this is so cool," I squeal.

I drop the psychedelic, tie-dyed collar shirt I am holding and sit beside her, mesmerized by the artwork; the intricate detail forming something grand and spectacular. The design looks difficult to imagine and create, yet is being created right before my eyes.

With each row of yarn, the masterpiece comes to life. Grandma diligently laces the loom with the yarn, and then gently pounds the yarn into place. And with each pound, there is that familiar thump, the thump that calms me within. It sounds like a soft drum beat, with no rhythm, just a plain old beat. Yet, it makes my inner spirit dance. I absorb the power and the beauty. The large, oscillating fan sitting near us blows warm air around the room, and whirs while Grandma pounds the yarn. The combination of the sounds makes me warm inside and I comfortably scoot closer to her.

The sound of the screen door opening and closing startles me and I curiously wander away to see who it is that is coming or going.

I step out onto the porch and recognize Mikah, casually walking on the beaten path, towards the outhouse. His hands are in his pockets, and he looks to be taking a stroll. Rather than return to my comfortable spot next to Grandma's side, I choose to sit on the porch and watch him walk down the path.

"Make sure you look for spiders before you sit down!" I yell after him.

He turns around and simply waves at me, before continuing down the path, and then disappearing into the outhouse.

As I sit, I think and sweat. *I miss my grandfather, my uncle, Paul, and of course, my mother. I wonder how much more enjoyable this day could be had they been alive still.*

My thoughts are abruptly cut short when Jonah steps out onto the porch and takes a seat in an old, wicker chair to my left. It's too hot to relax so I don't. I run through a few conversation starters in my head before I decide on something I figure is appropriate.

"Hot day, isn't it?" I ask nervously.

"Yep," he says, without looking at me. His blue eyes are looking straight ahead, either at the orange van parked in front of us or beyond that...into the open land, heavily covered with sage bushes.

"You and Grandma are the first real Indians I've ever

met," he says.

I am caught off guard and don't know how to respond, so I simply say, "Wow."

When I look at him, his head is angled as he looks back at me, and the smile which appears on his face is enchanting.

"I have to say you have very attractive features," he says calmly.

Is he flirting? It definitely sounds like a flirty remark, but I decide to ignore it and I respond by saying, "Thank you."

"I mean, I didn't mean like I'm checking you out or anything. I just think Indians have great features."

"Okay," I say, nodding my head, to portray my understanding.

"You don't believe me?"

"I do, I'm just nodding in agreement."

A few seconds pass as we both look back out to the land before us, with the outhouse being the only visible structure for miles.

"I would think there were other Native Americans who moved to San Francisco, besides my grandparents," I say.

"Oh yes, sorry about saying Indians, I don't know what the proper term is," he apologetically says.

I just smile and nod before saying, "Personally, I'm not offended…I'm just used to saying Native Americans."

"Well, I'm sure there are some in the city, I've just never seen any."

"You have to follow the smoke signals," I say jokingly.

He lets out a chuckle at my cheesy, desperate attempt

at a joke.

"So, I guess it's a good thing I didn't ask you where your tepees are," he says.

"Now that is funny," I say, with a laugh.

We both laugh.

"Oh, I would've told you our tepees are called casinos now," I say.

With confusion in his voice, he asks, "Is that good or bad?"

"It was a joke, a bad one."

Finally, he lets out another small chuckle before he adds, "I have some Native American blood in me, too."

"Oh, really? Were white people trained to say that or something? Every time I talk to white people about being native, they always say that."

"No, it's true," he explains. "My mother's great-grandfather was half Native American."

"So, that would make you a fraction, like one-eighth native," I say.

"It still counts for something, right?" he curiously asks.

"Not really, especially with your blonde hair and blue eyes," I say, followed by a giggle

Just then, Mikah emerges from the outhouse and begins his stroll back towards us.

Grandma joins us on the porch and asks, "What are you two talking about?"

"Oh, good, maybe you can clear something up for us," Jonah quickly says, as he gives up his chair for Grandma.

"What's that?" Grandma asks, as she takes the seat Jonah has offered.

"Well, my mother's great-grandfather was half Native American. Doesn't that make me Native American, too?" Jonah asks. He is now leaning against the frame of the porch, with his arms crossed.

Grandma contemplates the question for a split second and answers, "Yes, you are Native."

Just then, Mikah steps onto the porch. He must've heard part of the conversation. "Dude, we're Native?" he asks his brother.

"Yes, we are Native," Jonah proudly exclaims.

The two of them do a high-five with each other.

"Dude, whatever you do, do not call her an Indian," Jonah says, as he points at me.

I giggle at his remark.

"Actually, we are called the Diné, which means 'the people'," Grandma explains.

"Oh, cool, even I get to learn something new about myself," I say.

"Diné," Jonah repeats. "Cool."

"Is that the name of the tribe?" Mikah asks.

"Yes, that's our real name. We were given the name Navajos by Mexican people and it means 'thieves', which is not a name that sits well with a lot of Diné," Grandma explains further.

"But the official name of our tribe is still Navajo?" I ask.

"Yes, it is, unfortunately," Grandma answers.

"I wonder which tribe we are from," Mikah says.

"Yeah, I wonder, we'll have to figure that out," Jonah adds.

A Marshmallow Moment

That evening, conversation during dinner is light. Grandma does most of the talking, sharing simple details about her relatives and the neighbors. Of course, out here, a neighbor could live miles away. It's not like in the city, where your neighbor could reach out the window of their house and touch your house. Grandma's neighbors are her mother, her sister, Elsa, and a few families who don't share a common bloodline with us. All of their homes dot the landscape alongside the winding Little Colorado River, on the other side of the main dirt road.

Before long, everyone has eaten to their fill and there are more dirty dishes which need washing. This time, I leave the dishes and decide I will wash them later. Instead, I go outside, where everyone is sitting, under the tree, which sits on the south side of the house. And just as I arrive, Grandma rises from her chair with some difficulty and quietly walks towards the wood pile.

In the winter, the wood pile is usually standing at

least four feet high with wood, but now, there are only several logs and a heap of wood chips littering the ground. I can't imagine what she is going to do at the wood pile, so I don't try to figure it out.

"So, what do you guys think of this place so far?" I ask.

"Well, I know I enjoy the peace and quiet," Mikah responds.

"Yep, me, too, I feel comfortable here," Jonah says.

Adam remains quiet, simply nodding at his brothers' answers.

A few moments later, Grandma calls Adam over to the woodpile, with a wave and a holler. He dutifully responds and leaves us with a hurried walk before I can badger him for his thoughts.

I sit under the tree, on one of the folding chairs. Mikah and Jonah sit comfortably in worn, folding chairs on either side of me. For the short time we sit, they make more comments and observations about the land, and the peacefulness of it.

I nod and agree with their observations. I recognize I am learning to fully appreciate my origin and home. I am filled with pride suddenly and a smile stretches across my face.

"So what type of activities do people do for entertainment out here?" Mikah asks.

I ponder the questions for a few moments and finally answer, "Well, there are the traditional squaw dances which have become more of a pastime than a ceremony, the basketball tournaments at the nearby boarding school, and trips into town. Other than that, people have to be imaginative. For instance, Grandma weaves. My grandfather used to carve dolls, not toy dolls, of course. My uncle, Paul, was an artist and drew all kinds of landscape pictures. And I rode my bike a lot as a child."

"Any chance we will be able to do any of those activities while we're here?" Jonah curiously asks.

"I don't know, maybe, it sounds like we're going to take a trip into town here very soon," I answer.

After several minutes, Grandma returns and announces, "We built a fire and are ready to roast some marshmallows."

"Mmmm," I say, as I imagine gooey marshmallows with a nice crusty shell. The thought brings on a sudden hunger for sweetness.

With a bit of pep in my walk, I lead the guys to the wood pile, where the fire is crackling. Grandma has gathered five old chairs I never knew existed, probably from her shed house, which I call her stash house. The chairs, as old and worn as they are, look comfy now, covered with old quilts.

The evening air is cool, and there is stillness in the air. A calm breeze touches my face like pieces of cool silk. The flames from the fire are sweeping high, and the mild summer breeze is blowing the flames around in the wind. Embers are flying around the fire, and there is crackling from the flames.

I feel comfortable and protected as I take a seat on the quilt-covered chair closest to Grandma. The chair faces to the west, and I have a grand view of the last glimmer of light from the setting sun.

"Here, why don't you all get a stick, and let's cook some marshmallows," offers Grandma, as she reveals a large bag of marshmallows from underneath her chair.

Darkness settles in as the glow from the fire grows. The distant noise of barking dogs is the only noise for miles around.

Other than the erratic dogs, I am at peace and I feel refreshed, free, as if I am now loose of the city's grasp. I wonder if the Navarros feel the same as I do about city life. I wonder if their city taught them to keep their guards up, just as Los Angeles did to me. I wonder if they know what it's like to let their guards down, to truly relax.

The men settle, each one taking a seat and eyeing the ground for their own sticks.

I choose a stick which is not too wide and not too jagged. I watch Grandma as she spits on her stick to clean it off.

"We used to do this with our parents back home, when we went camping," says Adam, who seats himself on the other side of Grandma. He looks calm; his face expressionless and his body movement somewhat relaxed. Maybe he's already found the powers of relaxation this place holds.

"Oh yeah, I remember that," adds Mikah, who settles next to Adam on a squeaky, old chair. "Except I was the one who had to roast everyone's marshmallows and I was always burning my hands," he complains.

Instead of spitting on my stick, as Grandma had demonstrated for us earlier, I offer to clean everyone else's sticks off with some water inside the house. Jonah and Mikah take me up on my offer and I carry the sticks into the house for cleaning.

After I rinse off the sticks, I put a pot of water on the stove to boil. I will need it for washing the dishes later.

When I return to the woodpile, we all form a cozy circle around the fire.

While the three brothers share memories of their marshmallow roasting stories, I allow myself to slip into thoughts of L.A. and of my friends; Alex, Nicky, and Michael. I remember a time when we were sitting on a bench outside the Starbucks located a few blocks from home. We were laughing about nothing in particular, mostly events at school like the time I tripped with a handful of books because I couldn't see over the books and missed a step. Michael's eyes and mine met and we did not look away. Instead, we smiled at each other and that was the first twinge of attraction I have experienced with a boy.

I tuck my memory away and watch the fire. I wonder what my friends are doing now. I can picture them going to the mall, and watching a movie at our favorite theater, and then grabbing a bite to eat at our favorite spot, Subway, not far from home.

The evenings are probably just as mild right now in Los Angeles; a lot warmer, but mild. The city is probably beginning to light up with people of the night coming out to play.

As the evening goes on, I listen to Grandma and the Navarro men exchange stories of San Francisco while embers swirl around us and the darkness is kept at bay by the glowing fire.

Grandma portrays her experience of living in a small, cramped apartment above Market Street. She describes the street below as constantly noisy and busy. She describes her neighbors, the Navarros, the Japanese couple, and the Cherokee couple, as warm and nice people. By the tone of her voice and the smile on her face as she speaks of them, I gather she was fond of their companionship. She vividly remembers how her two children, who were three and four years old at the time, would play on the fire escape right outside her living room window.

She tells us, well, mostly the men, about how my grandfather slowly drank himself to death after moving back here. In her opinion, he thought moving back was a mistake and blamed her for it—for his depression, for his longing to be back in the city, and eventually, for all his failures after that.

Among the Navarro brothers, Adam is the only one who can relate to Grandma's memoirs. Jonah and Mikah are just as enchanted as I am and listen contently.

When it's Adam's turn to recount his tales of back then, he speaks of how he would venture to my grandparents' apartment and play house with Anthony and Jeanette. After they became tired of playing house, they would mimic super heroes like Super-Man and Spider-Man, and for my aunt, there was Wonder Woman. He also remembers the first time he tasted Grandma's delicious sweet cake during one of his visits.

And then he shifts his subject and in a dismal tone, he tells us about the last years spent with his mother, and how she slowly deteriorated right before their eyes and how "his father suffered most, from watching her slowly leave."

Grandma adds a comment about how their parents seemed so close to each other; that she isn't surprised their father died right after their mother.

Mikah and Jonah don't have much to say, and nod their heads in agreement, with a smile, every once in a while.

I can't tell if they're smiles stem from some distant memory or from an effort to conceal their grief.

At some point in the discussion, I realize I have something in common with the Navarro men; we are parentless. Although I'm sure my father is alive somewhere, the only thing I know about him is he's Navajo. Since I've never seen or heard from him, I figure I can't say I have a father so I just tell people he died.

And Grandma, well, she's seen her share of death. I look at her, as she sits cross-legged next to me, and I wonder if I can see the sorrow in her eyes. But I don't see a hint of it and I figure it's buried deep inside her, so I stop looking.

I feel a sense of closeness to everyone around the fire, and it makes me feel like we're connected at a higher level. Chills run down my spine, and I pull my knees up to my chin, and wrap my arms around them. I let the warmth of the fire surround me like a blanket being wrapped around me.

I quietly stuff gooey marshmallows into my mouth and just as I stuff the last one in my mouth, I remember I have water heating on the stove in the house. So I jump up to go turn it off.

"I forgot that I left the dish water heating," I say behind me.

Nobody answers. I'm certain they're dumbfounded by my sudden leap into action.

Before I reach the front door, I hear soft, quick footsteps behind me.

"Do you guys have mosquitoes out here?" I hear the person behind me say. I am startled. So I stop and turn around to see who is following me.

It's Jonah. And he apologizes as he catches up to me.

"Sorry, didn't mean to scare you."

"Yes, we do," I say hastily, still somewhat alarmed. "Grandma has some Off! spray if you need some," I add, doing my best to mask my nervousness.

Jonah follows me into the dark house. His presence spawns an awkward feeling within me and I try to shake it off. With nothing but the dim light from the flashlight to guide us, we carefully move across the living room and into the kitchen.

"I just came inside to turn off the water," I explain as I walk into the dark kitchen.

"It seems pretty dark in here and I figured you might need help," he replies.

"You think I need help turning off the stove?" I ask nervously.

"Yes, I think you do."

"Actually, I think I'm going to wash the dishes, too."

"I know how to wash dishes, do you need some help?"

"Umm, no. Thanks."

I do not know very many men who offer to wash dishes and think it's awkward, yet very polite of him to ask. As I contemplate more on the thought, I realize I do not know any men who would do such a thing.

Still confused as to why this young man is following me around in a dark house and asking to help me wash dishes, I say, "I got it."

And before he can offer again, I add, "Wouldn't you rather be outside, eating marshmallows?"

"Nah, I'm cool, being inside."

In an effort to change the subject entirely, I say, "I am sure you are tired from your trip and need some rest."

"We've been here for over 24 hours now. I'm over being tired from the trip," he says.

I fumble for some matches in the kitchen and finally light the oil lantern which I find on a shelf next to the table.

Jonah doesn't have a reply and I figure he must be thinking of something to say.

"Why don't you relax outside with everyone else?" I ask.

"I would rather be in here," he says.

I spot a little, pocket-size flashlight on the window sill so I pick it up, turn it on, and hand it to him.

"You can use this to find your way back to the wood pile, if you change your mind," I say, offering him the flashlight.

He takes the flashlight, flicks it off and back on, but doesn't leave.

I ignore him and go right about my business.

The water in the pot on the stove has boiled away half of the water. I decide I will use what's left anyway.

As I began pouring the hot water from the pot into the dish pan, he asks, "Maybe I can help you next time?"

Without hesitation, I say, "Yeah."

As much as I try to avoid making eye contact or looking in the same direction as him, my eyes wander to him. Him—the young man with the blue eyes and the baby face, standing quietly in the dark. I can see his eyes and I smile at him, hoping he senses my compassion.

"Is there something wrong with wanting to help such a beautiful, young woman?" he asks, to my surprise.

Unsure of how to respond to his question, I don't answer. I continue to smile at him for a moment.

"I hope that doesn't offend you," he says, leaning casually against the arch of the kitchen entryway.

"Well, it is awkward to hear that from someone I just met."

He stands and faces me, and I can tell he is sure of himself—very confident. His blonde locks loosely move as he takes a couple steps closer.

"I've never met anyone as beautiful as you," he says, in a low voice.

His words catch me off guard, and I stop meddling with the pot of water I'm trying to put back onto the stove. "So, let me get this straight. You want to help me wash dishes because you think I'm beautiful?" I ask, trying to brush off his remarks.

"Well, yes. And I just wanted to find an excuse to get to know you a little bit better," he says, matter-of-factly.

I feel butterflies in my stomach and in order to ease the tension, I move away from him, towards the kitchen cabinets. I try to relax and figure out how to respond.

"Are you always so forward with people you find beautiful?" I ask sarcastically as I turn to face him.

"Sometimes…it depends on how real and beautiful the person is," he says, retracting and moving away.

In the dimly lit kitchen, his frame looks bigger than before and his blue eyes are no longer blue, they look gray. His arms are crossed and his shoulder muscles look intensely larger than what I remember.

I hear voices. Everyone else is coming back into the house.

"It also depends on how approachable they are," he says, with a smile.

"I see, well, you caught me off guard," I say, defensively.

The screen door opens and closes after a long pause.

"Oh, yes, that reminds me, I need to get out some blankets for you guys," Grandma is saying, as she makes her way through the front door and the living room.

She has bad knees for as long as I can remember and her back seems to be in constant pain. Both conditions show themselves after she sits for long periods, like now. She walks slowly into the kitchen.

"You guys are probably tired," she says as she hands me a long stick with roasted marshmallows still hanging on it.

And then, slightly bent over, she strolls back into the living room and into her room. I can see that she is tired just by the way she moves, and I wish at that moment she didn't have to work so much or move around so much, that I can do everything for her, but I know her, and she wouldn't have that. I don't think being still is one of her fortes.

Adam and Mikah walk straight into my mother's old room, or shall I say, the guest room?

I quickly wash the dishes and Jonah helps with the rinsing and drying. We avoid discussion about what had just transpired moments before.

As Grandma shuffles into the bathroom, I decide to tend to her and leave Jonah in the kitchen to finish putting away the dishes. I feel horrible for responding to his comments in such a negative manner. I am sure his intentions were not to create a sense of discomfort and uneasiness. However, I make no attempt to explain my remarks.

"Sit down and rest, Grandma," I say, trying to sound

as authoritative as possible.

Of course, my best authoritative tone has no effect on Grandma. Instead, she walks to the guest room, peeks in and says, "If anyone needs to use the bathroom, use this flashlight to go outside, unless you guys have your own."

God knows she has an abundant supply of flashlights, and keeps an unusually large supply of batteries. She holds up her second favorite flashlight, for one of the guys to take.

"Thanks," Adam responds, as he meets her at the door, and grasps the flashlight. "I guess I better go before I head to bed. Anyone else wanna' join me?"

Mikah and Jonah take him up on his offer, and with that, they head out the screen door and to the outhouse.

Silence fills the house for just a few moments as Grandma and I shuffle about to prepare our sleep area. I fluff my pillow while Grandma quietly changes into her nightgown, in a dark corner of her room.

With the guys going to the bathroom, I decide I better empty my bladder now, rather than wait 'til midnight, or early morning.

"Grandma, I need to go to the bathroom, too," I say, in a low, hushed voice.

"Okay, we'll go behind the house," she says.

I can see her figure, moving about in the darkness. When she finally steps into the glow of light, she is wearing some sweatpants, and her night gown.

"Well, come on" she says, and summons me to follow her.

"What if the guys see us squatting back there?" I ask, hoping she would reconsider and say we use the outhouse instead.

"It's dark. No one will see us, unless the skinwalkers are out. I hear they can see in the dark," she says, half-way laughing.

"They're not real, so they don't count," I say, with a serious tone.

Well, then, no one will see us, for sure," she says, as she leads the way towards the back of her house.

The thought of one of the guys sprinkling on the toilet seat in the outhouse forces my mind to accept the squatting idea. So I follow along.

A Defining Moment

I follow her outside, to a spot about twenty feet from the back of the house. It is dark, and I look around on the ground, hoping the moonlight will reveal a spider or something horrible which will change Grandma's mind about squatting here. But there is nothing. I watch as Grandma naturally and easily takes her squatting position. I hear trickle and spraying, and my bladder pressure increases.

Why can't we just go to the outhouse?

As disturbed as I am about squatting here, in the bushes outside, in the dark, I scope out the area around me, searching for thee chosen spot. I choose a spot a few feet away from where Grandma is squatting, and unzip my pants.

Just as I start to bend my knees, and lower my body, I hear a loud BANG! It sounds like a firecracker. I look around but there are no sparkles in the sky. Another bang...my body jerks, my legs quiver, and my bladder lets go.

"Shoot!" I say out loud. My warm urine is flowing and my thighs are wet. I close my eyes and lose myself in the pleasure of letting my urine go. There is a loud shriek from the other side of the house.

"WHAT WAS THAT?!" I say in a loud whisper.

I hastily scramble to pull my pants up, only to find they are wet also.

"Shoot!" I whisper loudly. "Now I'm going to smell like pee."

There is no time to mull over my accident. I hear Grandma's feet shuffling towards the other side of the house, and I can see her silhouette moving away from me. A scary thought crosses my mind as I replay the sound in my head. Were those gunshots?

As I straighten myself out, and stumble after Grandma, I feel chills run down my spine, as I think of the Navarros. *Are they still at the outhouse?*

"Grandma!" I call out, when I reach the side of the house.

She has already reached the corner of the house and is peering around it.

"I'm right here!" she loudly whispers back at me.

I scurry over to her.

"Shh!" she says, without taking her eyes off whatever she is looking at.

There is loud shuffling of feet on the ground. It sounds like people running. I look around the corner, from behind Grandma. It's Adam, Mikah and Jonah, running back from the outhouse. I can see them in the dim moonlight.

As they near the front door, Grandma steps out into sight and I follow her cautiously.

"Did you hear that?" Adam asks, almost out of breath.

The look in Adam's eyes is more than enough to

scare me. Mikah and Jonah are right behind him, looking backwards, but still walking with quick steps towards the front porch.

"Yes, we heard it," Grandma replies in a hushed, but frantic voice.

I remember my little peeing accident and retreat into Grandma's bedroom to change my pants. I frantically dig through a small suitcase I packed some jeans into, which is lying open on the floor next to Grandma's bed. I quickly squeeze into a pair of jeans and cautiously walk back to the front doorway with urgency.

A muffled yell comes from out of the darkness in front of us.

I suddenly don't want to see whatever it is that made the noise, and I'd rather slip away into Grandma's bed and cover myself with her mismatched sheets and her light, hand-sewn quilt. Or better yet, take a shower. I can still feel dampness on the insides of my upper thighs.

Calm down…it's probably nothing.

In the next moment, I hear Grandma loudly exclaim, "Someone's hurt! There's someone there!"

I don't want to hear this. I don't want to see. I close my eyes.

Grandma, who was still standing near the front porch, now breaks into a run and fearlessly heads in the direction of the yell, in her nightgown and sweat pants.

"What's going on?" I ask out loud, no longer feeling the need to whisper.

"Someone's out there," Adam says, with a stunned look on his face, and points in the direction Grandma is running.

"Wait, Grandma!" I yell.

I squeeze past Jonah and Mikah. But before I reach the end of the porch, Jonah grabs my arm and says, "Stay here."

Mikah and Adam take a few steps off the porch, and dart down the path towards the outhouse, after Grandma.

"We better stay here," Jonah says, now pulling me inside the house.

I wonder what has happened. Who has been hurt? And was that really a gunshot?

The moonlight which was shining ever so brightly several minutes before is now hidden by clouds, and darkness covers the land in front of us.

Another yell comes from the direction of the outhouse, maybe a hundred feet away. It's a low, muffled yell. I can't quite make out the words, if there are any words.

The blood in my body is pumping fast, my heart is beating fast. I take one hand in my other and I crack my knuckles, something I do when I am very nervous.

"Let's drive the van down there," I say urgently, and look at Jonah. I can see the fear in his wide-opened, blue eyes.

"And do what?" he asks, stunned at my idea.

"We can use the headlights to see what is happening," I say. "I don't know what is out there, or who is yelling for help, or where Grandma and Adam are going, but I do know it's dark and when they find where this yell is coming from, they may need some light."

"Umm, okay…let me get the keys," Jonah says.

He quickly disappears back into the house. I stand. I look into the darkness. I listen for more sounds. I hear

Grandma's voice, calling out for help now. I can see the light from her flashlight.

A few moments later, Jonah returns, jingling the van keys. I follow him and swiftly move my feet, as we head towards the van.

I look at Jonah and I see the fear in his eyes still, as he takes his place behind the steering wheel and nervously puts the key in the ignition. He turns the van around and we drive.

"Go towards the light, where the flashlights are shining," I instruct him.

We make a hard left. And we bounce up and down as the bushes scrape the bottom of the van. The headlights expose the rough, bushy landscape and two figures bent over. It's Adam and Grandma. They are bent over something...a body. Mikah is standing near them. The van comes to a stop. Jonah and I quickly jump out.

"We need to get him in the van!" Grandma shouts at us, before we approach them.

"Come help us!" Adam calls out.

I suddenly feel panicked. I can see the body is that of a man. He is lying on the ground, face up, with his head tilted sideways. He is alive, and muttering something. Blood is drooling out of his mouth. Adam squats down to help while Grandma shines her flashlight on the man's face.

The man has long, black hair, which is covering part of his face. He looks to be a large man from where I stand, or maybe it's his clothes that make him look large. As Grandma shines the flashlight down the rest of his body, I notice that he is wearing a white t-shirt, cargo jeans, white Nike athletic shoes and mismatched socks; one with green stripes, the other with red stripes, and both are crumpled around his ankles.

He looks up at us. His eyes are lazy, empty and bloodshot. His face is distorted, and there is blood all over the back side of his hands, as he holds his stomach area.

I feel helpless and unhelpful, so I rattle my brain for ideas on how to help. "Why don't we get a blanket or something like a stretcher, to carry him into the van?" I blurt out, with a shaky voice.

"No, don't move him! We need to be careful not to hurt him anymore," exclaims Jonah.

"He will bleed more if we leave him like this. We need to stop the bleeding or slow it down," Adam says urgently.

I hurriedly walk to the back of the van, and fumble around for a blanket or some type of cloth. I find a rope and nothing else. Without thinking twice, I break into a run towards the house, just as Adam and Mikah are attempting to lift the man from the ground.

"I'm getting some towels!" I yell at no one in particular. I run in the dark clumsily, and I almost stumble over the bushes. I catch myself, but I can feel my legs getting heavier.

When I reach the house, I decide to search for towels in Grandma's room first and thankfully so, because I find an abundant supply of them in her closet on some shelves.

I race back out of the house and into the darkness again. I reach the van and wave the towels so Grandma is aware that I have them. She is overseeing the transfer of the man from the ground to the van. All I can do is look on as he is carried into the van and shoveled onto Grandma's lap in the middle row of seats.

"We need to get to the hospital!" Grandma hollers.

The man's face is slightly bloody. I can see his hair is long and it is scraggly, partly covering his face, and it's messy with blood. His t-shirt and jeans are covered in blood.

"Shannon!" I hear my grandmother yell. "Get in!" she demands.

I climb into the van, as does everyone else and we hit more bumps, up and down we bounce, over the bushes. Eventually, we reach the road, which leads towards the main dirt road.

Adam, Mikah and Jonah are like zombies. They are quiet and seem to go with the motions.

Adam drives the van, as quickly as he can. He strains to see the road, which lay right ahead of us. From where I am sitting, I can see his face has a serious, worried look.

I can't see Mikah's face. He is in the passenger seat, looking straight ahead at the road.

Jonah sits in the back of the van with me, and he looks straight ahead, expressionless.

I can only imagine how shocked they are about what is happening.

The pleasant place they thought they were visiting has turned into a place which will probably bring them nightmares for some time; a place they probably will not want to remember.

The thumping in my heart has slowed, but the blood is still rushing. I feel as if I am in a dream, as if none of what is happening is real.

Grandma cradles the man in her arms and says, "You're going to be okay."

Mikah sits at the helm of the van, next to Adam, and

looks back at Grandma and the wounded man.

Grandma is holding the man in her lap. She is whispering more words, words I cannot make out.

As we drive away from the house, I look back and the house is illuminated by the red taillights. It looks lonely and a little creepy. I turn back towards the front. The lights from the van are shining on the dirt road in front of us.

Who could've done this? And where is the shooter?

The wounded man is moaning and Grandma is asking him if he is okay, and what his name is. But all he can do is moan. Blood is still seeping out of his mouth, and I can see the blood in the moonlight, it looks dark in the night; dark and bubbling, dripping onto her clothes.

Grandma hastily tries to wipe the blood from the man. I presume she is trying to find the wound. After several quick strokes, she balls up a towel and holds it against his abdomen and rocks him gently.

I look at the road in front us, and I wonder what our neighbors are doing, if anyone else heard the shots. Surely, somebody else must have heard something.

"Give me another towel!" I hear Grandma frantically say.

I look at the wounded man in her arms and he seems to have fallen asleep. No more moaning, just silence, his chest slowly rising up and down.

"I hope he doesn't die," I say as I pass more towels to her.

"It looks like he's still breathing," says Mikah, observing from the front passenger seat.

Grandma removes a blood-soaked towel from the man's abdomen, and tosses the ball of bloody material on the floor, near the door.

The smell of blood from the towel and from the man's wound or wounds is climbing up into my nostrils.

"Drive faster, Adam!" Grandma yells. I look at her. She is sitting in the seat in front of me, facing forward, away from me, but I can see her facial features from the side.

"I'm going 55! The road is too rough!" Adam shouts back, with frustration in his voice.

The glow from the dashboard lights shine faintly to bring out the features of the wounded man's face. His eyes are closed now and his mouth is slightly open.

I look at Jonah and I notice the desperation in his eyes. My heart flushes, and I feel like crying right at that moment. I look away, out the window into the darkness, the darkness speeding by.

Although it seems we are already racing down the road, Adam speeds up anyway and we are now zipping by the first stretch of Sunflower Valley. Through the window next to me, the flower petals look gray and dark yellow.

I feel a knot in my stomach and I feel cold, so I close my eyes and pray for the man. I hope he lives. I hope he lives. I clasp my hands together, remembering that an old missionary who used to preach to us on Sundays at Grandma's house, once told me that if I clasp my hands together just right, it will help God hear me better. As absurd as I thought that sounded back then, I clasp my hands together and I pray the only way I know how.

Under my breath, I pray, "this man in Grandma's lap is a stranger, but I pray you keep him alive. I can't witness a death tonight...I don't want to."

Ahead of us, the headlights illuminate the sides of the

road and the last sunflowers from Sunflower Valley. This makes the flowers which are closest to the road a bright yellow color.

I focus on the bright flowers ahead and I don't look back out my window at the gray ones left in the darkness.

The Longest Ride

Except for the hum of the engine, a dead silence fills the small, crowded space in the van as Adam zooms down the dirt road and then down the last few miles of paved road into town. I squeeze my hands together again, and I look out the window, trying to grasp the situation.

Only one picture remains fresh in my mind: the look on the man's face when he looked right at me. It was an awful deep, empty, and dark look. It was as if he was looking right through me.

Then, as if the scene of a movie playing over and over in my mind has changed, I think of something nobody else has mentioned, the police.

"Hey, I can get off at the sheriff's office or the police station after we drop the man off at the hospital" I stammer, afraid someone else might beat me to the idea.

"We're going to the hospital first. We'll worry about all that later," Grandma says and in the same breath, asks, "Are we there yet?" She asks this even though she knows where we are, so the question is rhetoric and nobody answers.

She then takes a pouch from her neck, which was hidden under her blouse, and slowly unties a small string which clasped the pouch closed. I have seen her do this before and I know she does it when she is preparing for prayer, so I lower my head, close my eyes, and just listen to the words my Grandma speaks in Navajo.

"Great Spirit. Mother Earth. Father Sky. Spirit of the Fire. Spirit of the Winds. Spirit of Water. Take pity on this man in my arms, my human brother and son. He has been wounded for a reason we do not know. Whatever has happened to him or what he has done, everything, take it away. Be with him now. Go before us and bless our way. Thank you, Mother Earth, Father Sky, Spirit Gods. All is beautiful again. All is beautiful again. All is beautiful again. All is beautiful again."

I close my eyes tighter, and hold back the tears. I do not know this man, yet the thought of a man dying right here, near me, is sad—another life leaving this place is sad.

Grandma sniffs and wipes her tears.

Mikah looks to be wiping some tears away as well as he sits looking forward, in the front passenger seat.

A few more miles of riding in silence passes. No talking, just the hum of the engine and the pavement markings disappearing under the van.

The bushes and trees and the first few houses on the outskirts of town zip by, and the lights from the town illuminate the skyline ahead of us. The town inches closer, mile by mile, and so does the anxiety. I can hear a sigh from

Grandma.

She talks to the wounded man, on her lap, as if he can hear her say, "We're almost there."

He lets out a low, faint grunt.

I close my eyes and I beg harder, pray harder, and squeeze my hands together harder. I open my eyes and look out the window. I realize all we can do now is wait a few more moments. I turn back towards the road and we are in town. More houses zip by, and we make a few sharp turns, as Adam follows Grandma's directions to the only hospital in town. A left, a few more minutes, and another left. The wounded man starts moaning again.

Grandma starts crying again. "Don't die in my arms, young man, you are strong. We're here now. You will get help now," she is whispering to him in between sobs.

As soon as the van stops, I squeeze past Grandma and open the van sliding door. Adam runs towards the Emergency Room entrance. A minute or so passes as Grandma continues to hold the man and quietly pray under her breath. It feels like an eternity has passed when Adam finally returns with a nurse, who is running towards us with a wheelchair.

"Gunshot wound, I hear," she says to nobody in particular, as if to confirm Adam's story.

"Yes. We don't know how it happened, but he got shot," Grandma frantically explains, as the nurse and Adam lift the man from Grandma's lap and put him in the wheelchair.

"Hold him, he looks like he's lost a lot of blood," instructs the nurse.

Adam does as she says, with shaking hands.

90

"He can't hold himself up," explains the nurse, as she unlocks the wheels of the chair.

They quickly wheel him into the Emergency Room entrance. Mikah and Grandma follow, without hesitation.

My heart is pounding and I want to run after everyone else, but I stay behind with Jonah. When I let my eyes meet his, I can see the fear in his eyes and his face looks pale under the glow from the parking lot lights.

"I hope he is okay. I have never been through anything like this," I say, timidly, looking away, back towards the entrance of the Emergency Room.

I can hear myself talking and I can feel the cool air on my face. I can see and hear the semi trucks rumbling by on I-40, just a couple of miles away from where we stand. I am not in a dream. This is very real.

I look back at Jonah.

"Yeah, me too...that was one, very long drive," he says, emotionless.

We stand quietly next to the front of the van for a few seconds, looking at the door of the Emergency Room. It seems like minutes have passed since the wounded man in the wheelchair, the nurse, Grandma, and Adam all disappeared inside. Yet we stand there, as if we are waiting for further instruction or in a trance.

"I guess we better throw these towels away," I say, absent-mindedly.

"We better go find a parking space," Jonah mumbles.

"Yeah."

"I saw the visitor's entrance on the other side of the building," he says calmly. He walks around to the driver door, and gets back in the van.

I quickly remember something else. "We need to go to the sheriff's office!" I exclaim as I get in on the passenger side of the van.

"Oh yes!" Jonah says, with newfound excitement in his voice. Then he asks in an urgent tone, "Do you know where it is?"

"Yeah," I say, not really knowing, but quite positive it will come to me. I think and I remember. I do know where it is after all.

"Straight ahead, just stay on this same road," I direct.

The sheriff's building is a plain, single-story, brick building a few streets south of the hospital. The parking lot is occupied by two marked cars and a white Astro van. We park in the parking lot, right in front of the entrance.

When we get inside, I scramble for words. I want to tell the receptionist we need to file a report, but instead I say, "File report."

"Calm down, missy," the lady says as she rises from behind the large, wooden desk she's sitting at.

Jonah speaks and says, "We need to file a report."

"What kind of report?" the lady asks, in a soft, calm, Southern-accented voice. She is a middle-aged white woman, with a pink floral dress, and her hair is pinned up nicely in a big bun atop her head. She looks like she put on too much blush because her cheeks are a rosy red, and it contrasts with her light skin color.

"A gunshot report, I think," I say, unsure of the type of report it would be filed under.

I look at Jonah for support, and to my surprise, he looks just as calm as the lady behind the desk. His demeanor, his walk, and his face are not showing any signs of panic. He is cool and laid-back, as if nothing terrible was happening.

"We are not sure how it happened, ma'am, but a man was shot near their house," Jonah explains calmly, as he points to me as if to give me a cue to speak.

"Can you tell me exactly what happened?" the lady asks, looking at me with a concerned look in her eyes.

I begin to describe the scene and how we found the man. As I am talking, an old, very round, bald man steps out of an office behind the clerk's desk. He stands next to the clerk. He listens contently as the lady sits behind her desk and types what I'm saying verbatim.

After I finish my rant, the bald man speaks. "We'll get Marvin out on this one," he confidently says.

I assume he is the sheriff because he has a badge and a few other embellishments on his uniform. And I assume he is talking about one of his deputies.

After she has me review the report, the lady asks for a phone number, which I don't have, so I tell her we'll be at the hospital.

The Sheriff asks me to draw him a map of where we found the man, so I take a sheet of lined, yellow, notebook paper the lady is offering.

I draw a squiggly line to show the path of the curvy road which leads to Grandma's house. I draw a short line to cross the path of the squiggly line right in the middle of the line. Then I nervously draw a circle which turns out to be a somewhat squiggly line as well and write the words, *City Dump*, next to it.

"Just relax, your hands are shaking," the lady behind the desk comments.

"This is on reservation land?" the bald man asks,

with a confused look.

"Umm, yeah," I say, as I continue to draw a square for Grandma's house at the end of the squiggly line.

I continue with my map, by writing the words, *Sunflower Valley*, alongside the squiggly line which is supposed to represent the part of dirt road near the top of the plateau.

"This is out of our jurisdiction, but we'll send somebody out right away...Liz, call up the Navajo police headquarters," the bald man sharply says.

"Yes, sir," Liz responds, and she quickly picks up the phone on her desk.

I figure the bald man is disappointed with my map because he asks, "Why don't you just give us verbal directions?"

So I begin to describe the location. "It's about fifteen miles from here, on a plateau, a couple miles past the sunflowers." I let out in a shaky, cracked voice.

"Okay, you can finish drawing it on a map instead," he suggests with a smile. Then he steps back into his office and I hear what sounds like a dispatch call. "Marvin, can you stop by the hospital, we have a possible gunshot victim..." His voice trails off.

The drawing is not my best work, probably due to my nervousness, and the blood still rushing through my veins. All those years of drawing maps in Social Studies and I can't even draw a halfway decent map of a place I know like the back of my hand. In addition to the squiggly lines, the distance between town and Grandma's house seems disproportionate.

After a few moments, the sheriff returns from his

office and asks, "Were there any other witnesses?"

I think but I don't come up with anyone. Grandma Elsa, who lives about two miles away, near the river's edge, has jackrabbit ears and can hear an indoor argument from miles away, especially during the night. I figure this will not help in any way so I don't mention her name.

After I think for a few more moments, I look at the sheriff and say, "I don't know. There was no one else around, just us, his two brothers, and Grandma." I nod at Jonah, to show I am speaking of his brothers.

"That's good enough now," the clerk says, as she slowly pulls the poor attempt at a map drawing out of under my pencil.

"Sorry, I wish I could draw a better map."

"Thank you so much...this will be very helpful," she says, as she slides the map into a manila folder and hands it to the old, bald man.

"Thank you," Jonah quietly utters, as he shakes hands with the bald man.

Liz, the clerk, is now sitting back at her desk and waves at us as we leave the Sheriff's office.

As if I am in a dream or rather, a horrible nightmare, my body movements are slow and numb. I feel myself climbing into the van, but I don't know how my brain is telling my body parts to move, because my brain is somewhere else—lost.

Jonah drives the van back the way we came. We don't speak.

The small, shoddy houses, which are prevalent in this part of town, move by slowly as the wheels on the van turn. The darkness of the night is thick now. The clouds are still hiding the moonlight. I close my eyes and rest for a minute.

When we arrive back at the hospital, we sluggishly walk into the Emergency Room waiting area of the hospital.

Grandma's face lights up with excitement when she sees us and she sits up straight, smiling at us with her puffy eyes.

While Jonah fills her in on the details from our visit to the Sheriff's office, I let my eyelids close and mentally block out everything that is going on around me. I just want to rest.

Lost in Time

"Ma'am, I am Dr. Richards. This is Deputy Roberts," a man says, extending his hand to Grandma, as he walks up to us.

The two men who are approaching us are both white. The doctor, with a light green outfit and white, rubber clogs, looks to be in his late forties, early fifties and is taller than the man introduced as Deputy Roberts.

We had been sitting in the area marked *Waiting Room* for a couple of hours now and are anxious for an update on the wounded man's condition. Although we are not family or close to the man, it just seems right that we wait for him, maybe until his family comes to the hospital.

Grandma looks very tired. The bun on her head is unraveled a bit and the nightgown, which was clean when she put it on, is now spotted with dried blood stains. When she hears the doctor's voice, she sits up abruptly and attempts to straighten her clothes before she takes the doctor's extended hand and gives it a little shake.

As she shakes, she clears her throat and says, "I'm Ethel Scott."

"Are you the ones who found our gunshot victim?" Deputy Roberts asks. He is a short, white man with a receding hairline, who is wearing a brown and tan uniform with dark brown stripes down the sides of his pant legs. His voice has a deep Southern accent.

"Yes," Grandma answers.

"Do you know who the victim is?" Deputy Roberts asks, as he stands feet apart with his arms crossed.

"None of us know the victim," Adam answers. Up until now, he had been pacing back and forth a few feet away from where Grandma is sitting.

And then with a nod, Grandma looks up at the deputy and adds, "We don't know the man, we just found him. He was not far from where we live."

The doctor, a tall white man with a small, brown beard and beady, brown eyes, stands with his arms behind his back. He speaks with a raspy voice. "Well, we didn't find any identification on him," he explains.

He seems to wait for a reaction as he looks around the room at everyone, but nobody speaks.

Deputy Roberts then asks, "Do you know how he ended up by your house?" as he tilts his head a little to one side.

Grandma clears her throat again, this time in a nervous manner and answers, "We don't know. We were outside of the house and all of a sudden, we heard a noise—it sounded like a gun, you know?"

She looks at me as if to pull her memory from my face, and then continues her explanation, "It sounded like a gun was shot, and it sounded really close by, so we went to look."

She pauses for a second, long enough to take a breath, and then says, "He was a little ways from our house." She is now wide awake, and looks back to the deputy with a questioning look, as if he can somehow help her grasp the situation.

The deputy offers nothing but an inquisitive look.

"How is he doing? And will he live?" asks Adam, before Grandma or Deputy Roberts can speak another word.

"Well, I hate to be the bearer of bad news, but...he didn't make it," the doctor replies in his raspy voice. "He lost a lot of blood and the bullet went through his midsection."

And just like that...the mystery man is gone.

Is it our fault? Did we not drive fast enough? I rack my brain with questions. I'm upset. I'm confused. I'm sad.

As if to read my mind, the doctor says, "There is nothing more we can do, and try not to blame yourselves. You did well by bringing him to the hospital."

"Woah," is all Adam can conjure up. He had stopped pacing some time before and is now standing almost directly behind the doctor and I can see something which resembles defeat, on his face.

"Oh man," says Jonah, as he puts his claps his hands over his head, and walks away from us. He begins pacing back and forth in the room.

My heart sinks like an anchor. I feel pressure in my chest. The pressure is heavy and it numbs my body. I did not know the man, but I did not count on him dying right before us. I don't know what to say. I was sure he would live. All I could do is sit still with my hands on Grandma's shoulders.

"I can't believe the man did not make it. He had a pulse the whole way," Mikah says, with frustration in his voice.

"Do you know where he might have come from?" asks the deputy, who now has a pocket notebook and pen in hand.

"Well, he's not from any of our neighbors' houses, I've never seen him before," explains Grandma. "I guess I can ask around."

"In the meantime, I will need to take a report from each of you," the deputy states.

"And I'd like to thank you again for bringing him here," the doctor adds.

Mikah gets up from his seat, on the other side of Grandma, and speaks. "I'll go first," he says and follows the deputy towards the main entrance, which is in front of us.

Nobody else says anything for a few seconds, as we all seem to absorb the news.

"I want to thank you again. I would go home and try to relax now," Dr. Richards says, as he takes a few steps back from where he stood.

'Do you know what kind of bomb you just dropped?' I think of asking him. But instead of letting those exact words come out of my mouth, I ask, "How can we relax now?"

Dr. Richards turns his attention to me, and then looks around as if to address everyone, and then says, "It is important that you all try to relax and know that there is nothing more you can do. You did your best to save him. There is a chaplain here in the hospital…"

I can't listen. I cover my ears with my hands. In my

mind, I try to understand how any human being with feelings and emotions can relax after such a horrible experience. A chaplain? That's it?

Adam, who had stepped away from us a few moments before, comes back and stands next to the doctor. He looks like he wants to say something to us, so I uncover my ears. As if trying to find the right words to say, he moves his head in an awkward way, like he's trying to pull on a tight sweater. Then he says, with hesitation, "The doctor is right. We should go home and try to relax."

Hearing him say the word, 'home' as he refers to Grandma's house makes me feel some pride, and sorrow at the same time. I am happy that he sees Grandma's home as his home now, although it is still a little shocking. At the same time, I become filled with sorrow as I think of the dead man, who can't go home.

A page over the intercom calls Dr. Richards back to the Emergency Room. The lady's voice, coming from the intercom speakers, sounds dull and monotonous, as if she's just here for a paycheck and to sound as boring as possible.

The doctor nervously says, "Thank You," again, and then walks back towards the double, glass sliding doors, which open with a swooshing sound as he walks through them.

Deputy Roberts and Mikah return and Adam states, "I'll go next." Then he walks with the deputy to a circular table a few feet away.

When it's my turn to give a statement, I calmly explain my version of what happened. I give as many details as possible, but leave out the one thought that is still haunting me, the mystery man's eyes looking right through me.

After I give my statement, I remember that my thighs are still urine-stained, so I quickly walk to the bathroom, and take my pants off. I splash sink water on my thighs and make a mess on the floor. So I stammer to the paper towel dispenser and pull out a handful of paper towels. My hands are still shaking, but not as bad as they were at the Sheriff's office. I splash some water on my face. As I look at myself in the mirror, I notice how disheveled my hair looks so I try to fix it. I towel myself off, and put my wet pants back on. As uncomfortable as I feel, I understand I have to make the best of the situation, and return to the waiting area.

Nobody seems to care that I look like I just took a bath in the bathroom and I am content with that. We all proceed to slowly file out of the hospital through the sliding doors and into the van without a word.

The drive home is a quiet one as Deputy Roberts's car follows several hundred feet behind. The sun shines its first beams as it rises up over the horizon behind us. It casts a hazy glow as it breaks through the cloud cover. The closer we get to the house, the more daylight approaches.

When the house is in plain view, the sun is all the way up and I can see a marked car parked in front of the house. I figure my map was good enough after all. We park next to the car. It is a sheriff deputy's car, just as I had figured.

The man is not the man Jonah and I saw in the sheriff's office. This man is younger, with a receding hairline just like Deputy Roberts's, and a squarish-looking face. He gets out of his car, and I can see his frame is thin, yet muscular. He greets Grandma as she gets out of the van with some difficulty. She pinches her crumpled, blood-stained nightgown and holds it up a little to avoid stepping on it.

"Hello, I'm Deputy Smith," he says.

Grandma simply stands, where her feet landed and says, "Ethel Scott." Her face is one of uncertainty as she appears to be sizing the man up.

I wonder how long he has been waiting, and figure it couldn't have been long, because he is drinking a cup of coffee, unless he is drinking cold coffee. He bends over, reaching into his car for something. After I get out of the van, he pulls his head back out of the car, and stands up. He is holding a fancy camera with a long strap.

Deputy Roberts arrives shortly after we come to a stop and he parks on the other side of Deputy Smith's car.

"The Sheriff asked me to come and check out the area where you found the man you took to the hospital," Deputy Smith confidently says in a rugged voice.

"Ah, there are two of you," Grandma says, addressing the deputy. She wearily takes a few steps towards the house and stands closer to Deputy Smith.

Adam walks around the van to help her and stands next to Grandma, as if to represent her.

"Yes, I see you've already met Mike," Deputy Smith remarks.

I am exhausted and I do not care to know what other conversation takes place. Instead, I yearn to feel covers on me, and a soft bed under my body.

"Can you point me to the area where you found the man?" the deputy asks Grandma.

"I thought this was out of your jurisdiction," Jonah says. He is standing next to me and he speaks with a deep and hollow voice. He is still clad in clothes from the night

103

before. He is wearing long pajama-like pants, with a tie-string, and a loose-fitting white t-shirt, which is lightly smeared with blood. His tired eyes droop slightly and I can see he is exhausted.

"Well, it is, but we are helping the tribal police because they don't have an officer available right now. So we're going to start processing the crime scene for them, while it's still fresh."

As Deputy Roberts climbs out of his car, Adam points out the area and describes the location to Deputy Smith.

Jonah and Mikah add a few more details. They point out towards the road and re-live the minutes before they heard the gunshots ring out. Mikah's clothes are the cleanest of everyone's, no blood or wrinkles. His face, however, has worry lines and he is gingerly walking, as if to avoid pain in his right foot.

Grandma stands quietly next to Adam. When Deputy Roberts is finally standing with the group, and listening to the details, I notice he he is holding a roll of yellow tape.

"What happened to your foot?" I quietly ask Mikah, after he takes a few steps back and is now closer to me.

"I sprained it somehow when we were running in the bushes," he says.

Although I am weary, I manage to utter, "I'm sure Grandma has some home-made remedy to rub on it or something."

"At this point, my foot is the least of my worries," Mikah says, with sadness in his voice.

"I can relate. The past several hours have been unreal," I say.

I squeeze past the newly formed crowd of people

which is surrounding the porch.

"I just want to lie down," I say, loud enough for everyone to hear, and stroll into the house.

I let my tired feet guide me inside and I walk straight to Grandma's room. I stand at the foot of the bed and let my body fall face-down on the bed. I lie like that for a few moments, and then turn my head to avoid suffocating myself.

Before I fall asleep, my mind is overwhelmed with thoughts about the mysterious, dead man. I wonder if he had a wife, children, a mother, a father, a family. If he did, I wonder if they are searching for him.

I replay the events from the night before in my head. I remember hearing the gunshots and the pee accident. I am too exhausted to get my tired body up and take a bath so I don't move. I take a deep breath and let my body relax, and fall asleep.

I dream again that night. I am running through Sunflower Valley and I hear people talking so I stop in my tracks. The voices I hear are muffled at first, but soon gain clarity.

"Just shut your mouth. Keep your mouth shut and everything will be okay," one voice is saying.

"Who was that lady looking at us like a ghost? I hope she doesn't recognize us," the other voice says.

The voices sound like they are near and getting closer, so I step backwards slowly.

"There's something moving over there," another voice says.

"Run! Run! I am not going back to jail for this!" one of the voices exclaims.

My body is weak and shaking. I cannot move. I

don't know which direction to run, so I slowly sit down on the ground. I do not want to move. I wonder if anyone misses me, if anyone knows where I'm at. Where is Grandma? I decide to stay put long enough for the people whose voices I heard are long gone. Next thing I know, I'm slowly dozing off amidst the tall, graceful, and beautiful sunflowers.

Coffee and Conversation

When I wake the next morning, everybody else is milling around in the other rooms. As I lie in bed, with clothes from the day before still on, I can hear Grandma talking in the kitchen. I cannot make out her words. Someone is pouring water into Grandma's hollow and tall coffee pot. Jonah is talking to Mikah; it sounds like they are in the living room. They are discussing the events from the previous night.

I drown out the noise, the chatter, and the smell of brewing coffee. I just wish I can forget what happened. I wish I can close my eyes and just that act alone will change what happened, bring the dead man back to life. I wish I can open them again and the day would be a normal day, a day when we don't have to discuss the mystery man or his unfortunate death.

The smell of something yummy, maybe cake or sweet bread fills my nostrils. I can hear pots clanging in the kitchen. I know Grandma is at work, cooking up a meal. I look at the small, round clock-radio on Grandma's dresser. 12:37 pm. I roll off the bed and onto my feet. My shoes are still on my feet. I walk out of the bedroom and head towards the bathroom. I pass through the living room, walk by Mikah and Jonah, who are both sitting on the old couch. I turn the corner in the kitchen.

I pass through the kitchen when Grandma and Adam simultaneously say, "Good afternoon."

"Good afternoon," I muster up, as I walk by, rubbing my eyes, and make my way to wash up.

I hear another 'Good afternoon', louder than the first one, almost in unison from everyone. I suppose they expected more than a muster. But I keep on going, right into the bathroom.

I use the cold water sitting in a bucket next to the wash pan to wash up. The cold water on my face feels invigorating, yet harsh. I love it; the cold on my skin. It reminds me of my grandfather, and how he used to tell me to wake up with cold water. He'd say, 'The best way to start your day is with a splash of cold water on your face. It chases the laziness away.' And that it did this afternoon.

"Has anyone heard anything on the radio about the man from last night?" I ask out loudly.

"No, but the tribal police are outside now," one of the guys responds from the other room.

"How long have they been here?" I ask as I pat my face with a towel. I look at my reflection in Grandma's cracked mirror. Although I do not bear a strong resemblance to my mother, I have her eyes, and her nose. My face is narrow, yet well-rounded with high cheek bones, and a smoothly carved chin. I smile, and catch a whiff of my horrid breath.

"Oh, a few hours now, they got here not long after you came inside." I can't tell if it's Adam or Mikah whom is responding to my questions.

As I brush my teeth, I wonder what did happen last night, and who would want to kill another man. I have no answers as I stare into the mirror.

"Good afternoon," I say again, when I come out of the bathroom.

Everyone is at the table; all three men and Grandma. They are listening to Grandma's little, archaic radio which sits atop the window sill, with a bent clothes hanger for an antenna. They're all drinking coffee. A pan of fried potatoes, a large bowl of scrambled eggs, and several strips of bacon, with a few pieces of tortillas on a plate, are set on the table; breakfast in the middle of the day.

I guess Jonah wasn't able to convince Grandma to cook something non-fried this morning. On the contrary, he looks to be enjoying his meal.

I bet Grandma will fatten him up before he leaves. She is one of those people who feels the more of her food people eat, the better it must taste. And therefore, it's a reward or compliment if people finish all of the food she cooks.

I happily join the circle around the table. I smell that sweet smell again and ask Grandma, "Is there something in the oven?"

"Yes, I'm baking a cake, my imagination cake," she answers, with a mouthful of food.

I know from the times she's baked these cakes before that they are simply made from scratch and her imagination, hence the name. And they taste mmmm delicious, with just the right amount of ingredients. I don't know her recipe because she keeps it all in her head and she always seems to make the batter when I'm not looking.

"I can't wait to get some of that in my tummy," I say, before asking, "What have I missed so far?"

"It looks like the guy walked a little ways," Mikah says.

He takes a sip of coffee and then adds, "Jonah and I were looking at the foot tracks right around where we found him, and it looks like he walked and then crawled a little after he was shot."

"Yeah, and it looks like another set of footprints followed his, and then turned around about halfway between the road and here," explains Jonah.

I sit next to Jonah, who is already becoming my favorite of the Navarros. He scoots over a little. I presume he is trying to make room for me. On the other hand, I could have accumulated an offensive body odor by now, seeing how I haven't showered or bathed lately. Whatever his reason, I disregard it.

As I help myself to the food on the table, the conversation continues.

"How long have you guys been up?" I ask.

"I've been up all morning," Grandma says. "I made some coffee and fresh tortillas for the Navajo policemen and then I answered all kinds of questions for them."

"We didn't sleep much actually," Mikah says with a sigh. He is wearing a pair of bronze-rimmed designer glasses. They make him look older and somehow more sophisticated; boyish, yet mature.

110

"Well, I did dose off for a while," says Jonah, who appears rested. His eyes aren't red like Mikah's or Adam's. "But the smell of Grandma's cooking woke me up," he adds with a smile.

Of course, Grandma sops up all the praise and shyly smiles with a mouthful of food.

"Someone from the FBI should be getting here soon, too," explains Grandma, after she swallows her food.

After a few moments of silence, Adam says, "They should be getting here any minute." Then he rises to pour himself another cup of coffee.

"The FBI?" Jonah asks, with a confused look.

"Yep, the FBI," Adam replies nonchalantly.

"I thought that tribal land isn't governed by the federal government," Jonah says, looking even more confused than before.

Adam takes a bite of his food, and raises his index finger to indicate he will respond as soon as he swallows his food. And eventually, he replies, "Well, if you know anything about U.S. history, you would know that tribal land is still owned by the government."

"Well, thank you, Mr. Expert on Native History," Mikah says, mocking his brother.

Grandma clears her throat, then says, "They're all down the road, checking out the place where we found the guy."

"Who? The FBI?" I ask, now more confused than before.

"Not the FBI…just the deputy from the city and the Navajo policemen," Adam adds.

"The city? What city?" I ask.

"Winslow," Adam replies.

"Oh, we call it a town," I explain.

"My bad. Town, city, community, whatever," Adam retorts.

I don't remain at the table long. As soon as I am finished eating, I excuse myself from the table. "Well, I don't know about you guys, but I need a bath, for sure," I say.

"Me, too," Grandma adds.

It's not long before I am taking a sponge bath. When I'm finished, I pat myself dry and rub lotion over my ashy legs. While I do so, I hear a slow hum outside. I listen closer. It's the sound of a humming engine. It sounds like a new car; it's not rattling, and it's definitely not noisy.

I finish dressing, clean my bathing area in the bathroom and peek around the corner, into the living room. Adam and Grandma, who are sitting on the old, 60s style couch notice the sound, too and they both get up to see where the sound is coming from. Jonah and Mikah peek out from the guest room to see what the commotion is about.

"Sounds like someone's coming," Mikah says.

I listen harder. The sound is coming from the east. So I follow Adam and Grandma, wanting to see who's visiting us.

When I get to the door, I notice a white Chevrolet Tahoe is coming up the small sloped road about a quarter of a mile away. Adam, Grandma and I watch the truck as it gets closer.

The vehicle slowly pulls to a stop. A Navajo man in black slacks and a white Polo shirt emerges from the vehicle and approaches the front door.

"Detective James Yazzie from the FBI office in

Flagstaff," the man says, with his hand extended.

"Yá'áh'tééh, (Hello)," Grandma says, offering her hand for a shake.

A few moments later, I notice another car speeding towards the house. There is a cloud of dust trailing behind it as it rounds the corner of the turn about a quarter of a mile away. It's a marked, brown car.

"I'm here to investigate the murder and gather evidence and statements from witnesses," Detective Yazzie states. He is slender with thick, black, short hair, and a wide nose. He is wearing black Oakley shades that sit disproportionately on his face. He looks to be in his late twenties, maybe early thirties.

"I see," Grandma says, shading her eyes, as she looks at the brown marked car, coming towards us.

"This must be someone from the sheriff's office," Detective Yazzie says, looking back at the arriving car.

The marked, brown car pulls to a stop next to the white SUV. Marvin, the same white man with the receding hairline, gets out. This time, he is wearing dark shades that look very similar to Detective Yazzie's. When he smiles, slightly crooked and yellow teeth are revealed.

"Hello again, Marvin," Grandma says.

"Hello again, Mrs. Scott...Mr. Navarro," says Marvin, as he walks closer to us.

He nods at Adam and Adam nods back. Jonah and Mikah join us at the front door. Grandma and Adam move out to the porch to meet Marvin.

"Yes, yes hello again," Grandma answers anxiously.

"And you must be from the FBI office," Marvin says, offering a hand shake to Detective Yazzie.

113

"Yes, I got the call last night and came out here first thing," the Navajo detective says, in a gruff voice, as he accepts the hand shake.

"Well, let's get to work," Marvin says, looking at Detective Yazzie.

Marvin begins to lead the way on foot to the crime scene, which is located several hundred feet from the outhouse. There are a couple of vehicles already parked closer to the scene, several hundred feet from the house. One is a white SUV with tribal police markings and the other is a military-green Jeep Grand Cherokee with brown markings.

"We'll be here if you guys have any questions," Grandma says after them.

"Actually, it's good you mentioned that because I have some more questions about what happened last night," Marvin says and turns around. "Thanks to this guy here being pretty helpful yesterday, I was able to take some pretty good pictures of the scene," he says, as he nods in Adam's direction.

"My pleasure," Adam responds, with a smile.

Marvin walks back to the porch, puts a boot up on the porch step, puts his elbows on his knee, and then asks, "Do you guys remember exactly what time you heard the gunshots?"

We all look at each other, and Adam shrugs, and then answers first, "Well, it must've been about 10 o'clock or so, because the last time I looked at my watch, it was 9:40 and that was just before we headed to the outhouse."

The Navajo detective waits patiently for Marvin, several feet away, still within earshot of the questioning.

"So, you guys were outside around 9:40 or so?" the

deputy asks, taking his boot off the porch, and standing up straight.

We all look at each other again, and all nod yes. I don't know what time it was really. I just nod because Grandma nods.

"I have talked to some witnesses who said there was a truck parked on the side of the dirt road over there," Marvin explains, pointing towards the main dirt road.

Detective Yazzie, who looks like he was contemplating on whether or not he should continue walking to the scene, returns to the porch. Then he takes out a small, wire notepad from the back pocket of his black slacks, and pulls out the pen which was clipped to the pocket of his white, polo shirt. He slides his shades up to sit on the top of his head. His eyes have a light slant to them, and his eyelashes are thick and long. He quickly jots down a few notes.

"What witnesses?" Grandma asks.

Marvin doesn't answer her. Instead, he asks, "Did you guys happen to see any trucks?"

Adam starts to answer, "We didn't..." Before he could finish his statement, Mikah interrupts.

"Well, I saw some headlights…when we were walking to the outhouse," Mikah explains. "But I don't remember seeing them when we heard the gunshots."

"How long were you at the outhouse?" Marvin asks, looking directly at Mikah.

My god, why do they have to put their business all out like that? Pretty soon, he's going to ask them how long each of them sat on the bowl.

"Well, probably, about ten, fifteen minutes or so," Mikah answers. "We were all kinda' scared to go in at first, so we just talked outside for a while," he adds.

Poor white guys, city slickers, I bet they were scared. I'm scared to go into the outhouse during the daytime. I can only imagine what it must've been like at night. When I go, I usually kick the door or kick the toilet seat frame. Something about sitting on a wooden frame with a hole in the middle that leads underground makes me imagine spiders scurrying out. If that's how my imagination works, I can only guess what they imagined.

I think back and try to remember exactly how long Grandma and I were busy in the back of the house. And I figure we maybe spent about the same amount of time...ten minutes.

When I realize I am pretty unworthy of being involved in the conversation because I have nothing of value to add, I step back away from the door. I stand in the doorframe and continue to listen as more questions come.

"So these lights, what did they look like?" Marvin asks, as he pulls his small note pad from his shirt pocket. I can see that the silver, metal star on his shirt pocket is nicely polished as it generously reflects the sunlight.

"Well, I saw lights off in the distance, but nothing about them jumped out at me," Mikah explains, with nervousness in his voice. He runs his hands through his hair and stops on top of his head. He leaves his hands there, clasped together.

"They might have been headlights, but a few seconds after I noticed them, they were gone," he continues.

"Okay," Marvin says, as he thumps his note pad with his pen.

He looks back through his notes, and asks, "What

116

happened after that…after the lights went away?"

"Well, we used the bathroom. And just when we started walking back towards the house, we heard the sounds, the gunshots," Mikah explains.

Marvin looks at Jonah and Adam, and asks, "Is this what you guys remember, too?"

"Yes," Adam says.

"Yep," Jonah replies.

Adam gazes out towards the outhouse, as if he is remembering the events. He lowers his head and says, "We heard the man a few minutes later, calling for help. It was like a loud shriek or like a wounded dog whining."

"Yeah, it was an eerie sound and we didn't know what to do," Jonah adds.

"If you guys could come and point out where you saw those head lights, it would really help the investigation," suggests Marvin, with desperation in his voice, and obviously hoping Mikah would go.

"Yeah, sure, no problem," replies Mikah.

"Yep, I'll tag along, too," Adam offers.

Marvin nods, and turns to get back in his car.

Detective Yazzie, who has remained quiet for the past few minutes, finally speaks up. "I'll check the scene out right here while you guys take care of that," he says, pointing to the taped-off crime scene just beyond the outhouse.

"The tracks we found earlier look like they might lead towards the river, but I'll double-check again," Marvin says, looking at Detective Yazzie.

"Okay, well, I have another case to work on in Dilcon, so I'll probably be leaving shortly," Detective Yazzie says. Then he asks, "Can you send me a copy of your reports?"

"Sure, no problemo," Marvin replies, sliding his shades back down to cover his eyes.

Grandma, not having said anything throughout the whole questioning process, finally speaks up as well. "If anybody was driving around near the river, Ruthie from across the road will probably know something about it."

I am sure she is tired, so it doesn't surprise me that this little bit of information is all she has to contribute.

The slender, Navajo detective with his shades now lowered says, "Thanks," to Marvin and then turns to Grandma and says, "Ah'ee hee" to Grandma, which is "Thank you" in Navajo.

Grandma says, "A'oo, A'oo," (Yes, Yes) as she addresses the detective. Then with a wave of her hand, she says, "I need some more coffee, it's going to be a long day," and goes back into the house.

Adam slides into the passenger seat of the marked car and Mikah takes the back seat. Marvin takes the driver seat and they slowly back out of Grandma's dirt driveway.

As the marked car pulls away and Detective Yazzie walks down a bushy path to join the rest of the crime scene investigation team, I remain on the porch with Jonah.

A Story of Regret

I look at Jonah. He just sighs and follows Grandma inside.

After a few moments, I go inside as well. My breakfast is cold, but I make every attempt to finish it. When I can't stuff anymore into my mouth, I go back outside, but not before I remind Grandma her cake is in the oven.

I stand on the porch and look out at the valley which lay to the east, in front of the house. I scan the area for the deputy's car and finally spot it moving slowly across the main dirt road, heading west. I wonder what the conversation inside the car is about…three white guys on the rez, driving down a dirt road, to look for tire tracks which could be related to a murder. It's a very odd scenario. I can't even imagine what the conversation is about.

I stand on the porch alone just long enough to get those thoughts out, when Jonah returns. He stands next to me, and sips on a cup of coffee.

The smell of his coffee enters my nostrils and I inhale

it. I like the smell of coffee. I would drink it more often if I didn't know of its addictive powers. It seems like such an innocent drug, and I like the Frappuccino drink at Starbucks every now and again. But I clearly remember a vision of my fourth grade health teacher from the boarding school, Mrs. Castle, pointing at a cup of coffee from a picture in a magazine and saying, "This stuff is BAD, BAD, BAD!" And that is enough to keep me from becoming a regular coffee drinker.

The moment is awkward. *Hurry, come up with something appropriate to say.* Unable to come up with anything savvy or witty as a conversation starter, I finally say "Gee, this is all so crazy."

"Yeah, tell me about it," Jonah says. As mildly warm as the summer morning temperature is, I see a small upward swirl of steam coming from his cup.

"Have you ever seen another person die?" I ask, hoping he can offer me some advice on how to deal with what happened.

"Nope...and it's my first time involved in a murder investigation, just for the record," Jonah says, and then takes another sip of his coffee.

I didn't notice his eyes had a hint of green in them before, but now that I did, it added to his good looks. I try not to stare too long at his eyes.

"Yep, my first time, too," I say.

He takes another sip of his coffee and just looks out to the vast, open land.

And then before I can come up with my next genius question, he asks me, "So...Linda was your mother?"

I stare out to the valley before us again, and the hill

which slopes up slowly beyond it, then drops. Men are mulling over the crime scene, taking more pictures and talking amongst themselves. The shrubbery which covers the valley is a sage green and the shrubs sit on the ground in clumps. The sun shines brightly on both of us. I welcome the warmth from the sun, which is still breaking through the coolness of the night.

I sigh.

"Yes, Linda was my mother," I say and remember the day she left and how fast everything seemed to come at me after that; her death, my realization I am without parents, alone; my confusion and sadness.

I look at him.

He looks back at me as if to say he is sorry.

I think back and try to remember when I've talked about my mother's death. I can't remember a day. I feel uncomfortable talking about it to a person I just met a few days ago, who is from another world, a white man's world. In a lot of ways, he is still a stranger to me. I don't want to talk. I look back out to the horizon and build up strength within. After a couple of deep breaths, I decide I want to talk about it. I feel a hand on my right shoulder. It's a gentle hand, a hand putting just enough pressure on my shoulders to let me know I can talk.

I take another deep breath and continue, "I was at school, the boarding school not far from here, and I had just spoken to her before she left work that day," I say.

He doesn't interrupt. He just listens, waiting for me to finish.

I do not like talking about that day, and I wish he wasn't here, standing beside me, asking me...I know I want to tell him, somebody, anybody, about how my mother's death made me feel. I give into my overwhelming feelings and I go on.

"She worked at TDI, which is in the building next to where my dormitory was. I went to visit her when she got off work and spoke with her briefly, mostly about how the day went," I say and let out a heavy sigh.

The air is still and hot. I am uncomfortable, but I keep talking.

"She wanted to get home and help Grandma prepare dinner, and she asked me if I wanted to come home for the evening," I say.

I look at Jonah and see the sympathy in his cool, water-like eyes. I glance away.

"I had a Student Council meeting early the next morning, and wanted to get a good night's rest, so I told her I'd wait until the next evening. And she left," I finish as I lower my gaze towards the ground at the base of the porch.

"Wow, that must've been difficult to deal with," he says, with a compassionate look that defeats any resistance I was putting forth to hide my sadness.

I let the sadness come. Something about people feeling sorry for me makes me feel even worse about the situation. He shouldn't feel sorry for me. But I don't tell him that.

I had a chance to save my mother's life or to leave this planet with her and I chose to stay behind, for a stupid Student Council meeting. I should've gone with my mother that evening. I bang myself up for it every time I think about her death. Had I gone with her, things may have been different. I didn't deserve to be left alone because of one stupid mistake—a decision to stay the night at the dormitory. Although I could look at the mistake as being my mother's, I choose to make it my own. I didn't know that one decision would change my life forever at the time.

I look back at Jonah. I see his saddened eyes and I feel the pressure, the pressure in my chest and throat. I swallow with a big gulp and I shake it off. I look back out to the valley, past the vehicles still parked at the crime scene with men milling around, to the horizon beyond. I blink my eyes and swallow hard, hoping to push down the sad, painful emotions bubbling in my throat.

"Yep, it was difficult," I say. Not wanting to go into further detail, I make my attempt to tie up the conversation.

"After my mother passed, Grandma took me out of the dormitory at the school, and I caught the bus from here everyday for the rest of the school year," I explain, knowing he probably doesn't know what the dormitory is.

Sure enough, he curiously asks, "When you say dormitory, was it like a college dorm? Or how does that work?"

"Well, kinda', I guess," I reply, knowing very well it wasn't the same.

"Can you tell me about it?" he asks.

"The dormitory and the boarding school were depressing for most of the friends I had there. I didn't mind it so much, because I didn't necessarily have to go. I simply went there for the experience," I explain.

"Hmm, interesting," he comments.

"When the dormitory began to depress me or bring on feelings of loneliness, I simply went to my mother's work place and asked her if I can come home for the evening. And whenever I asked, she never refused to let me ride home with her for the evening. So I was privileged in that respect. My girlfriends would tell me 'You are lucky to have such a nice mother who works so close by,'" I say.

"You were probably lucky in their eyes, especially if they had to stay," he comments.

"Yeah, students who attended the boarding school stayed for a week at a time. They were checked in on Sundays and checked out on Fridays. Kinda' like checking into a hotel, except the hotel isn't glamorous by any means. Instead, it's a Clorox-smelling, disciplinary, and altogether, unfriendly facility," I continue.

"I see why you wouldn't put it in the same category as a college dorm," he says.

"Actually, it's nothing like a college dorm. Believe it or not, it's more penitentiary-like, which I suppose is the only way it can be, in order to work," I explain.

"Really?" he asks inquisitively.

"Yep," I answer.

He leans backward for a good, long stretch and then asks, "So, were you…I mean are you the only child your mother had?"

I sigh and answer, "Yep," with hesitation. God knows I had always wished for a sibling, and despised being the only child.

"Wow, how did you deal with it all?" he asks.

I look back to the horizon and notice the deputy's car coming back down the road which runs across the valley before us.

"Look! They're coming back!" I say, in a voice filled with relief and excitement.

"Oh yeah, I see," Jonah says and steps down from the porch.

He takes a few more steps away from the house and then looks back and says, "We'll have to finish our talk later."

"What didn't we finish talking about?" I ask.

"You have to let out more about your mom's death, trust me," he says.

I laugh and nod in agreement, although I know I don't want to talk about my mother's death at all. I would rather stuff it into my past, like everyone else has done, and simply forget about it. That's easier to do.

Let the Gossip Roll In

Mikah climbs out of the back seat of the deputy's marked car. He has a smile on his face. It's a curious smile.

Adam and Marvin talk for a few moments in the car, as Mikah walks towards us. We are still standing on the porch.

I call out to Grandma in the house, "They're back!"

"Well?" Jonah asks Mikah, his voice full of anxiety. He takes a few steps away from the porch and meets Mikah. They both walk back up to the porch.

After seeing that smile on Mikah's face, I'm just as curious as Jonah.

Adam finally gets out of the car, and walks over to us.

Marvin stays in the car, writing more notes on his notepad. He makes a call or answers a call on his walkie-talkie and then he slowly drives closer to the crime scene. He passes the outhouse, and crawls over several more humps of bushes before he parks next to the military green Jeep.

Grandma opens the screen door and asks, "What did

you guys find?" The apron she has on is wrapped tightly around her pudgy frame. Her hair is in a bun with wisps of hair around her face. It's obvious she hasn't fixed her hair lately.

Looking elated, Adam says, "I think we found the tracks of a truck which could be related to the murder."

"Wow, really?" I ask. *This is exciting. A real investigation.*

In my excitement, I forget all about the conversation with Jonah. I forget there is a man's murderer still free. I forget that a man's life is now non-existent…no more, gone. I can only think of how thrilling it would be to help solve a mystery, right here on the rez.

"News about a murder mystery would surely draw tons of attention to us if we solved it, or at least, helped solve it. Maybe the Navajo Times people will come. Maybe we'll be on the news!" I exclaim.

Nobody pays any particular attention to me. Grandma simply looks at me with an you-must-be-crazy look. And the discussion about the foot prints continues.

"Yeah, we found some tracks which lead off the main dirt road, like right over there," Adam says, pointing toward a section of the main dirt road. The section he is pointing to is in between the turn-off from the main road to here, and the point where the hill slopes upward a little, before it drops down the western side of the plateau.

Mikah, just as eager as Jonah is to tell us of their tracking experience, says, "And Marvin took some good pictures of them. They look like a pickup truck, maybe a four wheel drive."

"Did you see which way the tracks go?" Grandma

asks, stepping down from the porch. I suppose she wants to be close to the guys so she can hear them better. She picks her hands up to shade her eyes from the sun.

"Yeah, it looks like the truck went off the road just a little, and then backed up, and drove towards the river, turned around somewhere down by the river, and then headed west, where it came from," Mikah blurts out, as if Adam might beat him to answering her question.

"Well, it's good that you found something," Grandma says, nonchalantly. She stares out toward the river, with her hands still up to shade her eyes, and then asks, "Did you guys ask any of the people over there if they saw anything?"

"No, Marvin said he'll leave that to the tribal police and the FBI," Adam says.

It takes a lot to stir Grandma up in frenzy and I presume finding some tracks which look a bit suspicious doesn't do much for getting her excited about the notion. She makes a grunting noise and goes back inside.

"Did you guys find anything else?" I ask, still fascinated with the idea that we are in the middle of a mystery murder case.

Jonah must see the fascination in my eyes because he says, "Woah, woah, missy, don't get too excited now."

I smile shyly and return my attention to Mikah and Adam.

"Well, we did find some foot tracks, too," Adam says.

"What size?" I ask, acting as if I know what I'm talking about.

"Well, we found more than one size," he says.

He comes up to the porch and stands next to me. He hands me a Polaroid picture which reveals a pattern of elongated W's or a zigzag design with the name brand, CAT in the middle of the sole.

"Marvin wants us to pass the picture around, so we can all have an image to go off when looking for a suspect," he adds.

As he holds the picture out for me to observe, I notice the blonde hairs on his forearms. They're more like a bronze color than blonde. I had never paid so much attention to a white man's features before. I always walked right past them and avoided eye contact with them.

But now, as Adam stands next to me, I can't help but let my eyes wander. His hands are masculine, yet smooth. His forearms bulge with muscles, and I notice this as he makes hand motions to describe the detail of the sole and to point out the fact that it looks like a sturdy, work boot.

"I'd say the size we're looking for is a size 9 of 10," he is saying, when I let my eyes wander up to his face. His jaw line is smooth. His Adam's apple protrudes, as if a small rock is stuck in his throat. It moves up and down slightly as he speaks.

Mikah holds up another photograph, one of another track. This track is difficult to make out.

"It looks like the person who made those tracks went out of their way to cover them up," Jonah explains.

"They look like boots or some kind of utility shoe tracks," Adam says.

Grandma comes back outside and says, "Enough police work for now. We need a break. Let's all go into town and let the police do their job. Besides, I need to pick up some more food."

Adam and Mikah look at Marvin, whom nods at both

of them, as if to release them from their unofficial duty.

"Yes, good idea," Marvin says, as he collects his photographs from Adam and Mikah.

"But I want to get some of that yummy imagination cake in my belly first," I excitedly say.

By now, the sun has inched its way to sit on the west side of the sky, and the sunlight is beginning to scorch the land. Only a few billows of puffy clouds are scattered across the sky, not doing much for providing shade.

While the Navarros and Grandma continue their discussion of the pictures, I go back inside to help myself to the warm, delicious cake.

Eventually, everyone else comes back inside after me to prepare for a trip into town.

While I enjoy every bite of my cake, Grandma takes a brief sponge bath.

When she's done, I half-way placate my need for cleanliness with the same inadequate form of bathing. I figure at the minimum, it will take away any unpleasant stench I've accumulated so far.

A ride into town is always a treat. So I feel as if I am double-dipping on this day. First, I get to eat cake and now, a trip into town.

With everyone waiting in the van, I struggle with making a decision on which handbag to use. I would have never imagined me trying to decide on a handbag. In fact, I used to think having multiple purses was a silly idea. I finally grab my petite, floral print, strapless purse, and join the convoy outside, near the van.

Grandma and Adam are talking to Marvin and the two tribal policemen who are still working the crime scene. I presume they are telling them we are taking a trip into town. I don't see Detective Yazzie or his SUV anywhere.

We all climb into the van, one after another, and head on down the road. I sit next to Jonah in the back seat. Mikah sits in the middle row. Adam drives, and Grandma sits in the passenger seat.

Once we are a few miles down the road, Grandma begins talking about the land which surrounds us; her land and her ancestors' land. In an instant, she is transformed into a tour guide and proudly performs the task of narrating a historic commentary.

"This place was my Grandmother's land, and she claimed this land for her kids and grandkids," she starts out. "We used to live over there," she says, pointing to her right, to the far southeast corner of the plateau, "over in that hogan."

There is a hogan still standing, although it was abandoned years before I was even born. In the past, I had taken a few walks near it, but never built up enough courage to actually get close to it. It's a circular, mud house framed with logs that has a chimney sticking out of the dome-shaped ceiling. So with my vivid imagination, I've always imagined spiders and all kinds of creepy crawly things have crawled inside it from the hole in the roof. And that is enough to keep me from getting too close.

"Long ago, as the story goes, my grandmother came here from the Ft. Sumner. She ran away from her father and his wife once they settled in Shiprock because her stepmother used to constantly beat her. She traveled with other distant relatives until she came upon this land right here and settled down," Grandma explains.

She pauses for a moment as her eyes gaze over the land.

Mikah and Jonah hang on Grandma's every word as we bounce along, and Adam keeps his eyes trained on the road.

"This is where I grew up, I grew up all over this land…I used to herd sheep through here, right through here," she continues, motioning with her soft and fragile hands. She makes a circle over the area we are driving through. The land is a flat terrain for the most part, with a few large mounds.

"And back there, where our house is, I herded sheep through there, too," she adds.

"Wow, when was your house built?" Mikah asks. He is still wearing the bronze-rimmed glasses, and I wonder if he is wearing them for the look or if he has less-than-perfect vision and needs to wear them. Nonetheless, I like the mature, educated look they portray.

"A long time ago, I don't even remember how long it has been…about twenty-five years now. We built that house after we came back from San Francisco," she continues with her story.

"Twenty-five years sounds about right," Adam comments from the driver's seat.

Grandma keeps on talking. "Phillip and two of his friends bought the material, you know, the lumber and cinderblocks, all that, and they just started building a house," she says, as if it happened that easily.

We all listen contently, and although I've heard the story many times before, it is still intriguing and I listen. I imagine their life back then as she talks. It must've been a much more peaceful life than now, not having to worry about murders happening in front of their house. As we drive, Grandma keeps on with her story.

She tells of how her mother and father were in the medicine circle. Her father was a medicine man and her mother followed him to ceremonial events throughout the reservation. According to Grandma, his services were in high demand and were quite often requested at healing ceremonies across the river. And for transportation to all of those places, they rode in a wagon, drawn by a horse.

She tells of how she and her siblings were responsible for keeping their home clean, and how she took care of her younger siblings, how she cooked for the family, and how they all took turns watching the livestock. They used to let out the sheep early in the morning, before the sun rose, according to her, and they were to go find the sheep in the middle of the afternoon, and herd the sheep home before sunset.

Every now and then, someone would gasp, or say, "Wow," as if it is all too unbelievable. Her recount of the past was definitely interesting, and it made the ride go by faster.

"Nowadays, these girls around here complain about every little thing they do. They don't even wash dishes anymore. Instead, they run around after the boys and get pregnant," Grandma points out.

"Except for me," I exclaim, in my defense.

"Well, I'm not talking about you," Grandma says. "You are probably the only one that isn't like that."

"And I'm learning how to weave, and if we had sheep, I would herd them," I say, to further add proof that I am not like the other girls.

133

"Okay, okay, we get the point, you aren't like the other girls around here," Adam comments from the front.

I smile. I am satisfied that I have proven my point.

Before long, we are going over the last of two cattle guards, which marks the separation of federal and county land from the reservation land. Or what I call 'the line between white man's land and Injun land.' I don't even know where I got that phrase, probably from some old western movie.

The land in this area is desolate; flat and brown, except for a few acres of rocky hills and plateaus covered with light green shrubbery. It almost looks as if a large body of water once covered the low-lying areas, and carved out the plateau cliffs.

The rocky hills are like the plateaus, but with huge, boulder-like rocks all around the sides. As a child, I'd wonder what is under all those rocks, or I'd imagine there was a cave in there, which who knows, there probably is. I'd sit in my mother's lap, staring out the window, as my grandfather would drive us into town, with his old blue pickup truck, which Grandma sold not long after he passed away. I'd think up scary images in my head and then cover my eyes with my hands, afraid something of my imagination would appear out of the rocks.

We make our way around the towering rocky mountain walls, and come around the last bend before we reach the city limits, when Adam interrupts Grandma's story and asks her, "Did you ever come into the town as a kid? Or was there even a town then?"

Although I could've answered that one myself, I sit quietly and listen.

Grandma goes on to answer and tells him, "Yes."

This spurs her into a whole other scenario. She tells about how the town had pretty much one street and that was Main Street. She describes their bi-monthly trips into town and how they would come to the trading post to trade goods such as rugs, wool, and jewelry for food, and other white people products.

She tells us that her father worked for the railroad back then, so they would come to see him off to work. He'd catch the train from town and ride it to wherever his work was; in California or in New Mexico. He'd go on these trips for a few weeks at a time, although she didn't know exactly what kind of work he did.

In my mind, I imagine the town was bustling with saloons and dirt roads, and wooden everything; wooden stores, wooden houses, wooden sidewalks like the towns in old western movies. Wood and dirt.

Since Grandma's time as a kid, the town has grown quite a bit, but it's still small if you ask me. Businesses have come and gone as people came and went. And now, of course, the biggest and best thing in town is the Wal-Mart.

A New CD

"Woo-hoo, we're here," I announce, when we reach the city limits. We pass the Wal-Mart which sits at the end of town. I-40 is busy, as always with semi trucks, cars, vans, and all sorts of people in them making their way to wherever it is they are going.

"Isn't there a song about this town?" Mikah asks no one in particular as he looks out the window.

"Yeah, moron…it's by the Eagles," Adam says.

As cool as the idea might sound to the normal, average Joe Schmoe, it was not at all cool in my opinion. Of course, I come from a younger generation than the folks who listened with pride to the Eagles. So naturally, I am not as fond of the idea.

Now, if Janet Jackson, Madonna, or Beyonce wrote a song about this run-down town, I might've jumped at the mention of the song. But that wasn't the case. As Grandma revels in the notoriety, I cringe, and pay no attention to the guys singing the song out of tune.

When the guys stop singing because they don't know the rest of the words after the chorus, Grandma instructs Adam to stop by the post office first.

After the post office, we head to Safeway, one of two local grocery stores. As we drive around the little town, I yearn to be back in L.A., back to something bigger and more exciting, back to the sprawling malls, Asian grocery stores, jam-packed freeways, and where you can find a Starbucks on just about every corner.

"I just need to pick up a few things, and then we can go to Wal-Mart," Grandma says.

All I want to do is go to Wal-Mart, so I respond by saying, "I'll wait in the van."

"I'll wait, too," says Jonah.

"Do you guys want anything?" Adam offers, as he helps Grandma out. Mikah gets out and tags along.

We wait and wait, and while we wait, I tell Jonah about what it was like to come into town as a child. "I thought this was the most exciting place in the world, and the biggest, until I went to Flagstaff for the first time. Then I thought that was the biggest place, and then I eventually visited Los Angeles, and that was it, I knew there were more bigger places called cities," I tell him.

He laughs.

"So, what was your life like in San Francisco?" I ask.

"Well," he says, in a long, drawn out way, "I loved it, I loved growing up there. The city, and the people…they're all wonderful. I visited New York one time when we were little, and I missed home so bad, I cried for half a day. We were on vacation with my grandparents, and my parents were so upset," he adds.

"That's funny. So, did you hug your floor and bed when you got home?" I ask, trying to be funny, but not quite pulling it off.

"No, but I did lie down on my bed and I was happy to be home," he says, with a look of embarrassment.

"San Francisco sounds like a pretty nice place," I say.

"Yeah, it is."

"So, why do you keep avoiding discussion about your mother?"

"What's that?" I ask.

"You heard me."

"Yes, I did. I was just hoping you would magically change the subject again."

How else can I get out of talking to him about this? I better talk, before he calls me out again.

"Well, I'll tell you all about her eventually. Just keep bugging me."

He laughs.

"So, why do you like me?" I ask.

"Wow, you are straight-forward," he comments.

"Yes, I guess I am."

"Well, is it that obvious?"

"Yes."

He wiggles in his seat and then looks at me with his blue-green eyes, in a way that makes me nervous.

"Well, you are a beautiful girl and I am attracted to you," he calmly says.

"It's just that I've never known a white guy who liked me," I say.

"Okay, well, I'll be the first."

"Okay."

Grandma, Mikah and Adam return a few moments later with several bags of groceries.

Jonah opens the door and hops out to open the van's back door.

Grandma spots a neighbor, whom she waves at. I recognize the lady as Ruthie, who lives across the main dirt road, about three more miles on the other side. She is a large, round woman with an even deeper nasal tone than Grandma's.

The lady waves Grandma over to her parked vehicle, across the parking aisle from the van.

I get out and follow Grandma.

Once Ruthie greets Grandma, she asks about why the sheriff's car was at Grandma's house the night before. Apparently, she, too, like my grandma Elsa, has hawk eyes and doesn't miss a beat when it comes to strange activity in the area.

Grandma tells her about the shooting, and Ruthie adds her theories as to what might have happened; something about winos or a skinwalker.

In Navajo, Ruthie explains there was a squaw dance the same night of the murder, a few miles on the other side of the plateau. Then she adds, "Where there's a squaw dance, there's trouble."

Grandma's face looks surprised and says, "I didn't hear any noises or any loud drums."

When the lady reassures her there was a squaw dance, Grandma says she didn't see many cars going in that direction. Although, if it was on the other side of the plateau, that would explain why there were not many vehicles going back and forth on the main dirt road. They could've come from Leupp, which is to the west. Any of that traffic wouldn't have been visible from where Grandma's house sits.

"Yeah, there was one car that came by our house, too. I don't know exactly where it went, because the lights were off. But I heard it close by," Ruthie explains.

"I'll tell the police that," Grandma says in Navajo, as if she's found the missing key and the lady's theory is now a solid explanation for what might have happened.

"Did you see any other spooky cars driving around by your house last night?" Grandma asks. Of course, spooky to her means strange or extraordinary.

"No, not really, just that crazy grandson of mine, Petey and his friends were cruising around. They went to the Squaw Dance and came back late."

"I wonder if they saw anything. Maybe you can ask them if they know anything about what happened," Grandma suggests.

"Oh, him and his crazy friends, they're always causing trouble. I hate to ask them anything. They just laugh at me and think I'm crazy when I try to talk to them," Ruthie says, with discouragement in her voice.

"It was probably some aglanis (drunks) from the Squaw Dance, they're always fighting and causing trouble, too," Grandma frustratingly says.

People on the rez, especially the older women, always feel they have to be involved in every dramatic incident. If they're not involved in the scene, they want to be involved in drawing their own conclusions as to why something happened or how they happened, or who did what.

Of course, their conclusions are usually based off speculation and when the truth finally is known, and it's different from what they predicted, they don't admit they were wrong. And although Grandma has consistently reminded me not to draw conclusions until I know for myself what really happened, she falls right into her own trap and does the opposite of what she tells me.

Grandma eventually leads Ruthie back to the van and introduces the Navarro brothers to her. She tells Ruthie the men are visiting from San Francisco and she reminds her of the time she and my grandfather lived in San Francisco.

Ruthie vaguely remembers and then makes a joke about the Navarros coming over to her house and helping her with some manly tasks, and everybody laughs, as if it's really funny. To my surprise, the men actually entertain the idea, and offer their help.

"Sure, we can come over, and help you out," Adam offers, as he starts up the van and looks at Grandma for reassurance.

"Really? Are you sure? Is that okay, Ethel?" Ruthie asks. For sure, she knows Grandma, being the nice person she is, wouldn't be rude in front of these nice, young men.

"Oh, yeah, they're just visiting for the summer, as long as you don't keep them," Grandma says, jokingly, but meaning every word of it. And everybody laughs again.

I remember Grandma's promise to stop at Wal-Mart next and I ask impatiently, "Can we go to Wal-Mart now?"

I know it is rude and disrespectful, but I want to rescue Grandma from the conversation and I want to just get my hands around a new CD. I can tell Grandma is annoyed at the moment by the way the fingers on her right hand are tapping her pant leg.

"Okay, yeah, we better get going," Grandma says, and shakes Ruthie's hand.

The two women hug and everyone gets back in the van.

Finally, we are on our way to Wal-Mart, my place of consolation, the place I have been looking forward to stopping at.

When we get to Wal-Mart and everybody gets out again, I head straight for the CD section, and pick up the CD by one of the latest Rocafella stars, Kanye West; my latest obsession. Being a fan of hip-hop music is something many people in my family don't approve of; nonetheless, I listen to and love the music. The beat of the music and the rhymes pull me in and give me the urge to move, to free myself from the stillness of time.

Grandma says rap and hip-hop aren't good for my ears. She says 'the words are not words for smart, young women to hear.' I don't know really what she means by that...that dumb women listen to this kind of music? Or maybe she's just trying to kill two birds with one stone; tell me I'm smart and young, which I already know, and not to listen to the music. One thing about my Grandma; she is a simple woman and I figure she is trying to tell me the latter. So I listen to her words, but I don't agree with them.

I buy the CD, knowing Grandma will not approve, because I know Kanye West will not let me down and satisfy my yearning for something new and refreshing again.

Grandma buys some household items, and the Navarros pick up some toiletries, batteries, and a few other things. We all meet back at the entrance, and then Grandma recognizes another person she knows; her sister, Elsa, and they begin a discussion about the shooting incident in Navajo.

By now, word about the Navajo tribal police SUVs

and the marked cars sitting in our driveway must have traveled across the whole rez. A lack of electricity or phone lines on the rez has no bearing on the fact that gossip can't spread like a wildfire.

Any news around here is big news, of course. So, naturally, as did Ruthie, Elsa has her own opinions about the murder. She, unlike us that night, was watching the traffic on the dirt road, and said she saw the alleged truck come up from the west. She watched it stop and go, and stop again…not the truck, but the lights. She said it stopped for a long period so she took a break from her watch guard job, and when she finally saw the lights again, the vehicle was driving westward, in the direction of the alleged squaw dance. Of course, she doesn't know if the vehicle she saw driving westward is the same one she originally saw, stopping every few meters.

At this point, she also confirms the squaw dance, saying she saw the fire and all the action from her house. She lives on the edge of the plateaus, so she has the luxury of a pretty good panoramic view of the area. More importantly, she had access to view anything happening on the other side of the plateau.

At night, she keeps watch like an eagle and it's amazing what all happens on our little patch of land during the night hours, according to her records. She has supposedly seen people stealing other peoples' livestock, drunks breaking into homes, people stealing television sets…all of that, on our little piece of land.

I personally think she has bat vision at night and hawk eyes during the day, but makes up half of the stuff she sees.

The conversation eventually wraps up between the

sisters. They say their casual farewells, and we head home.

I am temporarily satisfied with my fill of the town experience. I clutch my newly purchased CD and wish I had brought my CD player. I anticipate our arrival back at Grandma's house as I hum a medley of Kanye's hit singles while the van travels down the road.

Unofficial Recruitment

On the way home, the sky is blue and orange; a pretty pastel blue mixed with orange ripples from the evening sun. The windows from the van let enough sunlight in to warm my arms gently. They also let the breeze in, and it is comforting. The warmth from the sun and the breeze make a comforting fusion on my skin and I absorb the combination.

I am excited about getting home. I don't know exactly why, but I am excited and happy. I flirt with the thought of taking my old bike out of Grandma's shed and going for a ride to the pond, just over the hill from Grandma's house. I'm sure I will have to pump up the tires. I don't flirt with the idea long.

Soon, we are approaching the driveway of the old, yellow house. The evening sun casts a shadow of the house in the front driveway.

A car from the sheriff's department is parked in the driveway, and the same deputy, Marvin, is standing against the car. With his boots crossed over one another, and a tilted cowboy hat which is shading his face from the sun, he reads a newspaper. He sets his paper down as we pull up.

The Sheriff I frantically blurted details to a couple nights before is observing the crime scene several hundred feet north of the outhouse. He stands with his arms behind his back, studying something on the ground.

The Navajo tribal policemen are nowhere to be seen.

After we all say our hellos to Marvin, Grandma approaches Marvin to start up a conversation while everyone else, myself included, carry plastic bags from Safeway and Wal-mart into the house.

"I have some more news and wanted to ask for a favor," I hear Marvin saying.

"Did you arrest anyone?" asks Grandma, curiously.

Knowing I cannot contribute to the conversation, I ignore the rest of the conversation and continue to help the men with the unloading.

On my way back to the van for more shopping bags, I hear the deputy ask Grandma if she can ask around in the area, to see if anyone else saw anything. His explanation for asking this is the sheriff's office and the Navajo police are not popular with a couple of the families, because they've arrested a few of their sons. He goes on to explain she would probably have a better chance, because she's from here also, and the people probably trust her more.

"They might be okay with the tribal police, I'm sure the people will talk to them," Grandma says, showing some hesitancy to the idea.

"They've already asked around and aren't getting anywhere," Marvin explains.

The Sheriff, slowly wanders back towards the house,

and stands next to Marvin, with his bald head glistening in the sun.

"Sheriff Johnson, ma'am," he says, as he extends his hand to Grandma.

Grandma eventually accepts the task Marvin requested assistance with and fills the deputy in on the conversations she had with her neighbors in town, specifically the details about the squaw dance that happened the night of the incident.

I carry the last two bags of groceries into the house and return to listen in on the conversation outside.

Jonah, Mikah, and Adam are casually standing around listening.

"We are looking for a murderer and this case has now taken priority," says Sheriff Johnson.

He adds, "Mr. Eddie Yazzie, the victim, was from the Dilcon area. His wife had filed a missing person's report yesterday, and we were able to piece everything together from there and figure out who the man is."

I sigh.

Grandma sighs.

Marvin reaches into the marked car, and brings out a photo. He passes it around. It's a picture of a gun.

As the photo is passed around, he says, "This is the kind of gun that was used. I figure if we show it around, it might help. If you guys see anyone carrying around a gun like this, let me know. It may have been tossed nearby, but we haven't found anything yet."

"That looks like a .38," Mikah observes.

"That's exactly what it is, son" the sheriff confidently says.

Marvin adds, "The killer may have gotten rid of it somewhere out here. Since the tribe doesn't have a dedicated office on this, I'll be out here more frequently, collecting evidence and doing what interviews I can. I'll be working closely with the F.B.I as well, so you may see Detective Yazzie out here again."

"Were we just recruited into the Sheriff's crew?" asks Adam, who is now standing behind me.

"Yes, unofficially, that's how we do things around here," replies the Sheriff in a gruff voice. "Because we're so out of the loop around here, we have to rely on the local peoples' information and help," he adds, as if to defend himself.

"And what do we do if we find this so-called gun?" asks Grandma, handing the photo back to the deputy.

"Come into town and report it," says Sheriff Johnson, and then after a short pause, continues, "I'm hoping we find it before anyone else does, of course."

"Don't try to arrest anyone yourselves," he adds, with a short laugh which makes his entire body jiggle.

"No wild west action or pistol-whipping?" asks Jonah, from the door. He is now standing in the doorway, with both hands on the top frame, as if he's holding the upper frame up.

Everybody laughs.

"I guess I have to put my rope away, too," says Grandma, adding to the joke. "I can tie really good. It's easy, like tying up a sheep, or roping a calf," she continues, as she goes through the hand motions of roping something.

Everyone laughs again. I laugh because she looks silly roping in the wind, with her round body slightly bent over.

148

"Alrighty now, don't try to be a hero," says the deputy, after getting a few laughs in as well.

"Well, we'll keep our eyes out," says Grandma, as she straightens herself.

Then she adds, "If I see any gun, I'll let you know for sure. Nobody really carries guns around here. Some people have rifles, but they don't use them really, unless there's a wolf attack on the sheep. One time, my brother-in-law, across the road here, pulled a rifle on a thief." She points to Elsa's house.

"You guys don't have any rifles, do you?" asks the deputy, looking at Grandma first, then around at everyone.

"No," says Grandma. "I'm scared of guns."

"Actually, I have a gun, a .38. It's registered, in California," says Adam.

With a look of surprise on her face, Grandma turns towards Adam, but says nothing.

The deputy looks at him as well and asks, "Can I see it?"

I am confused now. "Is he a suspect?" I ask.

"Oh no, this is just something we have to do. I'll actually have to take it with me, and run it through my computer at the office," Marvin warns.

"What? That can't be right," I say.

"We'll have it back to you in no time," Sheriff Johnson adds.

Adam just shrugs. "Oh, no problem, I'll get it for you. I know the routine," he says as he goes into the house.

"You had a gun in my house?" Grandma asks, in disbelief.

Adam is not in earshot and there is only silence for a

few moments.

"We just can't have another gun out here, with all the stuff going on, I would rather cover my butt, and make sure everything's good," the deputy explains.

Adam returns with the gun, and he hands it to the deputy.

The deputy sticks his head back into his car, and puts the gun in a plastic Ziploc-like bag, writes something on the bag, and tosses it onto the passenger seat.

While he's doing that, Grandma wants to know why Adam is carrying a gun, so she asks, "Why are you carrying a gun?"

"It's for protection, especially since we're in an unknown place," Adam explains. "You never know what will happen. The world is a crazy place."

"Well, I guess you're right," agrees Grandma.

"Okay, I better be on my way now," says the deputy, as he stands again, and extends his hand out to shake.

"I need to start cooking," states Grandma, as she shakes his hand, and thanks him for coming out.

"Can you give our condolences to the victim's family?" Mikah asks, as he shakes hands with the deputy.

What a proper thing to say. I like his words so much that I hear myself copying him. I try to sound as sophisticated as possible.

"Yes, I will. I should be seeing the family again soon, either today or tomorrow," says the deputy, looking at both Adam and I.

Everybody says farewell to the deputy and the Sheriff, as they get back into their car, and drive away.

Instead of pumping up my bike tires and riding to the

nearby pond, I decide to listen to my CD. So I go into Grandma's room, and take my CD player out of my bag. I find the track titled *The Good Life* and push play. I lie down on Grandma's bed, as I listen to the beats, the rhythm, the rhymes, and the flow of Kanye's voice on the track. I listen to the rest of the songs on the CD, and after I have gotten my fill of music, I take the headphones off, and go back into the kitchen.

Grandma is finished preparing dinner and I feel guilty for not helping her. She was the one who taught me at a young age that women, especially young ones, should help with the cooking, cleaning and any other home care duties. She drilled this lesson into my head every chance she had. So I didn't know why Grandma didn't chastise me this time, as she had normally done. I presume it has something to do with having visitors, but I don't ponder too much on the idea.

The guilt is soon overwhelmed by hunger, and by the smell of the food. I wander into the kitchen and find that Grandma has prepared pork chops, mashed potatoes, gravy, and tortillas.

Conversation at dinner is all about the events of the day and San Francisco, of course. As I watch the men eat, I wonder if one of them is capable of killing and if they could've pulled off the murder. Then I remind myself they don't have a motive. Why on Earth would three guys come all the way from San Francisco to kill a drunken Navajo man?

After dinner, I wash the dishes, and everybody else goes about their business. Grandma takes the trash out to be burned, and the Navarros retreat to their temporary room.

The dish water is hot, and my hands nearly melt as I stick them in the water, and take out dish after dish, rub them clean with my dish cloth, and stack them in another pile, soon to be rinsed, with more hot water.

It's not long before I'm finished with the dishes and decide to head out to the porch, where everyone else has congregated to relax in the coolness of the evening. Grandma sits and drinks a glass of Pepsi, with ice. The Navarro brothers have changed into more comfortable-looking clothes and appear refreshed.

The crime scene on the other side of the outhouse looks like a deserted post, with only the crime tape wrapped around four metal rods. The sun is going down, and a shadow has settled over the land. On the main road, we watch the cars, as they come up one side of the plateau, and disappear from view, as they get close to the other side of the plateau. Not many cars, just a few, maybe four.

Most people who travel this road choose it over the highway, to get from Winslow to Leupp; a community built around the government boarding school.

The school was originally built as a missionary school, to "re-program" us Indians. Its existence, to this day, is a reminder to me of how unfairly Indians were treated long ago. I despise the thought of common people having to endure sorrow and sadness, such as my ancestors endured at the hands of white people. Even after receiving most of my education so far from the school, I despise it and its origin. Nonetheless, it exists and people still attend it because they have no choice.

As my mind thinks about the school, Mikah and Jonah fill the rest of the evening with talks of their home town. They talk of the rolling hills in the Bay, the Bay Bridge lights at night, the ocean breeze, and colorful streets in

Chinatown, the smell of Asian dishes, the smell of the ocean, and the smell of seafood at a place called Fishermans' Wharf. Grandma joins in on the fishy smell part, telling us how she did not like the smell and how she would 'get sick to her stomach.'

Mikah talks about the apartment they share downtown; how small and cozy it is and how brilliant their view of the Golden Gate is. The more they talk, the more I want to see this city they speak so highly of.

Adam talks about his parents and I can hear a sense of respect in his voice. His father had become a professor at Berkeley, after going back to school for quite a while and teaching at several different levels of education. His mother was a seamstress for a few years, before she decided to open her own sewing supply store.

As the men continue taking turns to talk, they intermittently mention how fond their parents were of Phillip and his family, and how they had always wanted to see him, as well as his wife and kids again. This gives me a stronger feeling of satisfaction, of pride, as if I'm a part of this relationship. I wonder how my grandfather fit in, if he had to do anything special or if he was just himself. I don't ponder long on this thought.

The sun has set and my instinct to rest sets in, and I call it a day. A long day it has been and I am happy to rest my body.

Awkward Introductions

With the rise of a bright sun the next morning, I enjoy my breakfast of scrambled eggs, bacon and hash browns or as we call them, shoestring potatoes, and orange juice.

Jonah and Mikah enjoy two bowls of oatmeal each.

"I'm glad you two are leaving more food for me," I jokingly say.

"Yes, yes, me, too," Adam adds.

I am sure Grandma is disappointed that Jonah and Mikah aren't indulging in her homemade breakfast, but she seems content with their choice.

After a face wash and a quick sponge bath in lukewarm water, I join Grandma and the Navarro men on the porch after breakfast.

"So, what is this squaw dance thing you were talking about with the lady at the store yesterday?" Mikah asks.

He is obviously talking to Grandma and everyone quietly waits for an answer. Even I am interested in her response.

"The dance is a healing ceremony," explains Grandma. She sets the cup of coffee she is drinking down beside her chair.

Oh great, here we go…we are going to be sitting here forever.

"A long time ago, Navajos would have the dance, for soldiers returning home from war, and it was supposed to heal them of any bad things they saw in war," she starts out.

"But nowadays, it's a ceremony for anyone who is sick, and the ceremony goes for three days," she continues.

She bends down, picks up her cup, and sips her coffee while everyone waits in suspense. Then she resumes with, "There's a medicine man that does the healing and he sings, all night for the sick."

As she talks, I listen contently just as the Navarro men do.

"One of the days of the ceremony is for the family of the sick person, to give gifts to those who help with the ceremony. Another day is for feasting, and another day is for the celebration, that's the last day. They usually throw candy and all kinds of things out of a hogan, out from the top. And people outside catch the gifts," she states.

After a few moments of silence, Adam says, "That sounds like fun." His eyes light up and he's obviously captivated, just as I was when I first heard of this dance.

"You must've only heard the last part," I say.

Everyone laughs.

And then, with excitement in his voice, Jonah declares, "I'd like to go to one."

"Is there an actual dance? Or is that just the name?"

Mikah asks inquisitively. He doesn't appear to be as enthusiastic as Adam, but his voice suggests he is somewhat fascinated.

"Well, probably because the men dance one night, and on the second night, the men and women dance. I don't know how Squaw got to be part of the name, though," explains Grandma.

"People used to come from all over, but now mostly the local people come, and the women ask the men to dance, and the men pay the women for their dance," she says, with a gleam in her eyes as if she's remembering a dance she was paid for.

Adam is now smiling, and says, "Wow, that really does sounds like fun. How much does a dance cost?"

"Not much, just whatever, twenty-five cents or fifty cents, a dollar sometimes," says Grandma, as if the information she is giving is trivial and nothing big.

She doesn't realize she is sharing exciting information with the guys, and the gleam she had in her eyes is now transferred to theirs, noticeably Adam's.

"Yeah, that sounds cool...I want to go to one, too," says Mikah with the same tone of excitement as Adam.

Jonah joins in, and puts in his request to see one, too.

I am curious to know what other Navajos will think if Grandma takes them to one. The last time we heard of a white person attending a ceremony, it was such a big event and most of the locals were thrilled and many claimed they were the ones who invited the man. So, in essence, he was a sort of celebrity. But of course, there were haters, too, people who complained about their sacred dance being ruined.

As Grandma tells more about the Squaw Dance, I

think about a time when I was a child, and I went to one with both of my grandparents. I danced the night away, and made a little over five dollars, which was a lot of money for me. My feet hurt the next morning, but I remember having fun while Grandma and Grandpa danced with each other, taking breaks every now and again.

Grandma goes on to explain, "Nowadays, a lot of people get drunk at the dances, and every now and then, we hear about fights or people passing out, messing up the whole thing."

"That's unfortunate," is all Adam can offer.

"Yeah," says Grandma, with a sigh.

Grandma's comment about people getting drunk at dances reminds me of a moment from boarding school. I remember a girl I met there, who told me of a time she got raped at a squaw dance. As horrible as it sounds, the girl was very calm, when she told me of her encounter. I gasped at each detail she told me.

She had gone with her grandmother to a dance. Her grandmother was a drunk, and took the girl to the dance because she didn't have anyone to baby sit. After a short while of dancing, the girl realized her grandmother had left her alone at the dance. While her grandmother was gone, the girl went out to the dance circle, and asked an older man to dance…the man smelled of alcohol, she said, so she figured she'd get more money from him than a sober man. The man lured her to his truck, telling her he needed to get more money from his truck, and asked her to get in and help him look for his wallet. He asked her to close the door, so the bugs don't come into his truck. She didn't know what was really about to happen.

157

I could've told her that even as a little girl, I would've sensed something was wrong. But she did as the man told her, thinking she really was about to get more money. Naivety as its best.

Once both of her legs were inside, he locked the doors on her, as she was digging around on the floor for him. He pulled her by her hair, and after struggling with him for a while, she was soon under him, pinned on the seat. He stripped her naked, while she screamed, and kicked. The music from the dance, and the darkness all around did not help…nobody heard her screams and nobody knew she was in the truck. There was so much more going on near the bonfire. She had told me she just closed her eyes, while he proceeded to rape her. She could only scream.

Her grandmother eventually returned and apparently had left the girl to make "a run" into town, for drinks. As unbelievable as it may sound, yes, even grandmothers get drunk out here.

I cried for her as she told me her story. I wiped my tears away as they fell from my eyelids to my cheeks. She, on the other hand, sat on her bed, and didn't show an ounce of pain or sadness. She just talked about it as if it was a normal memory instead of one bursting with pain and shame.

I'll never forget the memory she shared with me that day as we sat on her bed while all the other girls played outside. It wasn't long after that when she was withdrawn from boarding school and sent to a foster family in Winslow.

I feel sad now just thinking about her story. I force myself to focus on the conversation at hand.

"Well, we'll have to find a dance so you guys can see what it is like," Grandma concludes.

"Yes!" Mikah and Jonah both say, jabbing their elbows backwards, to show their victory.

The conversation shifts to one about how Adam misses his friends, but not enough to go home yet.

I notice a car. It is on the main road and slowing to a stop. The brake lights come on, and I point to it, and bring it to everyone's attention.

"Look, there's a car stopping," I say, after everyone looks in the direction my finger is pointing.

"Let me grab my binoculars," Grandma says, and quickly goes into the house to retrieve her oh-so-famous binoculars, .the ones she claims she can see up to ten miles away with. I personally think her calculations are off and she is exaggerating. She says it has to be a clear day, no clouds, and the 'sunlight has to be j-u-s-t right.'

She quickly comes out again, binoculars hanging around her neck. She props them up and begins her diligent observation. "It looks like someone is getting out of the car," she mentions, with binoculars still propped.

With our eyes set on the car, we watch in wonderment. What looks like small figurines get out and a couple of them move towards the back of the truck.

"I can't tell who it is. It looks like they're walking around the car," Grandma says, adding more details.

"I hope they're not aglanis (drunks)," I say out loud.

The use of a Navajo word doesn't seem to concern any of the guys, so I don't bother to explain the meaning.

"Okay, let's just sit and watch; it's probably just someone who is changing drivers. They look drunk, though," she continues.

"Wow, you can see all that in those things?" asks

Mikah, now squinting.

"Yep, here, you want to look?" Grandma asks, handing him the binoculars, after taking them off her neck.

"Sure," Mikah says, and takes the binoculars, props them up, and starts his observation.

This observation pattern continues as everyone gets a turn. Sure enough, when it's my turn, I see there are a couple of men, who have gotten out of the car. By this time, they begin to walk towards us, as the car starts moving again, leaving them behind. One of them, with what looks like a bagful of stuff, resembles my uncle.

In this moment, I feel a twinge of fear run down my spine. This fear is mixed with anxiety. The two men continue to walk down the road towards us, and we all swap the binoculars again, trying to get a good look at the men.

After a few more minutes of watching, it is apparent that the men are both staggering.

"Oh dear! I hope that's not Anthony...it looks like him," observes Grandma. Her raised voice stirs up curiosity.

"Is he already out of jail? But how could that be?" I ask.

"Your son, Anthony?" asks Adam.

"Yes, it looks like him. He is supposed to be in jail, though," answers Grandma.

"Maybe he got out," add Mikah and Jonah in unison, with a chuckle.

"That wouldn't be funny," I say, not at all enthused about my uncle's return.

"He's not supposed to be out for another month, I think," says Grandma, not finding anything funny either. "That's what he told me when I visited him a couple weeks ago," she nervously adds.

"I just hope he's not drunk, but from the looks of it, he is," I say.

"Why is that?" Jonah asks.

Grandma sighs, and picks the binoculars up again to her eyes, and says, "He always gets crazy when he's drunk."

Yes, my crazy uncle. He actually does lose his mind from time to time, especially when he's drunk, and I can agree with Grandma on that note for a lot of reasons.

Grandma and I continue to sit on the porch, while everyone else moves about—Adam to take more stuff out of the van, or put something in; Mikah to go inside and Jonah to follow. Grandma continues her observations and makes minute-by-minute updates out loud.

Quietly, I sit and wonder what kind of stories my uncle will have this time. I hadn't seen him in quite a long while. The last time I saw him, he had come home and stayed with Grandma and I right after my mother had passed. He told me all kinds of stories about my mother when she was a child. They were funny and outrageous stories and they lifted my spirits.

Although I know he was very saddened by my mother's death, he showed very little sign of it. He simply carried on with life. He participated in the burial, and rubbed elbows with all the other men, mostly his cousins, during the funeral reception. And then, right after the funeral, he left, said he was heading into town, and that was it. He had hugged me and told me to 'hang in there.'

He rarely stayed home. Shortly after I was born, he had enlisted in the Navy and was gone for about 4 years. Then one day, when I was a little girl, in Kindergarten, he came home. He came walking up the road just like he was now, carrying a huge duffle bag, and Grandma met him halfway with the old truck she and Grandpa had then. Grandpa simply kept about the work he was doing at the moment, making Navajo dancer dolls, carved out of wood. He sat at his workbench outside, and held his hand up to shade his eyes from the sun, acknowledged his son was coming home, and went right back to work, while Grandma jumped up and into the truck, and drove off to meet her oldest son.

According to Grandma, after he came home from the Navy, he was not the same. He began drinking heavily, he was gone for days on end, and nobody ever knew where he was. He'd end up in jail sometimes or out on the streets for months at a time. Because of this, Grandma read through the police reports in the local newspaper anytime he was gone for more than a week; to find out if he had been thrown in jail.

Here he was again, staggering up towards the driveway; this time nobody is driving to meet and greet him. The Navarro men join us again on the porch, and we all watch my uncle and whomever he's with, get closer.

Grandma finally stands up and waves at him, and she waits for him to reach the porch.

My uncle's hair is thick, wavy and black. His eyes are bloodshot. His frame is thin and muscular. He is wearing an old, navy blue t-shirt, with khaki pants, and some brand spankin-new, tan work boots. They look like a pair I saw at Wal-Mart on the previous day's trip.

"Hello, shi'yáázh (my son)," Grandma exclaims, as she holds out her arms, to hug him.

He puts down the brown paper bag he was holding

162

with his right hand. It appears to hold a bottle of some kind of whiskey. He continues to hold the plastic bag with a six pack of Budweiser inside, and hugs his mother back.

"Who the hell are these people?" is the first thing out of his mouth. He stands back, takes out a pack of cigarettes, and pulls one out. He tries to light it, but his fingers can't seem to connect the matchstick and the narrow striking strip on the cover. He tries a couple more times and we all watch him. Nobody attempts to help.

"Well, here's Shannon," Grandma is saying, when he suddenly looks back up, stops messing with the matches, and gives me a big hug.

"Is that you? You look different. Come here, girl. Give your uncle a hug," he says, as he squeezes the breath out of me and I inhale the strong odor of alcohol.

My lungs feel like they're being crushed and I barely make out the words, "Good to see you, Uncle."

"Wow. Look at this girl. She has grown. How old are you now?" he asks, putting the unlit cigarette in his mouth.

"It hasn't been that long. I just turned sixteen," I mutter, as he releases the bear hug.

"Wow," he says again. The look in his eyes is sad, yet light with amusement. It's hard to tell what he could be thinking. The look could be a mix of different emotions.

I don't stare. I just smile and look away. It hurts me to see him this way, and I can't bear to look for very long.

My uncle's friend, who has been standing quietly next to my uncle finally speaks up and says, "Hello."

The man looks to be in his early twenties, much younger-looking than my uncle. He has a slight muscular build and I immediately notice that his right hand is bandaged

163

with white gauze. His hair is long, black, and touches the middle of his back. His eyes are squinty. His nose is straight and almost perfect, except for a small bump about halfway down in the middle. He walks with a slight limp and is wearing the same kind of boots as Anthony.

"Oh, oh, this is my friend, Kyle," my uncle mutters, as he clumsily pulls his friend closer to the crowd. "We just got off work."

"Work? I thought you were in jail," Grandma exclaims.

"I got out a couple of days ago and we just worked for two days," Anthony says, with a slight slur.

Grandma begins her introduction of our visitors. She goes through the Navarro brothers' names, as Anthony and Kyle shake each of their hands with a tight, yet clumsy grip. Neither seems to have good balance and they sway a little as they make their way around.

"You got off work or you quit?" Grandma asks, in a stern tone.

"Yeah, I quit," Anthony replies, with a smirk.

"No, no, we were fired," Kyle says, partly laughing as he speaks.

Anthony laughs as well and adds, "But we got paid!"

Grandma shakes her head in disapproval of either their behavior or their condition.

I am sad to see my uncle this way. At the same time, I am upset at him, for being a drunk, someone the kids back at the boarding school would have laughed about. I suppose they thought it was funny to see someone act belligerently. I, however, never thought it was funny. I thought it was sad to see a person, one of us, have little self-control and strength.

"You can stay if you don't cause any trouble," Grandma says, with a tone of voice that shows she is discouraged and upset. The cheerful face she wore not long ago is now one with a scowl.

"So you guys are tough guys, eh?" Anthony asks, eyeing Adam.

Oh great, here we go. Uncle Anthony—he always has to be a menace, always has to start something out of nowhere. And when he's drunk, it's usually something he can't finish, but he starts it anyway.

"Oh no, not tough guys, we're just visitors," Adam says, as he sits down, after having stood to shake hands.

"You want to be tough guys?" Anthony asks, now trying to straighten himself—his body teetering a little.

"No, we don't want to be tough guys," replies Adam, looking right at Anthony with an uneasy smile.

"If I knew there were so many people here, I would've brought more beer," Anthony says and then lets out a chuckle.

His friend, Kyle laughs as well and almost falls backwards.

"Oh, no, we're not drinking," Adam explains. I can see what looks like confusion in his facial expression.

My uncle does have a way of acting friendly and making you feel threatened at the same time and I recognize Adam's look immediately because I'm thinking the same thing.

Who does my uncle think he is?

"Shhh, these guys are our visitors. What are you saying? They're not drinking," Grandma says, out loud, with a bit of harshness in her tone. She holds her son steady, by putting her arm around him. The bun atop her head shakes as she steadies him.

"Well, then, how about one of you tough guys take my bag into the house?" Anthony asks, with another smirk on his face. He always manages to piss people off, and he pushes his limits to do it.

Before he can stir up trouble, Grandma jumps into the conversation again.

"Carry your own bag into the house!" Grandma says, raising her voice just enough to show her disappointment. And then in Navajo, she says, "I told you not to start trouble."

"I'll help," I say quickly, trying to help the situation and ease the tension.

I get up and pick up the bag with beer, but my uncle yanks it back out of my hand, and says, "I want him to take it," looking directly at Adam.

Adam stands abruptly and comes to my aid. He proceeds to carry the bag of beer into house without hesitation.

Anthony staggers to where Adam was sitting a few seconds before, and plops down. He props his elbows on his knees, and hangs his head. He sits like that for a few moments, mumbling under his breath.

Kyle just sits on the floor of the porch, against the wall. He lets his head fall backwards and his jaw drops open.

I stand and turn to leave, not wanting to be anywhere near my uncle.

So does Grandma.

"Yááh di lá!" (Oh great!) Grandma says to show her disapproval and disgust with the situation.

"What?" my uncle asks, as he wearily raises his head

for a brief moment.

"I'm going inside!" Grandma says as she walks past her son.

I hold the screen door open for my grandmother.

"Don't worry, Grandma, we'll fine, glad Adam and his brothers are here," I say, to console her.

Embarassing and Pitiful

Though I am also disgusted with my uncle's behavior, I wonder what it is that makes him this way. As a child, I had always thought people simply get addicted to alcohol after drinking it for fun. But the last few years in school have taught me otherwise. I have learned that people typically turn to alcohol for comfort. And in this search for comfort, they become addicted to the drug.

I wonder what makes him drink the stuff, and what could have been so bad in his life that he had to look for comfort outside of his mind and body.

I am already exhausted and figure a nap would be a great remedy. Instead of taking a nap, I go into Grandma's room, dig through my cosmetics bag and retrieve some Oil of Olay facial wipes. I lay one across my face, take a few deep breaths, and gently wipe my entire face in an effort to refresh and waken myself.

Mikah and Jonah eventually come back into the house. I presume they probably got tired of looking at my uncle, who is probably still slumped over on the porch.

I wander into the kitchen and find Grandma and Adam are in there, standing near the sink. I can see that Grandma is upset as she is talking quietly to Adam, in a whisper almost, about her oldest son.

"He's trouble when he's drunk. It's best just to leave him alone," Grandma is explaining, hands on her hips.

Adam just nods his head, as if he understands. But I doubt he really understands. After all, he is from a much more secure place, a place where people probably don't come home and pick a fight with him, just because they feel like it.

Nobody else utters a word. We all just look at Grandma as if she will have an answer for what to do next.

And she does. "Do you guys want to go for a ride somewhere?" she asks after a few seconds.

"Yeah, sure," Adam says, and he looks at Mikah, Jonah and myself for approval. We all nod our heads in agreement.

Grandma says, "We'll have to figure out how to get around them." She shrugs her elbow in the direction of the front porch, where my uncle and his friend are still sitting.

Adam, Mikah, and Jonah just look at her with confused looks. I am somewhat embarrassed that she has to act as if my uncle's a sleeping lion in a cave or something.

"Wait, let me check on them," she says and then steps out to the porch, to see what her son is doing. She comes back in and whispers, "Okay, let's all go out the back door...they're passed out."

"But the van is parked right in front of him," Adam says out loud.

"Shhh! If we wake them up, they'll want to go with

169

us," Grandma says, frantically.

"And we don't want that," I quickly say, shaking my head. "For sure, we definitely don't want that. There's nothing like driving with a drunk. They want to get out every few minutes to pee, and then they want to go into town, and get more beer or wine, or whatever it is they're drinking."

"So, we're going to sneak out?" Mikah asks in disbelief.

"I know. Let's go see if we can find a squaw dance," Grandma says excitedly, as if she just thought of some new invention. Her eyes light up as she looks around the room for approval.

"Isn't it too early for a squaw dance?" I ask.

Grandma replies, "No, they cook all day, too."

"Ahh-ha, that's what we're going for...food!" I exclaim.

We all giggle and laugh.

"Shhh!" Grandma says again.

"Yeah, yeah, I want to go," says Jonah. Mikah and Adam give similar responses.

"I wouldn't want to go looking like this," Jonah says, as he heads into my mother's old room to change clothes.

Almost in unison, Adam and Mikah say, "Me, too."

While the three men change, Grandma goes into her room to freshen up.

I can feel the filth on my skin and cannot be out in public, especially at a squaw dance, smelling like god knows what. So I opt for wiping my body down with a damp, soapy washcloth. I change into a new pair of khaki Polo shorts and a light purple tank top with spaghetti straps. I top off my get-up with a khaki baseball cap and grab a thin, dark blue sweater, for any quick change in temperature.

Grandma convinces the Navarros it would be best to bring my uncle and his friend inside the house, so all three men go outside, pick up an arm or leg, and literally carry the two men, who were both slumped over, into the house. My uncle mumbles and grumbles, almost wakes up, but for the most part, is still out of it. It's not until after we head for the van that he wakes up and staggers to the front door after us.

"HEY! Hey! Where you guys going?!" he hollers from the door.

We hadn't all gotten into the van yet, but it's very obvious we are trying to sneak away.

"We're going to see your Grandma!" Grandma says out loudly, as she turns around and faces him.

"Wait, hey, come back," Anthony says, waving his hand, signaling for us to come back into the house.

Grandma points towards her mother's house, and continues, "We're just going to go visiting!"

My uncle is swaying and holding onto the door frame, but is still very unbalanced. "The party's just starting! Come on back! Hey, hey guys," he says, in his drunken, slurred voice as he stumbles out the door and onto the porch.

Grandma climbs into the van. "Shoot!" she mutters. She hesitates for a moment as if she's thinking twice about leaving him.

Then she continues to get into the van, and yells to my uncle, "We'll be back in a little while! Just go inside and lie down!"

My uncle lets go of the porch frame, steps down slowly, and starts staggering towards us. Adam starts the van up, and Grandma gets all the way in, then slides the door shut.

Just as Adam starts backing up, my uncle bends down to the ground and picks up a rock.

"Oh crap!" yell Mikah and Jonah in unison.

"Go! Let's go!" yells Grandma.

Wack! The rock hits the front window shield and we all cringe.

The windows are rolled down and we can all hear my uncle hollering, "Come back, you losers! You can't leave me here!"

Adam stops the van, and is about to get out, but Grandma loudly says, "No! Don't get out! He's drunk! Let's just go!"

Adam starts the van back up, and my uncle goes to pick up another rock. This time, the van jerks forward and we speed off down the road.

I look back at my uncle, who looks like a crooked figurine now, with the house, the big elm tree, and the clear, blue sky as his background. He is waving his arms. He finally stops, as we get about a mile away, and I can see his figure stand still. He walks around, almost in a full circle, turns and staggers back into the house.

"You could've taken him, Adam," Mikah says jokingly.

Nobody laughs.

"I think Grandma just wanted to get out of there, otherwise, I would've taken him out in a second, but of course, he's drunk," Adam says.

"Yes, I did. I just hate it when he does that. He gets so crazy like that," Grandma says, to further state the point she was trying to make earlier.

"Crazy and stupid," I add.

"I am so sorry you have to put up with that, Grandma," Adam sympathetically says.

"Now I see what you mean about leaving him alone because he gets crazy when he's drunk," Mikah comments.

"Geez. Ugh. And I thought I was getting away from craziness by coming here for the summer," I say.

"I'm sorry you guys had to see that," Grandma apologetically says.

"It's not your fault, Grandma," I say.

"Yeah, don't blame yourself," Jonah chimes in.

We stop at the main road, and Adam asks, "Which way to your mom's house?"

Grandma says, "Oh no, we're going to find us a squaw dance." She signals with her hand for Adam to turn to the right.

"Okay...now we're talking," Adam says and turns the van down the road towards town.

I am positive my Grandma is still shaken up by the confrontation with her son. She's probably as embarrassed as I am.

"We'll ask the Begays down the road here, they're always going to squaw dances, they'll know where to find one," continues Grandma.

With that, we are on our way, down the road, to ask the neighbors for information. We are on a mission now, off to find a squaw dance.

Great-Grandma's Gift

The Begays are a neighboring family, who seem more introverted than the rest of our neighbors. According to my great-grandmother's stories, they were never supposed to be in this area. But they somehow managed to end up here. They begged her husband to stay on this land a long time ago, and my great grandparents agreed to let them live here until they found a more permanent home. Of course, they never left. Instead, they built a hogan and just began living here.

Because they never left, the family was indebted to my grandparents and agreed to pay them with some livestock and money, but they didn't keep that promise. So, there was fallout, of course. My great grandparents eventually told them they could stay, but anytime their livestock wander into our family's land, we would keep the livestock. The man of the house at the time, decided to give my great grandparents a few sheep right then and there. And according to the story, my great grandfather loaded the sheep onto his wagon, and drove them to his corral.

Back then, sheep were highly valued and could be traded in for money at livestock auctions. I guess that was the only payment my great grandparents ever received. And I guess that story would explain why the family members keep to themselves.

After a few minutes, we get to the Begays' house, or village, I should say. Over the many years they've lived here, they managed to build something of a camp. I had never been to their settlement before, but always saw it from the main road. They weren't too far from the main road, just a few bumps and we were there. They had what looked like a main hogan, a smaller hogan to the right of that, a man-made shed, a house to the left of the Hogan, and a couple of outhouses off in the short distance. There is also a small corral with about three sheep in it. And then, there are about twenty old hoopdies littering the land behind the main hogan.

We park next to a dark green Ford F-150 with humongous tires and a busted, rear window.

I can see that there are a few kids playing outside, and just as we come to a stop, a little girl in a muddied, white dress runs up to greet us. Her hair looks like she just fought with a dog; it's a mess. She is sucking on a lollipop, and her dirty hair is stuck to her face. With all that going on, she still manages to smile, showing off her rotten baby teeth.

Grandma is the only one who gets out of the van and goes to knock on the door of the hogan. An older-aged and round woman opens the door, and she shakes Grandma's hand. Then, Grandma disappears into the home. The rest of us sit in the van, and observe the little village or settlement, whatever it is. A few minutes pass, and we just sit quietly. Grandma comes back out of the hogan, and waves at us to come on in. So we all get out, one by one, and walk into the hogan.

We are introduced to the people inside; an elderly woman with missing front teeth, who I recognize as the Lady With Clumsy Hands, which is what my grandmothers call her; an elderly man with a balding head and thick glasses, who I recognize as her husband; and two men, who look like they could be her sons, but whom I've never met or seen before.

Both of the young men quietly mill around, careful to stay out of Lady With Clumsy Hands's way. Both are tall and thin. One of the men has a scar on his face. He is shirtless and I can see that he has a nicely sculpted torso. He has long, shiny, black hair and is either very reserved or very shy. He doesn't smile when he shakes everyone's hands. He simply nods. The other man appears to be younger, maybe in his early twenties, and is much thinner than the man with the scarred face. He has shorter hair, which falls into his face as he moves about.

Grandma explains that she called us in because the elderly woman just finished cooking dinner, and offered us some food. I think about the name, Lady With Clumsy Hands, and I pass on the offer, afraid to be fed some clumsily prepared food. This, I'm sure is an insult but I don't let that change my mind and I ignore the disappointed look on Lady With Clumsy Hands's face. The Navarros pass, too.

The hogan is somewhat small, there's a stove in the middle, a couple of beds that line the wall on two sides, and a table on another side, a cabinet with dishes on one side, and a washing area, with a tub of water, and a wash pan. There are a few pictures hanging on the walls, mostly old photographs of what looks like family.

I go to sit down at the table, and I notice a bulge in the scar-faced man's waist. He quickly pulls out a white t-shirt from a bag on the floor and pulls it on. I am somewhat shocked, and perplexed. Was that a gun in his pants? I try to re-focus my attention to the conversation between Grandma and Lady With Clumsy Hands. I look back in the direction of the two men and this time, I notice a small box of bullets, sitting on a chest diagonal to me, next to the scar-faced man.

Everybody is still talking, and nobody is paying attention to me or the two men. Grandma is telling the family about the Navarros, in Navajo. The Navarro men are quietly talking amongst themselves, making observations about the hogan mostly. They're probably wondering how all these people fit in here.

I don't want to stare at the peculiar, scar-faced man, but my eyes keep moving back in his direction. A chill comes over me, and I don't want anyone from the family to notice me looking around too much, so I stand up and I walk back towards the door to stand near the Navarros.

From that position, the scar-faced man is not within sight but the other guy is. I try not to look very long at him either. He stands to get more food, I presume, and I notice he has a limp in his walk.

I wonder who he is. His left hand is wrapped with some gauze, and he doesn't use it very much while he eats. When he sits back down on the bed, he holds a bowl of soup in his lap, and he sips it with a spoon in his right hand, while his wounded hand rests on the bed.

The scar-faced man is sitting on the bed next to him, sipping soup also. With their heads down, sipping soup, they exchange low voiced jokes, and chuckle every now and then.

The only two people who are really talking, Grandma and Lady With Clumsy Hands, talk about a squaw dance across the river. Lady With Clumsy Hands is telling Grandma in Navajo which family is holding the squaw dance, and that the next evening is the Second Night, the night of the dance. She gives Grandma some directions to the host family's home.

And with that, the Begay family members say, "Goodbye" to us in Navajo.

Grandma says her farewells to everyone else in English, and we all wave, and one by one, shuffle out of the hogan. Adam and Mikah have to dip their heads a little, to avoid hitting the top of the entrance to the hogan.

Once we all get into the van, I can't hold in my words any longer, so I burst out, "Did anyone see the gun?"

"What gun?!" Grandma and Adam both exclaim.

I can tell Mikah and Jonah are also surprised.

But one of them says, "Is that what that was? I thought I saw something bulging in one of those guys's pants."

"Yeah," I say, "Or at least that's what it looked like," I add.

"I didn't see anything at all, except that guy's hand," says Adam.

"I know. He looked creepy," I state.

"Are those guys their sons?" asks Jonah.

"I think so," Grandma says. "She didn't really tell me who they are and I've never seen them before," she adds.

As we drive back to the main road, Grandma decides it would be best to go to the squaw dance the following night, which will be the Second Night—the night of the dance.

"Tonight," she says, "there will just be a meeting and it will probably be too boring for you young people."

Instead of going home, Grandma suggests we visit her mother next.

Oh, this will be an interesting visit.

As excited as the men are about meeting the oldest woman alive in our family, I know my great grandmother is not a particularly affectionate or warm person. And I'm almost positive a visit from three strangers, white men at that, will not be anything tremendously exciting for her.

When we arrive at Great Grandma's home which is a traditional hogan, my expectations are met. As Grandma introduces the three men, she simply shakes their hands and says, 'White men…how nice," in Navajo.

The afternoon passes by while Grandma and her mother catch up on the happenings in the area; a dog attack on one of Great Grandma's neighbors, one of my cousins stealing some money from his mother, a sheep thief running wild; and the rotten mutton one of my aunts tried to pass off as good mutton at a potluck across the river.

As you can imagine, the Navarros have nothing to speak of in the company of Great Grandma, so they just sit and pretend to listen to Grandma and Great Grandma.

I cannot bear to see them suffer, so I ask Grandma if she can ask her mother to let us browse through my great grandfather's medicine man bag. I had seen it once before and thought it was an interesting collection of traditional and sacred tools.

Unsure of whether my great grandmother will approve of strangers looking through her dead husband's belongings, I patiently wait for Grandma to translate the request to her mother.

Surprisingly, Great Grandma agrees to give us a peek. So we wait for her to fetch the small, buckskin pouch from under her bed. It is stored in an old, wooden box, which is decorated with a drawing of a Navajo wedding basket containing heaps of turquoise jewelry, a drawing quite famous to the people.

Jonah, Mikah, and Adam crowd around her as she opens the bag right there on her bed. She explains in Navajo that she would have been reluctant to do this several years ago, but soon realized that the bag and its contents are no longer sacred to her, because she has adopted a Christian way of life. Yet, she keeps them as a reminder of her husband's craft, or gift.

I understand most of what Great Grandma says, but I wait, along with the Navarros, for Grandma to translate this in English.

As she translates, the bag is opened. Feathers, a bunch of deer toe nails tied together for a rattle, and a smaller pouch of corn pollen are revealed.

"Wow, that is cool," I hear Jonah say. He leans closer to get a better view.

Mikah and Adam follow with similar comments.

Great Grandma describes each item and explains the feathers were used for blessing people with smoke, the rattle was used for singing medicine songs, and the corn pollen was used for prayer—all of these are important in the healing of a person.

After we all get a look at the once sacred medicine bag, we retreat to the living room again and Grandma resumes her gossip talks with her mother.

The Navarros and I wander outside. While Adam and Mikah curiously walk around the hogan, dissecting the formation of the home, Jonah and I go for a stroll down to my great grandmother's old horse corral, which sits on a downward slope about sixty feet from her hogan.

"What a beautiful home your great grandmother has," Jonah says, as he picks petals off a wild flower he picked up.

"Yeah, it's a pretty cool dwelling," I say, proud of my great grandmother's hogan.

"I am so glad Adam convinced us to come out here, I am learning quite a bit and having fun," he says.

"Really? You're having fun with all this drama going on?" I ask. I am confused as to how anyone can think of having fun on a trip like this.

"Well, there's drama everywhere, but it's the way of life out here that has me intrigued and it's exciting for me to see this new lifestyle," he explains.

"I guess I can understand, I do take a lot of my family's traditional lifestyle for granted," I say.

For the next few moments, we walk around the horse corral and comment on the structure, which is deteriorating.

Before long, it's time to leave and Grandma comes out of the hogan, waving, to let us know it's time to go. So we return to the hogan, where Adam and Mikah are still observing the exterior of my great grandmother's hogan. Jonah joins them while I go inside to bid my great grandmother farewell.

I give my great grandmother, who is still sitting on her bed, a soft hug, being careful not to hurt her frail body.

She says, "Take care" in Navajo to me. Then she tells me to wait, while she unfolds a small bundle of leather.

She reveals an arrowhead stone, and hands it to me.

"She is giving that to you for protection. It will protect you," Grandma, who is standing a few feet away, explains.

"Ah'ee hee, (Thank you)" I say to my great grandmother as I grasp the stone.

I hug my great grandmother again and kiss her on the cheek.

She hugs me back and says "Take care" in Navajo.

Grandma says, "See you next time" to her mother in Navajo.

My great grandmother proceeds to stand, but looks to be having difficulty, so I help her up and she motions to the door. So I help her walk to the front door. She lets my arm go and waves to the young men, who have now congregated near the van.

"Bye!" Adam hollers. Mikah and Jonah scurry over to us and exchange hugs with Great Grandma. Adam follows, but instead of hugging her, he kisses her hand softly.

Great Grandma smiles and says, "Shooo!" to portray her delight.

We all laugh.

Grandma says, "She will think you're flirting with her."

"Tell her she deserves a kiss on the hand because she is a beautiful woman," Adam says.

Grandma obediently translates Adam's comment.

Great Grandma smiles again. She waves us off and says, "See you next time" in Navajo.

We get into the van and depart for our short trip home.

Great Grandma continues to wave as we bounce down the road. She is bent over with a hunch in her back and the skirt she is wearing is nearly touching the ground.

As we drive home, I clutch the arrowhead, and slide it into my purse. I will leave it there until I find a strip of sinew to tie it onto and hang it around my neck. I wonder what my uncle and his friend are up to. I wonder if they are awake now.

As if she is reading my thoughts, Grandma says, "I hope Anthony isn't awake. Or I hope he left again."

"I think three against two should be an easy one, if he still wants a fight," Adam jokingly says.

"I wouldn't put it past my uncle to attempt another fight again," I discouragingly say.

"No fights," Grandma sternly says. "We will ignore him and leave again if he is acting up," she adds.

The day has gone by quickly and the sun is setting, leaving the land comfortably cool.

Poor Memory

A few more moments later, we pull up to the front of the yellow, cinder block house again. The shadow in front of the house is dark. The air is calm and I hear dogs barking somewhere. I presume it is most likely the pack of sheep dogs from Grandma Elsa's house.

Grandma is first to go into the house. Just as I walk in the front door, I hear, "Hey, who's that?" from the kitchen.

"It's just us," Grandma says, as she makes her way into the kitchen, a few steps ahead of me.

My uncle is sitting at the table, and it appears he just finished eating dinner. An empty plate and a beer can sit in front of him. He looks a lot more sober than he had earlier that day, but appears to remain affected by the alcohol. His movements are uneasy.

His friend, Kyle, is passed out on the couch in the living room. He doesn't budge as we pass by him. He does not look comfortable as his body is halfway on and halfway off the couch.

The Navarro brothers eventually join us in the kitchen. They stand near the archway to the kitchen, silently, waiting to be introduced.

"Who are these people?" Anthony asks, doing a 'what's up' head nod to the Navarros.

"These are some visitors from San Francisco," Grandma tells him. I'm sure she's used to this by now, just as I am. There is no sense in talking to a drunken person, because you will only have to repeat what you told them, when they are sober.

Without questions, she goes through the introductions again, and tells him who their father is, and my uncle gets up to shake Adam's hand.

"I remember you," my uncle says, looking at Adam dead in the eyes.

"And I remember you, it's good to see you again," Adam says with a straight, but friendly smile.

Both men were quite young, maybe two or three, back then and I wonder how much they really remember.

Mikah and Jonah step forward to shake hands with Anthony as well.

My uncle says, "What's up?" to me, and gives me a hug again.

"You already gave me a hug earlier, but you probably don't remember," I say, showing my annoyance with his behavior earlier.

"I did?" he asks. He sits for a moment, with a puzzled look on his face. His thick, black hair dangles around his face and he runs his fingers through his hair.

No apology—just a look of confusion and emptiness.

"Yes, you did, but I'm sure you don't remember, you

185

were drunk," I say.

"So when did you get out of jail?" Grandma asks, as she takes a seat next to my uncle.

In between mouthfuls of food, he replies, "Umm, a couple of days ago."

Grandma simply nods. She looks down at the floor and her demeanor changes from one of cheerfulness to one of sadness. Her shoulders drop slightly and her chubby cheeks take on a sagging look.

Adam pulls out a chair at the table and sits to join in on the conversation.

"So, what were you in for?" Adam asks.

Anthony looks a bit perturbed by the question, but answers after a couple of seconds. "Theft...I stole a car from this guy who tried to run me over one time."

Without hesitation, my uncle begins telling Grandma and Adam his jail story. "I was supposed to be in for another couple of weeks, but they let me out for good behavior," he brags.

As my uncle begins telling us about his criminal friends and experience in jail this time around, Mikah and Jonah sit down at the table and are intrigued.

I busy myself with putting away the dishes in the dish drainer and I don't pay much attention to the conversation.

A few moments later, I hear my uncle say, "I ended up at a squaw dance on the other side of the hill after I got out."

Except for my uncle, everybody at the table freezes and all of our eyes light up.

"Really?" Grandma asks.

"The one on the other side of the hill from the other

night?" I ask.

"Yeah, me and Kyle were hitchhiking to Leupp, back to his place, and instead of taking us to Leupp, the people who were giving us a ride took us to the squaw dance."

"So, did you hear about the guy who was murdered?" Grandma asks.

Everyone's eyes are on my uncle. The forkful of food that is between my mouth and the plate stops in mid-air.

"What murder?" Anthony asks.

"The murder that happened right out here, in front of the house" Adam says, before Grandma can spit the words out.

"No, didn't hear anything," Anthony replies, with a facial expression of confusion.

"It happened the same night the squaw dance was on the other side of the hill," Grandma says.

"Huh. Nope, didn't hear anything about it," Anthony says, slowly shaking his head back and forth.

"You were probably too drunk to hear anything, if you heard it," Grandma says, in disgust.

"Yeah, probably," Anthony says smiling. "Or I was too busy trying to score another case of beer." He finds humor in his own joke and laughs while everyone else remains quiet.

I suddenly feel sick to my stomach. I can't stand that awful smile of his. So I retreat to Grandma's room, not at all enthused or interested in hearing anything else my uncle has to say.

On the way to Grandma's room, I pass Kyle, who stirs slightly, but is still sprawled out on the couch. His arm is dangling over the side of the couch with his palms up. A small area of blood-soaked gauze is exposed around the palm of his bandaged hand.

I lie down on Grandma's bed, and listen to the conversation and from the other room.

My uncle moves off the subject of murder and reverts to his jail stories. He begins talking about another time he was incarcerated and how he carved out a small hole in the jail wall using a nail and a rock, both of which were smuggled in from the outside. Once the hole was carved, he had convinced one of the jail mates to have his girlfriend, who was a frequent visitor, pour alcohol through the hole from the outside using a rubber hose. And everyone would meet at the "watering hole" for a good week before they were busted.

Although that is a clever idea, I don't think it's funny. Good behavior, yeah right.

I am disgusted with my uncle and his behavior. I wonder what the Navarros think of him, as they sit and laugh with him. I feel shame and wish he would change his behavior.

Instead of continuing to listen to the banter, I take out my new Kanye West CD, pop it in my player, and push 'Play'. I listen to the lyrics, the rhymes and the beats. I enjoy the music and let it wrap itself around me. I imagine myself in another world, hanging with Kanye West and his entourage at a concert, backstage, of course. I enjoy the music and close my eyes.

Speak Up

The music has stopped. The leather headphones are stuck to the side of my face. I look around. The CD player is on the floor beside me and the cord is tangled around my arm. Sunlight is beaming through the windows, and Grandma is not in the bed. I get up and untangle myself and test my CD player. It's still working.

I walk into the living room. Everybody else is already awake, so I go into the bathroom and wash up.

When I come back out, everyone is sitting down in the kitchen for breakfast. The talk around the table is about my uncle's friend, Kyle, who apparently walked out to the main dirt road earlier in the morning.

"Yeah, I've been in jail with him before," my uncle is saying.

"Where is he from?" Grandma asks.

"He lives in Leupp, and he's related to the Begays from down the road. I'm not sure who his parents are, though," he says.

"What was he in for?" I ask.

I proceed to fork out some fried potatoes with chopped spam from the skillet on the stovetop.

"He's in jail a lot, I know he was in for beating up his girlfriend—he told me he had to teach her a lesson about knives," my uncle says.

"Geez, what a horrible idea," I say, and cover my mouth, but not in time to get reprimanded for it.

"Don't interrupt my story," my uncle says sternly.

I notice that he looks sober with his thick, wavy hair combed nicely.

"Oops. Sorry," I say and take a bite of my food.

"That is a pretty blunt excuse for beating somebody up," Adam says. Then he asks, "With a knife? What exactly did he do to her?"

"He stabbed her a couple of times, knocked her around," my uncle explains nonchalantly, as if it's nothing.

Sounds a lot like something Anthony himself has done before, to his very own ex-girlfriend so I'm taken aback that he has anything to say at all. I wonder if he and the creep compared notes in jail. I suddenly feel sick thinking about it. I take a break from the grubbing, and listen to the rest of the conversation.

"Wow, that is horrible," Mikah says.

Jonah agrees and adds, "Yeah, it is."

There is silence for a moment.

"So, if he's related to the Begays, he must know those two other men who were at the their house yesterday," I hear myself say.

My uncle turns his head towards me with a quizzical look on his face. "What men? You guys were at their house?" he asks curiously.

"We were there yesterday…some creepy-looking guy and a younger guy," I reply.

"I dunno," he says and continues eating.

"I can't believe you haven't heard anything about the murder," I say. "I would've thought everyone would be talking about it on the streets."

"So who got killed?" my uncle asks.

"Somebody named Eddie Yazzie, from Dilcon," Grandma replies.

"Wow," my uncle says. He just looks at the food on his plate with a puzzled look. "He was another one of those guys who thought he was a tough guy."

"Actually, he's a very dead guy," I say, really intending to spark something in my uncle and hoping to make him feel guilty for saying what he just spit out. Of course, it doesn't work.

"Yeah, he was pretty crazy. He used to do stupid stuff like beat his woman and then get caught for it," my uncle says, before wiping his mouth with a napkin.

He sets his napkin down and then says, "His wife is actually pretty hot. What a shame."

The look on Adam's face becomes one of disgust, and he says, "Wow."

The urge for me to say something is strong now…I have to say something to this idiot I call my uncle. For the past couple of years, ever since he almost killed his ex-girlfriend, I had always wished someone would yell at him, or beat him for it. And now he sits here talking smack about someone who's just as bad as he is.

"Is that all you can say? Didn't you do the same

thing as him? Don't you even feel bad about what you did?"
I blurt out.

I show him all that outrage, and he says, "Since when
do you think you're old enough to talk to me like that?"

He has a glare in his eyes and he stops eating, food
midway between the plate and his mouth. He just holds his
food and looks right at me with those glaring eyes.

I don't answer. I just stare at him as if he's a stranger
to me. I don't know who my uncle has become, but I do
know he is unpleasant.

"Screw you!" he says angrily as he slams the forkful
of food down. He gets up and knocks his chair over.

"Hey, hey, no need to raise your voice at her," Jonah
says, coming to my defense.

I can imagine how angry my uncle is for being called
out like that in front of our visitors. But I don't give in to him.
I remind myself of how belligerent he can be and I want to be
just as bad, in order to show him how wrong he is. I don't
budge. I keep my stare.

"Damn right, I feel bad!" he blurts out, on his feet
now. His nostrils are flared and hist fists are clenched.

"Woah, woah, everybody, calm down," Adam calmly
says, as he cautiously stands up.

Jonah and Mikah stand also.

"Do you feel the same way?" my uncle asks, looking
at Grandma, who is now about to cry, hands folded in her lap.

"Well, do you?" Anthony repeats, his voice filled
with anger.

Grandma slowly covers her face with her hands for a
few seconds. She puts her hands back in a clasp and finally
says, "Just calm down."

"I think you don't have the right to judge anyone, even this guy you are talking about," I say. I want to say more, but I hold the words back.

My uncle unclenches his fists and he is staring right at his mother, but Grandma does not look up at him. Her head is lowered.

"I just wish you would stop ending up in jail and drinking and all this other stuff you're doing," I continue.

"Shhh, stop," Grandma says, raising her head and looking at me with disappointment in her eyes.

"I don't need to hear this," my uncle says.

Mikah and Jonah sit back down, with their heads down, as if they are embarrassed to be in on this conversation.

Adam is still standing, and speaks again, "Maybe we should leave the three of you alone to talk about this."

"No, don't leave. I was just getting ready to leave this place," my uncle says, and throws a balled up paper towel on the table.

Grandma just sits and begins to sob. Her hands are covering her face again and her sobs are heavier.

My uncle storms out of the kitchen, and into the living room. It sounds like he's getting his stuff together, mumbling something about how people are always judging him, too.

"Wait, I'm sorry" I say, and get up. I walk into the living room.

He doesn't look at me, but says, "I'm outta here!"

"Where are you going to go?" I ask.

No answer, just the screen door slamming.

I return to the kitchen.

"He'll be okay, I'm sure," Adam is saying as he rubs

Grandma's shoulders.

Grandma just sits and sobs, hands over her face.

I look out the kitchen window, and watch my uncle walk down a path that passes the outhouse, towards the main road. He doesn't have a car, so he walks, and hitchhikes just about everywhere. And there he goes, off to hitchhike, probably back into town to have some more drinks and get drunk out of his mind again.

"Shannon, why did you have to say those things?" Grandma asks, in between sobs. She lifts her head up now and wipes her tears.

"I couldn't sit and just pretend like everything is okay. I'm still mad at him for almost killing Sarah, even though he didn't do it to me. He never said anything about it. He just thinks we're all supposed to be okay with the fact that he used to beat her," I say and feel like I have said enough, so I leave the room.

A Natural Mural

I walk outside and take a deep breath, swallow down the bulge in my throat. I breathe. I look past the outhouse and past the abandoned crime scene. I watch my uncle's figure slowly shrink, as he walks down an old trail, and gets closer to the main road.

Why did I have to open my mouth? Why didn't I just let him go on and pretend everything is cool? He could've still been here, talking his nonsense. I wonder what makes him so ugly and mean. All these thoughts I think as I stand on the porch and hold onto the short wooden frame, which wraps around the porch. The porch was something he helped his father build, and I suddenly feel guilty for holding onto it.

Jonah steps outside with me, and offers his support. "What you said in there took some guts, and I hope your uncle finds peace," he says, as he stands beside me, and puts his hands on the same short frame I'm holding onto.

"I just had to get it off my chest. I couldn't listen to another word of his nonsense," I say.

I can't remember ever saying anything like that to my uncle. I was always afraid of him more than anything. I respected him a lot more when I was younger and would've never thought to say anything negative to him or about him. But times have changed.

Hearing him talk the way he talked was upsetting. He did say mean things before, mostly to his father, when his father was alive, and he used to get into fights with his cousins. Now I am sure I know why he was always getting into fights...his bad attitude.

"Yeah, I bet. It sounds like he's done a lot of damage," says Jonah.

"He has done damage to a lot of people; hurt peoples' feelings and stuff like that. He's just a mean person. And I don't think I ever realized how mean or how cruel he can be, I mean really realized it, you know?" say, looking into Jonah's blue eyes, which have a hint of green.

Jonah nods in agreement, "Yeah, I know."

"My other uncles were alcoholic, too. Paul was one and I was pretty close to him. He wasn't mean like Anthony, though," I say.

"Is he the one who died?" he asks. He lets his eyes gaze forward, and leans on the frame with his elbows propped.

It is still morning, and the sun is glistening on the land now, warming it up from the cool summer temperatures that covered the land the night before.

"Yeah, that's him...and my other uncle, Tom, is a recovering alcoholic," I say, feeling a sense of relief to talk about my uncles so freely. I keep talking.

"Tom used to fight a lot with Anthony when they got drunk. They'd be best friends one minute, and the next, they were each other's worst enemy. And it was always over something stupid, like who bought the whiskey, and who is supposed to get the last swig," I continue.

I don't know why I am telling this white man all about my family's alcohol problems, but I feel it is the perfect time to let it out. Something about Jonah makes me feel comfortable…already. I don't trust many white people, but Jonah has broken through that barrier. I decide it's not worth trying to analyze why I am spilling all this on him. Instead, I decide it's best to stop now.

"That's crazy," he says.

"So, anything like this happen in your family?" I ask, hoping to change the subject.

"Well, not really. My parents didn't drink, maybe a long time ago my father did, but in his later years, he didn't," he explains.

I admire his confidence when he speaks of his parents.

"Adam drinks every now and then, but I don't think he's anywhere close to what it sounds like your uncles do," he adds.

"Yeah, I doubt it. I know my grandfather drank a lot, too, when he and Grandma moved back from San Francisco," I say.

"Based on what Adam says about your grandfather, it doesn't sound like he was such a bad person when he was drunk," Jonah says.

"Yeah, I suppose he wasn't," I say. I pause for a moment. "He stopped eventually, after a bad car accident left him in pretty bad shape.

"Wow, that's not cool," Jonah says. He now has his back against the wooden frame and he is leaning on it with his elbows jutting backwards. He looks so cool standing there like that—his figure lean and relaxed with white, loose-fitting shorts, and a dark gray, v-neck t-shirt complimenting his look.

"Yeah, tell me about," I say.

I shift my eyes, and gaze out to the horizon. I look towards the main road, for a glimpse of my uncle. He's probably standing out on the road, still waiting for a ride to come along.

Awkwardness moves in as we stand quietly in each other's presence. It becomes too uncomfortable so I excuse myself. I go back inside to find Grandma, sitting in her room, on her bed, with a picture of Anthony in her hand.

It's a picture that was taken while he was in the Navy. Without hesitation, I go to sit next to her and put my arms around her. She doesn't move; she just sits. Her pudgy frame seems frail and her shoulders are soft. I cannot tell if she's crying or just thinking. But I continue to hold her as if she's crying.

After a few moments, with picture still in hand, she squeezes me back. Then she stands, takes a deep breath and walks back into the kitchen, leaving the picture on the bed.

I take the picture in my hand and study it. It is framed with a wooden frame. My uncle is holding up a peace sign. He is dressed in what I call his sailor blues. His hair is cut very, very short. He has a smile on his face and he looks cheerful. I see happiness in his eyes. I wonder when he lost that happiness or if it was ever really there.

I think of asking Adam if he can pick up my uncle at the main road, but dismiss the thought. Instead, I close my eyes and pray silently for my uncle.

The day wears on, with everyone finding their own activities to busy themselves with.

I want to tell Grandma that her son's actions are not her fault, but I figure she already knows that. Instead, I decide it's best to give her some space. She weaves for a couple of hours and then cleans outside for a couple more.

As for the rest of us, we play cards in the kitchen. I teach the Navarros how to play Rummy, because apparently, living in the city has kept them occupied enough and they never learned how to play cards.

Of course, out here, we found and played just about everything under the sun that didn't require money or electricity. As a kid, I rode my bike a lot. And when I got bored with that, I played cards. And when I got bored with that, I played marbles...with rocks. Talk about imagination.

Because the Navarros are new to the game, I don't find it strange that they are hooked after a couple of games. I was hooked the first time I played a card game. The first couple of rounds are practice rounds and all three brothers get the hang of the game eventually. Before the real games begin, I make fun by imitating Grandma. I spit on my fingers and make sputtering noises while I do so before I deal the deck of cards.

Mikah and Jonah look at me like I'm crazy and then both ask, "What are you doing?"

"I'm copying Grandma."

"Is that like a traditional thing?" Jonah asks.

He has a serious look on his face and I can't help but to bust out laughing.

"Of course not!" I exclaim after I get in a good laugh.

Before long, everyone else is copying me and we're

all cracking up. But our enjoyment is short-lived.

Grandma comes into the kitchen and announces, "The second night of the squaw dance is tonight. Who wants to go?"

Everybody gasps and I can tell from their gasps of delight, they are surprised and excited.

Adam smiles at Grandma and he looks back at the rest of us, and says, "Alright…now we're talking."

Of course, Mikah and Jonah are just as eager as Adam to experience a real squaw dance. So we don't turn down the opportunity to tag along. We all take turns using the bathroom for changing clothes and making ourselves presentable.

Amidst all the excitement of preparing to go the dance, I manage to find a lipstick I had received as a gift from Jackie. I had forgotten it was in the side pocket of my purse and when I find it, I decide now is a perfect time to try it out. Once we are in the van, I take the lipstick out of my pocket and use the small mirror from my makeup bag, to watch myself apply a generous layer of lipstick on my bottom lip. And just as my aunt, Jackie had showed me, I rub my upper and lower lips together. The new color on my lips makes me feel beautiful.

As we drive down the bumpy road again, the mood is cheerful. Everyone, including Grandma, has a smile. And the chatter is light. Adam, Mikah and Jonah grill Grandma on squaw dance etiquette and what to expect.

I just sit back and smile. I think about my uncle again. Although I am worried about him, I know he will be okay and I remind myself to not think about what happened earlier.

We pass Sunflower Valley and I admire the flowers once again. They are calm now. Some sway. Others are still. Each one, regardless of its size or the shape of its petals, is beautiful. They are calm.

The next area we drive through on the way to the dance has shrubbery covering each sides of the road, and a little bit to the left of us, is the wooded area, which runs alongside the river. It mostly has tamarack and cottonwood trees, which are good for carving, at least, for the local doll carvers.

After we pass the wooded area, we drive a little farther down the washboard road near the Begays' village, and make a left at a turn in the road. We take this road towards the river, and the evening sun glistens from the west. We cross the riverbed, which is very dry. There is some driftwood on the riverbed and the sand is thick so the van drives slowly and with a little extra power to get through it.

"The river was overflowing this past spring. It was way up high," Grandma says, as she uses her hands to show that the height of the river was five or maybe six feet high.

"Wow, how cool," Mikah comments as he delightfully observes the surroundings.

"Yeah, it was way up here, you couldn't even drive through it," she adds, raising her hand a little higher.

Knowing Grandma, she is exaggerating and the river probably barely reached three or four feet. Nonetheless, I remain quiet and pretend to be amazed.

Once we reach the other side of the river and are back on high ground, I am more excited about the dance. I'm gonna' be rich! Okay, maybe not rich. About five dollars richer, at the most. All I can think of is dancing as long as possible, and making a good impression on the drunken men at the dance. Wait a minute, those men probably can't tell their behinds from their heads, so it probably doesn't matter what kind of impression I make. I tell myself I'll stick to dancing and having a good time.

It's been several years since I've been to a squaw dance. As a little girl, I had been to a couple of them, and now I look forward to the experience again. My motivation for going to a dance when I was little was the money part and as far as I knew, things hadn't changed. As I come to this realization, I am disappointed in myself for thinking only of money and not the genuine reason behind such a dance. Shame on me. I remind myself that I am going to celebrate the well-being of another person and I wipe the lipstick from my face with my bare fingers.

We get farther away from the river, and we finally slow down. Grandma is directing Adam to a house, which sits on a slightly rounded hill to our right. I had been slouched down a little, so I sit up straight to see exactly where we are.

We are closer to the Painted Desert hills than I ever remember being and the sight of them is a beautiful one. They look to be about two miles away, but I know they are farther than that for sure, at least twenty miles. And in this beautiful evening sky, they look majestic and magical almost, with their different colors blending and separating, line after line of colored sand. I had always seen these hills from a distance, from the other side of the river, and I never really paid attention to the detail before. But at this moment, I can't help but pay attention and absorb their beauty.

After admiring the natural landscape for several more

moments, we arrive at the house where Grandma is supposed to get directions. It's a green, shabby, square house, which looks to be at least fifty years old. It looks like someone tried to paint the window borders white, but never finished the job. One window has a nice, white border while the other window has a faded green one. The door, however, is finished in white and it sits crooked on the door hinges.

There are some kids who could probably take on a gang of pit bulls, crouching on one side of the house. They look to be fixing what could be a bike. They don't wave at us. They just stare at us with their beady eyes and bushy hair for a few seconds. Then they get back to working on their contraption.

After Grandma knocks at the door a couple of times, it slowly creaks open and an elderly woman with a slight hunch in her back greets Grandma. A few words are exchanged, probably in Navajo. And Grandma disappears into the house, with the lady.

I notice the Navarros are swooning over the same view I admired a few minutes ago, the Painted Desert hills. Mikah gets out of the van with a disposable camera, and begins snapping away like a tourist.

I smile to myself, and explain, "Those hills are called the Painted Desert hills."

"Wow, what a scenery," Mikah says. Jonah and Adam drool over the sight, too.

I reach for Grandma's binoculars and hand them to Adam.

"Here, have a closer look," I say.

You'da thought these guys were going to explode with delight right here; their eyes are filled with amusement as they are hypnotized by true beauty.

"I wonder how the different colors in the hills came to be so colorful?" Jonah asks.

"Well, I do know one thing; a man didn't make them," I say, being sarcastic.

"Yeah, we got that part, smarty pants," Adam jokingly says as he lowers the binoculars and hands them to Mikah.

"For real, though, I believe the layers of sand were colored by water," I explain.

"That makes sense," Mikah says.

I smile again, and acknowledge Grandma who is walking back toward the van.

When she gets within hearing distance, she says, "The Squaw Dance is down the road from here. We better get over there before it gets dark; they are serving food now."

With that, we are all climbing back into the van again.

Before Adam maneuvers the van out of the dirt driveway, I attempt to make a connection with the kids fixing their contraption by waving at them, only to be disappointed. They just glare at us as we pull away.

A First Squaw Dance

We get to our destination a few minutes later. The land is flat all around and I can see land for miles. The sun is setting and there are a few Chevrolet and Ford pickup trucks as well as several dust-covered cars parked in a circle. A fire is being built by a few, strapping, young men in the middle of the circle.

As the last glimmer of sunlight illuminates the land, I can see more pickup trucks and cars trickling in. The sand is very fine on this side of the river, and there are a lot more bushes; sagebrush, yucca, and some other big, bushy bushes. As the vehicles move in, the dust clouds follow them, and then settle, as they park. The glow from the fire increases in strength as the crowd expands. The evening air is cool, and dry—a very pleasant condition after an extremely warm day.

When we are all out of the van, Grandma spots a lady, whom I presume is running the show or has something to do with running the show and we go over to greet her.

"Yá'át'ééh," (Hello) Grandma says. She draws out

the word, like she hasn't seen the lady in a long time.

The lady does the same and they begin updating one another on their family members' situations, then on who's having the ceremony and what's wrong with them, and most importantly, where we can find the food.

She points us over in the direction of a makeshift shed; four poles with some kind of a net on top, and tree leaves on top of the net, making the roof. Just to the right of that is a small fire, and a grill plate on top of four separate, upright bricks. That would be the equivalent of a grill in the white man's world.

After she is all caught up on the latest gossip, Grandma and I make our way over to the shed where Grandma picks up a paper plate from a table under the shed, and greets the cooking lady.

Apparently, she knows her, too because she says 'hello' again with a long drawn out voice, and they hug. The cooking lady offers Grandma some grilled mutton and tsii'kah bah (bread cooked over ashes). Without thinking twice, Grandma loads a couple pieces of mutton and one thick piece of tsii'kah bah onto a paper plate, which is about to crumble beneath the weight of her food.

Grandma instructs me to grab a plate also. So I do. I pile on enough food to share with the Navarro brothers, and we head back to the van.

The Navarro brothers have turned the van around so the back is facing the circle and they have opened the back doors of the van. They've even gone as far as spreading a blanket out in the back. I am impressed with their ability to adapt and I can only guess they backed up the van because it's what everyone else is doing.

Everybody except Grandma sits on the blanket; she goes off to greet more people she knows. The rest of us prepare to feast. I explain what we're eating; grilled mutton and bread which is cooked over ashes.

I take my piece of mutton and wrap it with the thick bread. Everybody else copies me. I want to laugh because I still can't believe all of this is happening. I can't believe there are three white guys at a squaw dance eating mutton with tsii'kah bah. It's all too crazy and I just want to laugh at the idea. But I don't. I simply enjoy the food and the moment.

For the next few minutes, we eat with little talk. There is a comment here and there about how Grandma seems to know everybody so far. There are no complaints from the guys about the food, so I figure it must be okay.

When we finish eating, I say, "Make sure you wipe the mutton grease off your faces." And I laugh.

Although their faces aren't greasy, they wipe anyway and don't seem to get my joke. Now if I was with a bunch of Navajo guys, their faces would have for sure been greasy, because they would've had the mutton all up in their faces, tearing the poor meat apart, and not caring about the mutton grease rubbing off on their faces.

"Now what?" Mikah asks, after taking a sip of some soda he brought from Grandma's house. He has a gleam in his eyes.

"Well, now, you wait," I say.

"Wait for what?" Jonah asks.

"For someone to ask you to dance," I calmly explain.

"Can't we just go ask for a dance?" Adam asks.

"No, you can't. That's not the protocol. You wait to

be asked," I say.

Disappointment covers Adam's face and I jokingly rub my eyes and pretend like I'm crying to show my pity for him.

He crosses his legs, looks at the watch on his hand and sighs.

"Yes, patience is a virtue," I say and smile at him.

To pass the time, I tell the brothers my few Squaw Dance stories; actually, I only have two. I tell them about a time when I tripped on a clump of bushes out on "the dance floor", and the man I was dancing with was so drunk, he couldn't even hold himself up. So I tripped and when I tripped, I pulled him downwards, and he fell right on top of me. And once he was down, he was down. And I was at the bottom, getting squished by him.

We all laugh at the story.

The other story is about how I was too young to count my money and got into an argument with a drunken patron because I didn't think he was paying me enough for a dance. Imagine that—a little girl trying to tell a drunken man he didn't give her enough money and the two of us, trying to count and re-count the change; the blind counting to the blind.

We laugh more.

"Dude, that chic over there is checking you out," says Mikah, as he nudges Jonah.

He is looking across the circle, at a girl directly across from us, who is sitting on the tailgate of a truck, her legs dangling and swinging. She has long hair and I can't make out her face too well in the dark, but she looks decent.

"No way, she's looking at the dancers," Jonah says, and shifts his eyes back to the few people dancing.

The flames from the fire are jumping high, trying to touch the roof of the sky; the fire continues to grow as men put more wood on the fire. The beat from the drums is mellow, and the dancers' feet pound the dirt to the beat of the drums. Slowly, they make the circle, and more dancers join in. Mostly young girls and older men in cowboy hats and cowboy boots make up the dancing crowd.

Oh, how the epitome of the American Indian has transformed; from war bonnets and moccasins to cowboy hats and pointy boots. What a transition. A transition I am almost ashamed of, but which almost every Indian has welcomed with open arms. My grandfather had the same style as a lot of men on the dance floor and Grandma loved it when he "dressed up"—cowboy hat, tight Wranglers, and shiny cowboy boots. All he was missing were the spurs and a horse.

I laugh to myself at the thought and turn my attention back to the girl across from us. She is gone and when my eyes search the area for her, I notice she is walking towards us. She looks pretty; long, dark hair; big, black or dark brown eyes; a creamy, caramel-colored skin, with pink, narrow lips. And young, I should add. Maybe the same age as myself.

I smile at her and say, "Hello."

She returns the salutation with "Yá'át'ééh."

Now that I know I'm dealing with a traditional Navajo girl, I say, "Aoó, Yá'át'ééh." The translation would be "Yes, Hello."

She approaches Mikah. She stands right in front of him, and asks him to dance with her, in English, of course.

He looks at me, as if I'm supposed to answer for him.

"Go," I say, shooing him away.

"Don't I need to have some money?" he asks, still looking at me.

"Yeah, don't you have some change?" I ask. I don't wait for a response. "Didn't you come prepared?"

"Ummm, no. I only have large bills," he says.

"You moron!" Jonah chimes in. "Here! Here's some change," he says, digging into his pockets, and offering a handful of coins to his brother.

Adam, who is leaning on the back of the van with his legs crossed simply snickers at his brothers.

"Well, I didn't know...I didn't think I would dance. I thought I was just coming to watch," Mikah says, defensively, as he calmly massages his goatee with his forefinger and thumb.

"Well, you thought wrong, brother," Adam says and pats his brother on the back.

The poor girl is witnessing all this and smiles shyly the whole time.

Mikah takes the change and holds it out to the girl, who lets out a giggle.

"Not now!" I exclaim. "Wait until you're finished with the dance."

He shrugs, puts the money in his pocket and escorts the girl to the dirt dance floor, his wavy, dusty blonde hair loosely bouncing as he walks.

"Wooo!" Adam cheers, as his brother leads the girl to the circle.

Mikah must've been watching the other peoples' moves because when they get to the circle, it doesn't take long for him to pick up the rhythm and move right along with the line. The girl slowly bounces up and down alongside him and her long hair moves with her body.

Jonah claps and cheers. His blonde locks bounce gently as he does so. Heads turn in our direction to see what the ruckus is about. This doesn't make him reconsider his celebratory claps and cheers. He keeps up with them for a few more moments.

Grandma returns to the van, and asks, "Why aren't you guys out there?"

"We're not as popular, apparently," Adam replies.

"We're not as rich either," says Jonah, with a laugh.

More laughter fills the air. Grandma doesn't get the joke at first, but we fill her in.

"Does anybody else need money?" she sarcastically asks, as she opens her purse.

A resounding "NO!" is the answer from both guys.

We laugh more.

Another girl approaches us, and I recognize her. She lives on the other side of the river, from the same area we're from. Though she lives close-by, she isn't related to our family. She is from another family who borrowed land from my grandfather similar to the Begays, except their name is Tsosie. She is a couple years older than myself, and wears her hair shoulder-length with no bangs. She is tall and thin, and pretty. The thing I always liked about her most was her smile. She has such straight teeth.

Grandma recognizes her, and says, "Hello" to her in Navajo.

The girl says "Hello" back to Grandma and nods her head at me as if to say 'What's up?'

I nod back and smile.

Grandma asks her about her grandmother, Alice. The

girl, Angie, points to where her grandmother's truck is and says, "She's over there."

"Did you come to ask for a dance, too?" asks Grandma.

"Yes…can you dance with me?" Angie asks, looking directly at Jonah.

Jonah puts down the can of Pepsi he's drinking, and shows his gratitude by bowing.

"I would love to," he says, as he takes Angie's hand and leads her to the circle.

I am certain Angie is on the verge of fainting when he takes her hand and leads her to the dance floor.

"Shannon, you better get to work," Grandma says. "All the old, rich men are being taken."

I smile and tell her, "I'm going on the prowl as soon as I get some fuel in me," as I take another sip of soda.

Just as I am walking away to start my partner selection process, Adam receives a dance request, and he leaves the van as well, with an older, plain-clothes woman who looks like she could be a teacher.

I make my way around the circle, and spot a middle-aged man, with his wife; they are selling some food out the back of their truck. I can tell this because they have an ice box, and a clear container of foil-wrapped items. I figure they must be burritos from their shapes.

I walk up to the couple and ask the woman if I can dance with her husband.

She's quite rude, and says, "Ask him!" in a mean, nasal, rezzed-out tone.

"Aoó (Yes)," the man says as he hops off the tail gate of his truck and leads me to the dirt dance floor.

We walk out to the circle and join the group of people dancing. The Navarro men are still dancing; Jonah with a different girl than before, Adam and Mikah right behind him with their partners.

The flames from the fire are still licking at the night air, higher than before. We move around the fire, and the heat from the fire is warming the left side of my body as I go around the fire in a circle. I move my feet and bounce to the beat. I look for Grandma and I see her, sitting on the bumper of the van, with the back doors still open. She is smiling and drinking her soda.

The singers and drummer are sitting under the makeshift shed, huddled in a small circle, and pumping out the music. They appear to be very enjoying themselves, and the music is flowing. It fills my ears, and pushes out the sound of fire crackling, embers sparking, and people laughing. I let the music fill my ears. All is good, and I smile.

I see a face I recognize in the crowd of people as I am dancing along. Where have I seen this face before? It's a man, wearing an army-green jacket; it absolutely looks like something the Army would issue. He is waving a can of beer in the air, and talking loudly to another man I don't recognize. They are standing about twenty feet away, in between a couple of pickup trucks, not in plain view, but in view. The other man has long hair, and is holding a beer can of his own.

As my dancing partner, the old, married man who smells like Ben-Gay and I make our way, stepping to the beat, around the fire, we get close enough to the two men, and I can hear them.

It sounds like an argument is brewing or has already started. Their voices are high-pitched, and the men are both waving their arms at each other. I finally remember who the man in the army-green jacket is. It's the man with the scar on his face, the man we saw at Lady With Clumsy Hands's house.

"You punk!" the scar-faced man is saying loudly to the other man.

"You guys are the ones who messed up! You were supposed to get rid of it!" the other man yells back. He turns slightly, and I can see part of his face. He looks familiar and I try to place his face. It doesn't take long to remember him. It's Kyle.

"That stupid friend of yours didn't have to cut me!" Kyle yells, waving his finger at the scar-faced man's.

"If you guys had finished what you started…"

I try to slow my steps down to listen more, but the music and the sound of people having a good time drowns out their voices and they trail off. I cannot make out what else they are saying. By the time we get back on the other side of the fire, the men are gone. They disappeared into the darkness or into the crowd.

I look back towards the van for Grandma, and I don't see her. I search the crowd and I can see that she is dancing with a younger looking man who's wearing a tall cowboy hat a few rows behind me.

After a couple more dances with a couple more men, I hear Grandma calling me. She calls the Navarro brothers also and one by one, we stroll back to the van. I collect my earnings from the drunk, middle-aged, chubby cowboy I am dancing with and jiggle the rest of the money in my pocket. It feels like it's about three or four dollars in coins.

When I'm back at the van, my stomach is growling

and I am tempted to go back to the mean lady selling burritos. Instead, I decide to avoid the mean lady and settle for a can of Pepsi.

"That was fun," says Adam, as he stands near the van's rear bumper, speaking mostly to Grandma.

"Yeah, I'm broke, but I had fun, too" says Mikah, wiping his forehead.

I remember the scene of the two men arguing earlier, but decide not to mention it. I would not want to dampen the mood. Besides, I doubt it is of any significance and figure no one will really care. We had enough drama already, and don't need anymore.

I look out at the crowd and can see the night is still young, and people are still making circles around the fire as their feet stamp the ground in tune with the beat of the drums.

"The squaw dance is just like I remember it as a little girl," I say.

"I think I got a little carried away myself," Adam says, with a small chuckle. He is trying to dust his shoes off as he is leaning against the door on the driver's side of the van.

"That rez dirt does not come off so easily," I say. "I hope that isn't your favorite pair of shoes."

"Well, then, these shoes will have to go into my hall of fame with rez dirt," he says. "I'll keep them for memories of my first squaw dance."

Butterflies In My Stomach

We all climb back into the van, Adam starts it up, and we drive back down the bumpy road, to the main dirt road.

Everybody tells their stories. Grandma tells us she danced with one guy, who didn't even pay her. She says she didn't complain and knows he is poor anyway.

According to Adam's account, he danced with five young ladies, and one older lady.

If this was a dance contest for who can dance with the most women, Mikah would have taken the title home. He danced with eight girls and says they were fighting over him and he had to make the girls take turns. He even danced with a couple of them twice.

And Jonah, well poor Jonah, he danced with two girls…one for only a couple of minutes, and the other, Angie, for the rest of the time.

"Woah, she was that good?" Adam asks.

"No! Not like that," Jonah refutes. "Well, yes, she is a good dancer," he adds.

"Yeah, we know you like her…A LOT", Mikah adds.

"She is a pretty girl and she didn't want to stop dancing with me," Jonah explains.

As I listen to them go back and forth, I feel my body being overcome by a new feeling I had not felt before, a feeling of aching in my chest, and butterflies in my stomach. I immediately realize I don't like the idea of Jonah being scooped up by another girl. I feel as if I have gotten closer to him in the past couple of days and I hope in that moment that he does not direct the new attention he's been giving me to someone else.

For a few moments, I sit and think to myself. *I can't believe I'm feeling jealous.* I ignore my feelings for the moment and turn my attention back to the chat.

"So…how much do you pay for dancing that long with one girl?" Mikah sarcastically asks.

Adam and Grandma sneak out a giggle.

"Ummm, five dollars…that's all I had left after I paid that other girl," Jonah says.

"What?! That's it?" Mikah asks. "I paid each girl I danced with two dollars, and I thought that was a bargain," he continues.

"Yes, I told you guys…that's all I had on me," Jonah says, in a defensive tone.

"I thought you only had large bills," I add.

"I thought I did…apparently, I left them at home, and had to bum money off Grandma and that's all she had," Jonah replies.

"You're such a moron," Mikah says.

"Well, at least he paid her something," Grandma says, coming to his aid, "Some of these guys are cheap…you might get fifty cents after you've been dancing for ten rounds and your feet are aching," she adds.

"Sounds like someone got stung before," Mikah says, mockingly.

"What's that? Who got stung? Were there mosquitoes out there?" Grandma asks. Of course, Grandma, not being hip with the latest terminology, doesn't know what Mikah is talking about.

"That means it sounds like that's happened to you before," I explain to Grandma.

"Ohhh. Yes, yes, that has happened to me before," she says.

We all laugh at her.

She adds, "I sure didn't get as lucky as the girls on the dance floor tonight."

"Yeah, me either," I say, taking out the money in my pocket. I count it. "Two dollars and seventy five cents," I say out loud. "Hmm, that is enough for...for an eyebrow pencil or a magazine, or a tall Starbucks Frappuccino, if I was in L.A." I jokingly add.

There is laughter again from everyone but Grandma.

"Starbucks? You drink coffee?" Jonah asks.

"Yes, I do," I proudly say. "I don't drink it regularly like some of my friends do, but I indulge every so often, when I have the money."

"I love Starbucks. I used to get a double shot latte with two sugars in the raw every morning on my way to class," he says.

"Wow, that's a lot of words for an order of coffee," I say, sarcastically.

"Yep, but I have to say all that to get exactly what I

want," Jonah explains.

"Where do you go to school?" I ask him.

"Berkeley, where my father used to work," he replies, with a sense of pride in his voice.

"Nice, I hear that's a good school," I say. Truthfully, the only thing I really know is that my school counselor received a degree from there.

"What did you study?" I ask.

"I'm studying the law. I want to become a lawyer," he replies. He is sitting next to me and he has on a look that says he is confident and proud of himself. I admire his look.

"Oh," I say, with nothing more to add. I turn away and look out at the darkness passing by.

We get to the river bottom again and cautiously make our way across the riverbed. The windows are rolled down in the front, and the back windows are propped open. I can feel the night breeze in the back seat and it feels wonderful. The rest of the ride home is pleasant, and Grandma makes the time go by faster by sharing another one of her famous recounts from the past.

She talks about how she used to herd sheep to the river to drink, and how one day, when she was getting ready to do just that, she decided to steal a can of Skoal from her grandfather.

She goes on to tell us that one of her sisters helped her herd sheep that day. When they got to the river, they let the sheep drink the muddy waters, while they sat back in the wooded area, and each took a pinch of Skoal, just as they had watched their grandfather do many times. They each put the pinches in their mouths, and waited and waited.

"So, what happened?" Adam asks.

She replies, "It felt like the world started spinning slowly, and it got really hot."

There is a burst of laughter from Adam and Mikah.

"So I stood up thinking it would help me feel better. Instead, I felt sick in my stomach so I spit the Skoal out, but that didn't stop me from feeling dizzy."

The story goes on. She tried to sit for a while, thinking it would help. But her head wouldn't stop spinning. Her sister was just as bad, and soon began crying. They drank water from their water jug. It didn't help. She finally dug a hole in the sand, and told her sister to put her head in the cool, moist sand.

"What?!" Adam remarks.

"How does that help?" Mikah asks.

"Shhh, let me finish the story," Grandma says.

Everybody gets quiet again.

We let her finish her story. She explains that the dirt cooled her head and helped stopped the spinning. I can't fathom how that worked, so I don't ask any questions. I just listen.

She and her sister both kept their heads in the sand for a while, and drank all the water from the water jug they had brought from home. After maybe two hours or so had passed, they were finally ready to head home, still uneasy. Once they got home, their grandfather asked them if they liked the Skoal. And they both started crying, knowing he already caught them, and thinking he would whip them. But he just laughed at them.

"That's hilarious," Adam says.

"So, you didn't get in any trouble?" Jonah asks.

"No, we learned our lesson, though. To this day, I

have never touched Skoal again," Grandma replies.

We are close to home.

The night air is still cool when we climb out of the van and drag our tired bodies back into the house.

I wash my face; brush my teeth and head on to bed, after saying 'Good night' to the Navarros, who are preparing for bed as well.

After everyone is finished using the bathroom, Grandma takes a quick sponge-bath and then comes to bed. I am not asleep yet when she comes to bed. She smells like Dove. I sniff the air to get a good whiff of her smell. And then I close my eyes.

A Fair Trade

When I wake, Grandma is already up, of course. She is sweeping the floors with her broke-down broom, and she has all the windows open. I rub my eyes and pull the covers closer to my chin to keep the cool summer air out. I remember my grandfather's idea of people who sleep later than sunrise. He never hesitated to call such people lazy. So I jump out of the bed. He would say 'they should've been cats instead of humans,' as if we get a choice during our creation.

I decide it's a good day for a run, although in Grandpa's eyes, I would've been a late-starter for a run. I had already missed the sunrise. I don't let this notion stop me, though. I take out an old pair of sneakers from my bag, do a few stretches I learned from Grandpa, and off I go.

When I return from my run, I heat enough water to take a full bath. I say 'Good morning' to everyone. Mikah and Jonah are in the kitchen, Adam is outside meddling under the hood of the van and Grandma is digging through her yarn, and sitting in front of her loom.

The bath is wonderful. The extremely warm water feels good, as always. And I allow myself to relax for a few moments. I quickly lather myself with some soap and rinse it off.

After my skin is refreshed and I am dressed, I head out to my favorite spot, the front porch. Grandma is still weaving in her room. Adam is building a makeshift ramp outside—the kind that mechanics use to crawl under their cars. Mikah is nowhere to be seen. And Jonah, my newest favorite person, joins me on the porch.

It is a calm morning, compared to most of our other mornings so far. Jonah and I sit and make comments about Adam's work. Mikah soon shows himself and begins helping Adam.

Curiously, I ask Jonah, "So what exactly does your oldest brother do? I mean for work."

He replies, after thinking about my question for a moment, "Well, officially, he's a financial analyst for a securities firm."

Not knowing what that means, I try my best to play it off like I know what it means.

I nod my head and say, "Ahh."

A few moments pass.

"Financial analyst sounds like something a person would do to make a lot of money, so why does he drive an old, rickety van?" I ask.

"Well, he doesn't live like a financial analyst. He believes in spending on needs only," Jonah explains, with a roll of his eyes, to show he disagrees with his brother's spending style.

"And you have a problem with that?" I ask, seriously confused by his comment.

"Well, he has a lot of money to play with, but he doesn't play, if you know what I mean," he says, with a sly smile on his face.

"What an interesting way to live," I say.

I admire Adam. I can now look at him with a different perspective. And I appreciate him more. I don't share any of my thoughts with Jonah. I simply stand on the porch, with my hands hanging over the porch frame, watching Adam work on his rickety, old van.

I decide to check on Grandma, and see how far along she is with her weaving, so I go back into the house while Jonah goes to help his brothers.

I sit down on a small, worn cushion next to Grandma and watch her pound the loom with what I call her fork. It's the fork-looking tool she uses to pound the yarn into the loom which is actually called a weaving comb or "bééh eh tsidi" in Navajo. Thump. Thump. Thump. She takes her strand of yarn and uses her fore finger to guide the yarn through the loom. She leans back to double-check her measurements, and then pounds the yarn into place.

A sophisticated design is emerging and I can see the patterns of different colored yarn working together seamlessly. They compliment each other. I stand and take a good, long look at her work.

I praise her work by saying, "It is coming along very good, Grandma."

She just nods and makes a grunting noise; a noise that says she agrees.

I watch until I feel as if I could fall asleep—like I

could just lie on her lap while she weaves just as I did when I was little girl. Instead of giving into the powers of relaxation, I retreat to the porch again.

Jonah is sitting on the porch again but rises and goes inside shortly after I sit.

I go to the van and try to figure out what Adam and Mikah are working on. I can't make heads or tails of anything. So I go back to the porch and watch them take turns bending over into the hood of the van, with their blonde-haired heads, bobbing up and down.

Jonah, who has been inside for the last few minutes, comes back outside to announce that Grandma has some bathing water heated.

"If anyone wants to take a bath, now is the time to do it," he says.

Mikah jumps at his chance to take a bath and quickly heads inside. Though a bath is definitely what he needs, I doubt he will enjoy it too much. I picture him washing himself in the wash tub Grandma keeps in the bathroom...the large, round circular, metal wash tub which although large, probably fits only one of his legs. Or maybe Grandma boiled enough water for him to fill the bathtub and he'll be sprawled out in the tub. I laugh to myself at the idea.

"I wish we had a shower," I say out loudly to Adam, who remains under the hood. I sound almost apologetic for Mikah having to take a bath in a wash tub, or in the bath tub, whatever he's using.

Adam takes his head out of under the hood, and walks over to me, wiping his hands, which look to be smeared with oil.

"I was thinking I could look at Grandma's plumbing

225

and see if I can fix some things," he says. "When I was in high school, I had a summer job doing some plumbing work part-time," he explains further.

"I know a little bit about plumbing, too," Jonah says. He has taken a seat back on the porch and is clipping his fingernails.

"If you call fixing a toilet knowing a little bit about plumbing, yeah, I'm sure," Adam says, and smiles at me with a mocking look.

I know he is poking fun at his brother, so I smile back shyly as if to concur with the joke. Adam takes a seat on a chair which is on the other side of Jonah.

I smile at Jonah as well, hoping it would convey my apology for going along with the joke.

"I'll have you know I've done more than fix a toilet, smarty pants," Jonah retorts, standing up.

"Alrighty, we'll just have to see what you know," Adam says, taunting his brother again.

"Yeah, we will. I'll even escort you to the hardware store and show you what to pick out," Jonah says, matter-of-factly.

I enjoy this good-humored banter. It's different from the joking I do with my friends. What my friends might find humorous are things like laughing about other people, making up yo' mama joke, and using the latest buzz words to make a joke seem funnier—all of which seem childish now that I think about it.

Before Adam can make a comeback, Grandma comes out to the porch and interrupts the flow. She stretches and asks, "So what are you guys up to?"

After a couple stretches and yawns, she transforms

and appears to be relaxed and cheerful at the same time. She unties the bun in her hair and runs her fingers through her hair. She dons a flowing skirt, a pink blouse and leather strap sandals I bought for her from Payless.

I fill her in on the latest development by saying, "Well, it sounds like you might have a working shower soon."

"Really?" she asks, and looks around at all of us, probably wondering if I'm joking or not.

"Yes, really," I say. "Adam and Jonah here volunteered themselves to fix your plumbing problems. I'm sure it will be a relief to have water in the bathroom again."

"Really?" she asks again.

"Yes, really," Adam says. He is standing at the edge of the porch and leaning back on the corner post with his arms folded casually in front of him. He looks at Grandma with a cheery smile which reveals most of his pearly whites. He has covered most of his blonde-haired head with a blue bandana.

"Wow. That would be so nice. I forgot what a real shower is like," Grandma says with a smile as she twists her hair back up into a bun.

In the past, whenever she wanted to take a shower, she'd go to a Laundromat in town. As odd as it may sound, they actually have a shower there. It's a great one stop shop...do your laundry and take a shower. I can assume that when the Laundromat first opened, there were a slew of Navajos without running water and whomever the owner was at that time, put two and two together. Of course, since then, only a handful of Navajos without running water remain and it's not such a high-demand service. But for two whole dollars, Grandma treats herself to one every now and again.

Mikah comes back outside, with some fresh clothes on, looking good in some khakis and a red t-shirt.

"Oh man, it feels so good to be clean again," he says proudly.

"Don't rub it in," Adam says.

I look at Grandma and I can see she has her thinking look on.

I look back at Jonah, who is rubbing his chest and shoulders, and says, "Man, I need a shower or bath…can someone just dump some water on me?"

Then as if to conceive a new idea, Grandma excitedly says, "We can go into town, to the Laundromat!"

"Oh no. Not the Laundromat," I say. I know it's a god-send for her, but I can just see the Navarros' looks of disgust when they see the place.

"Why? What's wrong with the Laundromat?" Grandma asks, obviously offended.

"Well, the shower is old and run-down. And the Laundromat is always swarming with a ton of Navajos. I'm sure it will look very out of the ordinary for three white guys to be taking a shower there," I say.

Adam, Jonah and Mikah all look at each other with puzzled looks.

"We can boil a big barrel of water or go to the Laundromat," Grandma says, now more offended than before.

Of course, in her mind, those were the only options. I, on the other hand, don't think the Navarros should be submitted to such fate. I mean it's a Laundromat for crying out loud. What if someone I know is there and sees our guests, three white guys, having to use the Laundromat shower…how would that look? I can't even begin to think what that would look like.

"Well, you guys can always rent a room," I say, trying to find a way out of making them go to the Laundromat.

"Oh yes," Grandma says, as if I just came up with the best idea in the world. And I did. Had I not said anything, she would've never thought of it.

"Okay, that sounds better," Jonah says.

"No. I am not going to try to escape to luxury," Adam says.

I am confused by his words and so is everybody else, or at least that's what it seems by their puzzled looks.

"Huh?" I ask him.

"What do you mean?" Jonah asks him.

Adam takes a step down from the porch. And then he says, "I am not going to rent a room, just to take a shower. If other people out here have to suffer by not having a nice shower, I am going to do just that."

"What are you talking about?" I ask in disbelief.

"Woah, woah, Adam, just because we're here, it doesn't mean you have to Survivor on us," Mikah says.

"I always wondered what it was like to live on a reservation, and now I'm here, so I'm going to experience it," Adam says.

Grandma has been listening to this little discussion all along, just standing quietly next to me. Then out of the blue, she speaks up.

"I'm tired of taking baths and showering at the Laundromat, so we are going to town and taking a shower in a hotel room," she firmly says. The cheer, excitement and calmness are gone from her face. She has a serious look, as if she's had enough of the banter.

Everybody bursts out with laughter.

"Okay, it's settled," Adam says. "I will give into my city slicker side and get a room," he continues.

We all laugh again.

That was it. No more discussion, no more bantering, no more arguing. It was settled.

I laugh inside one more time about how Grandma has the power to put everything in perspective. I knew she was sick of that Laundromat shower.

"Before you came outside, we were just talking about helping Grandma remodel her house while we are here," Adam says, updating Mikah of the discussion from earlier.

"Cool, sign me up," Mikah says.

"Where am I going to get money for the materials?" Grandma asks, with a worried look on her face.

"Oh, don't worry about. It'll be our payment for staying here," Adam says.

How amazing. What a generous offer. I am stumped, and I smile at Grandma, who has a huge smile across her face.

"Wow, really? Are you sure it's not a problem? I don't want you to feel like you have to do something like that just for staying here," she says, knowing very well she'd like it.

"Oh yeah, no problem...think of it as a fair trade," Adam says.

Nothing but Speculation

Just as the conversation is winding down, we notice a car driving up the road. It's a white SUV.

"I wonder what they want this time," Grandma says, nervously.

"I'm kinda' glad to see them, I want to mention those two creepy guys from the Begays," I say.

"And what are you going to tell them? That you saw a bulge in a man's pants?" Jonah asks, with a faint laugh.

I giggle at the thought and say, "Yeah, that's what I will tell him."

"Really? And you think that will fly?" Jonah asks, this time with a more serious tone.

"The man did tell us to look for any guns or anyone suspicious," I say defensively.

"Well, it is a good idea," Adam says.

As we all take up space on the porch, some of us standing and a couple sitting, the white car pulls up. The FBI detective who had paid us a visit a few days earlier is in the driver's seat and Anthony is in the passenger seat.

"Howdy, everyone," says Detective Yazzie in a relaxed, yet flat tone, as he gets out of his car.

We all say our hellos.

"What is my son doing in your car?" asks Grandma, just as curious as me. She steps down from the porch and walks toward Detective Yazzie.

"Well, I picked him up right outside of town. He was telling me about a gentleman in town who has been claiming to be the murderer," the detective explains.

"Who?" Grandma asks, looking surprised. The wrinkles on her forehead deepen and shift for just a few seconds as she raises her eyebrows.

"Garrett Benally," my uncle answers, as he reluctantly gets out of the car.

"What?! But he's not in his right mind," Grandma declares.

"Garrett Benally from across the road? How?" I ask, just as confused as Grandma.

"What do you mean 'not in his right mind'?" Detective Yazzie curiously asks. He's wearing the same shades he wore the other day and removes them from his face to expose a stern, confused look. He slides the shades into his shirt pocket and then puts his hands on his hips, and gives his attention to Grandma.

"He's retarded," Grandma says.

"He's mentally challenged," I say, hoping to remind Grandma that 'retarded' is too offensive of a word.

She doesn't bother to correct her statement. Instead, she comments, "Gee, Garrett, huh?"

"He couldn't hurt a bug even if he wanted to," I say.

"Maybe he was attacked and was just defending himself."

"Well, I'm just telling you guys what I heard," Anthony states, as he walks towards us. His left eye is slightly bruised and puffy with a light purplish color to the skin around it.

"No jumping to conclusions…I still have to interview the man," the detective says.

"He's still a boy actually, probably no more than seventeen or eighteen," I say.

"I'll be heading over to his house after this. But I also came to see if there are any new developments on you guys' end," the detective states as he pulls out a small tablet and pen from his back pocket.

Grandma rushes to her son's side and asks, "What happened to your eye?" She raises her hand to his eye.

Anthony blocks her hand from touching his eye and walks right past her.

"You need to put some ice on that," Grandma says, not at all thwarted by her son's actions.

She turns her attention to the slender Navajo detective and says, "He doesn't know what he's talking about, he probably had DTs. Garrett can't do something like that."

"What is DT?" Mikah asks.

Grandma doesn't respond.

Instead, Detective Yazzie responds and says, "DT stands for delirium tremens, and hallucination is one of the symptoms…it happens to people who are hard alcoholics."

I nod at his explanation, along with the Navarros.

"I am just kidding," Grandma says as she opens the screen door.

She invites the FBI detective inside. He takes her

offer and I'm sure it's because he'd rather be inside than burning up under the hot sun.

I follow Grandma and Detective Yazzie into the house. Jonah, Mikah, and Adam fall in line as well. Adam pulls out a chair and sits down at the table next to Anthony, who is holding a plastic Ziploc bag full of ice over his left eye. The rest of us stand around and listen while Grandma recounts the visit to the Lady With Clumsy Hands's house.

When she finishes her recount of what happened that day including Anthony's threats and violent behavior, I tell my version, specifically the part about the bulge in the shape of a gun hidden in the scarred man's waist line.

The detective jots the notes down and says, "I'll stop by there on my way out and see what I can find."

"I've never seen those two guys that were sitting there when we stopped by," Grandma says. She is brewing a fresh pot of coffee on the stove, for the young detective, I'm sure.

"Has anyone else seen any other guns, small handguns?" the detective asks, as he looks up from his tablet, and around the room.

Everybody shakes their heads no.

"Oh, by the way, I have your gun in my car. The sheriff's office said it came back with no flags, so you're good to go. I did take the prints off, though."

Adam just nods his head, and takes a sip of the coffee he's drinking. I can see he could care less about his gun. I'm sure he had nothing to worry about from the beginning, and I'm sure he's more interested in figuring out who the murderer is.

Detective Yazzie shifts his attention to me, nods, and

asks, "Is there anything you'd like to share? You look anxious, like you have something to say."

Grandma busies herself with pouring fresh coffee for the detective, and then brings out a box of donuts she apparently had stashed away in the cupboard, which she sets in the middle of the table.

"I saw the man with the scar from the Yazzie's and that Kyle guy arguing at the Squaw Dance last night. They seemed pretty upset with each other," I say, unsure of whether or not the information is helpful. I look around the table to see if anybody else has anymore comments.

"Kyle?" my uncle asks, with a puzzled look.

Nobody says anything. They all just look at me.

I casually answer, "Yes, your friend, Kyle...the guy who was here with you the other day."

"Hmm," my uncle says under his breath.

"Kyle Who?" Detective Yazzie asks.

"Kyle Chischillie," Anthony answers.

With this, Detective Yazzie props both of his elbows on the table and says, "Good, this is all good information. I will give Kyle a visit and hopefully, he will have some valuable information as well. I know his family pretty well."

The detective shifts in his chair and looks back at my uncle and taps his pen on his notepad, where he has scribbled down Kyle's full name, the words 'squaw dance argument' and a few more scribbles which I can't make out.

"I bet that other guy is Johnny...Johnny Begay," my uncle says, now with an I-know-for-sure look on his face.

Grandma asks, "Johnny Begay from the Begays' down the hill?"

My uncle sets the makeshift ice pack Grandma gave

him earlier on the table. "Those two hang out together all the time, they're always drinking together, and they ended up in jail one time together...for raping some girl, but then the girl dropped the charges, so they didn't go to prison," he says, confirming my creepy notions about the scar-faced man.

"I knew he was shady," I say out loud, referring to the scar-faced man.

"He's shady alright. He's been to prison before, too. But I think that was like ten years ago," my uncle adds.

"Which guy are we talking about?" asks Detective Yazzie.

"Johnny Begay," Anthony replies.

"How do you know so much about him?" I ask, curiously.

He hesitates and then says, "Well, because he talks to me. I see him on the street, and we were in jail together a couple of times, and one time, we shared a cell," he says. "He's always yapping, talking about what he did, almost bragging, you know," my uncle continues, with a crooked smile.

"What is so funny about that?" asks Detective Yazzie, obviously distracted by the crooked smile on my uncle's face.

"Nothing, he just brags a lot and he's a punk, so it would be funny if he got caught for murder," my uncle replies, and wipes the grin from his face.

"What a mean thing to say," I quickly comment.

"Well, I'll check out this Garrett guy, pay the Begays a visit and question Kyle for now, but stay on the lookout. I don't like to put my eggs in one basket, if you know what I mean."

"Oh boy, I wasn't counting on all this when we

decided to come here," Mikah says out of nowhere.

"We weren't counting on using an out-house either," Adam says jokingly. He smiles and reveals his pearly whites.

There is some nervous laughter.

Jonah offers only a generous smile, as he sits at the other side of the table, a ways back, with his legs lazily spread out, and his arms behind his head.

"I'd like to interview some people from the Squaw Dance," the detective says. "So if you guys can remember some names, I'll jot them down and start asking around."

As I sit and try not to think of that ugly smirk on my uncle's face, I let my mind wander to thoughts of the Squaw Dance. Of course, I don't remember any names, except for Angie's so I give her last name, and I point in the direction her grandmother lives.

Adam, Mikah, and Jonah name off the girls they danced with, well, the ones they remembered.

Grandma names a lot more people, names and house directions at that.

While Grandma soaks up the spotlight for several minutes, I get up from the table, go into the adjacent living room and sit down on the couch. I can still hear the conversation and see everyone in the kitchen.

Detective Yazzie quickly writes each name Grandma reads off, adding to his list of notes. His small tablet looks pretty full by now, pages and pages of notes. Good for him, it looks like he is doing his job. Then he gets a beep on his walkie-talkie/radio device, and goes out to his car.

As for the people still gathered in the kitchen, they speculate about what could've happened. For all the inside information my uncle knows about the suspects, you would think he would have figured out who the murderer was, but he doesn't have any good input, just off-the-wall theories.

"Who was murdered again?" my uncle asks, with a quizzical look on his face. I suppose he wasn't quite himself the other day when Grandma told him so I don't find it surprising that he is still behind with the details.

"Remember, Eddie Yazzie...from Dilcon, I already told you," Grandma says in a frustrated tone.

"Ohhhh yes, I know him," Anthony says out loud.

"We know," I say even louder than him. "You told us that the other day."

"I guess I did," he says proudly. Then he takes on a thinking look and continues, "But I've never seen Eddie hanging out with Kyle and his buddies."

"You mean Kyle and *your* buddies?" I ask.

Everybody looks in my direction.

"They're not all my buddies. I just hang out with Kyle sometimes," Anthony replies.

"So how do you think they could be linked?" Adam asks my uncle.

My uncles pauses, as if he's trying to remember something.

Then as if to remember all of a sudden, he waves his index finger in the air and says, "If I remember correctly, Eddie was messing around with this girl, Liz or Lynn, and I know she's related to the Kyle."

"I doubt that's motive for murder," Adam says.

"Yeah, I guess it's not," Anthony states.

I'm confused by now, so I don't throw anymore questions my uncle's way.

I just observe him. He looks scraggly still. I didn't

notice this before, but his face looks whiter than before. He seems lighter. Maybe that is what happens when you're in jail for a couple of months. It makes sense, though—he's been out of the sunlight and able to shower every day. I suppose it's possible to wash the brown away.

As embarrassed as I am of my uncle and his alcohol addiction, I realize he is just a lost soul, but still human and still my uncle.

Adam and Grandma re-fill their coffee cups, Jonah goes to the outhouse and comes back, and the detective rejoins us.

"So where did we leave off?" Detective Yazzie asks, once he's reseated himself at the table.

Grandma and Adam fill him in on the latest clues we have pieced together or didn't piece together.

"All of this information is good," Detective Yazzie says. He thumps on his notepad after he's done writing down a few notes. Then he looks up at everyone and nods.

"If it wasn't for this guy right here, we'd still be at square one," Adam says, shrugging his elbows towards Anthony.

More speculation around the murder continues, but it's just that, speculation and I'm bored with it. Blah, blah, blah…yes, they were probably all drunks in town…blah, blah, blah, they're all buddies somehow or linked together somehow by a girl whose name my uncle doesn't remember.

"If you ask me, I say Johnny whatever his name is pretty suspicious," I suggest.

"Yeah, that's what it sounds like. But we don't want to jump to conclusions," says Adam.

"There was more than one set of foot tracks out in

that dirt," Jonah states.

"True, true," I say, and everybody nods in agreement.

As Detective Yazzie stands, as if to dismiss himself from the table, he adds, "By the way, I double-checked those tire tracks and the same tracks we found around the murder scene head towards the river, and back to the main road where I lost track of them."

"Which way do they go to get to the river?" Grandma asks.

"It looks like they pass by one of those houses over there," Detective Yazzie says, pointing out the north window, towards the houses that dot the riverside.

"Which one?" Grandma asks, standing up to see which house the detective could be pointing at.

"Come outside, I'll draw a map for you," the detective suggests.

He and Grandma go outside, to his car I presume.

Once Detective Yazzie and Grandma are gone, Adam announces, "Well, we're going into town to start looking for some supplies." He drinks the last of his coffee and sets his empty coffee cup down on the table.

Mikah and Jonah, who were both leaning against the wall stand up, as if they were just told they can stop holding the wall up and begin moving about.

"What supplies?" my uncle asks, as he rises from his chair.

"We're going to help your mom remodel this house a little bit," Mikah replies with a sense of pride in his voice.

"Don't forget our showers, too," I add.

"Ah yes, we are also going to bathe, at a hotel room, thanks to Shannon," Mikah says.

"Oh…can I help with the remodeling?" my uncle asks. "Maybe I can stick around and help out," he adds.

If you ask me, he was probably feeling a little guilty for his behavior the other day.

"Sure, sure, the more help, the better," Adam replies.

A Trip Down Memory Lane

It's not long before we are all packed into the van and bouncing along down the dirt road again.

"So whose house was the FBI guy talking about?" I ask Grandma, who is sitting in the front passenger seat. She looks comfortable in some jean shorts, a blue t-shirt, and white tennis shoes.

"Ruthie's house," she replies.

"Maybe it's a different truck with the same tire tracks," I say.

"Maybe," she says in a dull tone, which shows her boredom with the subject.

"Let's talk about something else," I suggest, hoping this will liven up Grandma again.

Anthony reads this as his queue to start up with his stories from the road again.

Instead of listening to my uncle's jokes and everyone else's laughter in the van, I tune everything out and pop one of my older CDs into my player and hit the forward button on my player until I get to *Baby Baby* by Ashanti. I slide my headphones on and escape to a land of hip hop tunes, of melody, of harmony, and where Ashanti's sweet, womanly voice surrounds me and I can feel her pain, her love, and her music.

Once we get to our destination, I wake from my nap and stretch like a cat that just woke up from a nap under the warm sun.

Best Western is the grandest hotel in town, so I am not surprised it is the one Grandma chooses to go to. We all climb out of the van and wait near the registration desk while Adam pays for two rooms.

Although I don't feel I desperately need a shower, I indulge in one anyway. After my shower, I sit and watch MTV on the television. Grandma, then Anthony showers after me. Adam and Jonah use the room next door to shower and change. After watching a couple of heavy metal videos, I am instantly bored so I step out to the courtyard of the hotel.

I spot Jonah, who apparently had first dibs on the shower in the room next door, and is already showered. He is playing the archaic game of Pac-Man near the hotel lobby. I don't see Mikah or Adam anywhere and I figure one must be in the shower and who knows where the other one is. I walk over to Jonah. As I get closer to him, he throws his hands up in the air and I figure this is a sign of defeat.

Knowing he probably needs a break from the machine, I ask, "Do you want to go across the street to Dairy Queen?"

"Sure," he says.

The thought of eating some cold, Dairy Queen ice cream on a hot summer day has to be better than fretting over

243

Pac-Man. So we walk across the empty street. Since we're the only customers, our order is filled right away. Two chocolate dipped cones.

We both take a seat on one of the old, ceramic benches outside and after a few licks of his ice cream, Jonah asks, "So, can we talk about your mother again?"

Not knowing how to respond, I look across the street at the hotel, and pause for a moment before answering. I knew this subject was going to come back up again.

"Yeah, I suppose," I say hesitantly.

I can see Mikah come outside the hotel across the street. He walks over to the van, and stuffs some clothes into a bag in the back. He looks to be freshly-showered. Not that he needed one—maybe the bath at the house wasn't good enough after all.

"Do you mind if I ask how she died?" he asks.

"Yeah, I do," I say and wait a few seconds before I crack a smile. He smiles when I smile. His eyes are blue and mesmerizing.

"Oh no, if you don't want to tell me, that's cool...I'm cool with that," he says, almost apologetically, but in a casual manner.

"I don't mind," I say, turning to look back at the orange, VW van parked across the street.

Mikah notices us and waves.

I wave back. Jonah simply holds up his hand, and I giggle as I imagine him saying, 'How' like an Injun with a war bonnet.

"What is so funny?" he asks me, with a smile on his face and eagerness in his voice, as if he desperately wants to be let in on the humor.

"Oh nothing, I am just imagining you saying 'how'," I explain, as I put up my hand to show the Hollywood version of an Injun greeting.

"Ha ha, very funny. I thought that type of stuff would be offensive to you, Miss Native American," he says, sarcastically.

"Okay, okay, no more fun. I'll get to the story about my mother," I say, quickly changing the mood to a more serious one.

"Yes, good idea," Jonah calmly says.

And then I start my story of my mother's death, or at least, how I remember it.

"Well, on that day she asked me to go home with her, she never made it home. Instead she went into town, and met up with some friends, and partied the night away," I say, remembering the day.

I shift my butt on the ceramic bench, and take another lick of my ice cream.

"What a horrible and unforgettable night that turned out to be. The next day, her body was found dumped on the side of a road outside of town, just up the road," I say, pointing to the north of where we are sitting.

There is a gasp from Jonah. "I thought she died in a car accident," he says, confused.

I don't look at him. I just look at the hotel across the street and lick my ice cream again.

"No, but that's what Grandma tells most people, at least people who don't know the real story."

"So, did they ever find out exactly what she died from?"

"Nobody knows exactly what happened to her that

245

night, but the police found evidence of foul play and told my Grandma someone had raped my mother and then killed her," I say, looking down at my ice cream cone.

"I am so sorry for your loss," he says and then puts his hand on my shoulder.

"Yeah, I've gotten used to not having her around," I say. I blink away the tears forming in my eyes and I just look across the street. I don't want him to see my eyes.

"I'm sorry I had to ruin our ice cream trip," he says.

His hand remains on my shoulder.

And then he speaks again. "But you look relieved, like you've wanted to tell that story."

I say nothing. I breathe calmly, careful not to stir up anymore emotions deep inside which might push the tears out.

I do feel relieved and I say, "Thanks...for listening."

I don't look at him although I want to.

He takes his hand off my shoulder.

I take another lick of my cone, and I make my best 'I'm okay' smile. I have to shade my eyes a little when I finally look at him because the sun is so bright.

"So, did they ever find the people who did that to her?" he asks.

"Nope, of course not. According to the police officer, who came to our house a couple weeks after they found her, 'they had a couple of leads, but weren't able to come up with any solid evidence.'"

For the next few minutes, we don't talk. We just lick our ice cream and crunch away on the cones.

When we return to the hotel, bellies satisfied, Grandma informs us that Anthony decided to go on another drinking binge, and left a few minutes after he showered. As upset as she is about this, she manages to smile and say, "The good thing is I'm clean again."

The wrinkles which form around her eyes remind me of her tender age and I suddenly feel sympathy for her again.

Adam, looking like a new man, with damp, clean hair and a fresh set of clothes rejoins us shortly after I seat myself comfortably on one of the queen-size beds, with my head propped against the headboard.

"Maybe shopping for supplies is a bit much for today, don't you think, Grandma?" Adam asks, as he glides across the room and stands next to Grandma, whom sits on the bed opposite the one I'm sitting on.

Cheerfully, she answers, "Yeah, let's get something to eat instead."

So, instead of going to shop for supplies, we settle for a couple of taco value packs from Taco Bell. We call it a day in town and agree to head home.

On the way home, I find myself wondering what San Francisco is like. I imagine the city the way Grandma describes it; rainy, cold, and noisy. I picture the Navarros' apartment; a small, yet cozy place. I picture the trolleys I've seen in the Rice-A-Roni commercials.

A sudden jerk of the van forces me to snap out of my daydream.

"Woah!" yells Grandma.

I sit up from my slouch in the backseat, and it appears we swerved to avoid hitting a cow, after coming around a sharp bend at the rocky mountain area. I relax, and Adam speeds back up, after having slowed down to a crawl, and shaken everyone up with his swerve.

"I didn't see it. I didn't expect a cow like that,"

explains Adam, in defense.

"You have to go really slow around that curb," advises Grandma.

"Whew!" Adam says, with a sense of relief.

"One time, me and Phillip were coming around there, and he was going too fast, and we almost ran off the road, Grandma says.

Jonah and I look out the back window at the cow, which slowly crosses the road, as if he had right of way to begin with.

"There was another time when we hit a cow, too...up here near the cattle guard. That's another dangerous place," she says, adding validity to her advice to slow down.

And on we go, while Grandma begins her story-telling again. She captures the young mens' minds, as they sit and listen.

The story is about how another truck Grandma owned broke down when she was with all six of her kids. They ended up hitchhiking into town but couldn't seem to get a ride because there were so many of them. So, they formed a single line and pretended to be one person as a truck slowly approached. The guy driving was known to have bad vision and hearing, yet he still drove. According to Grandma, he drove so slowly, one of her sons, she couldn't remember which one, was able to latch onto the tailgate as the truck slowly rolled past. I'm sure he did that out of desperation. The man, unaware of what my uncle had just done, kept going. Because the man was going so slowly, everyone else was able to run after the truck and latch on as well. Of course, when they arrived in town, they couldn't simply bang on the window or the side of the truck to signal their stop as was usually done. So when the man stopped at the first stop light, they quickly climbed out. And the poor man never knew they rode with him. How the man was never in a car accident is nothing but a miracle...or maybe he was and just kept on going.

We all laugh at the story. I cherish the moment and am glad to see everyone is happy.

It is not long before we are zooming past Sunflower Valley again. Once again, I admire the beauty of the flowers and am grateful to see such natural beauty. Their brightness livens the entire area. I smile and say out loudly, "Don't these flowers look beautiful?"

"Yes, yes, they do," Grandma replies from the front passenger seat.

"Why is this area so different from all the other areas around here? I mean, there is no other place with so many flowers," Mikah states.

"We call it a gift from our Mother Earth," Grandma says.

"And a beautiful gift it is," I say.

With that, I enjoy the rest of the ride home, with a smile across my face.

Soon, we arrive at home again. By this time, the sun is setting and a slight breeze is coming from the west.

Adam helps Grandma out of the van once we pull to a stop again.

"Hey, I think I see something on the door," Grandma says, as she points to the front door.

Mikah walks to the door and returns, with a note in his hand.

It's a note from the FBI detective.

'Stopped by. Will be
back tomorrow morning.'
– Det. James Yazzie.

"What else do they need from us?" Grandma frustratingly asks.

"I'm sure they need more help," I say.

"Whatever it is, I'm sure we'll find out in the morning," Adam says.

I slowly follow Grandma into the house and then into her room.

"Can I practice weaving?" I ask, as I take a seat on her pillow, in front of her loom.

"It's going to be dark soon and it's not the best time to weave," Grandma reminds me.

"Ah, man, I need to learn more weaving. But with all this crazy stuff going on, I am worried I will not learn much this summer," I whine.

"Be patient, Shannon," Grandma calmly says, as she sits on the edge of her bed, and takes her shoes off.

"Okay, I will be patient," I say, as I sit on the pillow, cross-legged, watching her slide on her house slippers.

"Well, shall we get started on dinner?" she asks.

"Yes," I say, as I stand.

"Come help me stand up again. My legs and back are aching," she says, as she reaches around and attempts to rub her lower back.

I help her up from her bed and follow her into the kitchen.

Grandma turns on her old radio with the wire hanger

for an antenna and tunes it to a local radio station, which is streaming country music. I recognize the song as one from George Strait, titled 'Friends in Low Places'.

Grandma hums along to the song while we go about cooking our next meal.

Once dinner is prepared, and the table is set, I call the Navarro men from their rooms. One by one, they slowly join us at the table.

There isn't much conversation at dinner. Jonah mentions his relief from answering questions about the investigation. Adam makes a comment about how relieved he is about not having to take a bath in Grandma's round bathtub. There is no more talk of the investigation.

The evening is calm and quiet.

After dinner, I practice my cleansing ritual. Then I slip into Grandma's bed. I don't fall asleep right away. Instead, I lie with my hands behind my head and consider how alcohol has affected my family. It has been significant in keeping us off track and messing up most of my family members' lives. And to this day, I despise the people who make beer and wines. They are probably some rich, white people who sit behind big, wooden desks and live in elaborate homes, and sip on their drinks, the drinks they make, which have almost no affect on them.

I sigh, knowing there is nothing I can do to change things.

That night, I don't dream. I sleep.

Dramariffic is the Word

The birds are chirping outside, and I can see that dawn is on the horizon, the sun is about to make its glorious appearance. I close my eyes and lie still. I don't want to wake, but I know if I let myself lie here, I will dose off again, and that would make me lazy. So I roll off Grandma's bed.

Breakfast is savory and filling, as usual. The talk around the table is about how the kitchen will look, and what Adam needs to buy. I am excited about the outcome, but not the talks.

I hear the sound of an engine, a car coming. So I get up and walk into the living room. The front door is open, with the screen door closed, and I look out to see a truck driving down the road towards the house. It's coming fast. So I call out Grandma's name.

"Graaandma!" I yell and walk back to the kitchen as fast as I could.

"What? What?" she says. She is obviously annoyed. I'm sure she'd like to continue dreaming about how her kitchen will look rather than deal with another visitor.

"Somebody's coming," I say, excitedly.

"Who is it?" she says, wiping her hands with a paper towel.

"I don't know!" I exclaim. "I just looked out the window and here comes a truck, driving down the road towards us."

"It's probably just that Navajo guy, Detective Yazzie," she says and reluctantly walks over to the screen door.

"It doesn't look like him," I say.

"Hmmm, I can't tell who that is," she observantly says. She opens the screen door and steps out to the front porch to get a better look.

Everyone else remains seated at the table; Adam still talking about what he needs to do with the house and how he's going to do it, Jonah and Mikah listening contently and probably imagining what Adam is talking about.

The truck comes to a stop near the house. A middle-aged Navajo lady with a long, white skirt, blue blouse and a ponytail gets out. In the truck, a girl is sitting in the passenger side. She looks as if she's been crying. Her head is lowered and she is covering her face slightly.

I shade my eyes; it looks like the girl from the squaw dance, the one who danced with Jonah almost all night, Angie.

"Yá'át'ééh," the lady says, as she comes up to the door.

Grandma has propped the screen door open, and is standing in the doorway. She is shading her eyes, too.

Before the lady can start talking, I already know it has something to do with Jonah.

253

"Yá'át'ééh," Grandma says in return.

"Who are you?" Grandma asks in Navajo.

"Mary Tsosie…from across the river…Joe Tsosie's daughter," the lady says in English.

"Oh, yes, hello. What can I do for you?" Grandma asks in Navajo.

"My daughter here," the lady says, pointing to the girl in the truck, "she came home the other night with some big hickies on her neck and I want to talk to the man she was dancing with at the Squaw Dance."

"Who? Jonah?" Grandma retorts in English, obviously shocked by the implication.

"She won't tell me his name. One of the white guys who was with you," the lady says.

From her looks, I can tell she is stressed. Her hair appears matted and her eyes are puffy.

Jonah, Adam, and Mikah emerge from the house, probably to see what the ruckus is about.

I can see that Jonah notices and recognizes Angie after a glance in her direction.

"Hey, what's going on?" he asks in a low voice.

I look back and whisper, "Shhh, It's about you."

He is in some shorts, a t-shirt, and some cute manly, house slippers. I didn't see his house slippers at the kitchen table, but now that I see them, I have to take a double look because I don't see him as a house slipper kind of guy.

The lady looks at Mikah and Jonah, as if she's trying to figure out which is the guy she came to confront. She is still standing near her truck and Grandma is standing near the porch. The lady takes a step forward as if to get a closer look at the guys.

"What do they want?" Jonah asks, in a whisper.

"That girl you were dancing with the other night at the Squaw Dance...she's here with her mother," I say quietly.

Grandma is telling the woman she doesn't believe her, while I fill Jonah in on the discussion so far.

"No, Jonah didn't give her those hickeys. He was with us all night, and I watched them dance!" exclaims Grandma.

"They could have snuck off when I wasn't looking," the lady says angrily.

At that moment, I feel like bursting out and telling the lady she should watch her daughter more carefully. But I don't. I let Grandma handle the situation.

"Well, I can tell you right now, that didn't happen. I watched Jonah, both of his brothers, and my granddaughter the whole time," Grandma says, raising her voice.

I know she is thinking the same thing I'm thinking, about the lady watching her daughter more carefully.

Before the lady can interject, she continues with her rant. "And none of them snuck off. We all sat together and left together. Your daughter wasn't even around when we were leaving," she says...not taking a breath.

I can see she is furious by now.

How dare this lady come zooming up to our house, and start mouthing off at Grandma. I want to say something in Grandma's and Jonah's defense, but I figure Grandma has it under control. And that she does.

She tells the lady to ask her daughter who else she can blame, because it wasn't Jonah. And before she comes up with another accusation, she needs to basically check herself. That was it.

That's all it takes, and the lady walks back to her truck, gets in, and is about to drive off.

We hear her yelling at her daughter. "You little wench! What do you think you're going to do? Sleep around with guys?!"

Then smack. She slaps her!

The poor girl cringes and puts her face in her hands. She begins sobbing up a storm.

"Is all that necessary?" I ask, feeling sorry for the girl.

Just then, Grandma darts off towards the truck, and yells at the lady, "Hey! Don't hit her!"

I take a step down from the porch. Jonah briskly walks right past me, and towards the truck, after Grandma.

The lady looks up at him, says, "You! You are the one!"

"You don't have to hit her," he says in his loud, but calm manly voice. His hands are folded across his chest and he looks authoritative. He is still in his shorts and t-shirt and doesn't seem to mind the morning breeze coming from the west.

The girl looks up, and wipes her tears. Her eyes brighten when she sees him.

The lady still looks very upset. She opens the door of her truck again, and gets back out.

"You can't tell me what to do with my daughter!" she says to Grandma and Jonah, in a high-pitched tone.

"You don't have to hit her. You are supposed to watch your kids. You're the one who needs a slap in the face!" Grandma exclaims.

I can see the lady is still upset. Her skirt is blowing in the breeze. She looks at her daughter, and then back at

Grandma and Jonah.

"You're going to tell me what happened. You better not be pregnant!" she yells to her daughter, who has her head down again.

I am sure the girl is very embarrassed by now. And I feel sorry for her.

The lady gets back in her truck, and they back up with a jerk. The lady speeds off, with her F-150 pickup leaving a little cloud of dust in our face.

"Geez!" I say out loud. I look at Grandma and Jonah.

Mikah adds, "Geez is right, you'd a thought we committed a crime."

I laugh and say, "Dramariffic" under my breath. That is what my friends back in Los Angeles would call the whole incident.

"What a way to start the day," Adam says, nodding his head to show his disapproval.

Grandma and Mikah go back inside and I can hear Grandma adding her two cents to the comment pile, by saying, "What a crazy lady."

Adam and Jonah go back inside as well.

I stay on the porch and watch the dust cloud disappear.

When I go back into the house, I hear Jonah say, "Wow, I didn't know I was going to cause all that." He is sitting on the couch in the living room with his head in his hands, holding his blonde locks in place.

"Yeah, me neither," I say, sitting down next to him.

Grandma fixes another pot of coffee in the kitchen, and comments, "That lady needs to keep an eye on her daughter. That's the problem. If she wasn't so busy dancing around and carrying on at the Squaw Dance, she might've seen what happened to her daughter."

She comes back into the living room and sits on the other side of Jonah.

Adam is in the bathroom, washing up. I can hear him splashing the water around in the little wash pan. Mikah is in the guest room, doing who knows what.

Grandma reassures Jonah that what just happened was not his fault.

After a few moments of sitting with his head in his hands, he sits up straight and agrees he isn't responsible for what happened to the girl.

Adam returns from the bathroom, and announces, "I will be going back into town to buy some supplies."

Mikah hollers from the room, "I'll go with you!"

"Supplies for what?" I ask.

"Supplies for my project, you know, for the house," he says.

I look at Jonah and Grandma, as if to ask them if they're going, too.

Both look at me with blank stares and then at each other.

"I'm gonna' stay," Grandma says hesitantly.

I can see the weariness in Grandma's eyes. I know she must be tired from all the events over the past couple of days. I don't want to leave her by herself. So out of consideration, I offer to stay with her.

"I'll stay, too," I say.

Adam smiles at me and says, "Good idea."

I smile back and wipe a dangling strand of hair from my face.

Adam says, "Okay, well, we shouldn't be long. Jonah, can you stay and watch over these ladies?"

Jonah remains seated next to Grandma and accepts his honorable duty.

Before leaving, Mikah asks Grandma, "Don't you want to make sure we pick out the right things?"

"I trust you guys. Besides you guys are paying for it. I don't want to be picky," she says, and laughs a little. That's just like Grandma. She has always reminded me to be grateful for anything I receive and not to ask for anything I'm not entitled to.

"Okay, if you say so," Mikah says.

Say What?

　　While Adam and Mikah prepare for their short trip into town, Grandma continues talking. "You never know what will happen around here, especially with the squaw dances, with all those men around...old, horny men," she says.

　　I gasp and laugh at the same time. How Grandma got onto such a subject, I don't know.

　　She isn't disrupted by my gasp, and adds, "And then, there's the young guys, they're even worse than the old ones. They can't keep their weiners in their pants for more than a minute."

　　"Oh my gosh, Grandma!" I exclaim and cover my mouth. I am shocked that I am hearing this from an old, Navajo lady, who was always telling me to watch my mouth.

　　"Wow...Grandma," Jonah says. "Don't count me in on that crowd," he says, and smiles. "I know how to control myself."

　　"Yes, yes, I know, you're not like that," Grandma

says. "But the guys around here are like that, most of them at least. Some of them are decent, but not many," she goes on.

She gets up from the couch, pours herself a cup of coffee, and walks out to the front porch to see Adam and Mikah off. I follow her out to the porch and so does Jonah.

As we watch the van slowly pull away from the house, I decide now is probably a good time to talk about my experience with the horny boys from boarding school. As soon as the van is a few feet away from the house, we wave several times at Adam and Mikah and go back inside.

When we are back inside and I'm seated on the couch again, I say, "Speaking of horny boys, when I went to the boarding school, this one boy tried to make me touch his thing."

"What!?" Grandma gasps. "Shannon! You never told me that!" she exclaims, freaking out and almost dropping her cup of coffee.

"Well, I didn't know how to tell you. I was little then," I say. I really didn't want to tell her, because I thought she'd think I was misbehaving somehow, and although my reasoning was not the best, I really believed I was at fault somehow.

I remember the day this event happened just like it was yesterday.

Jonah looks at me with a surprised look on his face and says, "Do tell us more."

And so I start to tell about that oh-so nasty day. "It was a Friday and I was waiting to be picked up after school," I say.

I take a deep breath, knowing this is probably the type of story most people would want to hear. But I go on.

"I was sitting in the living room at the dorm and he came over and sat by me. This was when our dorm was mixed and I imagine the administrator figured we weren't at the age of curiosity. We were watching TV, He-Man was on," I continue.

I don't look at Grandma or Jonah. I just look straight ahead and try not to laugh about feeling so silly.

"And this boy started talking to me...And then he started scooting closer to me, and he was making me laugh. So, I'm laughing away, and he got really close to me and then, he started tickling me," I continue.

Jonah lets out a small giggle and Grandma is smiling when I look at her. It's as if she's anticipating the end of the story, but already knows the outcome.

"Nobody was around. The dorm-aides were all busy checking out students, and running around after other kids. It was just the two of us sitting at the TV. The couch we were sitting on was facing the TV, and it was facing away from the rest of the room. So only our heads were showing. Anyway, I got a cushion and I put it in between us, and I told him to stop tickling me," I say.

Jonah and Grandma are listening contently, waiting patiently for me to get to the part about the touching of his thing.

Grandma takes a sip of her coffee.

"And then he started putting his hand under the cushion, and tickling me again," I continue with the story. I'm getting embarrassed now, just telling the story. I smile, and remember the moment again.

"And then all of a sudden, he grabbed my hand under the cushion, and he whispered in my ear, 'Touch my private part.'"

Grandma gasps and says, "What!? That little horn dog."

There is a burst of laughter from Jonah and he almost falls to the floor. He steadies himself before falling off the couch and places his hands over his belly, to show that the laughter is hurting his stomach.

"So what did you do?" asks Grandma.

"I pulled my hands away, and got up from the couch," I go on, trying to be serious. "Then I walked away from the TV section, and found some other girls to hang out with."

"Oh my," Grandma says.

"Yeah, it was crazy, but I guess that's normal...to be a horn-dog at that age," I say, and shrug. I really didn't know whether or not that was really normal.

"I don't think so, it's not normal," Grandma quickly says, in a serious, flat tone.

"I figure boys start feeling their urges in their pre-teens and that kind of behavior is normal somehow," I say.

"No, that's really young...you said you were how old?" Jonah asks, after catching his breath.

"I must've been about 6...I think I was in the first or second grade," I say.

"Yes, that is definitely too young," Jonah says.

"See, I told you...these guys out here are horny little dogs," Grandma says, now certain of her accusation.

"Well, I guess. I'm sure all the guys aren't like that," Jonah says. "I know I wasn't doing that at that age," he adds.

"I would have slapped that little boy right then and there, and then I would have told on him," Grandma says.

"Oh yeah? Would you have thrown some salt and pepper in his eyes, too?" I ask jokingly. I am referring to a time when she once told me to do that if I ever get into a fight. I laugh at the thought. I remember laughing at it then, too.

"What?" Grandma asks.

I remind her of her advice. And we all laugh. Jonah is really cracking up by now. He's holding his stomach.

"Like who carries around salt and pepper with them all the time?" Jonah asks, laughing and barely making out the sentence.

Grandma is laughing, too.

"And who has time to shake out the salt and pepper while someone's beating you up?" I say, trying to control myself.

We all laugh more, and Grandma says, "Well, I must've thought it was a good idea at the time."

"A good idea, if you want to get beat up," I say. I finally gain control again. Jonah is still halfway bent over, still holding his stomach.

"Oh, that's hilarious," Jonah says, straightening his body, and letting go of his stomach. "That is the funniest thing I've heard for fight advice," he says, in between breaths.

After Grandma and Jonah get a good laugh, Grandma retreats to her bedroom and I can hear her pounding at her loom after several moments.

Jonah busies himself with straightening the guest room, while I clean the rest of the house. He helps me by sweeping the living room and taking out the trash. He asks Grandma for instruction on how to burn the trash. She simply tells him to pour some lighter fluid in the metal trash can several yards from the house, and then light the trash on fire. As bizarre and dangerous as this may sound to him, he does just as she says.

It's not long before Jonah and I are outside taking a rest on the porch when Grandma comes outside to instruct Jonah on cutting some branches from the tree. According to her, the tree branches are getting too long. So he does as he's told while she and I watch.

We soon turn our attention to the hum of another engine. It is a white SUV, bouncing up the road towards us. When it pulls to a stop, Detective Yazzie and another gentleman with long hair, tight jeans that do nothing to hide his belly overhang, and a white-collared shirt get out.

"Yá'át'ééh," they say in unison, as they approach the big, elm tree.

Grandma meets them halfway between their truck and the tree. She shakes their hands.

"We stopped by to see if we can talk to your son," Detective Yazzie says, lifting his shades, and propping them on his head. "I brought another detective from the FBI along with me this time."

Grandma shades her eyes with her right hand, as she nods at both of them.

"I'm new to the case, I'm Detective Chavez," the man with long hair explains. His face is oval, and when he talks, his neck muscles move as if they are being strained.

"We think your son can give us more information on this case," Detective Yazzie says, standing with his hands on his hips.

"Okay, he's not here right now," Grandma explains. "Do you want to come in for some coffee?"

The two men look at each other. Detective Yazzie

nods at his cohort and they follow Grandma.

Jonah and I follow the procession into the house. We sit on the couch in the living room while Grandma leads the two men into the kitchen.

"Sit, sit," Grandma instructs the men.

Detective Yazzie slowly sets his shades on the table, and relaxes in the wooden chair. Detective Chavez props his elbows on the table, and looks to be ready to get down to business.

"Anthony left us yesterday, he's probably in town somewhere," Grandma says, as she pours coffee from a pot on the stove.

"Well, it's our understanding that he knows a couple of the suspects and we'd like to question him further about them," Detective Chavez explains.

Detective Yazzie asks if he can wash his hands, and Grandma directs him to the wash pan in the bathroom.

"Yeah, he was here, telling us about a man named Johnny Begay and Garrett from across the road," Grandma says as she seats herself next to Detectibe Chavez.

"Garrett isn't a suspect anymore," Detective Chavez says. As he talks, I notice that his jawline is a bit crooked and it makes his mouth look crooked as well. He has what I call an Indian nose, a bulgy and round nose.

Jonah and I look at each other with raised eyebrows.

"I knew it," I whisper.

Just then, Detective Yazzie returns from the bathroom and makes an interesting comment. "The gun we ran tests on came back positive and is the one that was used in the murder."

"Which gun was that?" Jonah asks.

"The one we picked up from just down the road," Detective Chavez explains, as he looks in our direction.

"Where was this?" Grandma asks, looking confused.

"Down by the river, it washed up a few miles down the river," the detective explains.

"So, the one that Johnny Begay had wasn't the one?" I ask.

"No, but we are still trying to get some prints off that gun. Of course, we don't know if the one he gave us is the same one you saw," Detective Chavez comments.

"But now that we found the matching gun, it doesn't matter what we find on the one you led us to," Detective Yazzie says.

Grandma grunts a little and makes a noise that sounds like, "Heh."

The conversation is interrupted by the sound of another engine. So Jonah and I go to the door, to see who it is.

It is the orange van, bouncing up the road towards us.

"Here they come," Grandma says, from the kitchen.

"I guess she's psychic," Jonah whispers.

I giggle.

"She can tell who's coming from a mile away, without looking to see who it is," I explain.

"I heard that," Grandma hollers from the kitchen.

There is a trail of dust behind the van as it lurches up the road towards us.

The van pulls to a stop, and Adam gets out first. Then Mikah climbs out and there's one more person, Anthony.

Oh great. I am soon relieved to find that he is not

drunk this time.

They start unloading the back of the van right away.

I notice that Anthony is looking much, much better than before he left. With a new haircut and a set of new clothes on from who knows where, I think he's a new person.

When Mikah gets out of the van, he has a bagful of stuff—soda, chips, dip, and coffee. He is also carrying a Wal-Mart bag and a Cellular One bag.

"Is that a cell phone?" I ask, curiously, knowing that Cellular One is the only local cell service carrier.

"Grandma, we got you a surprise!" Mikah says excitedly as he opens the bag, and takes out a cell phone. He hands it to Grandma.

"Wow! A cell phone?" she says, sounding surprised, yet confused.

Grandma takes the phone into the house and we all follow. Everybody comes inside, Anthony and Adam dusting their hands off. We all watch as Grandma opens up the package and looks at the phone, admiring it for a moment, still looking confused.

"It comes with a service plan for a whole year," Mikah says, as he hands her a piece of paper, which looks like a receipt.

She is still surprised, and says, "Thank you guys. Wow, this is nice."

"Adam bought it…he thinks it's best to have one, especially since all this crazy stuff is going on…you know, the murder and all that," Mikah explains.

The commotion surrounding the phone soon ends as the two detectives come out of the kitchen, and into the living room.

Grandma introduces Adam, Mikah and Anthony to the new detective.

"These guys came by to ask you some questions," Grandma announces, eyeing her son.

Anthony's face changes from one filled with delight to one of confusion.

"Umm, okay," he says.

The two detectives look at one another.

"We'll need to take you down to the sheriff's office in town," Detective Chavez states, looking at Anthony.

"What? Can't you just interview him here?" Adam asks.

"No, we'd rather interview him in a place where there are no disturbances," Detective Yazzie replies.

"Unless he's a suspect, he shouldn't need to go anywhere," Adam says, with a confused look on his face.

The detective looks back at his partner and then back at Anthony.

"Well, I suppose we can use the truck as an interview room," Detective Yazzie states.

"That sounds a lot better," Adam says.

And with that, the three men get into the truck. My uncle takes the back seat.

As for the rest of us, we focus our attention on the supplies just bought.

"Come on outside, guys. We need to finish unloading the van," Adam says, and leads Mikah and Jonah to the van.

I, on the other hand, admire the phone with Grandma.

"Now how do I use it?" she asks, looking at me with a perplexed look.

We head into the kitchen after a few moments of drooling over the phone. I look over the instructions, and she begins preparing dinner. She takes out some pork chops from the ice chest and begins making the dough for tortillas.

"Well, let's see here," I say, as I open the box and take out the cellophane casing, along with the car charger and wall charger.

"A phone, I've never had a phone before," Grandma says.

The afternoon passes as the men sort out the supplies by room. The bathroom is slotted to be remodeled first, followed by the kitchen area. Adam unveils a new sink and some white pipes, along with some cabinets.

After about an hour or so of interviewing my uncle, the detectives let my uncle out of the van and he comes back inside to let Grandma know they're done.

Anthony lends a helping hand to Adam and his gang while Grandma says farewell to the detectives.

I set Grandma's new phone on her charger and watch the food on the stove. When the pork chops, mashed potatoes and mixed veggies are all cooked, I set the table.

Several moments later, everyone returns from outside.

"So what did they ask you?" I ask my uncle, who looks relaxed and not at all worked up about the interview or interrogation.

"Well, they just wanted to know how I know Kyle and Johnny and a few other people," he says casually.

"Did they say who their main suspect is?" Jonah asks.

"No, I don't think they want to give out all their information just yet," Anthony replies.

"Enough talk about the investigation," Adam says,

after washing his hands in the bathroom.

With dinner ready, we all sit and serve ourselves. Grandma fills everyone else in on the event of the day—the visit from the erratic lady and her daughter.

"Sounds like you've got some Injun revenge coming," my uncle says, laughing. Since there isn't enough room at the table to seat everyone, he sits in the living room, with a plate of food in his lap.

"How would I be a target for revenge if I never did anything to the girl?" Jonah asks, obviously disturbed by my uncle's statement.

"I'm joking," Anthony says.

"Oh, no, that kind of stuff doesn't get to me anyway," Jonah says.

"If it doesn't get to you, why did the joke get you all worked up?" Anthony asks.

Adam and Mikah are obviously hungry, because they shovel food into their mouths and just listen. They do not indulge in the discussion.

"I just thought it would be odd that anyone would consider revenge," Jonah says.

"It was just a joke," Anthony adamantly states.

"Okay, okay, enough about the joke. Let's eat," Grandma says, as she offers Anthony more meat.

When dinner is all eaten up, everybody resumes what they were doing before. The men put all their energy into laying out the work ahead. Adam starts marking on the walls of the bathroom.

Grandma and I clean up the kitchen and take a rest on the front porch. We sip on iced tea, and snack on cantaloupe slices. The men join us every now and then, each one taking turns for a break. They nibble and sip, and get back to work.

Eventually, the sun goes down and we all take a seat on the porch. We all listen to Anthony's tales from his travels. He talks about the time he spent in the Navy, and how he was stationed in Alameda. As he talks about the Bay Area, the Navarro men chime in every now and then, and they compare stories. Anthony was actually in the area when Mikah and Jonah were in high school, and when Adam was in college. But since he didn't have their contact information and had probably forgotten about them, he didn't visit them.

As interesting as the conversation is, I retreat to Grandma's room and briefly mull over the day's event. I soon doze off, without brushing my teeth or washing my face.

No Longer Immortal

The next several days are spent working on the house. Everyone pitches in and it keeps us busy, keeps our minds off the murder and everything else. The days are sunny and warm. The nights are cool.

Anthony shows to be a hospitable person after all. He shares more stories of his time in the Navy with the Navarro brothers. He also manages to stay sober, and helps out in the kitchen with cooking, as well as with the remodeling. He isn't good with carpentry, or plumbing, so he learns where he can, watching the Navarros display their skills, picking up bits and pieces.

Adam tackles the plumbing work. He has to make another run into town to exchange some parts, but for the most part, it is a smooth process. The sink is soon replaced, and a new cabinet is put in to go along with the new sink. The kitchen is closed off for a few hours each day as the men work.

And during lunchtime, Grandma makes sandwiches

in the living room and we eat off paper plates; some of us sitting on our knees, and others sitting out on the porch.

Grandma also manages to chip in on directing the remodeling work, but only because Adam insists. He keeps telling her it's going to be her bathroom and kitchen, so she should have some input. And she does. Boy, does she have some input. All of a sudden, she wants the sink to be moved over a little bit farther from the bathroom door. She wants a softer toilet lid. And she wants a deeper sink basin for the kitchen sink.

All of this requires Adam to make a couple more trips than he expected into town, to exchange equipment. But he does not complain at all...or at least he doesn't complain in front of us.

After two weeks of working on the bathroom and kitchen, Adam unveils his work.

"Everybody, come see the latest and greatest bathroom," Adam announces from the porch, just as the hot afternoon sun is cooling down.

Jonah and Grandma are burning trash in a barrel which is our makeshift dumpster,

Anthony and Mikah, who have been helping Adam pick up the last few pieces of paper from the kitchen floor and make way for us to take a tour, are now standing next to Adam.

I am doing nothing spectacular, simply sitting under the tree, taking a break from sorting the leftover supplies, which Adam has instructed me to pack into a large cardboard box.

As soon as everyone is gathered on the porch, Adam invites Grandma in first.

"Right this way," Adam says, as he leads Grandma into the kitchen first. There are beads of sweat on his forehead, which he wipes off with a red handkerchief.

"Should I close my eyes?" Grandma asks, as she slowly walks into the house, with everyone else following.

I head into the house last and pat Anthony, who is right in front of me, on the back.

He turns around and smiles.

We all congregate at the doorway of the kitchen while Adam counts down from three to one.

Grandma, who has her eyes covered with her hands, slowly removes her hands from her face and opens her eyes.

"Wow, oh my god, this is so beautiful!" she says, surprised and excited. I can tell she is about to cry...her voice becomes muffled, and she turns around and hugs Mikah, and Adam, and then Anthony. She wipes her tears, and goes back to finishing the tour.

"What did you guys do in here?! It is so pretty. The sink...the sink is so big," she exclaims.

Although she picked out the sink basin herself from a catalog, she hadn't seen it sitting in her countertops. She turns on the faucet and the water comes out perfectly fine. The knobs and the faucet are new also...much prettier than before...very fancy-looking. She plays with the knobs for a while, and steps back to admire the countertop and the cabinets. The delight in Grandma's eyes is more than enough to let us know she is satisfied with the work.

"Come see the bathroom," Adam calls out from the bathroom, and he steps back so she can enter.

I admire the new kitchen as the rest of the convoy continues into the bathroom.

"Oh my gosh, this is pretty!" I hear Grandma exclaim.

Everyone watches Grandma as she lets out compliment after compliment, and admires her bathroom.

"I love this bathroom. I will spend a lot of time in here," she says as she looks at every detail.

I eventually squeeze my way into the bathroom to see first-hand Grandma's reactions.

The sink is new; the cabinets under the sink are new. The toilet is new. Grandma flushes it and it works. The bathtub works and so does the shower. The tiles that cover the walls are new. Before, the paint was peeling from the constant pressure of the shower head water. Then, after the plumbing stopped working, there was no reason to fix it. Now, the tiles are gleaming and they look oh so beautiful.

"Anthony painted the walls, too," Adam explains, proudly putting a hand on my uncle's shoulder.

"No more outhouse, and no more peeing in a bucket," Grandma says.

"When did you have to pee in a bucket?" Anthony asks his mom.

"When I'm alone and don't want to go outside in the dark," Grandma says, not at all ashamed of her confession. I don't think she cares a bit what anybody thinks of her at that moment. She is probably too overwhelmed and way too happy to care.

"Wow," Grandma says again. "Now everybody out, so I can use the bathroom," she says and laughs out loud and her chubby body jiggles.

Everybody hurries out, and we all laugh. I laugh mostly because it feels so good to see Grandma finally get something she very much deserves.

"Go ahead, Grandma, it's your bathroom. You can do whatever you want with it," Adam says, as he closes the door behind him. He takes his handkerchief from his back pocket and wipes his forehead again.

I stop in the kitchen and admire the work again. What a beautiful job. "This is amazing," I say.

"Ahh, it's nothing. I've done the work before. And I love fixing things," Adam says, as if it really is nothing. But it is. And I am so thankful he has made Grandma happy and has given her a beautiful gift, when he didn't have to do anything at all.

"Hey, thanks man," Anthony says, stepping to Adam and shaking his hand.

"No problem, man. Your mom is a very deserving woman," Adam says, shaking my uncle's hand.

Jonah and Mikah take a seat in the living room, on the couch and share comments about the wonderful work also. They look like they have both turned a shade darker. They take turns wiping sweat from their foreheads with the back of their hands.

I stay in the kitchen again and admire it again.

The sun is going down, it's shining in from the west window. It brightens the room with an orange shade, and it brings out the beauty of the white, wooden cabinets. The stainless steel sink, with the curvy faucet, and crystal-like knobs, compliment the countertop, which is granite—gray with speckles of brown and black.

I am sure Grandma cannot wait to start cooking in the kitchen, not that she doesn't ever hesitate to cook.

"Now all we have to do to make this kitchen even more wonderful is get a new stove, and maybe a new table, and maybe a pantry," I excitedly say, to no one in particular. "Of course, that is all a ways off," I add.

"Don't get ahead of yourself now," Jonah comments, from the couch.

I get an idea. I silently pledge to put my Social Security checks towards Grandma's house. I've already saved more than three-thousand dollars since I started receiving checks, after my mom's death. I can afford to put some of it towards helping Grandma. I just have to convince my aunt, who is the manager of my account. I doubt that will be an issue, although I know how serious she is when it comes to saving for education versus spending my money.

I hear a thump in the bathroom, and Grandma yells, "Help!"

It's a low call for help, but I hear it just enough and run to the bathroom. The door is locked, and I bang on it. "Grandma! Are you okay?!" I yell, through the door.

"Help!" She says again, in a loud whisper almost…like she can't breathe too well.

Adam and Anthony are right behind me. Adam gently pulls me back from the door and he vigorously wiggles the knob of the bathroom door.

"Move, move!" my uncle yells.

Adam backs away from the door.

Anthony charges the door and it gives. He breaks the lock and the knob falls to the floor. The wooden frame of the door is cracked and so is the door where the knob was.

Grandma is sitting on the floor against the wall opposite the sink. She has a towel wrapped around her, and she is holding her chest.

"I – can't – breathe," she says, in between short breaths.

"What happened?!" my uncle barks. He helps her stand, and guides her out to the living room couch, where she lies down.

Without contemplating too much about what to do, I run into Grandma's room and dig through her dressers for a bathrobe. I find one after a few moments and run back out to put it on her.

Anthony yanks the robe from my hand and manages to roll her sideways and back a couple of times to get her robe on.

Adam turns on the new, partially charged cell phone, and dials 9-1-1. It doesn't work. So he slams it on the counter in the kitchen. He mumbles something about forgetting to activate the phone. I remember him saying something about his and Mikah's cell phones not working out here, so I ask, "What about your phones?"

Mikah darts into the guest room and comes out with two cell phones. Both Mikah and Adam begin dialing.

I cautiously walk back into the bathroom, fearful of what I might see.

"Yes, hello?" I hear Adam saying from the living room.

"How strong is the pain?" Anthony asks Grandma, who is propped against the wall in the bathroom. She is still trying to breathe and has a look of panic in her eyes.

Grandma doesn't answer. Instead, she clutches her

279

chest.

"Yes, yes, I need an ambulance," Adam tells the person on the other end of the line. The person must have asked him for directions, because he comes into the bathroom and hands the phone to my uncle, who gives directions to the person on the line.

"Help me get her up," Adam instructs. Mikah and Jonah push their way into the bathroom as I step back out into the kitchen.

My uncle hangs up the phone, and stands with his hands on his hips for a moment. "Let's get her in the van. An ambulance is on the way. We can meet the ambulance halfway or something," he says, with a strong sense of urgency in his voice.

I rush to Grandma's bedroom, find her bedroom slippers next to her bed, and run back to the bathroom just as Adam and Mikah are helping Grandma into the living room. I quickly slide her slippers on her feet while Adam and Mikah hold her up, with each of her arms slung around their shoulders.

My heart is pounding.

Anthony and Jonah hurry outside to get the van ready. Mikah helps Adam carry Grandma out the door to the van.

I grab her purse from her bedroom dresser. I grab a blanket and pillow for her. I try to think of anything else I can bring. I cannot think of anything else so I go out to the van.

Grandma is lying across the middle seat. Anthony and Mikah are in the back seat. Jonah and Adam are up front. So I squeeze way into the backseat, between Anthony and Mikah. And we speed down the road. Adam drives faster than he has before.

"It must be a heart attack," Anthony says, with urgency in his voice.

I look at him and ask, "Can it be?"

"Yeah, that's what it seems like," he says, almost out of breath.

"Oh my god!" I gasp. "Grandma can't die now." Tears form in my eyes, and I can't hold them back so I start weeping.

"Shhh, don't add anymore stress to her. We need to just be calm," Anthony says, and puts his arms around my shoulders.

I fight the tears, I think of Grandma…of how she held me when my mother died. It makes me want to cry more, so I try to think of something else.

Think about Los Angeles. Think about school. Think about something else.

I wonder what all my aunts would do if Grandma passed away. I wonder what they are all doing at this very moment. My favorite aunt, Jackie, is probably at work now. My other aunt, Jeannette, is probably at work, too. It is a weekday, so they would have to be at work. I try to focus.

What day is it anyway? It's a Thursday or Friday. Thursday. Yeah, for sure, everybody's at work. My uncle, Tom, is probably the only one at home.

"We must make some calls at soon as we get to town," I say frantically.

My uncle rubs my shoulders again, and says, "Yeah, we will." In this moment, I couldn't think of how he beat his wife, or how he was so angry with me for calling him out. I could only think that he and I could lose Grandma soon and we were in the same boat. I didn't hate him. I let him rub my shoulders, knowing he meant well.

Mikah, and Jonah remain calm and silent. They just stare ahead as Adam speeds down the road.

I reach over the seat in front of me, and hold my hand out for Grandma. She looks up at me and gives me her left hand. I squeeze. I squeeze. She squeezes back. Her hands are soft and wrinkled. There is fear in her eyes as she gasps for air. She squeezes again.

We swiftly pass the sunflowers that welcomed me home several weeks before. I don't admire them this time. I watch them pass and their faces droop. There is no breeze to make them sway. In that moment, I think I'd rather be one of them than to know death as a human and to be riding in the van at this moment.

We drive through an extremely bumpy area of the dirt road, right next to The Lady With Clumsy Hands's house, and the van bounces up and down vigorously as it skids across the washboard road. I hold Grandma's hand, harder than before. Her head slightly bounces around but she keeps looking at me. I smile at her, with tears in my eyes. She gasps for air and looks at me with fear in her eyes.

We pass the cattle guard, the last bump on the road. The rest of the road is paved, so I release my squeeze a little, and let Grandma's hand take a break. She looks a little relieved, with not so much fear in her eyes anymore. Something about passing the cattle guard makes both of us feel better. Maybe it's because we know we're closer to getting help.

She breathes deep. Time ticks. She breathes deep. She breathes again. I look at Anthony. I look up front at

Adam and Jonah. The landscapes are zooming by so fast: the city dump to the right, the mountains to the left and the right, the valley to the right, after the mountains. We drive over the next cattle guard.

She breathes. I hear relief coming with her breaths. The fear that had gripped her a few moments earlier seems to have disappeared.

She lifts her head and looks straight ahead. Her breaths come easier.

"Just relax," I say to Grandma, sitting up, closer to her.

She keeps breathing.

Lights are flashing ahead of us. An ambulance is coming towards us.

Adam slows the van down, and we finally pull to a complete stop, right near the mysterious rock mountains, with the big boulders looking down at us.

We get out one by one and make room for the medics to help Grandma out of the van. The medics are running, and moving quickly. They bring a stretcher from the back of the ambulance, and park it right next to the open sliding door of the van, and they slowly lift her and put her on the stretcher.

More relief. I can breathe. I can relax. She has help now.

Anthony is standing next to me, and I reach over and put my arms around his waist. He hugs me and keeps his arms on my shoulders. The bulge which was down in my gut somewhere pushes its way up my throat. I release my cry and as I hug my uncle's chest. I let out the fear.

"She's gonna' be okay," he says, reassuringly, patting my shoulder.

"Thank God," Adam says.

Jonah and Mikah seem to be in shock still, and are still quiet. They just mill around the van, and watch the whole transition from the van to the ambulance. Jonah runs his fingers through his blonde hair and holds his hands in place on top of his head for a few seconds. His bright eyes are not as big and beautiful as before. His face is cringed.

Once Grandma is in the ambulance, Anthony quickly climbs in with her and the ambulance swiftly turns around. The rest of us move quickly to get back into the van. I feel like a zombie and I let my feet guide my steps.

We follow the ambulance and its flashing lights.

I look at the rocks on the mountains; the boulders. They look at me. I smile and wipe my tears. They don't smile back.

I close my eyes and say a small prayer...not a prayer for forgiveness or for help, but for thanks. No words, but simple thoughts and clasped hands.

I am grateful for all I have...for the people in my life, for the Navarros, for my uncles, for my aunts, my cousins, and most of all, for my Grandma. I thank the spirits for my Grandma.

I open my eyes. We have passed the boulders and we are going over the last hill before the town spreads before us. I close my eyes again, and I listen to the hum of the engine. I can feel the air blowing in from the open windows. I smell the air. It has no smell. I breathe. I open my eyes.

Jonah turns around—he is sitting in the front seat with Adam. And Mikah is sitting next to me on the middle seat.

I smile at Jonah. He smiles back. Mikah is looking

out the window and Adam is at the wheel, as always, keeping his eyes on the road.

"I know she's going to be okay now," Adam says in a flat tone, just when I think the silence is too much to bear.

The town passes us, or we pass the town—the Wal-Mart, the Mobil gas station, the first street light—the only major intersection of town, the Safeway and Bashas', the first residential houses, and the Presbyterian church. We follow the sirens.

The few people on the streets stare at us as we pass. The drivers in their cars are stopped and stare at us just the same. The town seems to have come to a halt and we are the only moving parts.

The racing in my heart has slowed and I breathe deeply.

Back to Our Favorite Spot

We get to the hospital, the same hospital we brought Eddie Yazzie to…the man who almost died in Grandma's arms—the man who whirled us into a whole other world of murder and mystery.

I notice that the light from the sun has left us, and darkness has crept in just as we park in the area designated as "Emergency Room Parking". It's about fifty feet from where the ambulance is already parked, and we get out, one by one. We meet a plain-clothes lady who is waiting for us at the Emergency Room entrance. She asks for Grandma's name and insurance card. I hand her Grandma's purse.

"You sit down, I'll handle it," Adam says, as he pats me on the shoulder.

Jonah and Mikah walk me to a row of empty chairs along a wall of windows, next to the TV and vending machine.

The Emergency Room waiting area is empty—a small, white room, with floor-to-wall windows on the main entrance side, and potted trees located every few feet—a comfortable place, with chairs that don't have arms. I can rest. I can lie across the chairs and I don't hesitate to do so. I like the waiting room instantly. It feels good to lie down, even if it only lasts for a few seconds. I close my eyes. I can hear the television set and what sounds like Barbara Walters's voice, but I don't pay any mind.

Adam returns shortly and he begins talking with Mikah. They stand near the main entrance and give their diagnosis evaluations on what happened to Grandma.

Jonah sits down on the chairs, next to my feet. I can feel his presence and don't have to open my eyes to see it's him.

I keep my eyes closed and I breathe. I think about Grandma. Grandma: what a wonderful woman. I remember how comforting she was after my mother passed away. She made sure I was fed, amidst all the confusion and mayhem surrounding the funeral. I cried on her shoulders just about every day for a good week. She held me. She cradled me. She played with my hair. She told me I can cry and still be strong. She told me it was okay to mourn for my mother, even if it takes the rest of my life because she is who I came from. And I will mourn for as long as I have to.

The minutes pass, the television set blares on, the clock on the wall ticks, almost in beat with my heart. The sliding doors down the hall open and close. The vending machine hums like a refrigerator. I slip away, to a world beyond the real one—to a land of dreams and thoughts, maybe just deeper into my brain, but somewhere other than this waiting room.

I see an empty room, and a woman in tight-fitting

jeans and a black t-shirt facing away from me. There is a sliding door between us; the room has windows, lots of small, square windows letting in sunlight. I can smell hospital all around me, like Clorox mixed with strong urine.

The lady's hair is up in a hairclip, and she just stands there—looking down a long hallway; and the sliding door is open. I call out to her, 'Hey' but she doesn't respond. It's like she can't hear me.

I move my feet forward, one step at a time. My feet are heavy. It feels like someone tied a brick to each foot. I lift, and step, lift and step. It seems like forever before I get close enough to her to hear her heartbeat. I stand and lift my arms to touch her. She turns around. It's my mother. She smiles at me. I hug her hard. I don't want to let her go. I squeeze her and cry. Then I look into her eyes. There is sadness and happiness in her eyes. She lifts her arms and takes both of my hands.

She squeezes and says, "You will be okay."

I cannot speak—my tongue is stuck to the bottom of my mouth. I have words to say, but they will not roll off my tongue. I want to scream, but I have no voice. Mom! Wait!

The sliding door opens. I jerk out of my dream. I sit up and look around. I am still in the waiting room, and Jonah is still sitting at my feet. Adam and Mikah are outside, talking. The TV is still blaring. The vending machine is still humming. I don't see Anthony anywhere. It is dark outside.

A doctor is walking towards us, out from the sliding doors behind us. "Excuse me," I hear him say.

Jonah and I both stand abruptly as if just called to attention.

"Yes, doctor?" Jonah responds.

"Are you the grand-daughter of Mrs. Scott?" the doctor asks, looking right at me, with his arms behind his back.

"Yes, yes, I am," I say as I straighten my clothes and my hair.

"Your grandmother is going to be okay. She suffered from something called a Pulmonary…" I don't understand the last word. It sounds like elbow list. "But she will be okay," he says, with a smile. He reaches out to me and puts an arm on my shoulder. His arms feel heavy on my shoulder.

Jonah stands to the other side of me, and he looks at me and smiles.

"Is it severe?" Jonah asks.

"Not as severe as a heart attack…it's basically caused by a blood clot," the doctor explains, as he runs his fingers over his left eyebrow.

"Good," Jonah says, with a huge sigh of relief and calmly takes a seat again.

The main entrance sliding door opens. Adam and Mikah, who have been outside somewhere, re-join us. Jonah shares the news with them, and the doctor explains his diagnosis and the treatment to all three of the guys while I sit and relax my shoulders.

Before the doctor in the green garb leaves, I stand to thank him, with tears in my eyes.

"You are welcome. She is a strong woman, your grandmother," he says, as he takes my hand in his, as if to shake it.

"Yes, we know," Adam confidently says. He is no longer shaken up, but is calm. He is still wearing the dirty white t-shirt he had on earlier, with a stained pair of jeans, and brown work boots.

"She will need to stay here for a couple of days, so we can observe her and make sure she's in the clear," the doctor adds. He looks at me and smiles again.

"Can we see her?" I ask.

"Well, she is sleeping now. It's probably better to come back in the morning. She really needs some rest," he replies and smiles.

I thank him again and he goes back to wherever he came from, back through the sliding door; back to making sick people well, I suppose.

Everything is going to be okay. I feel my chest as it rises and I take a deep breath.

"Where is my uncle?" I ask Jonah.

He hesitates, then looks out at towards the entrance and says, "He left. He said he'd be back after he gets a drink."

I can hear the disappointment in his voice and I understand.

I know it's hard for my uncle to deal with hardships and when he faces any kind, he turns to alcohol. I suppose it soothes him somehow and all I can do is nod at Jonah. I know Anthony will not be back anytime soon.

"He will most likely not be back. Once he starts on a drinking binge, it could be days before we see him," I discouragingly say.

"I understand," Jonah says, and pats me on the back.

I use the payphone down the hall from the waiting area to make calls to my aunts and my uncle, Tom. Jackie is surprised to receive a phone call from me so soon, and says she is grateful it wasn't a heart attack. She mentions that she is in Florida and will be home in a few more days. So I tell her not to worry, that we have it covered. I also tell her about our visitors and this surprises her as well. She says she wishes she was here with us. By the end of the phone call, she promises not to worry.

I leave a voicemail on my aunt, Jeanette's home phone. Her voice on her message sounds so happy and I feel bad for leaving semi-unfortunate news about Grandma's situation. I tell her not to worry and let her know she can call the hospital directly if she has any questions for the medical staff.

I leave a message with Tom's wife, who doesn't sound too distraught by the news. She informs me that Tom is still out fighting fires and says the most she can do is leave a message with his boss. As long as she's been with my uncle, which would be about seven years, I still don't know her well enough to share details of our new visitors, so I don't.

Making Do

The sun rises with extra shine the next morning. I wake right before it fully rises and I watch it finish its daily ritual of emerging. I take in the daylight with pleasure, with comfort, and with relief, right from Grandma's bedroom window.

I take my arms off the windowsill, once the sun is all the way up, and briskly fix Grandma's bed. Grateful that Grandma is going to be okay, I pompously make my way to the kitchen and dutifully wash up in the new bathroom.

I change into a relaxing outfit of denim, stone-washed jeans, a light blue tank top with a loose-fitting purple top.

What can I make for breakfast? I am sure I will find something in the kitchen. No sweat, right?

Nobody else is awake yet. I'm sure the Navarro brothers are very tired from the prior day's events and I don't bother to wake them.

I stride back to the kitchen where I wash the dishes

from the day before. After rummaging through the ice chest, I decide to cook some eggs and bacon...no tortillas. Definitely not ready for tortilla-making yet. Grandma makes the tortillas and I don't make very good ones. She doesn't buy bread from the store because it usually goes to waste. Hardly anyone eats the store-bought bread over her wonderful tortillas. The eggs and bacon alone will have to do this time. I put on a pot of coffee and slice up a juicy cantaloupe, which Adam brought home from one of his supply excursions.

Adam emerges the room, rubbing his eyes.

"Good morning," I say, showing as much delight as possible. The sight of him floods my mind with images of Grandma enjoying her newly updated home. Absolutely certain she would be relishing in the new kitchen right now, I picture her with a smile, spreading from one cheek to the other. I immediately miss her presence.

Adam comes into the kitchen and compliments on how good the food looks and returns the 'Good morning.' Then, he asks, "You going to take a shower today?"

I laugh, and remember the bathroom is finished...I really can take a shower.

"I am!" he exclaims before I can answer.

We both laugh. Sad thoughts which had moved into my brain a few moments before are replaced with anticipation to try out the shower.

Adam and I indulge in the minimal breakfast.

Breakfast is filling, probably not a breakfast Martha Stewart would swoon over, but good enough for me. I was hungry. So was Adam.

I pour a cup of coffee

Adam, looking shocked by my choice of beverage, asks me, "What are you doing? You don't drink coffee."

"I do, remember? I drink Starbucks coffee," I say, taking a sip of the hot coffee. It is refreshing, in a weird, hot way and it tastes good.

"This isn't Starbucks coffee," he says, holding his cup of coffee up. He has a smile and raised eyebrows, as if he's questioning my decision.

"I know that, but it actually tastes pretty good," I say.

"Is there some kind of traditional, Navajo ritual for this? For you becoming a coffee drinker?" he asks and then lets out a laugh.

"Ha ha ha, no, there is not…smarty pants," I counter.

Jonah and Mikah eventually traipse out of the room, just as Adam and I finish eating. They both trudge past us and into the bathroom to wash up before joining Adam and I at the kitchen table.

I take a bite of the sweet, juicy cantaloupe and I savor the taste. Adam indulges in the fruit as well. I smile coyly at Jonah when he sits down across from me at the table. I hope Mikah doesn't take notice and he doesn't. He is too busy stuffing his mouth.

"Well, it looks like you guys will have quite a story when you get back to San Francisco," I say.

"Yep, and nobody's going to believe us," Mikah says.

I excuse myself from the table. Mikah and Jonah remain. I retreat to Grandma's room, where I plop myself onto her cushion, in front of her loom. I cautiously uncover her loom and admire her work of art once again. I let my fingers playfully run back and forth across the loom. A gentle whirring sound fills my ears and I welcome the sound.

Excitement fills my stomach, as I imagine Grandma sitting here again, passionately weaving—pounding the yarn, spinning wool with her spindle, stringing the loom, pounding the yarn again.

A few minutes later, I hear Mikah and Jonah walking through the living room, commenting on how much better they feel after eating breakfast. I take that as my cue to clean up after everyone has eaten to their fill and dutifully go about washing the dishes. Then I take a shower after Adam gets out of the shower.

The water is wonderfully warm and it is unbelievable. I take a shower shorter than the ones in Los Angeles, because the water starts to cool sooner. I figure it must have something to do with the size of the water heater. Grandma's Dove bar goes on nicely, and it smells like flowers. I bathe as quickly as possible and I get out.

"You guys might want to wait a while...the water is cool," I say, as I pass Jonah and Mikah, who are sitting in the living room with rolled up towels in their hands. They laugh and ask me how my shower was.

"Excellent," I reply with a smile of satisfaction. I am wearing a fresh set of clothes and my hair smells nice and clean. I feel refreshed.

Jonah darts into the bathroom, obviously unable to wait for the water to warm. Mikah and I both laugh at Jonah's actions.

I go out to the porch after I put my dirty clothes away. I remind myself we will need to go to the Laundromat in town after I see how high the pile of dirty clothes in Grandma's hamper is.

The sun is already up high in the sky, spreading

warmth over the land. Adam has turned on Grandma's radio inside and the weather man is predicting rain today, although it doesn't look like rain is anywhere nearby. There is the sun and a few puffy clouds dotting the sky.

The men are still inside and I secretly enjoy my few minutes on the porch. I can hear the shower—the little bathroom window is open, and it is a few feet to my left and about two feet higher. So it's nearby enough that I can hear the trickle of the water. I imagine Jonah in the shower. I imagine his nude body. I have always thought of fish when I thought of naked white people. And somehow, it deterred me from desiring them or thinking they are sexy.

But Jonah, he is different. I picture a tan body underneath the clothes. I imagine muscles and more muscles. I snap out of my daydream when I hear the screen door close behind me.

"When we go into town today, I want to buy some plants," Mikah says to Adam, as they step out onto the porch, each with a cup of steaming coffee.

"Okay, that's cool," Adam says.

I put in my request to stop at the Laundromat.

"Okay, it sounds like we will be busy today," Adam comments and goes back inside.

"It is so peaceful out here," Mikah says, taking a deep breath.

"I know...I love it. I feel a lot better here than I do when I'm in Los Angeles," I say.

"Oh, I bet you do. I miss San Francisco, but there's something about this place...it is really growing on me. I could see myself living out here," he says.

"What?! Really? You? City slicker dude? I don't

believe that!" I exclaim, knowing very well he would be tired of the place if he really had to live here.

"Yeah, I could. I could get me an Injun woman, have some half-breed kids, grow some corn, maybe buy some horses or some kind of livestock, and just live," he says, as if he's contemplated all of this in his head.

I laugh at his idea, and he looks offended.

"What's so funny about that?" he asks, looking at me with a peculiar look and smile.

"Grow corn? Where did you come up with that?" I ask.

"Isn't that what you guys do?" he asks.

I laugh again. Then I realize he is serious.

"Woah, woah, you sound like you've actually thought about it," I say, trying to be more serious and more polite. Although the idea of a white man living on the rez strikes me as something funny and unbelievable, I don't want to make him feel bad for actually considering the thought of living on the rez.

"Of course," he says earnestly.

"With all this craziness that's been going on, you think you can actually be cool out here?" I ask, now looking at him for his expression. He looks calm and serious.

"Yes, I'm sure it's not always this crazy...there must be some times when everything is mellow, right?" he asks.

"Well, yeah, of course," I say.

"What are you guys talking about out here?" I hear a voice from behind me say. It's Jonah, and he looks like he's definitely come from the shower. His cute locks are tighter than normal...still damp. His eyes are blue as the ocean. He has on some khaki shorts, a white t-shirt, and a ball cap in his hands.

"What's the game plan today?" he asks, and shakes his head, as if to shake the dampness from his hair.

"Well, it sounds like we have quite a bit of business in town," Mikah says.

"Visit Grandma, do some laundry, and buy some plants," I say and take my eyes off Jonah. I don't want to stare too long. So I look back out to the land in front of us.

"Cool, sounds like fun," Jonah says sarcastically, as he puts his ball cap on and walks briskly towards the van. His demeanor has 'cool' written all over it and I feel chills running down my spine just watching him.

The drive into town is routine by now, and we make the most out of our short trip. We talk, laugh, and talk some more. Adam and Mikah poke fun at Jonah about Angie, the girl who accused him of making hickies on her neck. Adam calls him a vampire, and Mikah says things like, 'Who even makes hickies anymore? I didn't know they were even in style'.

I add, "I don't think they were ever supposed to be in style."

We laugh about Jonah and he answers by saying, 'It wasn't even me,' after every remark from his brothers.

On the way, Mikah also sketches out his landscaping plans for the house.

When we get into town, we make our first stop at the Laundromat. The guys help me with the two large trash bags of laundry. Adam and Mikah wait while Jonah and I put the loads of clothes into the washers. Most of the clothes are theirs and some are mine and Grandma's. I decide not to separate them by owner, but by color to keep the cost down.

Once we get everything out of the bags and into the washers, we get back into the van and back on the road.

Our next stop is the hardware store, where plants and pretty much everything related to a house; building supplies, lawn mowers, and the likes are sold...so I'm confused as to why it's called a hardware store; it should be called a houseware store.

Mikah leads the way, and picks out some potted flowers, a potted, baby apple tree, a potted weeping willow tree, some potting soil, some peat moss, a small gardening shovel, and a bag of dirt—yes, a bag of dirt...they actually sell that.

I picture what the house will look like once he puts all this stuff in the ground. I can't picture it so I just hope it all comes out better than it looks now.

After the hardware, or houseware store I should say, we return to the Laundromat to put the clothes into the dryers. It is there that I spot Angie and her mother. And once again, Angie's mother is disappointed with her daughter. When Angie spots me, she reluctantly comes over and asks me, "Where is Jonah?"

I am not sure if I should answer her truthfully at first, but the outcome is soon decided by fate. Jonah walks through the door and instantly recognizes Angie.

I tend to the clothes while the two of them greet one another and make small talk.

Angie's mother glares at them over a few rows of washers, but continues to fold clothes on the opposite end of the Laundromat.

While I continue to transfer clothes from the washers to dryers, Angie approaches me and asks, "Are you guys going to the dance for the Yazzies?"

"Which Yazzies?" I ask.

"Dorothy Yazzie, she's having one next week," Angie replies.

I recognize the name. It's the real name for Lady with Clumsy Hands. "Oh, I don't know, it's up to my grandmother."

"I saw your uncle at the other squaw dance, the one by your grandma's house," she says.

"Really?" I ask. I'm a bit surprised, but try not to show it.

"Yeah, he was with Kyle."

Jonah is directly behind her and asks, "You know Kyle?"

"Yeah…I dated him for a while," Angie responds.

Her mother approaches us and sternly says, "I need your help, Angie." Then she walks away, after giving Jonah a good stare-down.

"Oh, nevermind her, she's like that with everyone," Angie says, in defense of her mother's behavior.

"Anyway, yeah, they were running around with a bunch of guys, and one of their friends tried to pull me into their truck after I danced with him," she says.

"Oh my goodness," I say.

"Yeah, Anthony told us about them going to the dance. Of course, he left out the part about his friend trying to kidnap you, though," I say.

"He was ugly, with a big old scar on his face. When you see your uncle, tell him he needs to keep his friends under control," she says, with a smile.

Not knowing how to take her statement, I simply

respond by saying, "Yeah, sure."

"Well, I gotta go," she abruptly says, and then turns to leave.

"If there was any such thing as a squaw dance groupie, I would say she qualifies," I say jokingly.

"Maybe she's just a very traditional girl," Jonah says, as he loads the last of our clothes into the last available dryer.

"That sounds nicer," I say, as I turn on the dryer.

With our official business out of the way for the most part, we make our way to the hospital, and when we arrive, we converge on Grandma's room. Mikah brings a flower pot with some gorgeous tulips for her, and I bring her clean clothes. Adam brings her a can of soda, and Jonah brings her a bag of pork rinds from home; her favorite snack. Of course, they are only her favorite if they have some hot sauce. And apparently, she must've told him this, because he brings a bottle of hot sauce from home also.

Her eyes lighten up when we walk in the door and we all give her a hug. Then we present our gifts and she looks at them one by one. With every gift she receives, her smiles gets wider, and her eyes light up each time. She doesn't have any tubes connected to her, but she does have an IV in her arm.

"So? How are you doing?" Adam asks first.

"Ohh, I'm doing well. Did the doctor tell you guys what happened?" she asks back.

"Yep, a blood clot?" Adam says, fishing for more details.

"Yes, it scared me, but I'm okay now," Grandma says, taking a big sigh as if saying 'the worst is over'.

"Yeah, you scared us there a bit, too," I say. I stand

301

by her bed, and hold her hands.

I look at a note on the stand beside her bed that has the words "Pulmonary Embolism" scribbled on it.

Grandma informs us that she has had a few visitors, including her sister Elsa, and her mother.

I hold her hands as she talks. Although I really want to cry, and tell her that I thought I was going to lose the most important person in my life, I don't say anything. I just listen to her and thank the powers that be for letting me be with her right now.

I smile inside again and I am happy because she is happy. The Navarros are all smiling, and the moment is special. I wonder if it was by chance or by a powerful act out of our control that these men came into our lives when they did…just in time to provide some level of comfort and help for me and Grandma. Actually, some help is an understatement. They have been a lot of help and I am so grateful.

Grandma always did tell me I need to count my blessings and not just for a day or a moment, but for all time. She always told me that things happen for a reason and there are some things we have no control over, like when people depart this planet.

I look at Grandma again and she is crying, not out loud, but tears are rolling down her cheeks. They must be tears of happiness because she still has a smile.

Oh great…here we go, I can feel my heart in my throat. Seeing Grandma's tears make my tears start to form, and I blink, look away and try not get pulled into the crying moment. I look at Jonah and he is crying also. The emotion is overwhelming and I feel powerless. I hug Grandma and I sob like a baby.

Jonah puts his arms around my shoulders and rubs them.

Adam and Mikah also join in. They don't sob like babies. But they make almost-sobbing noises.

"I am so glad you're alive," I say, with a cracked voice.

"Me, too," says Grandma. She isn't crying as hard as I am. She just holds me and says it again, "Me, too."

The room gets a little bit too quiet for just a moment and then Adam breaks the silence by saying, "No squaw dancing for you for a while."

And we all laugh.

I wipe my tears. Jonah wipes his tears. The sadness is lifted and in settles happiness and joy.

We visit with Grandma for as long as we can. We sit with her through lunch and we talk. We listen to more of her stories about her younger years.

The Navarros talk about their family; and it turns out they don't know their parents' families well or at all. Their father's family is from Iowa, and their mother's family is from Connecticut. The brothers have met family from both sides, but only a couple of times, when they were kids. Their parents both came from poor families, who pretty much did not stay in contact with them after they left home. Their parents met in California, in San Francisco, working at the shipping docks. Their mother went to school while their father worked. Then, their mother supported the family, while their father went to school, and became a professor. Typical common family story, I suppose, but not what I expected. I had this idea they were from a rich family to begin with.

As I listen to their accounts, I wonder what it is that really makes us different from them. I feel small compared to them, yet, we do very similar things. Their parents worked hard to make a good living, and it took years to build up what they had. Their parents owned a home, which the guys recently sold. My grandparents worked hard. They or at least my Grandma still owns the home Grandpa built.

I decide the differences are opportunity and location and in this case, the two kinda' work together. They grew up in a city, a major city, with tons of opportunity. My family grew up here, well not here in town, but on the rez, and although they work hard to make a living, the rewards are not the same as they are in San Francisco. Instead of going to school like their mother, my Grandma focused on raising her kids.

As for my grandfather, I am almost certain he simply became depressed over time, probably from living on the rez, and just started drinking alcohol on a regular basis because of his depression. Their father went to school and became a professor.

I figure the differences between our families are not opportunity and location, but opportunity and alcohol instead.

I try to cheer myself up again by letting positive thoughts flood my brain. *I am glad that Grandma is going to be okay. I am glad she's still here.* My mind wanders back to the alcohol again. *The darn alcohol.*

As a kid in school, I used to wonder what would happen if there was no alcohol, if it never existed. I would sit at my desk and wonder what my family would be, what my grandfather would have become, and what my uncles would have become. Like a promise made but never kept, I was sad about our family's future, about the way they lived, about the people around us, our neighbors, and the pains they've endured, thanks to alcohol.

And then one day, I asked my Social Studies teacher, Mr. Thompson, a gray-haired white man, what he thought would happen if alcohol was gone. I remember his answer so well. It was something I didn't want to hear. He said, 'We've already seen that…it was called the Prohibition, and it was not pretty.'

As ambitious and outgoing as I was, I lost so much hope that day. Before that day, I remember going home on weekends and sharing my lessons about alcohol with my grandfather. I'd tell him, 'If you save the money you spend on wine, you would have more money for Christmas gifts.' He'd laugh. I never knew why he thought the idea was so funny. But I learned it that day.

Mr. Thompson made the Prohibition a topic for a whole week almost. By the end of that whole lesson, I was upset, upset that humans are so damn weak. I still did not accept that things just have to be the way they are, with alcohol poisoning people; humans and the communities.

Before I get more upset, I decide to stop contemplating on the subject and I force my mind to focus on Grandma, and the house…oh yeah, the house. She is going to love the house and the trees. I get excited and want to spit it out, but I bite my tongue and I hold it in.

"So, when will you be coming home?" Adam asks. Home? What is he saying? Home? He's calling Grandma's house home.

"Yeah, Grandma, when are you coming home?" I ask,

too.

"Oh, I should be ready to go home the day after tomorrow. I just talked to the doctor early this morning and he said they would like to do some more tests on my blood and they want me to do okay on my own for at least forty-eight more hours," Grandma says.

Adam nods his head, as if he agrees with the doctor's orders. And he adds, "Well, we all miss you."

"Yeah, we miss your tortillas," Mikah adds.

We laugh and talk more. The sun shines into Grandma's hospital room, and it warms the room nicely. After the day progresses quite a bit, a couple of nurses come to check Grandma's vitals. She finishes her lunch and another nurse comes and takes her tray.

The doctor comes in a little later. He is a thin, short white man with gray hair and gold-rimmed glasses. He tells her she needs to get some rest. We take that as our queue to leave her alone. So we say our farewells, and we all give her a hug.

"Watching you eat your lunch made me hungry, so we're going to get some late lunch and head home," Adam says to Grandma before we walk out of the room.

"I love you guys. You come back tomorrow, okay?" Grandma says, as we leave the room.

"Yes, yes, we'll be back tomorrow," Adam says to her, as he closes her door.

It makes me feel good to know Grandma will be home tomorrow.

"We better get those trees and flowers home," Mikah says, putting in his two cents on what we should do next.

"Oh yeah, I almost forgot about those," Jonah says.

Adam walks ahead of the three of us, and waves at all the nurses at the nurse's station. They all wave back and smile at him.

"I'm hungry for a burger," I say, as we follow Adam out the main entrance sliding door. Adam wearily climbs into the van and starts it up.

The rest of us get in the van, and Mikah says, "Burgers sound good. I'm cool with that."

"Mmmmm, burgers? Is that the unanimous vote?" Adam asks, as we pull out of the parking lot.

"Yep, that's what it sounds like," Jonah says, as he settles into the seat next to me, on the second row. Mikah sits up front with Adam and we all agree on Sonic as our late lunch destination.

We enjoy the rest of the hot afternoon sitting outside of Sonic and talking about how great of a woman my grandmother is. Then we stop by the Laundromat on the way out of town and fortunately, nobody stole any of our clothes. Before I know it, we're home and the sun is going down.

I do not have to worry about dinner, so I get ready for bed, while the Navarro brothers unload the van and sit outside on the porch.

The house is not the same without Grandma. It is empty. I try to imagine her beside me as I curl up in her bed, close my eyes and wish tomorrow comes quickly.

All in a Day's Work

I am woken by the roar of thunder and the drops of rain on Grandma's window. I look out the window to see that the morning sun doesn't have a chance to shine through the clouds which are dominating the sky.

As hot as the summer sun has been, I am sure the ground is thirsty so any rain is good.

I find Mikah and Adam in the kitchen, eating Kellogg's Special K cereal. So I join them and we talk about our plans for the day.

Mikah declares the day will be spent planting.

After our light breakfast, Adam and I follow Mikah out to the porch. We watch the pouring rain in silence.

Then Mikah pushes me out into the pouring rain. I nearly stumble to the ground because I wasn't expecting a push from behind. At first, I'm surprised, but when I turn around and realize it's Adam, being playful, I laugh.

Adam laughs. Then he pushes Mikah into the rain as well.

"Serves you right," is the only thing I can think to say.

Jonah comes outside. Still half asleep, he is immediately pulled into the frolicking. And eventually, Adam joins us on the ground as we dance in the rain.

My hair is soon damp and so are my clothes. Not wanting the men to see through my clothes, I cut my fun short and go inside to change into some dry clothes.

I am certain everyone is outside still because I hear the chatter through the bathroom window. But to my surprise, Jonah is in the kitchen, toothbrush and toothpaste in hand, when I come out of the bathroom.

He is standing a few feet away from the door, next to the kitchen sink, and he looks as if he's about to say something, but can't get the words out.

In the few moments of silence, I strain my brain for something to say that would keep the moment from being too awkward. "Do you need to get to the bathroom?" I ask nervously, closing the bathroom door behind me.

"No, I'm already finished brushing," he says.

Then he just stands there, looking at me.

I realize he needs help getting his words out, so I ask, "Is everything okay?"

"I...I...ummm, I don't know how to say this, but I like you," he mutters, as if he doesn't want to say it too loud. I see his lips moving, and I see the endearing look in his eyes, but I can't believe what I am hearing.

"I like you, too," I say, with a long drawn out tone, hoping he doesn't mean in a boyfriend-girlfriend kind of way and hoping I don't lead him on.

"I mean, not in a regular way," he says, as he steps even closer. I can smell his fresh breath from where I stand,

and I don't know how to react.

I pull all my confidence out of my gut, and I hear myself ask, "You mean in a boyfriend-girlfriend way?"

"Yes, I guess you can say that. I am really attracted to you," he says. And then adds, "but you are younger than I am."

With this, my heart stops for a second and I try to keep calm. My heart is fluttering, like a butterfly in a cage. I wonder if he knows how I feel. I wonder if he knows how I've grown attracted to him in the past few weeks.

"I know what you mean. I feel the same way," I quietly say.

He takes a couple of steps towards me. His blonde hair is a bit bushy but he looks cute nonetheless. His lips look so big, right there, close to my face. His eyes are bluer than the ocean, and I stare right into them. For a second, I can almost see them sparkle like sapphire jewels. I blink and take my eyes off him, and I look out the kitchen window to my right. I breathe a deep breath. I feel my heart being crushed.

"I am glad you said something first, because I would have silently admired you forever if I could," I say in almost a whisper. Before I can go on and tell him I want him to kiss me, I hear the screen door slam shut.

Jonah moves back as if he was just bitten by a snake. I open the cupboard beside me, and say, "Here you go," as I reach for a cup.

"Thanks," he says and steps backward towards the table.

"Hey guys, come look at this rainbow!" Mikah says excitedly. He comes to the sink to wash his hands, as Jonah busies himself, acting as if he was about to make a fresh pot of coffee.

We follow Mikah outside. As Adam and Mikah try to point out the location of the rainbow to us, I realize I didn't even notice that the rain had stopped. The smell of the wet dirt fills my nostrils.

I close my eyes. I inhale and exhale. "Ahh," I say with a long sigh.

As I admire the rainbow, Mikah goes into the house and returns with a drawing; a plan for what he wants to do with the landscaping. The drawing has a detailed picture of the house, and he has dotted the landscape with rose bushes, small shrubbery, flowers, and the trees. He has a small fence around the flower bed, which is going to be around the front of the house. And below that, on lower ground, he has the shrubbery, and this is lined with some small bricks in a slight curve.

I am impressed. And I close my eyes for a quick moment to imagine the picture in my head. It looks wonderful. I open my eyes and imagine it again. It will be beautiful.

"Wow," I say.

"This will take a couple of days at least, but it will all be worth it," Mikah says, as he proudly holds his drawing up and matches it up to the house, as if he's putting it in place.

"I can't wait for Grandma to see it," I say.

"Yeah, it will be a nice surprise....a good homecoming gift," Adam says.

"I wish my uncle and aunts could be here to participate in the work," I say. I figure they are busy with their lives and wouldn't have time to help out anyway.

We spend the next few hours doing all the groundwork—digging up the muddy ground, and clearing the rocks. Mikah directs us as we do each task. Jonah looks content digging in the mud. The ball cap he has on hides his locks, but his ocean blue eyes look right at me whenever he has the opportunity to gaze in my direction.

I shift my attention to find Adam who is pushing around Grandma's old wheelbarrow. He uses it to take sand from the dig to a pile he has created about thirty paces away from the house.

I help with digging up the old dirt.

Mikah pours the new dirt into the ground that we have already dug up and he blends it, mixes it with his cute, little gardening shovel.

Afternoon comes and goes as we finish the row for the taller flowers. I take a break to prepare some bologna and cheese sandwiches for lunch.

After a quick lunch, we follow Mikah outside again and he quickly begins ordering us around. We fill the ground in the front of Grandma's house with the new sand, after Mikah carries the old sand away. Mikah busies himself un-potting the flowers. I am not sure what the proper term is, but it makes sense to me to call it un-potting, since you take the flowers, potting soil intact with the roots, out of the pot. Every few inches in the dirt, Mikah sets one of the flowers in the ground and covers it all around with the new dirt. The new sand looks so much richer than any sand around, and it feels wonderfully rich.

I don't care that my fingernails are dark brown with dirt packed tightly under them or that my jeans have dirt stuck to them, from my kneeling. I stand back and admire the fresh dirt with the pretty, small flowers of all colors decorating the ground. Already, I can see Mikah's vision taking shape.

After all the flowers are planted, I am impressed. The front of the house now has a difference look, a face lift almost. It is no longer boring, but now festively beautiful, with flowers dotting the ground. All we have left to plant are the bigger shrubs, which Mikah says will go on the outsides of the flower bed, on either side, so the shrubs will look as if they are protecting the flowers from the right and left side.

The sunlight is slowly fading away and giving into the power of the darkness. As I sit up and take note of this, Adam decides to let the work rest for the day and although I am enjoying myself, I am relieved it's quitting time.

"We can finish up tomorrow," Mikah says with a sort of grunt, almost as if he's disappointed in our progress.

I stand. My knees are wobbly, my feet are heavy, and I stretch them out before I take small steps into the house. Just as I get in, I leave my shoes at the door, and slowly make my way to Grandma's room. I let my body fall onto the bed, and welcome the softness of Grandma's pillows. I lie for a long moment as I let the fatigue and heaviness leave my body. I let my hair, my body, my feet, my mind be still. I regain my strength and focus, and turn over to look up at the ceiling. I am reminded of Grandma, and I let my mind wander through the waves of memories I have of special moments.

I lie for only a few more moments before I realize it's time to start making dinner. When I go into the kitchen, all three men are waiting, to help me prepare dinner. I light the oil lamp and the lantern. And we get started on dinner.

We cook pork chops in the oven, which is something

Adam suggests. He says it is much healthier than fried pork chops, which I am accustomed to eating. Mikah prepares mashed potatoes with gravy. Jonah and I decide to tag-team a vegetable dish—frozen carrots with butter and brown sugar. According to Adam, "a meal is not complete without vegetables."

After dinner is devoured by us all, I began my routine of clean-up, as everyone else retreats to the living room or outside. When the dishes are washed and the table is clean, I allow myself to retreat to the porch, where I find the guys unwinding.

The air outside welcomes me and I welcome it. Fresh air. I think about Grandma again and feel a little excitement come through the air and touch me me. I smile at the thought of having her home.

By now, darkness has taken over, and the night is magnificently comfortable. To the east, there is an even more magnificent wonder—a rising new, orange moon. The moon is large and in that moment, I am sure millions of other people see this same beauty and all are probably just as entranced as I.

"Wow, look at that moon," I say.

For a few moments, we sit in silence and just stare at the moon. I find it intriguing how we all seem to know beauty when we see it. I can accept this idea for myself, but it is difficult to contemplate for city people. I did not know they can be just as intrigued as I by the beauty of nature. However unbelievable, I am impressed with their recognition of beauty, and I appreciate their sense.

We eventually make our way to bed. I look forward to the next morning and anticipate Grandma's homecoming.

I go back into Grandma's room and lie down on the bed. I let my exhausted body fall into a deep sleep.

A Sweet Surprise

The next morning, after a small breakfast of toast and eggs with orange juice, I walk over to the old elm tree to absorb the morning. The day is cooler than the day before, and the ground is dry. I'm sure that tells you how dry the land was—it soaked up every bit of moisture in one evening. The tree is on the side of the house, so when I hear the front screen door open, I cannot see who it is. But soon, Adam comes around the corner, and unfolds a chair of his own and shakes it.

"So, how often do you come out here?" he asks, once he settles comfortably in his chair.

"You mean out to the tree or to Grandma's?" I ask.

"To the tree…I want to know exactly how often you come out to the tree," he says, sarcastically. "No, silly, to Grandma's."

Just then, the door opens and closes again.

"Well, I hope I'll be coming out here every summer until I'm done with school," I say.

"When will that be?" he asks.

I smile. *What a silly question.* But I answer anyway.

"In a couple of years," I say.

"Maybe next summer, we can come back to see you guys again," he says.

I am surprised, but I smile and say, "That would be nice."

"I am really, really glad I decided to come out here," he says.

Unsure of how to respond to his statement at first, I eventually nod my head after a few moments and say, "I'm glad you guys came and stayed."

"We should probably get going into town," he declares, as he rises out of his chair and folds it up.

"Great idea!" I exclaim, as I fold up my chair and lean it against the tree.

We go back inside and dress ourselves with enthusiasm, as if we're on our way to a celebration of some sort. Adam persuades Mikah that he should stay behind and finish planting the trees. It doesn't take much persuasion. Mikah quickly agrees, as if he was thinking the same thing.

"This way," Mikah says, "everything will be planted by the time Grandma comes home."

I can hardly believe these three men have become so passionate about pleasing Grandma. It seems they have a high opinion of her. I respect their actions, and I am even more enthusiastic about what the final result of all the planting work will look like.

I imagine how delighted Grandma will be to come home again and see her front yard, as well as shower in her updated shower. I make a point to buy some new towels for her at Wal-Mart before we come home. I cannot bear to see the raggedy, tattered towels she uses. I decide some new towels will give her bathroom a lift on top of the one it's already been given.

We arrive at the hospital about a half hour later, and I walk fast-paced ahead of everyone into the hospital. I arrive at Grandma's room to find her dressed in the clothes we brought for her the first day, and she is sitting on her bed, with her legs dangling down, watching the morning news show. When she hears my footsteps, she turns towards me and reveals an enormous smile. She is ecstatic and rises slowly from the bed just when the rest of the gang enters the room. She gathers her belongings, what little bit she has accumulated.

I notice there are a couple vases of flowers on her bed side table; one from my aunt, Jeannette and one from Jackie. I give her a giant hug, and hold her for a few seconds longer than normal.

"I'm so glad you're okay, Grandma," I say, finally letting her go.

"I am glad to be alive," she cheerfully says.

The sun is shining into the room and it gives the room a cheerful ambiance.

Adam quickly assumes the responsibility of helping Grandma with her plastic, drawstring bags which bear the logo of the hospital. He takes the bags from her hands, and gives her a gentle hug.

"Grandma! It's time to go home!" Jonah and Mikah say in unison, as they enter the room.

"You guys, it's good to see you," Grandma says, with a smile, as she wipes tears from her eyes.

Both young men embrace her.

A nurse in a pastel pink uniform enters the room, and

says, "Farewell, Mrs. Scott." She looks around the room and asks, "Do you have all of your beautiful flowers?"

There is a heavy Mexican accent in the nurse's voice and her hair is what I believe is the darkest black hair I've ever seen, with perfect, bouncy curls.

"Yes, yes, I think I have everything," Grandma replies.

The nurse gently puts an arm on Grandma's shoulder, while Adam's holds Grandma's left hand and they both escort her out the door.

"You have a safe trip home now. You seem to have enough people who care about you and I'm sure they will take wonderful care of you," the nurse says.

Before we walk through the double doors, which have to be opened with the push of a silver square button on the wall, all the nurses who are seated at the nurse's station individually say, "Goodbye!"

"Bye!" Grandma shouts back.

We walk her outside and Adam helps her into the van, while the rest of us stand back. She gets in with some difficulty, and I come to the realization that Grandma is now more fragile than ever and I cannot view her as I did before, as a vibrant old woman, but rather a delicate woman. And this is heartbreaking, because she is changing.

I always revered her as a strong old woman, who was unbreakable, but just now, she looks weaker than I'd ever seen her and I do not know how to accept this.

After stopping at Safeway to stock up on food and supplies, we stop at Wal-Mart for more shopping and I pick out some pretty, pink towels on sale for $8.88 each. I spend the last of my money on the towels, but am very satisfied with my choice.

The mood on the way home is jovial as we joke and laugh with Grandma about the last couple of days without her. Adam has quite a few jokes about how Mikah, Jonah and I wouldn't have survived without his "expert" cooking skills or without his sense of humor. Although he is only joking, I can't help to think he is somewhat right, in that I wouldn't have survived without them and I couldn't begin to think what I would have done if I ended up on my own for even a couple of days. I laugh right along with everyone else as we travel the rest of the way home.

Once we arrive at the house, and after Mikah helps Grandma out of the van, everyone except Grandma helps to carry groceries and our newly purchased wares into the house.

I head straight for the bathroom to see how well the towels look hanging on Grandma's new towel rack. The towel rack is a brass rod, with small flower-like structures on the ends. Simple and modern. I finish hanging the towels just when Grandma comes into the bathroom.

She is in awe all over again, and expresses her joy. "I am so glad to be home," she says delightfully.

"Please don't have another attack," I say.

"I will try not to," she says, as she makes her way past me and towards the toilet.

I take this as my cue to leave, so I do. I join the guys outside and we admire our work, well mostly Mikah's work.

Grandma joins us again, and I notice she is thinner than before, when she steps down from the porch. She has to hold onto the frame of the porch, as she steps down. Adam rushes to help her, and he walks her a few feet away from the house, so she can take in the entire scene; the trees and plants, which will grow into grand structures to fill the once plain landscape. Mikah had spaced the plants out quite nicely so they weren't too close and not in any particular pattern.

As I stand in my place, waiting for Grandma to find a spot in front of the house, I sneeze, and there is a warm sensation, something warm is released from between my thighs, and I find myself wondering what happened. Oh geez! It's that time of the month for me, my menstruation period. And I'm wearing white shorts! Luckily, there is nobody behind me; everyone is either at my side or in front of me.

Just as Grandma and Adam stop, and they take their place to view the spectacle, I slip away as slyly as I know how. I take a few steps backward to the porch and hurry into the bathroom. I quickly go about cleaning myself up, only to realize I don't have any spare clothes. So, I slip back into my blood-stained shorts, and scurry into Grandma's room to change my clothes.

Outside, I can hear the cheerful conversation about the wonderful landscaping while I tend to my personal hygiene matters inside.

Although I had been experiencing my menstrual cycle for a few years now, I hadn't learned how to forecast the beginning of each cycle yet. It seemed to fluctuate, some months it started at the beginning, other months it started in the beginning, and sometimes, at the end. Although I could have probably used one of Grandma's new towels from the bathroom to cover myself, I didn't want to risk leaving a mark on any of them, so when I feel moistness from the pants on the inside of my thighs, I regret not using the towel after all.

Blood-stained shorts still on, I hastily look through

my bag in Grandma's closet for some clean panties and some clean pants. I don't button up my shorts when I emerge from the bathroom, so I have to walk bow-legged to avoid touching the blood stains. As I bend over and dig through my bag, the shorts manage to slip down from my hip. I dig faster.

Just as I find what I am looking for, I turn around, only to see a man peeking in from the window next to Grandma's bed. I jump at the sight and my shorts slip farther down, while I clutch a clean pair of shorts. I cannot tell right away who it is in the window, but I soon realize it's an older second cousin of mine, Alan, one who is mentally challenged.

I am shocked, and my face must have shown it very well, because Alan jerks away from the window, and walks toward the front of the house. I manage to regain my composure and fumble to get my clothes on before I go back outside.

It turns out Alan walked over from my Grandma Elsa's house, and wandered over to Grandma's bedroom window, as he usually does when he comes to visit. I suppose it is his way of checking to see if anyone was home. I don't know, but whatever his reasons, I didn't expect it this morning, and apparently, nobody else knew he was even at the house.

When I get back outside, Alan begins hollering. "Nasty! Nasty!"

Everyone looks in the direction he's pointing, at me.

My face immediately feels hot. My jaw drops.

Everybody looks confused, as he continues to yell and point at me.

Grandma finally goes to hug him and calm him down.

I immediately feel I have to explain the incident, so I

322

do. And I feel so embarrassed.

When I've gotten out all the words to describe the incident and my shock, Mikah and Adam begin to laugh uncontrollably.

Jonah doesn't laugh at all. Instead, he comes over to me and puts his arms on my shoulders, as if to protect me.

I don't mention anything else about the incident and we all get back to admiring the landscaping.

For the rest of the morning and part of the afternoon, Alan sticks around the house. He occasionally helps out with raking rocks, watering the flowers and whatever else he is able to do. He doesn't talk. He just does as Grandma tells him to do. He eats lunch with us, and sort of wanders around before heading home.

Adam convinces Grandma she needs to rest, although as stubborn as she is, was hard to convince at first. Once Adam gets her into her bed, and reassures her that she has nothing to worry about but sleep, I go into her room and tell her how embarrassed I am about the incident with Alan.

"Oh, Alan, he's not right...his mind is you know...messed up," Grandma says. She is laying on her side, with her elbow propped, head resting on the palms her hand.

"Yeah, I know...but he scared me," I say, as if to defend myself, for an unwarranted reason.

"Do you want to know how he got like that?" she asks me, as she sits upright and scoots herself up in her bed. I help her put a couple more pillows behind her.

"Yeah," I say. As odd as it seems, I never wondered how he got to be the way he was. I just assumed he was born that way.

So I look at her and ask, "He was born that way,

323

right?" just to make sure I have the story right.

"Well, his parents…your cousin, grandma Elsa's daughter, Olivia, and her husband left him alone with another cousin, Julie. She was really young at the time, and she was babysitting him. I don't remember where Olivia and her husband went, but they were gone for two days. I guess Alan got sick somehow, he got a fever, and Julie, you know she was too young to know he was sick," she says. "She said he just felt asleep and he was tired…that's what she told Olivia. She just thought he was really tired, but he had a really high fever and she didn't know it," she continues.

I gasp.

"He was like that for a couple of days before Olivia and her husband came home, and they rushed him to the hospital when they found out he was sick," Grandma says, telling her story, probably for the hundredth time now.

"Oh my god," I say, gasping again. I already know how this story is going to end, but I don't know how else to react. I listen.

"His brain was messed up…that's how he got to be brain damaged…retarded," she finishes.

"What a horrible story," I gasp. My face takes on a shape of its own as I try to comprehend how something so unfortunate can happen, something so preventable, something so terrible.

My god, I never knew what pushed my cousin, Olivia, to become an alcoholic. I now know why she goes on alcohol binges and maybe why she and her husband had split. I can't imagine what kind of irreparable damage that kind of incident can do to a person. But I knew it had to be very bad.

All in one moment, I want to run to Grandma Elsa's

house and apologize to Alan, for something somebody else allowed to happen. I want to hold him. I want to cry for him. I let the sadness linger for a moment before I let anger towards his parents settle in. I become sad once again, knowing there isn't one single thing I can do to make the situation better.

"Gee, that's a sad story, Grandma," I say, with a low, shaky voice.

"Yeah, it's a sad story," she says and slides down a bit in her bed.

Grandma changes the subject, back to her newly updated bathroom and kitchen. I tell her I am happy for her, and she finally got what she deserves. "I want to show Elsa," she says excitedly.

The next day, Grandma and I take a ride in the van with Jonah to see Elsa. Mikah and Adam stay behind to work on touch-ups and on mistakes they see in their work.

If you've ever been to a farm, you would have an image to start with for my grandma, Elsa's house. The house is on the highest ground in this area, and it faces to the east. It is made out of cement, and has a few high windows. It has a plain, wooden porch which looks like it can provide just enough shade for one person.

About a hundred yards to the side of the house and close to the river's edge, sits the sheep corral. To the east of the house sits the horse corral, which works hard to stay intact. It looks to be older than the sheep corral and much shabbier, yet I suppose it does its job. In between the house and the horse corral sits a chicken coop, a nicely sized one at that, made out of wood and wire.

And then of course, there are the sheep dogs, about six of them, parading around, barking at us as we arrive at the house.

When we finally get to the front door, Jonah helps Grandma inside and I follow. Elsa is cooking on her antique, wood-burning stove. She uses it for heating the house and for cooking. She stands in the kitchen and says 'Hello' in Navajo, as we file into her house. She pushes up her glasses on her nose to get a better look at us.

Grandma introduces Jonah.

I spot Alan in the hallway, peeking out from behind a stack of boxes. It's almost as if he's hiding from us and I remember of the story Grandma shared with me. I feel sorry for him, but I don't run to him and hug him as I wanted to do earlier.

Grandma and Elsa converse in Navajo, laughing here and there. Although I could understand about sixty percent of what they talk about, I laugh every time they laugh.

Grandma explains a few jokes to Jonah and I every so often throughout the conversation.

Before leaving, Grandma invites Elsa and her husband to come visit her newly remodeled home.

As I sit in Elsa's house, I can't help to wonder what life on the rez full-time would be for me. I have grown so accustomed to living in the city lately, that I have to re-think my desire to be on the rez every day. Could I do without the stores? Could I do without everything being so close? Could I do without having so many things to do? I don't wonder for very long. Jonah speaks and interrupts my thoughts.

"So…what does your Grandma do?" he asks, referring to Elsa.

Not wanting to be rude and carry on a conversation in English, I nod to the door, and ask him if he wants to go outside. I tell Grandma we'll be outside and we step out.

"Well, she stays home, and takes care of the livestock, I guess," I say.

"That sounds so cool. So, is this like a farm?" he asks curiously, looking over the surroundings.

"What sounds cool? Staying home or taking care of the livestock?" I ask.

"Both," he says.

"What kind of livestock does she have?" he asks, now shading his eyes from the sunlight and gazing at the horse corral.

"Well, she has horses and sheep, and cows," I say. As I say this, I wonder where the cows are kept. And then I remember after a few jogs of my mind, that the cows graze on their own, mostly down by the river.

I point to the sheep corral and explain to Jonah that is where the sheep are and before I can continue through the rest of the structures, he heads off down the path to the corral. So I follow.

"And over there is the horse corral, thus the horses inside," I say.

"Well, the house with the dog inside must be a dog house then," he says, as he looks at me with a smile.

We both laugh. We get to the sheep corral and observe the sheep. Then we go to the horse corral and pet the horses. All the while, I explain as much as I could about how

Elsa uses them, which I know very little about. The only thing I really know is the horses are used for herding sheep sometimes.

Jonah states he's only seen a horse once, and has never actually seen a sheep, except on TV. The experience seems fulfilling to him as he takes in the surroundings. Just as we decide to walk back towards the house, Grandma steps out and waves at us.

"I would have thought none of this is interesting to you...seeing how you're from the city," I say, cracking a smile, as we walk back to the van.

"Yeah, it's all interesting. I like learning new things, especially stuff like this...it's all intriguing," he says and looks back at me with a smile.

"I would think you'd rather be at home, in that big city or a place much more modern than here," I say.

"Quite the opposite, actually...I'm a very simple person and I perceive the way of life out in a positive light, it's cool out here," he says.

As we ride home and Grandma explains to Jonah what most of the jokes were about, I sit in the second row of the now comfy and familiar VW van, considering my conversation with Jonah. I find it hard to believe that a white person, a cool white person from San Francisco would actually perceive life on the rez as cool.

The Aftermath

A few more days pass as Grandma continues to recover, and as Jonah starts on a new project, replacing Grandma's back door off the kitchen, with a newer, sturdier door.

The old door was blocked by a shelf because the frame had been damaged somehow, and the door didn't stay close on its own, so Grandma tied it up with wire. I can't even tell you how she did it or how the wire held it in place because it all looked too jumbled to me. Once Adam unties the wire, and finds the problems, he fixes the frame, and puts a new door on the hinges. It fits so perfectly and gives the kitchen an entirely different look, a much cleaner look.

After the new door is in place, Adam says, "The only thing left to do is to repaint the walls."

So once he finishes with the door, he buys some cream-colored paint, and starts yet another project, of painting the walls. This project is one which everyone gets involved with, except for Grandma, who continues to rest for the next week or so.

On a day when Grandma feels strong enough to take a walk, she asks me to join her on a visit to Elsa's. I happily agree to join her and am certain it will be refreshing for both of us.

Jonah hadn't shown anymore advances since Grandma's return, and I yearn for his attention. So I take it upon myself to ask him to join us on our walk. I find him helping Adam in the kitchen; he is squatting down by the kitchen sink, and fidgeting with something under the sink.

I tap him on the shoulder and he answers with a frustrated tone in his voice, "What is it?!"

Fearing I had somehow upset him over the past few days, I try to recall my actions and what might have stirred this frustration in his voice. I can't think of anything, so I tap him again. This time he turns around.

"Oh, it's you…I'm sorry for yelling at you," he says, wiping his forehead with his forearm.

I accept his apology and smile bashfully. I ask him, "Wanna go with us to Elsa's?"

He looks at his brother, Adam, who says, "Go ahead, bro…I got this."

Jonah looks back up at me and then jumps to his feet. He wipes the sweat from his forehead again and I notice that his cheeks are pink…pink from the heat, I guess. I hadn't seen him like this before. I admire him. His skin is glistening with sweat and he has no shirt on. His jeans fit him so perfectly and his skin is tan, just like I had imagined. His abs are rippled with muscles.

I realize I am drooling. I want to touch him. I want to let my brown skin touch his skin. I feel goose bumps on

330

my arms. Even the hot, dry summer air can't keep me from getting them.

Summers on the rez aren't extreme, but they are warm. Temperatures often reach the upper 90s and on this day, it must be about 95 degrees. And since Grandma doesn't have any air conditioning units, she uses an oscillating fan, which she moves from room to room, depending on where it is needed most. The fan sits in the kitchen now, but it isn't doing much to keep Jonah or Adam from sweating. In fact, it blows nothing but warm air.

Jonah takes a few moments to freshen up. I step out to the porch and find Grandma waiting for us, ready to go. She is standing outside with a wide-brimmed hat on, binoculars around her neck, and wearing shades.

"Grandma, you look like you're going on a safari trip," I say.

She smiles and mentions something about not knowing what a safari is.

Out here, she needed all that, though. So I don't joke anymore about her get-up.

After Jonah joins us, dressed in a clean, white t-shirt and khaki shorts, the three of us walk towards the main road, heading in the direction of Elsa's house. The road we walk down is not traveled frequently, so it is covered with an overgrowth of shrubs. We walk past the pond, cross the main dirt road, and up a long, steep, rocky hill which leads right up to Elsa's front door.

While Grandma goes inside the house, Jonah and I explore Grandma's Elsa's property. I take him to the sheep corral, where he pets a baby lamb and then to horse corral. There we find Elsa's sheepherder, Alvin, who greets us.

"Ha Ho!" Alvin cheerfully says, as we approach the horse corral.

It is not long before Alvin is describing his sheepherding routine to Jonah. Meanwhile, I use Grandma's binoculars to indulge in a little bit of spying. I scan the area and scope out the nearby home of Ruthie, the woman who greeted us at Safeway and was entertaining the thought of having the Navarros do some work for her. Her house is located on the same side of the river as Grandma Elsa's house, about a mile eastward.

With so many wrecked or non-working cars littering the land around her house, I find it difficult to spot her rubble of a house. When I do, I notice a couple of parked cars in front of her house, and I immediately recognize her grandson, Petey, who is at least twenty years old by now. I had only known him a short while, when I was at the boarding school, but he had always seemed withdrawn. Apparently, he isn't so withdrawn anymore, because now, he is surrounded by a gang of people, at the rear of a brown Chevy Malibu with tinted windows.

"I usually let the sheep and horses drink from the river, so I don't have to haul water from the windmill," Alvin is saying to Jonah.

Jonah nudges me and I acknowledge him with a short glance.

"I am spying," I say, keeping steady, with the binoculars propped up to my eyes.

"Alvin is going to show me the river," Jonah says.

I let the binoculars drop around my collar, as I give my attention to Jonah.

He is pointing in the direction of the lightly wooded and bushy area which lines the river's edge. "We're going over that way somewhere," he says, as he walks away.

"Okay, cool, I'm scoping out these people next door," I say, and return to my binocular viewing.

When I focus in on Petey and his friends again, I notice there is an exchange of what looks to be small, pink and blue bags going on. There are two girls, one with short hair who looks to be suffering from a severe case of malnutrition, and another one with long, curly hair who is extra friendly with Petey.

Then I see money change hands and I'm confused. Two guys are leaning on a dark green Chevy S-10 pickup which is parked directly behind the Malibu. One guy, with baggy, black pants and a white tank top passes a roll of money to Petey, who unrolls the money, counts it and then slides it into his pocket.

I let the binoculars drop down and hang. I look around me. There is a flash of guilt that overcomes me and I move out of eyesight, behind the sheep corral I'm still standing next to.

Did I just witness a drug deal? I ponder the idea of such a thing happening here, on this peaceful place. *Maybe it's not so peaceful anymore.*

Instead of positioning the binoculars back on Ruthie's grandson and his friends, I decide to mind my own business and head back into Elsa's house.

Before I reach Elsa's front door, Grandma comes out of the house and yells something like, "Let's go." She could've been saying, "Ho," or "No." Whatever it is, I meet her on the porch, to find out that she has purchased a sheep from her sister.

"I want to butcher a sheep for those guys so they can have some fresh mutton and see what butchering a sheep is like!" she explains excitedly.

"Who? What guys?" I ask, still disturbed by the scene from Ruthie's house.

"You know, those guys," she replies, pointing towards her house.

When Jonah and Alvin return from the river, I share the news of the sheep butchering with them. Jonah is excited about the news while I am instantly disgusted.

I cannot stand seeing a sheep getting butchered, at the hands of some hungry, mad humans. It's heartbreaking and plain old disgusting. Yet, it has been the livelihood of many Navajos over many years. On another hand, I am a carnivorous person so I can't argue with why the butchering has to take place.

With the deal made and the sheep butchering set for the next day, we walk back to Grandma's house and talk casually along the way.

I tell the two of them about what I witnessed back at Elsa's and Grandma isn't surprised.

"They're probably selling drugs, that Stevie uses that crystal meth stuff," she says.

I gasp.

"He is always getting into trouble," Grandma says.

"I can't believe what I'm hearing. Not the innocent Stevie I knew," I say.

'He's not so innocent anymore," Jonah states.

"He used to be so quiet," I say, remembering Stevie from my boarding school days.

"Those are the ones who usually get into drugs," Jonah says, as he walks on the other side of Grandma, with a stick in hand. He taps the ground with the stick as he walks.

"Crystal meth? Out here?" I ask.

"Yes. It's all over the rez. The Navajo police were out here questioning us a couple months back. They wanted to know if we knew anyone who sells crystal meth," Grandma says.

"Really?" I ask, still in disbelief about drugs actually being something people out here would use.

"And what did you say?" I ask.

"I told them I didn't know anybody, I don't want to get mixed up in that," she says.

The afternoon sun beats down on us and I shade the right side of my face as I walk.

"How do you know they're dealing?" Jonah asks.

"Ruthie's house has a lot of cars come and go," Grandma answers. "What else can they be doing?"

"Wow, that's crazy," I say.

"Your uncle was telling me about how he helped Petey sell some of that stuff, too," Grandma adds.

As we continue our walk, Grandma changes the subject and tells mostly Jonah how the Spanish introduced the Navajos to sheep; they were the first to bring them to the local trading posts a long, long time before. And once the Navajo people figured out a sheep can give them meat, wool for weaving, and sheepskin for sleeping mats, they valued the new commodity and began buying up sheep like crazy. And since then, Navajo people consider sheep to be extremely valuable and the more sheep you have, the wealthier you are as a person.

When we get home, Jonah informs his brothers of our purchase and about their chance to witness the butchering of a sheep, which according to him is "sacred." They are ecstatic, as if they won some kind of a prize.

I find their excitement disgusting. It must be their barbaric side coming out is all I can guess. I retreat to the outdoors after we get home, taking a chair out under the tree, and sitting to enjoy the light, dry breeze from the west.

The air is settled and warm in between breezes. In my comfort, I let my mind wander.

I had never expected the Navarros to come to the rez, nonetheless, getting to know them and considering them family, but it was happening. And I welcomed the closeness. They are all such jovial, relaxed, and wonderful people. Anytime before now, I would not have allowed myself to become so close to white people, and always regarded them as something I cannot touch, people I cannot know, or people who I could not relate to, people who are my enemy.

Ever since I sat in class one day, listening to the torture and torment we suffered at the hands of the white man many, many years ago, I had grown to dislike them very much. Yet, here are three white guys, so warm-hearted, and easy-going. I feel close to them, as if we have known each other for years and I decide I cannot treat see them as replicas of their ancestors, but rather as friends and family.

We Are Savages

The next morning, I am greeted with a bright sunrise and a cool breeze as I lay in Grandma's bed, with her windows open. I wake early to the smell of breakfast cooking, or at least the smell of bacon. I join everyone in the kitchen after washing up. The Navarros are still excited about butchering a sheep and that is what they are talking about when I sit down.

Although I do not want to watch the big event, I decide to tag along to Elsa's after we finish breakfast.

I wear some faded, tattered jeans which I find in one of Grandma's boxes of old clothes, and a long sleeved white t-shirt. I advise the Navarros to wear something they wouldn't mind dirtying, because butchering a sheep will surely mess their clothes. That's of course, if they participate.

Once we get to Elsa's, we park next to the shed, where the sheepherder, Alvin and Elsa are standing. Both look like they're prepared. Alvin is wearing some tight Wrangler jeans and a long-sleeved brown, button-up shirt.

Elsa is wearing what looks like her oldest Navajo skirt, with a long-sleeved blue t-shirt. This isn't her everyday attire. She is usually wearing a fancy get-up; a Navajo skirt with a traditional blouse and turquoise jewelry.

Alvin already has the sheep tied up on the ground, next to a large tub of water.

After we get out of the van, and the Navarros observe the sheep, Alvin makes small talk with them, mostly about how the butchering will happen.

He is wearing a brown and white cap that says, 'This Way to Mutton'. He smiles and reveals brown, crooked teeth which look like they've been waiting to be let loose. The front ones dart outwards. He has buckteeth. He smiles nevertheless, not ashamed of his teeth.

The sheep is wiggling and baa'ing on the ground. I immediately feel sick and run to the outhouse. I can feel my breakfast making its way up my throat and I don't hold it back. I let it come. After I spew out my breakfast and I emerge from the outhouse, Elsa summons me to go inside the house for water. Once I'm cleaned up and have taken a few drinks of water, I finally work up enough nerve to go back to the butchering area. I avoid looking directly at what is happening. Although I cannot see, I can hear Elsa ordering the Navarro men around, and Grandma translating the orders.

"Hold the pan still!"

I hear feet shuffle.

"Hold that leg!"

I hear Adam commenting about the leg slipping from his grip.

"Move over here and hold this."

And I can imagine what is happening because I have

seen a butcher happen. It was a horrible sight to see at age five and I will never forget seeing the blood squirt from the sheep's neck as its throat was cut. The sight spurred all kinds of thoughts, and I asked Grandma why we had to kill the sheep. She pulled me aside after the throat was cut, and kneeled down to look me in the eyes and she explained, 'It was the sheep's time to die.'

Once the worst part is over, and the sheep's body parts are separated, I finally find enough courage to look at the butchering area. Elsa and Grandma hurry around, carrying sheep parts into the house for cleaning. Alvin and Elsa's husband, Harry carry the sheepskin to a nearby clothes line and hang it to dry, after wiping a few drops of blood from the inside. Adam helps by spilling out the bloody water. Mikah and Jonah just stand back from the aftermath, under the shed roof. They make comments about their experience.

I walk over to Jonah, who is washing his hands in a pan of water Elsa has brought out for everyone to wash their hands in. The water is a pinkish color, from the blood.

"So how was it?" I ask him.

"It was cool, kinda' disgusting, but cool," he says.

"Yeah, you have to have a strong stomach to do that kind of stuff," I say. Inside, I am trying not to think of the blood, and the wails I heard from the sheep before its final breath.

Adam proudly exclaims, "I helped to hold the sheep down," and after a sigh, he adds, "It's not like anything I've ever done before."

When I ask Mikah for comments on his experience, he doesn't appear to be fascinated with it. He simply says, "It was okay."

In the next second or so, I notice how flush his face looks. I don't ask him if he's sick. I know he's sick. So I pull him away from the shed. I pull him towards the bushes that are nearby. And he vomits. His pale, muscular body jolts with each jerk.

"I'm glad I'm not the only who cannot hold it in," I say, after he is done vomiting.

I lead him into the house and he goes into the wash room to clean up. Apparently, Elsa has a working plumbing system, because I hear the water running as he washes up. He comes back out, looking refreshed with his face back to its normal color and his blonde hair patted down with water.

I smile and say, "You are now an official butcher."

He just smiles.

After the meat is cut and cleaned, it is cooked. When it comes to butchering sheep, Navajos do not waste any one thing from the sheep, so Elsa prepares a different dish from all the organs, and insides. Of course, she has to empty the stomach contents before using the stomach. She pours the blood from the pan taken from under the sheep's slit throat, and uses her fingers to clean any clumps from the blood. Then she pours it into the stomach, which is then tied with a piece of intestine. She takes this balloon-like thingamajig into the house, where she will boil it and make blood sausage. As most Navajos think of this as a delicacy, I only think of it for what it is, blood in a stomach.

I am sure my grandma, Elsa would say I think I'm too good for blood sausage, but I could care less what she would say. It is what it is and I'm not a blood eating person. The rest of the organs, except for the heart are cooked as well. The head is cooked as well, in the oven. And so are the feet.

Nothing is wasted. Not even the wool. Elsa gives the wool to Grandma, for weaving.

While we wait for the food to be prepared, we talk more about the butchering.

Adam says he should've brought his camera, and I am grimace at his comment. Why anyone would want a picture or even a memory of such a nauseating act is beyond me.

Grandma makes some tortillas while Elsa cooks the meat on her makeshift grill.

After the food is ready, we eat and the Navarros comment on how unusual, but good the meat tastes. Of course, the taste is unusual as they have never tasted mutton before. Although I do not enjoy the taste of mutton, I force myself to eat a rib and it is satisfying, for I am hungry once again. I wonder if there will ever come a time that I will gladly enjoy this food. I think not. And we eventually head home.

When we get home, I feel dirty for some reason. I don't know why exactly, because it wasn't me who did the butchering. I disregard figuring out why, and I run the water in the bath tub. Before I can fill half of the tub, the hot water turns cold. So I boil some water, and pour it in, to make it nice and toasty.

I slide my petite frame into the water and I fit perfectly into the smooth ivory-finish tub. As I soak in the bathtub of semi-hot water, and let the heat burn my skin, I let my mind wander off and I find myself thinking about Stevie and his friends.

I wonder if his grandmother, Ruthie, knows about his business and if so, how she allows it to happen right in front of her house.

I wonder what Grandma would do if I was to do anything of the sort. I imagine she would yell at me, like she does to Anthony. And then she'd probably slap me and kick me out of her house. The thought of all that happening is enough to keep me from even thinking about dishonoring my grandmother.

As I continue to soak in the water, I wonder how crystal meth came to be a popular item on the rez. In my naivety, I thought drugs were only used and sold in the cities. I had never imagined anyone on the rez, especially one of our neighbors, using it, nonetheless, selling it.

The water is still somewhat hot and I splash my face with it.

I lather myself with the bar of Dove soap, which is sitting on the side of the tub, and I rinse myself.

I towel myself off after my bath and drain the dirty water. I realize I didn't bring my clean clothes into the bathroom. I contemplate on calling Grandma over, but decide to listen for her voice before calling her.

I strain my ears and listen for voices, I don't hear anything. I wonder if anyone's even inside. Instead of yelling for someone to bring me some clothes, I decide to tip-toe into the kitchen. I'd rather do this than put on the dingy clothes I had on before. When I get to the corner that separates the kitchen from the living room, I peek around it and see only Grandma, who is asleep on the couch. She is halfway sitting up. Her head has fallen back on the couch.

I tip-toe over to her shake her gently to wake her. When she wakes, I tell her to lie down on the bed in her room, and she does so lazily, still half asleep.

In the transition, she mumbles, "The guys went back to Elsa's."

With my towel still wrapped around my body, I help her to her bed and I tell her, "Shhh." When I stand up and turn towards the closet, I notice a figure in her bedroom doorway. It is Jonah.

Shock. On my face. Shock. On his face. His eyes widen. My eyes widen.

I gasp. "I thought you guys left!" I exclaim. I know I'm not naked, but I feel naked. And I wrap my arms around my towel, as if to cover myself more.

He shuts his eyes and says, "I'm sorry," and then he turns around.

I scurry to the closet and dig through my bag for some clean clothes.

I can hear him in the next room, still saying he's sorry.

I clumsily and quickly put my clothes on.

When I go back into the living room, he is standing in the middle of the room, with his back turned and his hands in his back pockets. He looks nervous and just stands there, waiting patiently.

I admire him for a few seconds and then I say, "Okay, you can turn around now."

I laugh. I am relieved the embarrassing moment has passed. He smiles and says he's sorry again.

"Your shoulders and thighs look good," he says sarcastically.

"Uh-huh, you're lucky I had a towel wrapped around me. Otherwise, you would've gone blind."

"What?" he asks, confused by my sarcasm.

"Grandma used to tell me as a child, that if I see a naked person, I will go blind."

We both laugh.

He walks towards the front door just as I take a few steps to go back to the bathroom.

A strand of hair is dangling in my face and I don't recognize how close we are to bumping into each other. But he does, so he stops. Then I stop. And he waves his left hand outward and in a circle, then bows, as if to give me the right of way in a majestic way.

I smile and nod. I start walking towards the kitchen again. As I pass him, I can feel him, his energy, and his stare. I wonder if he feels the closeness I feel. I wonder if he can feel my energy.

I feel his hand, as he reaches out and takes hold of my left arm. My heart stops. I turn towards him and I can't believe he is holding my arm. My body is in shock and I feel as if I will melt, right onto Grandma's pewter green rug. The only thing I can think is, *don't look into his eyes.*

My eyes don't listen to my brain and they wander. His eyes, so beautiful and blue stare right at me. The look in his eyes…he looks as if he wants to give me more than he can, as if he wants more from me. I want to reach out and touch him. But I don't.

He pulls me closer to him and I let my feet and body move with his pull. In that moment we are so close to each other; I can feel his breath and he can feel mine.

Then I remember Grandma is in the next room. And I jerk…I pull away from him.

He lets me go. Then he looks away as if he's ashamed of what he has just done.

I don't know what to say or do. So I just walk away. I get behind the kitchen wall, out of his sight, and I lean against the wall. A rush of mixed feelings comes. There is shame, guilt, pleasure and excitement. I don't know what to think. I know I can't like him. I'm too young.

I finally gather up enough courage to step back out to the living room. And when I do, he is sitting on the couch, with his head in his hands.

I sit down by him and say, "I like you, too, but I am sure we cannot do what we want to do."

With his head still in his hands, he mutters, "I know."

He stands, walks over to the screen door and then out onto the porch.

I follow him.

He looks so cool, wearing his khaki pants and a red Polo t-shirt. The color of his t-shirt brings out his features so well. In that moment, I imagine he is a model who just walked out of a magazine. I smile inside as I take in the sight of him, standing here on my Grandma's front porch. He looks distraught but I focus instead on his lips, and his handsome face—big, blue eyes, his straight nose with a perfect bulge at the tip and his smooth skin.

I have to turn away. I look out at the valley.

"Want to go for a walk in the fields?" he asks.

Somewhat confused, I ask, "What fields?"

"Out there," he says, pointing out to the bushes.

"You mean go for a walk in the bushes?" I ask, even more confused.

"Bushes, fields, whatever," he says.

Who would want to go for a walk in those bushes? I don't speak my mind. I am still confused and surprised at his question. "We don't go out there. I've never known anyone who wanted to go for a walk in those bushes," I say.

"But it's so open and beautiful," he says, looking out to the valley, mesmerized.

I have no desire to take a walk in the bushes, so I ask, "How about we go for a walk to the pond?"

"That sounds like an even better idea," he says. I am sure I would have taken him, if not all of the guys to the pond by now, if we weren't so busy with all the craziness going on.

And with that, I trot down the porch step and around the back of the house to lead the way.

He follows me and walks with his hands in his pockets.

I slow down and we walk up the hill behind Grandma's house together. As we walk, we talk. He talks about school and how he can't wait to finish school and start making some real money. I tell him I'm excited for him and it's wonderful that he has a bright future. I tell him that I look forward to going back to school, but not back to Los Angeles.

When we reach the pond, he picks up one of the millions of glassy rocks from the ground and throws it towards the water. The rock bounces on the top of the water. We both watch the rock disappear, and then he asks, "So, will you miss me when we leave?"

My heart flutters.

He picks up another rock, throws it and it skips on the water top again.

"I suppose," I say shyly.

I look up and take in the grand view of the land. There is another valley on this side, and a view of the majestic San Francisco Peaks, rising up towards the sky, like jaws of a shark protruding from the ground.

I feel Jonah taking my hand, and I turn to him. He smiles at me and says, 'I've liked you since the minute I first saw you and I think you're an amazing young lady."

I start to speak, but he softly puts his index finger up to my mouth. I want to tell him I can't think about our attraction right now.

I think of my grandma, Elsa and her hawk eyes. I think of Mikah and Jonah, who are probably still at Elsa's house, and can probably see us from there. I imagine Ruthie's son, Daniel, a.k.a. "Peeping Tom," from across the road, with his binoculars trained on us. I want to take a couple steps back, but I don't.

"I thought you were beautiful the minute I set my eyes on you," he says.

I move his finger from my mouth and I say, "You can't like me."

"You are not like any girl I've ever met before," he says.

In an attempt to lighten the subject, I say, "Duh, I know...I'm probably the only Navajo girl you've ever met."

"You know what I mean," he says. Surprisingly, he takes a step away from me and lets my hand go. I want him to be close to me and hold my hand. I want his attention for a few more seconds at least. But I let him walk away, knowing I cannot indulge.

"Not wanting him to feel rejected, I apologetically say, "I do know what you mean, but we're from different worlds." I pause and can almost hear his heart break. "Not to mention, I'm still a child, as you so eloquently put it."

"I didn't mean a child in the literal sense, I meant underage."

"I know what you meant. I'm just being a pain."

"So, we're from different worlds, huh?" he asks, as he nods slowly, as if he shows his disapproval of the words.

"Yeah, I mean look at this place, look at me, we are different," I say.

"We're not as different as you think," he says with a smile.

I pick up a rock and throw it. It doesn't skip on the water. It sinks.

We both laugh.

"We better get home and check on Grandma," I say, turning back in the direction we came.

We make the walk home, with no more talk of our attraction to each other. He mostly makes observations of the plain land.

When we get back to the house, we both quietly go back inside. I go to Grandma's room and check on her.

She is still snoring away.

"Ahh, poor Grandma," I whisper.

She is always running; cooking, cleaning, and caring for everybody else but herself. She still has her apron on. I know she must be ready for a bath. So I fill up as many pots as I can fit on the stove, and turn the temperature up to high on all four eyes. I will add this to the water I fill up in the bathtub for her. I know she will need extra hot water since the running water cools quickly.

I step back into the living room. The house is still. And I remember why I love being here, the peace and quiet.

Grandma eventually wakes and rolls out of bed.

When I tell her the bathtub is ready for her, she is surprised and heads right to the bathroom.

Adam and Mikah come home eventually, and tell us they had to return Elsa's bowls which they had used to bring leftovers home with.

We eat sliced mutton with gravy and tortillas for dinner that evening and the long, hot day ends.

Nobody complains about not having vegetables or a side dish to go along with the mutton. We quietly eat the butchered sheep's meat.

Peace, At Last

Another few days pass with all of us pitching in to finish painting the kitchen, and then the living room, and eventually the other two rooms in the house. Finally, the house is ready. What a dramatic effect the new paint has on the house…it seems so much more beautiful, transformed from a dull, old house. The change is like from a rusty, broke-down car to a brand new one.

As the last of all the painting supplies are removed from the house and the floors are cleaned, Grandma suggests we invite some family, which means her sister and maybe her mother. Everyone agrees the idea is a good one, so Grandma and Adam make their rounds of visiting people and inviting them for a cook-out, which is set to happen that evening.

While Grandma and Adam are out inviting relatives, Mikah and Jonah build a fire near the small wood pile, then put cinder blocks around it, and lower Grandma's grill plate over the blocks…voila, a homemade fire pit. As I sit on a wooden log near the wood pile, I wonder if they enjoy the work.

"Where did you guys learn how to build a fire?" I ask.

In between huffs and puffs, Jonah replies, "Well, our father taught us."

And so their stories of camping in a place near a place called Lake Tahoe begin. Each recounts their memories of the few visits to the area with their father. Their stories of putting up tents, building fires, fishing, and hiking all seem to run together, because by the time Grandma and Adam come home, I can't remember any one exact trip they spoke of. But it turns out, each of them learned to build fires at a young age, and I had to compliment them on their fire-building skills.

The flames from the fire grow, and the fire itself looks marvelous.

Before long, a couple of vehicles are parked in the driveway of the house, and more people sit around the fire, as Grandma cooks the beef steaks.

Elsa, her husband, Harry, Great Grandma, and an older second cousin of mine, Ann, who is Great Grandma's caretaker all sit around and joke with Grandma in Navajo.

As for the rest of us, the younger and modern crowd, we stand in a circle a few feet away from the fire, and talk.

Although we could have taken our conversation into the house, Adam suggests we stay near the fire and Grandma, just in case she needs anything. And it is a good thing we do, because she needs quite a few things; a pan for the cooked meat, a longer fork than what she started out with, more wood on the fire, some paper towels and so on.

"What is Grandma going to do with all that wool?" Jonah asks me.

"Spindle it," I proudly say.

The next few minutes we spend talking about how

the wool is spindled, and then woven into a rug. He is impressed with the art of weaving and says, "It must be a great skill."

I laugh and say, "Yes, it is."

"Do you know how to do all that?" he asks.

"No, not yet, but I want to learn soon," I reply.

Indeed, it will be a great skill for me to learn.

Facing Grandma, I ask, "Can you teach me how to weave?"

As she pokes at the meat on the grill, she answers, "Yes, whenever you're ready to learn."

Grandma Elsa, her husband Harry, and Great Grandma all sit quietly and observe the Navarros. Ann helps Grandma with the cooking.

As the flames lick at the sky and fight with the darkness, I shift my attention towards the main road and notice a person walking towards us in the dark.

I let out a small yell of fear, before recognizing the person as Anthony.

Everybody turns around and Grandma lets out a small yell as well.

"What are you doing out here?" she asks my uncle, who is only a few feet away now.

He is drunk, and staggering towards us, with a bottle of whiskey in his right hand. He waves the bottle at us and takes a seat next to his mother, on the ground. He hangs his head.

He doesn't say anything. He just sits there and lets his head hang. His shoes have dried mud on them and as he relaxes his legs more, I notice a familiar pattern. The elongated W's and the letters CAT.

I look in the direction he came from and this time, I notice a set of headlights in the dark. *Oh geez, now who's coming?* Before I can say something to alert everyone else, Jonah speaks up.

"Hey, somebody's coming!" he blurts out excitedly.

Everybody else turns their head in the direction he is looking and they acknowledge the headlights. There are a few grunts and a sigh. I am almost sure it was Grandma who sighed.

Jonah on the other hand, is still excited that he made the discovery. Adam and Mikah don't seem too thrilled about the vehicle coming up the road; they just stand and observe.

Grandma gets up and walks towards the house with Adam, Mikah, and Grandma Elsa. The rest of us stay behind, but keep our eyes on the approaching headlights.

It appears there are two vehicles. As they get closer to the house, I stand and walk towards the house. Jonah follows.

When the vehicles come to a stop, I realize the first car is Marvin's and the second vehicle is Detective Yazzie's.

My uncle remains on the ground back at the wood pile, with Great Grandma and Grandpa Harry.

Detective Yazzie quickly gets out of his car and approaches Grandma.

"We came to arrest our suspect," the detective says in a flat and demanding tone.

"What?" Grandma asks in disbelief. She puts her hands on her hips.

I am a few feet away from her and the detective.

Jonah and Mikah are standing on the porch and

Adam has gone inside the house.

Grandma Elsa asks her sister in Navajo, "What are they saying?"

Grandma doesn't answer her. She keeps her eyes on the detective, as if she's still waiting for him to repeat himself.

"Where is your son?" Detective Yazzie asks. In the darkness, his eyes look more slanted than before and he appears uptight.

Marvin is out of his car by now and explains, "Your son is a suspect," in his strong, southern accent.

"That can't be," Grandma says, still in disbelief.

I am just as confused as she is.

"How did he come to be a suspect?" Mikah asks.

"We can't share the details right now," Marvin calmly explains.

Without thinking twice, I run back towards my uncle. In that moment, I want to save him rather than send him away. But I know I can't. I shove him. I hear footsteps running after me. He doesn't budge. With his head hanging low, his wavy hair is covering his face. I shove him again. This time, his neck jerks back to hold his head up. He looks at me. The flames from the fire shine just enough light on him and I can see that his eyes are bloodshot.

Within seconds, Detective Yazzie and Marvin are pushing me out of the way and dragging my uncle to his feet while my uncle curses at them.

Great Grandma and Grandpa Harry just sit and watch all of this from their seats. They don't move. I imagine they are too old and tired to jump up for the action.

I look back towards the house and I can see Adam holding Grandma close to his chest, as if to protect her from the sight.

My uncle grumbles and curses. "Get your hands off me. You want a fight?!"

He is quickly cuffed by Detective Yazzie, who makes no hesitation to begin reading my uncle his rights.

My uncle struggles with the officer and ends up getting pinned to the ground. Detective Yazzie kneels on the small of his back while Marvin opens the door to the white SUV, the one with the tribal seal on the side of the door.

Without much effort, in the next minutes, the two men drag my drunken uncle's limp body to the white SUV while we all watch in astonishment.

In that moment, I become angry at my uncle. How can he get involved in such a horrible incident? What did he do? Why?

"What is going on?" Grandma cries out.

Adam pulls her closer. "Shhh," he says.

"We're arresting him because he is a suspect," Detective Yazzie explains, after he catches his breath from the struggle.

Adam lets Grandma go. She reaches out for her son. Adam holds her back again.

"I…I don't understand," Grandma says. "Be careful with him."

The door to the SUV closes. My uncle wiggles in his seat.

Marvin is speaking to Detective Yazzie when he asks, "Can you handle him?"

Detective Yazzie, answers, "He's drunk. He can't fight. I can handle him."

The beams from headlights shine on the detective's

midsection and the gun propped in its holster as he makes his way around the front of the SUV.

Marvin apologetically says, "Sorry guys." He lowers his head and climbs back into his car.

The engines start.

The two vehicles depart.

My heart sinks as I listen to Grandma's uncontrollable sobs.

Dinner is littered with small conversation, as Grandma mostly talks to her mother and sister in Navajo. I can hear confusion and frustration in her voice, and maybe even some fear.

I am sitting next to her and I can sense her frustration through the air. I immediately become worried about her and fear she might have another attack from all the extra stress so I scoot my chair closer to her and embrace her.

"Are you okay, Grandma?" I ask, wrapping my arms around her and nestling my head on her shoulder.

"Yes, I'm okay," she replies with a warm, yet unsettled voice.

"I can't believe what happened," I say.

Jonah and Mikah are nowhere to be seen. I presume they are probably outside somewhere. Adam is in the guest room. I can hear him making thumping noises. It sounds like he could be moving stuff or stomping. I want them to come in and tell Grandma everything is going to be okay.

Grandma's sister shows nothing resembling

sympathy for her sister. Instead, she makes note of how nice the kitchen looks.

Grandma smiles and says it's all because of the hard work from our visitors that she has such a nice kitchen.

After Grandma, her sister and her mother finish eating dinner, Jonah, Mikah, and I clean the kitchen by the glow of a lantern, while Grandma continues to visit with her family on the porch.

I try to focus on cleaning the kitchen, but my mind runs through the events of the day, and I try to figure out how and why my uncle is a suspect in the murder of Mr. Yazzie; the man who looked straight through me, not long before he died.

"I am so sorry about what happened today," Jonah says, as he stands in the middle of the kitchen, between the sink and the table. The look on his face is filled with sympathy and compassion. The bright, blue eyes I have grown accustomed to seeing now look sad and not as bright.

I do not know what to say to express my ball of emotions. I can't even decide on what it is I am feeling. Is it anger? Is it confusion? Is it sadness?

"Yes," I say and nod.

After the cleaning of the kitchen is complete, and all the dishes are nicely put away in the cupboards, Jonah refreshes himself with a shower while Mikah and I go outside and join everyone else on the porch.

The night air is cool.

Not long after we get out to the porch do Great Grandma and Grandma Elsa announce they should be heading home. So Grandpa Harry starts up his truck and the three of them leave us.

"I can't believe Anthony was arrested," Grandma says.

"I'm sure he is innocent. He'll probably be back here tomorrow," Adam says. He had been in the room all this time and finally makes his appearance, stepping out onto the porch.

And right after him, comes Jonah, with a towel loosely covering his broad, muscular shoulders. He is wearing some casual, sporty shorts. He is without a shirt, and his chest looks perfect—not too muscular and not too flat. The bulges are just round enough to show he works out.

"Let's not talk about that…let's talk about the stars, or the moon," Jonah says, shifting the mood.

"Yeah, that's a good idea," Mikah says cheerfully.

And so we do. I get up and step down from the porch to gaze at the stars. Mikah and Jonah do the same. I am mesmerized by the beauty of the night. As we stand and peer up at the sky, we point out which constellations we know and Mikah knows the most.

Grandma doesn't sit with us long. She appears to be bored with the star-gazing, and rises out of her chair to go inside the house.

"Don't worry too much, okay, Grandma?" I say.

"Yeah, we don't want you to end up in the hospital again," Mikah says somberly.

"I'll be okay," she quietly says.

The screen door closes. Then there is silence. The night air blows.

"Well, good night, everyone," I say and silently retreat to Grandma's room, where I change into my nightgown and slip into bed.

And just like that, the murder suspect is arrested and whisked away. I try to sleep, but I toss and turn instead, thinking about my uncle's actions and wondering how he could've killed another person one day and be back to normal the next day. I am disturbed by the fact that we joked and laughed with him.

At some point during the night, I finally doze off.

The Calm After the Storm

The next morning is a reserved one. There is little talk. Everyone finds their own space and for the most part, everyone stays within their personal boundaries.

Adam busies himself with tidying up outside the house. He straightens the old shed, to the point I don't recognize it when I walk inside. He puts in a couple of hours updating the outhouse with a new roof and a little window. The outhouse looks more like a little house than the old, smelly outhouse it used to be.

Jonah reads an old, worn book from Grandma's personal library of Louis L'amour books. I can only guess where she got her books from, most likely the remnants of her daughters' old reading material.

Mikah tends to the flower garden. He gives Grandma tips on how to do this and do that, how to keep bugs away, and all kinds of fun, gardening knowledge.

Grandma quietly weaves and then treats herself to a mid-morning nap.

With no one paying any mind to me, I decide today is a good day to take a long shower and pamper myself. I begin my pampering with the plucking of the hairs from my armpit. I move onto a good shave of my leg hairs. I can't forget about the plucking of my eyebrows and a facial mask. I finish with a long, warm shower.

When I emerge from the bathroom, I hear voices outside. So I step out to the front porch.

I hear Mikah saying, "So...the man must have been running to this house for help."

Marvin, with a cowboy hat hiding his receding hairline, and his Oakley shades covering his eyes, is standing next to his car. Detective Yazzie, in a black suit with a white, collared shirt, is outside too, standing next to Marvin. They appear to be deep in discussion with Grandma and Adam, who are standing near the deputy's car, facing the two men.

"Probably...well, your uncle allegedly told Kyle and Johnny he would get revenge, and that is exactly what he did," the deputy explains.

"Wow, that is horrible," Jonah says.

Grandma lets out a small gasp and covers her mouth with a cupped hand.

As the deputy spills the details of the murder, I can't help but wonder if he is being so informative only because the Navarros are here. I wonder if he would even give us the time of day, nonetheless, share the details of the case with us, had it not been for a few white guys staying with us. Before I let the thought carry me away, I shift my focus back to the conversation.

"So, how long will Anthony be locked up?" Grandma asks.

"Well, once he is convicted, it will be a long while," the deputy replies.

Detective Yazzie speaks up. He is chewing on a toothpick and has to pull it out before he says, "We are holding him for now, but he has confessed to taking part in the murder. We don't know how long he'll be in, not until he's sentenced."

Grandma begins crying and covers her face entirely with both of her hands.

Adam quickly puts his arms around her and holds her close, as if he is protecting her from the news.

I inhale and I hold my breath. I can't breathe. The sadness and the anger overwhelm me at once. But I don't cry. I don't yell. I don't gasp. I don't breathe.

"When can we see him?" Grandma asks.

"Probably not for a few days…after a couple days, you can come by the jail in Window Rock," Detective Yazzie explains.

"Window Rock? That's too far," Grandma says.

"Yes, he'll be in Window Rock and then if he's found guilty, which I'm sure he will be; he'll be moved to a federal prison."

As the deputy puts the notepad he is holding back into his chest pocket, Grandma sobs and sobs. Her shoulders move up and down with each sob.

The sun shines brightly. There is no breeze.

Federal prison. The words ring throughout my head. Federal prison. The words seem so severe. I have always thought of federal prisons as places nobody I know goes. They've always seemed so far away, in another world. Yet, here are those two words, being said to Grandma, in reference to somebody we know, somebody from this very house.

Mikah and Jonah stand quietly on either side of me. I

feel their presence, but I don't acknowledge them.

Marvin reaches his hand out to Adam and they shake hands, before he says, "Thanks so much for all the help you guys gave me." He goes on to shake Mikah's, then Jonah's hand. "If it weren't for you guys, we would've probably still been working the case."

"I don't know if that's a good thing. I didn't know my old playmate would be the one to get arrested," Adam says disappointedly.

Marvin shakes my hand, and says, "And thank you, young lady." His hands are rough and he has a firm grip.

I breathe. And I shake his hands.

He doesn't shake Grandma's hand. Instead, he gives her a soft rub on the shoulders as Adam continues to hold her close.

Detective Yazzie gives his head a little shake, to move his thick, wavy bangs out of his face. He doesn't shake hands with everyone. Instead, he waves from where he stands and says, "Bye and thanks."

When the two visitors are in their vehicles and on their way, I whisper to Jonah. "How did they find my uncle as a suspect?"

He sighs and then answers, "Well, they looked at their jail records and found that he spent time in jail with the victim, and that there was a complaint from him about rape that same time."

"A complaint from who?"

"From Anthony."

"Umm, okay?"

"Well, put two and two together, and your uncle, was the rape victim and Eddie Yazzie was the rapist."

"Oh my god!" I exclaim. My heart sinks and my chest feels heavy. The information is disturbing.

"Oh my god," I say again.

"So, with a little help from his friends, he killed the man for revenge."

Marvin and Detective Yazzie leave us again.

"And he confessed to the murder?" I ask.

"Yep," Adam answers.

I sit on the porch and absorb the news. I let my head fall back and I roll my neck.

The screen door opens and closes. I don't look back to see who it is.

Suddenly, I feel hands touching and then gently rubbing my shoulders. I let my head fall back again and recognize Jonah's face. His small patch of a beard is directly above me. My head is pressed against his rock-hard abs.

I exhale and release the tension. I let him rub my shoulders.

Just as I'm getting comfortable, Grandma hollers from the kitchen, "Dinner time!"

"A couple more seconds of that and I might've fallen asleep," I calmly say.

I slowly rise.

"Don't worry about your uncle too much, not much you can do," he sympathetically says.

"Yeah, I know," I say, with a sigh.

Playfully, he puts his arm around me, and squeezes me, as he pulls me into the house.

"When do I get my return on investment?" he asks.

"Your who?"

"My shoulder rub."

"Umm, when you finish with my rub," I say and bust out laughing.

"That's actually not funny," he says as he follows me into the bathroom. "And for your information, I'm already finished."

I laugh shyly and say nothing else.

After a quick wash of my hands, we are sitting at the table, once again, ready to indulge in some fried chicken.

Jonah and Mikah take a seat on either side of the table. Adam and Grandma sit at the ends of the table.

I sit by myself on one side, and the chair that Anthony was sitting in several days before is empty. I hope my uncle is safe wherever he is, and I hope he is well. Hope, that's all I can do. It's all Grandma can do. It's all any of us can do, so we do it, silently.

The food on the plates shrink, and everyone is looking like they've had their fill of fried chicken, when Adam makes an announcement.

"I got my old job back," he says, after setting the paper towel that was draped over his lap, on the table.

His expression is one of satisfaction. He takes off the ball cap from his head, to reveal his misshapen, dusty blonde hair. He gazes all around the table, waiting for a response.

Mikah and Jonah look at him and Jonah says, "Congratulations?"

Adam replies with a nod of his head, "Thank you…it is a congratulations." He adjusts the glasses which sit on his nose.

A round of "Congratulations" comes from the table.

As it turns out, Adam, at some point during his supply excursions, had checked his voicemail on the phone back home and received a message from his previous boss, who offered him the job he was laid off from.

"I bet you're ready to go home," Grandma says, sitting back in her chair, as if to show relief or satisfaction from the food.

I wipe the fried chicken grease from my mouth, and I smile before I ask, "So, I take it you guys will be leaving soon?"

"Yes, we will actually need to leave tomorrow," Adam replies.

Jonah and Mikah just sit, with their eyes on their food. Both of them look surprised. The surprise is soon replaced by disappointment.

"So soon?" Grandma asks, looking disturbed by the news.

"Well, we have to leave tomorrow if I want to start my job on time," Adam replies. "I only have a week before I start."

After a short sigh, Jonah says, "It's so like your boss to give you very little time to prepare."

"Wow, I wish we didn't have to leave so soon," Mikah says, with heaviness in his voice.

"What a summer it has been...I almost forgot it all has to end," I say.

Adam looks at Grandma and says, "It was so wonderful to get to know you and Shannon."

"Yeah, it was so nice of you guys to let us stay," Jonah says, with what looks like a forced smile.

"We loved having you guys here," Grandma says, with a slight quiver in her voice.

"We'll have to come back again," Adam says.

A bit of silence follows as we chomp on our food.

"Or, maybe they can come visit us," Mikah says, after a few moments. His eyebrows are raised as he looks at Adam.

"Yeah, that's a good idea. Maybe for Christmas or for next summer…when Shannon's out of school again," Jonah adds with a bit of excitement in his voice.

I feel as I might choke on my food and have to take a drink of Kool-Aid, before speaking. "I would love that, wouldn't you Grandma?" I ask, hoping she agrees.

"Yes, yes, that sounds good…I can't leave this place for a long time, though," she says.

I can understand Grandma's concerns, but I am excited about the opportunity to see San Francisco and I figure I will need to convince her leaving this house for a short time will be okay.

"It will be fun," I say to Grandma. "And besides, Grandma Elsa can watch the house for you," I add, hoping to ease her worries.

Adam's eyes lighten up. Jonah and Mikah look at Grandma as well, and they smile at her answer.

"Yeah, maybe for a week, or something like that," she says, showing little enthusiasm about the idea.

"Maybe I can stay longer," I add, looking at Adam for approval.

"Yeah, that's cool, too," Adam says, with a nod.

"It sounds like you'll have to get a bigger apartment," Mikah adds. "He only has a two bedroom and we all squeeze into it during the summer months."

I quickly finish my food and begin cleaning my area. Adam, Mikah and Jonah brainstorm on ideas for the next summer, while Grandma eats the rest of her food in silence. She smiles every now and then at their ideas. But I know she is not very enthused and I know I have more convincing to do.

I decide I will worry about the convincing part when we're alone again. For now, I am in good spirits and excited about the idea of visiting the Navarros next summer. It doesn't bother me that I have a whole year to wait. I am excited.

When the kitchen is clean again, and all is calm throughout the house, it is dark outside and Grandma lights a lantern for Mikah to use for reading a book before bedtime.

I go out to the porch and instead of sitting down as I usually do, I step out to the open driveway. The stars are out again, shining bright above us. The moon has moved to the other side of the sky. I wonder if my mother is looking down on me as I gaze up into the night sky. I wonder if she misses me as much as I miss her. I wonder how much she regrets leaving me here on this planet, in this dimension. I wonder if she is even up in the sky, or if she is floating around me, as Grandma often says she is. Or is she just lying in her grave, with no thoughts or no spiritual presence? I wonder how she would have taken the offer made by the Navarros, for me and Grandma to go to San Francisco.

That night, I lie in bed and wait for Grandma to come to bed. As I lie still, I dread the thought of having to go back to school, of having to leave Grandma by herself on the rez again, of the Navarros leaving. I feel the sorrow again, deep in my bones. I toss and look towards the window. The curtains are drawn but I can see the moonlight glimmering through the window.

I hear Grandma's voice in the darkness. She quietly

asks, "Are you asleep?" in Navajo.

"No," I say. My eyelids are heavy, but I don't want to fall asleep yet.

Grandma sits down beside me and we both look out into the night, out the window.

"I hope Anthony is okay," she says, as she unties the bun atop her head. Her long hair comes falling down around her shoulders. In the moonlight, I can see her hair is thinning at the top of her head...not something I can tell when it's up in a bun.

"I hope so, too," I say, forgetting my own sorrows. I think of prayer and the power it holds. I ask Grandma to say a prayer for him. And she does so, without hesitation.

She clears her throat first, lowers her head and quietly begins talking. She holds my hand in hers. Her wrinkled skin is soft and tender and I rub the wrinkles.

"Great Spirit, we ask you to watch over our son and uncle, and bless him during his journey in prison," she says. She pauses. She sighs.

"Show him a good way of life, and help him realize his sins and please, please forgive him," she adds, finishing her prayer. The prayer isn't as desperate or elaborate as the one she said for Mr. Eddie Yazzie, but it is enough.

After a few more moments of silence, she speaks again. "Thank you," she says. Then she slowly lifts her head.

I sit up and scoot closer to her. "Grandma, I don't want to go back to Los Angeles," I say, with my head buried in her chest.

"Oh, poor baby," Grandma says, in a whisper.

"I'm going to miss you again," I whimper.

"You're not going back right now," she says.

"I know…but…" I whisper.

"Shhhh, you're going to be okay," she says, interrupting me, as she squeezes me.

I don't share anything else with her. I just let her hold me.

After I calm down and regain my composure, I clear my throat and say, "Here I am crying…over something so small and there are so many more people with less fortune than me."

"Yes, some people have worse problems," Grandma says. "It's okay to be sad about all that has happened to you. But you should be grateful for all you have," she goes on to say.

A quick feeling of relief comes over me. She doesn't have to mention specifics, but I know she is referring to Eddie Yazzie's family, his kids, his wife, my uncle, Alan, Angie, Stevie, and the girl from boarding school who was raped at a squaw dance.

"You are very blessed," she quietly says as she plays with my hair. "You have me, you have a roof over your head, food in your belly, and when I'm gone, you'll have your aunts."

"Don't say that, Grandma," I say, not wanting to hear about her death.

"I'm not always going to be around, that's all I'm saying," she calmly says.

"I don't want to think about when you will leave me, too," I whisper.

"I'll be with you in spirit, just like your mother is," she says.

"I love you, Grandma."

"I love you, too, shi' yazhi' (my little one), and I am proud to have you as a grand-daughter."

I hold her. She holds me. For a few more moments, we sit in the dark, hugging each other before we give into our fatigue.

I slip easily into sleep that night. Grandma's tossing and turning doesn't disturb me, and neither does her snoring. I let myself fall, fall into a deep sleep.

Love in A Letter

The sun rises slowly the next morning, as if it is holding back, not wanting to start another day. I sit on the front porch, reflecting on the past summer days. I consider asking Grandma if I can stay with her for the school year, and I wonder what her response would be. Before long, I am joined by Jonah, cup of coffee in hand.

"So, I guess you'll be going back to Los Angeles to finish up school?" he asks, putting his cup down on the porch shelf. As much as my eyes want to wander in his direction, I don't let them.

Instead, I just reply, "Yep."

"I really can't wait to see you guys again. I am going to miss you and Grandma a whole lot. I will even miss the rez. I feel like it's a place I can call my second home."

"Yeah, it's funny how it grows on you," I say, keeping my gaze ahead, out to the valley of bushes and tall grasses.

"I'm going to miss hanging out with you, too," he says. I can feel his eyes on me, but I stare straight ahead and take in the brilliant sun's rays.

I let the sun warm my skin. I can tell the day will be a nice, hot one.

I nod. I don't know what to say and I don't really feel like talking, so I nod again.

"As much as I'm going to miss this place, I can't wait to get back to school myself," he continues.

"Yeah, I suppose you can't wait to get back to cable, too," I say.

"Yeah, that, too," he says.

I finally let myself look at him again, and his eyes look right through me. I can feel them unpeeling my outer layers of presence. I feel helpless. I want to hug him or kiss him, but I don't. I just admire his eyes, his blonde locks, the eyebrows that accent his eyes so well, and his oval, baby face.

I glance away and gaze at the land before us again.

"You know you can call us anytime. I left our phone number on Grandma's dresser," he says.

"Thanks," I say.

The screen door opens again and this time, Adam comes out, and hollers, "It's time to load up!"

Mikah begins to carry bag after bag past me, and into the van.

The smell of breakfast—sausage or bacon, and potatoes, is coming from inside the house. I can hear Grandma yelling from the kitchen, "Breakfast is ready!"

The smell makes my nostrils tingle. Before I can savor the smell, I hear the hum of an engine. There is no one coming from the east, so I walk around the side of the house, and recognize Elsa's truck rumbling towards the house. I presume they are coming to bid farewell.

The dull hum of the engine comes to a stop right in

front of me, and Elsa gets out slowly. She is of old age, older than my Grandma, and she moves cautiously.

"Ni' Ma'saní shá?" she asks me…which translates to 'Where is your grandmother?'

I point to the house, and she wobbles right past me.

Jonah says "Yá'át'ééh" to her, and she just nods at him.

I wave at my grandfather, Harry, who remains in the truck, behind the wheel. He waves back and smiles. His hair is a silvery gray, and he is a large, slow-moving man. Most of our relatives call him, "Ho' zhóo'o', which means "slow" in Navajo.

With the sun now farther up in the sky, I go back to the porch and sit down, to keep from taking direct sunlight. I can hear my aunt, Jackie's voice in my head, telling me 'It's not good to be out in direct sunlight. Your skin will burn.'

Jonah quietly tends to packing, along with his brothers.

I hear Grandma speaking to her sister inside, in Navajo. I don't try to make heads or tails of what they're discussing.

As soon as the Navarros are all packed up, Grandma hands them a large Ziploc bag with warm tortillas and frybread, which Elsa brought. They give us each tight hugs before they all load themselves into the van.

As Grandma and I stand on either side of the van and wish the men a safe trip, Elsa waves to the Navarros, while Harry waves from the truck. Elsa climbs slowly back into the truck and they drive away.

Adam gives Grandma a kiss on the cheek, and Jonah slips me a folded note. Mikah is in the back seat, and says he doesn't like farewells.

Jonah whispers into my ear. "Don't open it until we're gone."

I nod and smile shyly.

With that, Adam starts up the engine, and they drive slowly away from the house. He honks the horn and waves again.

I am overcome with sadness, but I continue to wave. I put the note in my pocket before Grandma asks about it and I go back into the house.

"I don't know what to do with myself, now that they're gone," Grandma says, following me into the house.

"Yeah, it's so sad...I'm going to miss them," I say, with heaviness in my voice.

"Yes, but let's not talk too much about it, or we will both be crying our hearts out," Grandma utters.

"Okay, let's talk about something else then," I say, trying to jerk my mind away from the sight of the van driving away.

"Well, I asked Elsa to give us a ride into town later, so we can call Jackie, and find out when she will be back for you," she says, reminding me again that my stay will come to an end, too.

"Okay," I say, trying not to show my disappointment.

I help Grandma tidy up the house while we wait for Elsa and Harry to come back and pick us up. In order to keep my mind off the loneliness surrounding me, I wash the dishes.

As I finish rinsing the last of the dirty dishes, I remember the note in my pocket. My heart excitedly jumps at the thought and I dry my hands off before I fumble for the note. I find it, and I take it out. I open it slowly. It is nicely folded into a small cube and as I pull back each fold, I anticipate Jonah's words. Will it be a short letter? A long one? Did he put down his true feelings on paper?

I reveal a short note when I fully open the folded paper. The paper has no lines, but the writing is perfectly straight. My anticipation grows and I read as fast as I can.

My dearest Shannon,

I hope you will miss me as much as I will miss you. I want you to know that I have grown to like you very much.

I couldn't sleep for the last couple of nights. I tossed and turned and thought of how much I will miss this place and you

I know Grandma would probably disapprove of you dating. I have great respect for your grandmother and I will miss her very much as well. I will never forget you and I hope to see you again soon. I hope you keep me in your heart as I will keep you in mine.

The note is signed with a fancy, but legible signature. His phone number, I presume his home number, is at the bottom of the letter. I smell the letter and to my disappointment, it doesn't smell like him. I wipe the tears which are running down my cheeks.

I fold the note back up and focus on rinsing the rest of the dishes. I put the note in my pocket and make a point not to show it to Grandma.

I don't have to busy myself for long, because Grandma Elsa and Grandpa Harry come back after I finish with the dishes.

Without much discussion, Grandma and I squeeze into their truck with them, and all the way to town, Elsa and Grandma laugh about people they know; a man who lives down by the river, another man who supposedly is somewhat of a ladies' man, and of course, The Lady With Clumsy Hands.

I don't understand everything they are saying, but I understand enough to know they are making fun.

I notice something about Grandma and her sister during that ride into town. They are uneasy around each other. They don't speak of circumstances at hand. And they laugh a lot. They don't talk of my uncle's arrest, the murder, or how much Grandma already misses the Navarros or how she will miss me, they simply avoid the obvious and divert their talks to other people, which I find unusual.

I, on the other hand, want to talk to Grandma about how horrible I feel for having to leave her again and about how my stomach twists and turns every time I think of the murdered man's fate and of my uncle's worst sin yet. But I hold my words and just listen.

I look out the passenger-side window at the sage-green bushes. I admire the sunflowers as we pass them. They are bright and erect, peacefully swaying in a light breeze coming from the south. As we continue down the road, I watch the inches of dirt road disappear under us.

I consider the murdered man's family; their sadness and sorrow. I wonder what kind of life he led, what kind of person he was as a child. I wonder why innocence in humanity disappears so quickly.

I wonder why my uncle couldn't restrain himself from killing Mr. Yazzie. I wonder what it is that makes people do such horrible things to each other. I have no answer to any of my thoughts, so I just ride.

Once we arrive in town, Grandma asks Harry to stop at the first pay phone, near the Safeway grocery store. Then she hands me a worn, AT&T 200-minute calling card.

"Call your aunt and ask her when she is coming," Grandma instructs me.

I obediently get out of the truck and take a few steps to the pay phone. I dial the code on the card, and then my aunt's number. There are only 25 minutes left so I figure I better make it short and sweet.

Ring, ring.

A voice picks up and I almost don't recognize my aunt's voice.

"Hello?" the voice on the other end says.

"Hi," I mutter.

"Hey sweetie," she says cheerfully, once she recognizes my voice.

"Hi, Auntie. I was calling to find out when you will be by to pick me up," I ask nervously.

Without hesitation, as if she was expecting my call and that question, she says, "Well, I can come by whenever you're ready."

"Okay, I'm ready," I say, in what I think is a voice too low to hear. So I clear my throat, and repeat myself. "I'm ready."

"School doesn't start until next week, but it might be a good idea to get back this weekend, so we can get you ready," she says.

"Oh, okay," I say.

"That way, we can go shopping and all that."

"Okay, I'm ready," I say again.

"What's the matter, sweetie? You do not sound happy at all."

"Sorry, I am already missing the rez."

"Alright, alright, I'll go out there this weekend then," she says, with a short laugh.

Then she asks me, "So, how was your vacation?"

"It has been a very interesting one. I'll tell you all about it when you get here."

"I heard about Anthony and what happened," she comments.

"Yeah, it's been a long summer."

"Can I talk to Grandma?" she asks after a deep breath.

Before I call Grandma over to the phone, I tell my aunt, Jackie I can't wait to see her. I wave Grandma over. When she takes the phone, I get back into the truck, and wait. Elsa converses with her husband in Navajo and a few moments later, Grandma squeezes her body back into the truck.

The next few days I spend hanging out with Grandma, and watching her weave. She shows little sadness, although I am sure she recognizes she will soon be alone again, out here on the rez, which can be a depressing and lonely place. As

379

tranquil and beautiful as the land is, it can be a merciless place when you're alone.

As I sit and watch Grandma weave on the days that she busies herself doing so, she gives me careful instruction on how to make sure the rug is tight, but not too tight, how the designs should come naturally, and how to keep the rug from shrinking in the middle. I admire her movements, her fingers working diligently and carefully to create a masterpiece. When she finishes this rug, maybe in another week, she will probably visit a few of her usual buyers and sell it for around a hundred dollars, just enough to buy some food to hold her over until her next Social Security check comes.

"Do your fingers hurt from weaving?" I curiously ask, as Grandma laces her loom with strands of thin wool.

"Yes, I have arthritis," Grandma explains. "But this is all I know how to do," she adds as she puts her weaving comb down to take a break. "When I was a little girl, my mother used to tell me and my sister we need to learn how to weave so our families will never go hungry."

Grandma sits back as she stares at her loom, as if she's going back in time. "A long time ago, rugs were traded for food, clothes, or livestock. My mother used to bring home flour, sugar, meat, and some cloths for sewing. She sewed all of our clothes."

"Wow, and how long would the food last?" I ask, amazed at the history.

"It would last us about two weeks. We didn't eat a lot of meat, mostly potatoes and bread. In the summer time, we grew corn and all kinds of vegetables. Before winter came, my father used to make beef or mutton jerky and every once in a while, we ate the jerky. I miss those days."

I can see the sadness in her eyes as she speaks of her past.

"It sounds like things were easier back then," I say.

Grandma closes her eyes and sighs. "Oh, it wasn't easy. It was hard work, but it wasn't crazy like it is nowadays," she discouragingly says.

"I know, Grandma," I say, sympathetically.

Grandma adjusts her cushion, spits on her fingers, and resumes weaving.

"Grandma, I had fun this summer, being here with you and the Navarros. Even though it was crazy, I enjoyed my time."

"I am glad you came back," she says, as she pounds at her loom.

A Bittersweet Farewell

On the day of my departure, I take a walk, a walk to the same pond that I introduced Jonah to. I walk with my head down, looking at the hundreds and thousands of glassy rocks under my feet.

The rocks beneath my feet make a crunching noise with each step.

As I approach the small pond on the other side of the hill, I pick up a handful of glassy rocks, and when I reach the pond, I throw the rocks one at a time as far as I can, like Jonah had done the day he professed his attraction to me. With every throw, I release my anxiety, my fear, my jealousy, my anger, my sympathy, and my sorrow.

I am sure Grandma is wondering where I am by now, so I take a long look at the pond once again and softly whisper, "Goodbye." In the winter, it will be frozen, holding the plant life in it prisoner. I say a prayer for the plants, another prayer for my uncle, one for the Navarros, and one for Grandma.

On my walk home, I feel anxious to go back to Los Angeles, back to the city with all its glamour and all its lights, or its darkness and filth, if you're in the wrong part of town. I am anxious, yet afraid and nervous of the coming school year. I will cling to the memories from this past summer break. I will remember Jonah and his brothers and what seemed at first like a strange visit from strange people. I do not want to leave Grandma. But I know my aunt is right. I know I will not receive the best education here and I know Grandma wants only the best for me. I will remember my grandmother's stories, for as long as I can. I promise my spirits and my mother, that I will never forget where I am from, and who I am.

As much as I will miss Grandma, I know she will miss me more, because she has no one else here. The thought saddens me again. I don't like the sadness. I want to be happy. I want Grandma to be happy. I don't cry. I just swallow hard.

When my aunt arrives later that day, I am excited and give her a generous bear hug. She is dressed nicely in a white, linen summer outfit and her black hair is dangling with loose curls. She comes into the house for a bite of some meat Grandma prepared. She takes a sip of soda and grimaces.

"I don't know why I try to force down soda, it so harsh," she says.

"Because that's all Grandma keeps around for beverages and we love it," I retort. "Of course, we are not uppity like you, we don't have cranberry juice on ice," I add.

Jackie looks at me, makes a smug face, and says, "I am not uppity."

She gives me a good tickle. "Take it back," she demands.

"Okay, okay, you're not uppity, we are just soda-lovers," I say, in between giggles.

She then takes a few moments to wander through the house as Grandma shows her the newest updates in the kitchen and the bathroom. Her thoughts seem to be elsewhere and she doesn't seem too thrilled with the work, or at least she shows very little animation when she compliments on it.

While Grandma fills Jackie in on the events of the summer, I pack my bags. Once my bags are sitting neatly in a row by the front door, I go into my mother's old room, sit on her bed, and reminisce the summers when she was around.

"I'm going to miss you and thanks for the dreams," I whisper, as I stare at her picture on the wall.

The room is clean and neat. I straighten the bedspread before I leave the room, leaving it nice and taut. As I make my way out to the porch where Grandma and Jackie are now standing, I stop in the living room to take a look around and I whisper, "And goodbye, old house."

I pick up my bags and tightly pack them into the back of Jackie's car. I return to the porch to give Grandma the tightest hug I can give her without hurting her.

I whisper in her ear, "I'm going to miss you."

She lets a couple of tears drop and says, "Oh, you'll be back soon enough," as she wipes the tears away. She takes a deep breath. I know she is trying to be tough. So I don't say anything else.

I climb into the car and Grandma gives my aunt a soft hug as she says, "You ladies, take care of yourselves and don't forget to call. I don't really know how to work my cell phone but if it rings, I will push the green button, just like Adam showed me."

The three of us chuckle.

Jackie and I wave to my grandmother, as the car pulls away from the house.

I leave Grandma's house with confidence, knowing I will be back before long. We travel down the same bumpy road we had driven all summer with the Navarros; the same road to town; the same road to the hospital, which turned out to be a popular hangout spot for the summer. From town, we will go west on I-40 and then south on I-17, back into the thick of the city, back to the sprawling malls and the identical rows of stucco houses in the suburbs, back to the choking, brown smog and the congested freeways.

"Aren't you excited to be going back to Los Angeles?" my aunt asks me as we drive through Sunflower Valley.

I can almost hear my mother's voice in hers, and I tell her, "Yes." Although it's a lie, she doesn't know that, and I don't tell her. I let her drive.

"I bet you can't wait to get back to the malls, to see your friends, and to go shopping with them," she says in a delightful tone.

When I think about it like that, I realize I can't wait to get back to those things. Yet, I feel the pull from Grandma's house, from the rez, from my mother's land. I want to go back, I want to stay. I let the pull from the road win. I am going back to Los Angeles. I remind myself that I need a good education and being back in the city will give me the opportunity to get just that.

As I look out the windows and silently bid farewell to the flowers which line the road, and spread for miles on either side, I breathe and think. They wave in unison, and I imagine they are bidding me farewell, too. I will miss their beauty. I will miss the hope their beauty gives me. They stand and grow, out here, in the flat lands, in the boonies, where there is little hope for survival. Yet, they grow and wave. I silently cry inside. And then I breathe.

I wonder if I will be able to endure and outsmart any adversities that come my way throughout the year. I wonder if I can make it in this world without my mother; with only my grandmother as my rock; my rock on the rez. A fast realization comes to mind; I have made it this far and I am okay. I smile at this thought.

The urges of the city will soon be nipping at my heels and I know I will have to be strong in order to keep a balance between both worlds; my modern world and my traditional one. I don't want to be a lost Navajo girl drowning in a sea of modern life.

The thought of being someone I am not or my reflection of such pushes me to ponder on the thought of not going anywhere, of simply staying here with my grandmother.

"Do you really think I will be smarter if I go to school in the city?" I ask my aunt, as we roll past the dry sage bushes and the barren strips of land on either side of I-40, just outside of Winslow.

I turn my gaze from looking out the window to look instead at my aunt's expression.

Her expression is calm and she acknowledges me by looking directly back at me.

"Why would you ask such a silly question?" she asks.

I don't answer. I just smile an awkward smile and shrug my shoulders, as if to say 'I don't know and I'm silly for not knowing.'

"You are smart, period," my aunt declares, with confidence in her voice. "And yes, I think the city schools will be better for you, but I didn't realize you would actually want to stay out here, I mean at your grandmother's house."

"Yes, I would love to stay with Grandma," I say, not wanting to miss another moment of driving in the wrong direction.

"Are you sure?" my aunt asks, as she studies me for a quick moment.

I ponder her question for a moment and answer, "Yes, yes, I am positive."

She keeps her eyes on the road and brakes to slow the vehicle down. She signals to exit on the next freeway exit.

My heart skips a beat and I feel a shot of happiness, as if it is a drug that was just shot into my arm, and I loudly exclaim, "Yes!"

Jackie smiles and then laughs and says, "If you want to go home, I will take you home, back to Los Angeles. But if you know for sure you want to stay with Mom, I will take you back to Mom's."

"Yes, I want to stay with Grandma."

"Okay, it's a done deal."

We make a u-turn at the next freeway exit. I stare out the window at the white, dome-shaped building which is the only building in Meteor City—a small tourist stop a few miles west of Winslow on I-40.

About thirty minutes later, we are approaching the yellow, cinder-block house once again.

When we pull into Grandma's dirt driveway, I see Grandma's silhouette in her doorway and my heart is racing. I cannot wait to share the news of my choice with her.

"Grandma, Grandma!" I exclaim as I hop out of the Camry and dash towards her.

She greets me on the porch and looks surprised.

"I am staying with you!" I say loudly, as I hug her.

"Oh, really? You want to stay here with me?" she asks, still surprised. Her eyebrows are raised and she looks to my aunt for validation.

"Yes, yes, she wants to stay with you and I told her it's okay," Jackie explains, as she walks towards us.

Now I see relief on Grandma's face and she smiles.

"Well, I better get started on dinner for two," she says happily.

I embrace my aunt as she steps closer to me and I utter, "Thank you for everything you do."

"And I love you, too, Shannon," she says with a generous smile.

"I love you, too, Jackie," I proudly say.

"Mom, you should prepare dinner for three. I am going to stay. I can drive home tomorrow morning," Jackie says as we both enter the front door of the yellow, cinder-block house, followed by Grandma.

You would think Grandma just won the lotto and has only a few seconds to claim her prize. She hurriedly walks into the kitchen, and returns in an apron within a minute Her hair is nicely tightened up in a bun and she is ready to cook.

She excitedly proclaims, "Dinner for three it is!"